POP CLUTCH

Thrilling Tales of ROCKABILLY, MONSTERS, & HOTROD HORROR

Additional Anthologies Edited by Eric J. Guignard

A World of Horror (Dark Moon Books, 2018)

After Death... (Dark Moon Books, 2013)

Dark Tales of Lost Civilizations (Dark Moon Books, 2012)

The Five Senses of Horror (forthcoming) (Dark Moon Books, 2018)

+Horror Library+ Volume 6 (Cutting Block Books/ Farolight Publishing, 2017)

Exploring Dark Short Fiction (A Primer Series) Created by Eric J. Guignard

#1: A Primer to Steve Rasnic Tem (Dark Moon Books, 2017)

#2: A Primer to Kaaron Warren (Dark Moon Books, 2018)

#3: A Primer to Nisi Shawl (Dark Moon Books, 2018)

#4: A Primer to Jeffrey Ford (forthcoming) (Dark Moon Books, 2019)

#5: A Primer to Han Song (forthcoming) (Dark Moon Books, 2019)

#6: A Primer to Ramsey Campbell (forthcoming) (Dark Moon Books, 2019)

Fiction Written by Eric J. Guignard

Baggage of Eternal Night (JournalStone, 2013)

Crossbuck 'Bo (forthcoming) (JournalStone, 2019)

That Which Grows Wild: 16 Tales of Dark Fiction (Cemetery Dance Publications, 2018)

Pop the Clutch: Thrilling Tales of Rockabilly, Monsters, and Hot Rod Horror

Edited by Eric J. Guignard
Illustrated by Steve Chanks

DARK MOON BOOKS
Los Angeles, California

POP THE CLUTCH: THRILLING TALES OF
ROCKABILLY, MONSTERS, AND HOT ROD HORROR
Copyright © Eric J. Guignard 2019

Edited by Eric J. Guignard
Interior layout by Eric J. Guignard
Cover design by Eric J. Guignard
www.ericjguignard.com

Interior illustrations by Steve Chanks
www.stevechanks.com

First edition published in January, 2019
Library of Congress Control Number: 2018908254

ISBN-13: 978-1-949491-05-0 (hardback)
ISBN-13: 978-1-949491-01-2 (paperback)
ISBN-13: 978-1-949491-02-9 (e-book)

DARK MOON BOOKS
Los Angeles, California
www.DarkMoonBooks.com

Made in the United States of America

(V010919)

This anthology is dedicated as always, and with love,
to my family—Jeannette, Julian, and Devin.

Thank you, also, to the hip cats
who penned for this book.
Your imaginations are outta sight.

TABLE OF CONTENTS

THE '50s.

One vision of this era has gone down in history as an idyllic time in America where middle class was one of prosperity and uniformity, and most people knew their place and they stuck to it. Girls shopped for Prom dresses, and boys played ball, and men worked, and women kept house, and no one spoke up about the ills of society for fear of being labeled a *Goddamned Commie*.

Another vision is this, where the seedy underbelly of the nation wasn't just glimpsed by some wayward scandal of the bespectacled elite, but rather once-and-for-all laid entirely bare and, further, *flaunted* by the tassel-covered chests of go-go dancers on roller skates, while Satan smoked a reefer right behind and gyrated his hips to the latest Elvis hit.

INTRODUCTION

BY ERIC J. GUIGNARD

Welcome to the "cool" side of the '50s . . .

Wanna guess what vision this anthology leans toward?

Not the Cronkite or Chet Huntley broadcasts of the night, that's for sure. Not the *Happy Days* and homogenization of mid-American cultural norms, oh no. And, surely, not the checkered leisure jackets and smoked pipe with your feet up on the ottoman, while Tommy and Judy play tiddlywinks at your side . . .

Not here, where the fast cars and revved-up movie monsters peel out in the night. Not where outlaw vixens and jukebox tramps square off with razorblades and lead pipes. Not where rockers rock, cool cats strut, and hot rods roar. Not where you howl to the moon as the tiki drums pound and the electric guitar shrieks and that spit-and-holler jamboree ain't gonna stop for a long, long time ... maybe never.

In other words, welcome to the "cool" side of the '50s, where ghost shows still travel the back roads of the south, and rockabilly has a hold on the nation's youth, where lucky hearts tell the tale, and maybe that fella in the Shriners' fez ain't so square after all ...

Where exist noir detectives of the supernatural, tattoo artists of another kind, Hollywood fix-it men, and a punk kid with grasshopper arms under his chain-studded jacket and an icy stare on his face.

This is the 1950s of *Pop the Clutch: Thrilling Tales of Rockabilly, Monsters, and Hot Rod Horror.*

This is your ticket to the dark side of American kitsch ... the *fun* side.

But before we descend into yesteryear, a few words further from your intrepid editor.

This is the sixth fiction anthology I've edited and, for many reasons, one of my favorites. Being a rockabilly-listening, tiki-collecting fan myself, this era has always resonated to me as one of the heralds of chic and the prelude to 60s-all-out-strangeness. Of strengthening Civil Rights and the mainstream rise of rock 'n' roll. Of television sets invading every home, and space exploration turning from a wistful dream to that God-inspiring realization. Of the stories my parents told of growing up which, regardless what you say, is the sort of thing that will always leave an immutable impression in your mind for the rest of your life.

The 50s were—for better and for worse—a turning point in the nation, and they are an era which half of Americans today lived through, and the other half can only imagine.

... and I don't know about you, but my imagination can run pretty wild.

So can the authors included within.

Normally (as I've done in prior anthologies), I like to write a little introduction prefacing each author's story, explaining my rationale for selecting it, or what it means to me, but that just didn't seem to fit this time around. Because, simply put, these stories are just badass. There's no higher ambition or lofty ideal, no need to pad around, but just to read 'em straight through, and my intermissions would probably kill the buzz, like that annoying Ovaltine commercial popping up in the middle of every *Buck Rogers* episode.

But I'd still feel remiss not to at least cue you in (i.e. *brag*) a little now about what's in store <cue the dropping checkered flag>:

Seanan McGuire knocks it out when she shows us that high school cheerleaders are more than tumbles and pom-poms... *waaay* more. Weston Ochse infuses his military tradition into a tale of Korean War veterans who must rescue certain aquatic damsels at the behest of a talking fish. Joe and Kasey Lansdale, who never let a reader down, share the melancholy of an aged rockabilly musician and what happened the night his band returned to play in the home town where the band was bullied as teens.

Pulp-pro Gary Phillips pulls out all the stops as the Korea War's first black jet ace fighter pilot returns home to race hot rods and battle a creature of the night. Thriller writer Jason Starr gives us a mild-mannered man, whose psychotic family all have something in common. Then, not everything is what is seems when Nancy Holder slyly tells of dreamboat Johnny Morris and his all-American (and beyond!) romantic escapades.

Duane Swierczynski lets loose a monster that only Hollywood could create...and perhaps destroy. David J. Schow gives new meaning to the term "Draggers," where the only rule is: You die, you lose. A dimwitted sheriff comes to us by mystery author John M. Floyd, who discovers that several gruesome deaths lead to an abandoned drive-in, and its cache of old horror movies.

Lisa Morton (who can do no wrong) reminds us that those who call upon ghosts most often find them, even when mirrors and smoke are involved. Grand Master Bill Pronzini knows no limits, and nor does his mean-streaked race car driver who feuds for a mysterious beautiful woman. Yvonne Navarro delivers a quiet high school superstition where tradition meets curse (and atmospheric writing trumps shock and awe).

Steve Perry continues his forty-plus year tradition of cutting-edge fiction when the roadie of a greaser rock band gets revenge on his band's abusive lead singer, with the help of weather control. Mystery bestsellers, Max Allan Collins and Matthew V. Clemens, collaborate to create a case where the investigator is just as mysterious as the matter he's inspecting. Comedic horror author Jeff Strand writes of the tough gang rivalries over sidewalk turf, and which of their patron mad scientists is better.

Amelia Beamer slows the juice with a beautiful, introspective view of a teen's emerging feelings, and her place—or lack thereof—in this world. Gonzo author Will Viharo continues the legend of a certain deformed fish-man when he falls in love with a heroin-addicted burlesque dancer who's "owned" by the jealous nightclub's mobster owner. And Brian Hodge (master of blending humor, action, and the unexpected) closes out this book with an homage to the last greaser in a world of hippies, who deals drugs, mayhem, and his own sort of social justice.

And let's not forget the art, the amazing illustrations electrifying each tale that take this anthology to a whole 'nother level. Steve Chanks is an ace of the inks.

So now continue on, dear reader, and leave my cube-talk behind.

It's time to start your engine, and Pop that Clutch!

Midnight cheers,

—Eric J. Guignard
Chino Hills, California
July 15, 2018

"**R**EADY? OKAY!" SIXTEEN GIRLS IN KNEE-length orange skirts and long-sleeved white sweaters struck a pose on the field, half kneeling, the other half with their arms up, forming a perfect *V*. Every hand held a pom-pom, half green, half orange, and every face bore a brilliant, white-toothed smile. They were the golden girls of fall and they knew it, even as the days were getting shorter and the nights were getting longer, winter claiming its territory one day and one hour at a time.

Only a few more games left in the season; only a few more turns on the field. That made practices like this one all the more important,

THE GOLDEN GIRLS OF FALL

BY SEANAN MCGUIRE

The Fighting Pumpkins cheerleaders walked like they owned the halls . . .

because when it was over, it would be over for good for almost half the squad, seniors all, who would finish out the school year shaking their pom-poms at pep rallies and trying not to envy the junior varsity girls as they trained, day after day on the field, for next year's football season.

It wasn't fair. It wasn't *fair*. Football should last the entire school year. That, or cheerleading should be for all sports, not just one of them. Most of the squad would have been willing to cheer for the *chess club*, if it meant they got to keep doing it.

Their coach clapped her hands. The standing girls folded backward into perfect cartwheels, while the kneeling girls bounced to their feet, waving their pom-poms wildly, trying to get an imaginary crowd to stand and cheer.

If anyone could have managed it, it would have been the Johnson's Crossing Fighting Pumpkins. Worst mascot in the district, as far as anyone with eyes was concerned, but try telling that to the cheer squad, who acted like being the living avatars of a vaguely menacing cartoon squash was the best thing that could ever have happened to them. It was surreal, to say the least, and a little bizarre, to say the most.

At least they were all good girls. The coach looked out upon the bouncing, cheering squad, and didn't see a single teased hairdo or slouched sock. When someone caught a group of girls behind the gym smoking or talking with boys, was it her Pumpkins? No sir, it was not. Good girls one and all, who had chosen healthy athletic outlets for all those buzzing hormones and confused teenage feelings.

She blew her whistle. "All right, ladies! Time to hit the showers and get back to class!"

Laughing and waving their pom-poms, the Fighting Pumpkins cheerleading squad turned and trotted for the locker room. One of them—Andrea, who was in the running to be team captain after Iris graduated—turned and blew their coach a cheeky kiss. Then they were gone, vanishing as quickly as they'd come.

The coach sagged, a sudden wave of exhaustion sweeping over her, and barely managed to catch herself on the bleachers before she fell. It wasn't fair, really. These girls got younger every year, and she was still expected to keep up with them.

Every year.

"I THINK YOU MIGHT have hit her too hard, Andrea," said Iris, stripping out of her uniform sweater and stuffing it into her locker before digging out her blouse. "Be careful, okay? We don't want to break in a new coach because you broke the old one."

"*Literally*," said Laura, and giggled vapidly. Laura did everything vapidly. It would have been annoying if she hadn't been so good-natured about it, and if she hadn't had good reason. Earth didn't have enough oxygen for her. No matter how much she inhaled, she was basically half-giddy from suffocation all the time.

Not that a little suffocation was going to get her to go back to her home planet, no sir. She had come here for a high school education. They all had, and by whatever dark and terrible gods they happened to follow, they were going to *get* one.

Andrea rolled her eyes and took another swig from her thermos. "Lighten up, okay? I know how hard it's safe to push. I've never broken a Renfield, and I'm sure not going to start with the *coach*."

"Is she really your Renfield, though?" asked Mary, digging the grease from under her nails with a file. "I mean, does she drink your blood?"

Andrea looked abashed. Mary's eyes widened.

"Oh," she said. "How . . . ?"

"She always leaves her lunch in the teachers' lounge fridge, and it's not like the door locks, and *anyway* it's easier to keep her in thrall if she's a little bit mine, *okay*?" Andrea hunched her shoulders defensively. "It's not my fault if she looks sort of confused sometimes. This school is confusing."

"Says the girl who keeps coming back for another stay," said Iris. "Mom says hello, by the way, and wants me to remind you that you never returned her biology notes."

Andrea rolled her eyes. "That was twenty years ago."

"Yet still the notes go unreturned." Iris pulled a pack of cigarettes out of her locker and tucked it under the strap of her bra. "You girls ready to get back to skipping class?"

As it turned out, they all were.

The Fighting Pumpkins cheerleaders walked like they owned the halls. Sixteen girls in white blouses that were just a trifle too tight, in short pants that were just a trifle too short—baring calf more than halfway to the knee, well, their mothers would *never*, even though every single one of their mothers absolutely would have, absolutely had, according to the fashions and standards of their own sweet, bygone days. Youth was like a school year: it seemed like forever when you were standing at the start, but before you blinked, it was homecoming, it was prom, it was graduation. It was standing on a stage, clutching your diploma, and asking yourself what you were supposed to do now.

For most people, anyway. Teachers looked away when they saw Andrea Lomax coming, staring at walls or other students or anything at all to keep themselves from thinking, *I know her, why do I know her?* Knowing how they knew her would mean admitting that things like her were real, could really exist. So much about the world would have started to make sense if they'd been able to do that. So much about the world would have turned instantly, eternally inimical.

Better to be a little confused, to look a little foolish, than to admit that they had seen that girl before in graduating class after graduating class, her hemlines bouncing up and down like basketballs as she shifted herself to fit the times, but her smile—always a little bit too full of sharp white teeth—remaining always, awfully the same. Better to live in the sunlight than to admit that they had seen a glimpse of the things that owned the shadows.

Cheerleading was still a new thing in Johnson's Crossing, at least as far as the faculty was concerned. For the squad, now midway through its fifth year, cheerleading was something that had always been and would always be. Cheerleading was eternal. It only made sense that their once and future team captain should be equally everlasting.

Andrea herself watched the girls who moved around her with a predator's eye, assessing them each, measuring their strengths and weaknesses according to a scale that predated anything so plebian as high school. She had been considering moving on to another town, another set of daily routines, when the paper had run the announcement that *cheerleading* was coming to the local high school, and she had decided to come back for one more year—one more year that had transformed, after her customary break to let the minds of the faculty recover, into another four-year trip through the halls of academia.

Cheerleading was *fascinating*. It was like the humans had suddenly figured out that they couldn't fly, and were trying to figure out a way to make up for it. It wasn't there yet, but part of being a vampire was learning how to see the places in the pattern where the shape of things to come hadn't quite appeared, and Andrea could see them soaring. The tumbling and pom-pom shaking of today would give way to the death-defying stunts of tomorrow, and it was going to be amazing, and she was only sorry she wouldn't be there, flying with them.

Being a vampire meant passing for a human teenager for a long, long time, but by the time cheerleaders learned to fly, she would be past this stage in her life, off to spend a decade or so repeating her missus degree at some middle-of-nowhere college with easily enthralled registrars. It was a pity. She liked this town, and she liked this school, and she liked these *girls*. Oh, these girls, these bright, brief birds, who were more like attractive chickens than the parrots their children's children would be, but still. They did the best they could with what they had. They did the best they could.

There were already people behind the auto shop—greasers in their black leather jackets, vocational study kids in their white shirts with the rolled sleeves and their old jeans with the pegged cuffs, like rolling something was the same as repairing it—but none of them *mattered*. They'd come around the corner to find the quarterback there once, all golden boy glory and the possibility of getting caught while in company so elevated that an example needed to be made. Worse, he'd been there with some tarty little thing he must have scraped off the drama department floor, all popping gum and teased-up hair, when he should have been there with Mary if he was going to be there with anyone.

The Pumpkins took up their usual position along the wall. Iris produced a pack of cigarettes. About half the girls took one, while the other half brushed their hair, or checked their lipstick, or did any one of a dozen other things that signaled "too cool to be in class, yet still too cool for you" to anyone who happened to wander by. Andrea waved off the cigarette she was offered, choosing instead to rest her shoulders against the wall and watch the others with a possessive predator's eye.

These were *her* Pumpkins. They wouldn't be hers forever, would move on to the protectorates of other monsters, other ideal lives, but for now, for the moment, they belonged entirely to her. She didn't have to share if she didn't want to, and upon careful consideration, she found that she didn't want to.

Which was why it was such a problem when the hot rod roared up on the narrow stretch of asphalt behind the auto shop and the boy in the black leather jacket leaned out the window, grabbed Iris around the waist, and hauled her, shrieking, into the car. Iris kicked and fought the whole way, to no avail: in a matter of seconds, the hot rod was shrieking away again, leaving only a few tire tracks and a single Mary Jane to show that it had been there in the first place.

Andrea pushed away from the wall, eyes wide and mouth hanging open, like she couldn't decide between shock and fury. The rest of the Pumpkins were squawking and fluttering like the birds she'd always fancied them to be, stunned into meaningless motion.

It was Laura—pretty, vapid Laura, who never met a question she couldn't answer incorrectly—who seemed the most collected, possibly because she spent so much of her time confused that a few unexpected events simply weren't enough to throw her.

"I think Iris just got kidnapped," she said, as calmly as if she were remarking on the weather. "Maybe we ought to go and get her back?"

CUTTING CLASS WAS ONE THING: leaving school grounds before the final bell was something else altogether. It was likely to attract attention if the whole squad tried it, no matter how much they all wanted to be a part of Iris's daring rescue. *Especially* since there was always a chance some teacher would suddenly get a bee in their bonnet about talking to Iris, and when that happened, they'd need to have people in place to make excuses and shuffle her supposed location from bathroom to bathroom as she fought valiantly against a scourge of "girl troubles."

In the end, only four of them—including Andrea, of course; she wasn't captain yet, but everyone knew she was going to be, just like everyone knew the squad was *hers*, had been since the beginning, would be until her preternaturally slow aging took her away from high school at last—were able to cram themselves into Mary's car, with Mary herself behind the wheel.

"So try not to die, okay?" said Mary, flicking her cigarette out the window. That was the whole of the warning she gave before she slammed her foot down on the gas and roared out of the student parking lot at a speed that would reduce the occupants of the car to mere brightly-colored blurs in the eyes of anyone who happened to be looking. Andrea, who was in the front passenger seat, squeaked loudly and grabbed hold of the dashboard, clutching it until the indents of her fingers were pressed into the leather. The girls in the backseat shrieked and clutched each other.

Mary didn't seem to notice any of that. She was *driving*. Outside of a car, she knew everyone thought of her as mulish and stupid and a little bit useless, and maybe they weren't wrong: she was all those things, and it didn't bother her, most of the time, because she knew that at the end of the day, she'd be back behind the wheel, back on the open road. Her father had stopped paying for her gas after her first report card of the school year, saying that no daughter of his who couldn't even pass home economics deserved to have her own car. She hadn't put a penny in the tank since then, and her baby handled better than ever, taking the curves like a dream, unbeatable on the highway. Unstoppable.

She liked being a Fighting Pumpkin and she liked her squad well enough to put up with them, but sometimes she thought life would have been an awful lot better if she'd just been born a boy. Boys were allowed to be stupid and a little bit useless and love their cars more than they loved anything else in the world. They had permission, and she didn't.

But oh, none of that mattered when she drove, in her souped-up hot rod that she'd rebuilt herself in the auto shop, with the tank as dry as a bone, running on hope and hormones and *need*.

Andrea clutched the dashboard a little tighter. When she spoke, there was a strangled note in her voice. "Maybe try not to kill us all today?"

"You're a vampire," said Mary, with her customary bluntness. "You're hard to kill."

"'Hard' is not the same thing as 'impossible,' and everyone else in this car is *human*." Well, one reanimated corpse, one alien in a vat-grown body, but human for all intents and purposes. Human in the sense of a car crash would end with a trip to the morgue for some, if not all, of them.

Mary sighed. "Spoilsport," she said, and slowed down a little.

The girls in the back seat heaved a sigh of relief.

"Why did they take *Iris*?" asked Emily, leaning forward. She was one of the younger members of the squad, still new to the orange and green, and the delicate web of nonsense and improbability that bound them all was still revealing itself to her. She'd technically been at school before joining the Fighting Pumpkins, but as she'd been three separate students at the time, it didn't really count. "She's only barely team captain anymore. Everybody knows it."

"They probably knew that taking Andrea would end with nobody having a throat anymore," said Laura, and yawned, pulling in as much air as she could manage. "People need throats. All the biology studies agree."

"I don't know, but we're going to find out," said Andrea grimly. "All the hot rodders hang out down by the levee. I've seen that car before, I know I have. We're going to find it, and then we're going to find the driver, and then we're going to explain why you don't touch a Fighting Pumpkin."

"Explain with fists, right?" asked Mary.

"We spend two hours every day kicking higher than our own heads," said Andrea. "I think we can get our point across."

"Only if we get there before they hurt her," said Mary, and bore down on the gas again.

If any of the rest of them had driven like that, they would have had the fuzz on their bumpers in seconds. Not Mary. She drove like the road was her personal property and she was only deigning to share it with the people around her out of pity, because if she didn't share, they'd be relegated to horse trails and gravel driveways. The police never bothered her. Andrea privately suspected that they were afraid to.

The town zipped by outside the windows in a blur of bright color and brighter sunlight. Andrea let go of the dashboard long enough to dig her sunscreen out of her purse and apply a liberal amount to her arms, rubbing it in until the vague tingling that had started there faded away. Mary gave her a sidelong glance.

"So, if you lost that, would you just, I don't know, burst into flame?"

"No. But I would get a very, very bad sunburn, and then I would get very, very hungry, and since the symbiont that's responsible for vampirism isn't as picky about where its next meal comes from as a human would be, I'd start to see you all as potential lunch partners. In the bad, messy, bloody, dead way." Andrea smiled, and her teeth suddenly seemed a little pointier than they were really meant to be. It was probably a trick of the light, and yet . . . "So someone who thought hiding my sunscreen on tryout day would be a good way to keep a vampire from being team captain, well. That someone would have to be prepared to attend a lot of funerals. Including her own."

"Can you really attend your own funeral?" asked Laura.

Andrea kept her eyes on Mary. "I don't know," she said. "Maybe it's time for us to find out."

Bit by bit, Mary's smugness melted away, replaced by unease. She switched her gaze back to the road. "I was just asking," she muttered.

"Stop asking," advised Andrea.

Silence fell across the car. They spun past the city limits, and into the surrounding farmland, flashing past strawberry fields and artichoke patches and cows that didn't even lift their massive heads to watch the hot rod full of cheerleaders zoom by.

The fields fell away, replaced by unirrigated scrubland. Looming out of the landscape ahead of them like a warning came the boxy shape of the old military complex, wreathed in a heat haze that seemed to shimmer there no matter what the weather did. It stood barely ahead of the slash of the levee that tore across the land like a scar. It didn't rain as often in California as it did in so many other places—sort of funny, given how much food they produced, but true. When it did rain, the soil was often unprepared, and couldn't take the volume. The levee kept everything they loved from being washed away.

One day, it would fail. Andrea glanced at Mary again, this time with the gentler eye of the much older and much wiser and much wearier. All these girls would likely be women by the time that happened, their youths burnt out like fields of stubble in the fall. They might not even be alive when the flood came. But it would come all the same. The flood always came.

Cars began to appear out of the heat haze as they drove closer. It felt like they were moving toward some great confrontation, something that should have happened in the grace of twilight, not in the glaring light of day. Andrea tensed. This *was* the sort of thing that was better done by night. Iris would have been just as easy to snatch from outside the diner, or from the picnic tables in front of the burger joint downtown. All the Pumpkins went there after school at least three times a week. So why take her from behind the auto shop, unless it was to force this confrontation during the daylight hours?

Suddenly, this felt like the jaws of some great and terrible beast, gaping wide for now, but ready to snap shut the moment they were too deep to turn back. Andrea gripped the dashboard tighter. It didn't matter. They needed to keep going. Iris was counting on them, and Iris was a Fighting Pumpkin, and if there was one thing she had learned from cheerleading, it was that you *did not leave a teammate behind*.

"Loyalty is a plague," Andrea muttered.

"What?" asked Mary.

"Drive faster," snapped Andrea.

Mary drove faster.

THEY WHIPPED AROUND the last curve like a carload of avenging angels, skidding to a halt barely fifteen feet from the line of hot rods that were already parked there, waiting for them to arrive. Most of the drivers looked like they had barely finished their own high school educations, hair slicked back and piled high, jackets missing their sleeves and dripping with chrome chains that were too short to be used as weapons in any kind of proper fight.

Still, they made an intimidating picture.

The four Pumpkins, in their pegged pants and their orange and green accent scarves, did not. But they climbed out of Mary's car all the same, hands clenched into fists, pretty faces contorted into scowls. It was not, perhaps, a showdown for the ages. It was a showdown all the same.

"One of yours took one of ours, and she didn't go willingly," called Andrea. "Give her back and this is all over. No one has to get hurt."

The greasers laughed. A few of them made obscene gestures in her direction. Andrea looked serenely on, as did Laura. Her planet boasted several gesture-based languages, and none of them included profanity: on her world, all profanity was spoken. Thus far, the rest of the squad hadn't seen fit to enlighten her on the many ways Earthlings could tell each other to fuck off. It wasn't about preserving her innocence; more about making sure she didn't start flipping teachers the bird when they displeased her.

"Sorry, sweetheart, but this ain't a negotiation," rumbled the man Andrea took for their leader. He was tall and broad and if not for his baby-face and the class ring still glittering on his hand, he would have seemed far too old for the gang around him. Like her, only with his years written on the outside, not the inside. "We bought the little witch fair and square."

"Iris is a witch?" Laura cocked her head as she turned to look accusingly at Andrea. "I wasn't told that. I should have been told that. I have questions."

"I think he means 'bitch,' and doesn't want to cuss in front of girls." Andrea narrowed her eyes. "Iris isn't for sale."

"I don't care about swearing in front of you, *sweetheart*," said the man. "I care about swearing in front of my lady. Mary, baby? You want to come over here?"

"Sure do, honey," said Mary, and skipped around the front of her car to stand next to the man. In case that wasn't a sufficient signal of where her loyalties lay, she bounced up onto her tiptoes and pressed a kiss against his cheek before turning and offering a poisonous smile to her fellow Fighting Pumpkins. "Oh, by the way, I won't be in class tomorrow. Or at the game this weekend. Or ever again."

"You're dropping out of school?" Emily sounded horrified. "But we're supposed to get a good education so we can take better care of our kids! And what about the squad? We need you for the pyramid!"

Andrea, who remembered a time when the good education wouldn't have been a part of that sentence, somehow managed not to groan.

Mary rolled her eyes. "As if any of us are getting a good education in that place. Isn't that right, Frank?"

"You know it, baby." Frank kissed the top of Mary's head before looking blandly at the remainder of the squad. "You should go. Gonna be a long walk home. Unless..."

"Unless?" asked Andrea.

"We could give you a car and a driver. And your girl back, of course. No point in coming all the way out here without getting what you came for. It'll cost you, but maybe you're willing to pay. How strong is that sense of ownership, dead girl? You willing to go one for one if it gets your precious squad out of here?"

Andrea hesitated. Then she cocked her head to the side, looking at the bruiser thoughtfully. "What's your grandfather's name?"

"Abraham Harker."

"*Mmm.*" She shook her head. "I thought Abe and I had buried the hatchet. How is he?"

"Dead." Frank scowled. "You should be, too."

"So you kidnapped one of my cheerleaders, all so you could lure me... where?" Andrea made a show of looking around herself. "The middle of nowhere? I'm a vampire. That doesn't mean I don't know about camping."

"Danny." Frank snapped his fingers. Another of the greasers appeared, standing anxiously by, a bucket of clear liquid in his hands. Frank pointed at it. "This stuff's designed to take the oil off an engine. It'll clean anything. Even the filthy skin of the damned."

"I'll have you know I bathe regularly, not that it's any of your business," said Andrea.

"Don't care." Frank looked at her coldly. "That's the deal I'm offering. Your girls go free. You stay here, wash off that sunscreen of yours, and burn."

"You didn't say anything about killing her," said Mary, doubt creeping into her voice. "You just said you were going to get your own back, for your gramps. She hasn't done anything worth *killing* over."

"You don't know anything, Mary," said Frank, and shoved her away from him with one meaty hand. She cried out a little as she stumbled, trying to keep her feet. In the end, gravity won, and she fell—

—only for Laura's hand to grip her wrist, stopping her before her face could hit the ground. The perpetually vacant cheerleader looked down at Mary, a small frown on her lips. "I do not believe he is an optimal mate for you," she said. "You should consider another."

"What the hell's wrong with *her*?" asked Frank. "You cheerleaders are a gang of freaks."

"You have no idea," said Mary, glaring at him as Laura pulled her to her feet. "I'll drive the girls home. Whether or not you let us take Iris."

He snorted. "Loyalty lost that easily? Isn't that just like a girl?" He returned his attention to Andrea. "So. What's it going to be? You or her? I promise she won't suffer, if you decide to be selfish. My boys can be fast."

"I take it your 'boys' won't be dropping her off safely on her front porch," said Andrea coolly.

"Now she gets it."

Andrea glanced to the others. The rest of the squad—now including Mary, who looked confused by her easy reacceptance into their ranks, as if she'd expected to be shut out for longer, held at arm's length and refused their protection, and that alone made Andrea want to scream— was arrayed behind her, out of uniform but united all the same. How she loved them. How she treasured them.

How she needed to protect them.

"I'll stay," she said, bowing her head. "Let Iris go, let my squad drive away, and I'll stay here and wash off the sunscreen and let what happens . . . happen."

Frank's eyes shone with triumph. "Get the girl," he snapped.

Several greasers hurried to obey, dragging Iris out of the back of one of the cars and bringing her to Frank's side. Her hair was a mess and her blouse had a tear in one sleeve, but she appeared otherwise unharmed as she struggled against the men holding her arms.

"Andrea, I'm sorry!" she cried.

"It's not your fault." And it wasn't, not really. It was her own fault, for letting Abraham live without infecting him; for staying in the same town, following the same routines, loving the same sweetly predictable things. This had always been coming. It was just too bad it had come now, when there were innocents in the line of fire. Andrea forced herself to smile, meeting Iris's eyes and pushing, just a little, to make the other girl listen. "Go back to school. I'll join you there as soon as I can."

"But your sunscreen—"

"Go back to school."

The greasers shoved Iris toward the other Pumpkins, and they hurried to gather her up, ushering her into the waiting car. For a moment, Mary looked like she was going to say something. Then she focused on Frank's cold, scowling face, and got behind the wheel, and drove away, leaving Andrea alone with the kidnappers.

Frank pointed imperiously. Danny dropped the bucket in front of Andrea, never coming quite close enough for her to grab.

"Clean yourself," snapped Frank.

"Your funeral," said Andrea, and crouched to pick up the sponge and begin wiping her exposed skin clean.

The bucket was full of brake cleaner. Of course it was. Cheap, easy, stocked in every auto shop. And it was cold. It would have been pleasant, if not for the burning sensation that followed it as the sun found more and more of her exposed skin. She left her face for last. The pain didn't care where on her body it happened, but she *hated* when her eyelids blistered. It was inconvenient and unsightly, and she wanted to avoid it if she could.

After wiping the sponge only lightly across her face, she dropped it back into the bucket and straightened, holding out her arms, which were already turning red, already growing ripe with a harvest of fluid-filled boils.

"Happy?" she asked.

"Delighted," said Frank.

Things began to happen very quickly then.

The pain, which had been building since the first swipe of the sponge across her skin, reached a fever pitch. Conscious thought yielded before the flames, and Andrea went willingly. She knew the truth of what she was, had known it for a hundred years and more, and while she was perfectly happy to embrace both the good and bad aspects of her nature, there were some things she did her best to avoid and hence had no living desire to see. Agony woke the symbiont, woke the hunger she was home and heir to, and the last thing she heard before her body was no longer her own was screaming, shrill and pained and virtually inhuman.

It went on for a long, long time. But Andrea, in a very real way, was no longer there to hear it.

WHEN SHE CAME TO, the sun was down and she was sprawled, completely covered in blood and surrounded by corpses, on the dusty ground next to the levee. Andrea looked at herself and sighed. There had been plenty of time for the blood to set; this was one more really nice sweater down the drain.

Gingerly, she stood. Everything seemed to be working fine. That was swell. She needed all her limbs for the rest of the cheerleading season.

Andrea turned to the nearest body. Frank, his throat gone and his eyes open in endless, sightless surprise.

"Well, *honey*," she said. "How about you loan me your keys so I can drive myself home?" Turned out he had no objection. She folded herself into his car and cranked the radio high, and all the road was ahead of her, and she was going to be young forever. In the end, what else mattered?

"Go, Pumpkins," she muttered, and hit the gas.

SEANAN MCGUIRE lives, works, and watches way too many horror movies in the Pacific Northwest, where she shares her home with her two enormous blue cats, a ridiculous number of books, and a large collection of creepy dolls. Seanan does not sleep much, publishing an average of four books a year under both her own name and the pen name Mira Grant. Her first book, Rosemary and Rue, *was released in September 2009, and she hasn't stopped running since. When not writing, Seanan enjoys Disney Parks, horror movies, and looking winsomely at Marvel editorials as she tries to convince them to let her write for the X-Men. Keep up with Seanan at* www.seananmcguire.com, *on Twitter as* @seananmcguire, *or by walking into a cornfield at night and calling the secret, hidden name of the Great Pumpkin to the moon. When you turn, she will be there. She will always have been there.*

THE SOUND OF HEAVY FEET SLAPPING THE ground behind him came closer and closer. He was out of breath, but he'd been chased before down Old Baldy and Heartbreak Ridge, so he'd become used to running for his life. But that was Korea, not the ass end of Oregon in the old fishing town of Astoria. And he'd been carrying a carbine back then instead of the slippery yet voluptuous mermaid, her lips pressed against his neck sending thoughts that would make an eighty-year-old keel over for the sheer preposterousness of the position. Even now, with the Columbia River within reach, his cock was hard and his body twisted with the need to react to the mermaid's

Sea Lords of the Columbia

BY WESTON OCHSE

*"So give it. What are the Finns
doing with mermaids?"*

advances, his mind acting out the fantasy until he was left gasping and out of breath and barely running. The only distraction was an odd track from the new Carl Perkins' song, "Dixie Fried," slashing through his head: *Rave on, children, I'm with you, rave on, cats, he cried. It's almost dawn and the cops ain't gone, and I've been Dixie fried.*

A shout from one of the burly Finns chasing him gave him new energy as he surged forward. The Columbia was less than fifty yards away. And, magically, Hemmo was already halfway there and waiting with a length of two-by-four in each hand. All Doogie had to do was reach the river and they'd all be free.

But let's not get ahead of ourselves . . .

THE STORY REALLY STARTED two days ago in the Desdemona, a bar where anything and, often, everything happens. The low-ceilinged wooden building built from the lumber of its namesake, a ship that foundered on the Columbia Bar fifty years earlier, is full of roughnecks, fishermen, and hookers from upstairs. Leather and chains are what the guys wear. Leather and lace is what the girls wear. Everyone has a story to tell, and it's to the short Japanese man talking to the immense Finn where the story takes us, and you can tell right away that it's a well-worked tale.

"The morning mist rising from the Columbia River met the fog rolling in from the Columbia Bar, creating a fabric of unreality. The normally troublesome waves had flattened, making the water around my boat as pristine as a mirror. I should have known something was going on, when a monster snagged at my line, almost breaking my arm with the force of it. Five, ten, fifteen minutes passed as I fought the fish, letting it drag as often as I would reel. When it finally landed, we were both exhausted. I noosed it and pulled it into the boat, then things got real interesting." Doogie Nezumi, second-generation Japanese-American and Korean War veteran then lowered his voice and said what had been burning a hole inside of him for the last two days.

Hemmo slapped his beer down and open-mouth-ogled his war buddy and best friend. "What do you mean the fish spoke to you?"

Hemmo Saarsgaard was an acre tall compared to Doogie and as angular as a pike. They each wore a white t-shirt underneath leather jackets. Blue jeans and combat boots finished their ensemble. Doogie couldn't help note that they were still in uniform albeit not the same uniform they'd worn in Korea. The difference was that back then they'd been part of something—part of something special. Now they were just—they weren't part of anything. They were just drifting like every other war-aged man in America back in the Land of the Big PX with no focus and no prospects.

Doogie pushed the ennui aside and stood a little straighter. "Just as I said. It spoke to me."

"I mean, did its lips move? Did it swim up to you and begin a conversation? I mean, come on, Doogie, you can't just lead with, *Did I tell you what the fish said?*"

"It didn't swim up. I caught it. I just told you. And no, its lips didn't move. It spoke to me in my head."

"How do you know that it wasn't just in your head? Why attribute it to the fish?" Hemmo eyed Doogie. "You took a fair bit of abuse over there. Remember when we were mortared that one night near Kaesong? You were raving about seeing Chinese in the trenches for days."

Doogie shook his head. "Fucking Third Battle of the Hook. You had to remind me. And there were like a billion Chinese in the trenches."

"But they weren't wearing pink leotards and attacking us with claw hammers like you screamed they were."

Doogie gave himself a self-depreciating smile. "Okay, I might have been a little out of it then, but I swear to you I am not crazy."

"Was a hard time, my friend." Hemmo spun as he heard the clatter of chairs. He tossed back his beer, then threw his glass into a conflagration of men and pool sticks.

Doogie watched as the Finn used his ham-sized hands to pound belligerents into the floor. Within seconds, he was the only one standing. He glanced around, as if checking to see if anyone wanted more, then strode back to the bar.

Hemmo was always like that. He was the brute who'd take down anyone who stood against him or his friends.

Doogie felt the same way, but because of his size, he had to concentrate on speed and guile.

Sandra slid a fresh beer in front of the Finn. "Thanks, Hemmo." Then she winked. "On the house."

Hemmo grinned. "It's what I do, Sandra. Hey, you up for something later?"

She flashed a grin. "I might be."

"See you at one then." He leaned over the counter and ogled her as she went to help another customer, then he stood straight and shook his head. "A good fight never fails to get them all hot."

"I think *you're* all hot, Hemmo," Doogie said. "You know she's married, right?"

"To a fisherman who never comes home."

"Don't you think it's wrong?" Doogie asked.

"That he won't come home and be with his woman? Hell yes." Hemmo sipped his beer, then asked, "Where were we? Oh yeah, how do you know that the talking fish wasn't just something you made up?"

"Because the fish told me that it got caught on purpose to deliver a message and would I please let it go when it was done."

Hemmo took a long slow drink of his beer, using the opportunity to gauge Doogie.

Doogie took the moment to break for the bathroom. The door to the head was to the left of the jukebox. The combatants had already risen from the floor. A biker from M.C. Portland Joes was leaning over and making his selection. Probably something Elvis who was all the new rage. A hooker from upstairs came down smelling of roses and sweat. Doogie wrinkled his nose. He'd had enough of them back in Pusan when they'd been waiting to come home. Only, instead of Roses, they'd smelled of a different flower, something remarkably Asian.

After he was done and back at the bar, Doogie ordered another beer.

It wasn't until it had arrived and he'd had a drink before Hemmo asked. "And did you?"

"Did I what?"

"Let it go?"

"Oh, hell no. Who lets go a thirty-pound salmon?"

"So you killed the talking fish," Hemmo stated, both eyebrows raised.

"Evidently all fish can talk. Does that mean I'm going to give up fishing?"

"Who told you that all fish can talk?"

"The talking fish told me."

"And you automatically believed him?"

"Based on talking to the fish who told me they all could talk I was inclined to do so, yes."

This time it was Hemmo's turn to go to the head.

Sure enough, Elvis crooned from the Juke about a "Mystery Train." Sometime between the time they'd gone to war and returned in '53, the music had changed. Or at least Doogie felt that way. He thought about the way he was telling his old friend the story and hated drawing it out this way, but he knew he had to in order to achieve the effect he desired—to get him to do what he wanted him to do.

Hemmo took his time, so the Juke cycled through Carl Perkins' "Dixie Fried" and Tennessee Ernie Ford's "Sixteen Tons" before he returned. Then he downed the rest of his beer and turned to face Doogie, not saying a word, just staring.

When it looked like he was about to ask the question Doogie was waiting for him to ask, Doogie interrupted. "What do you think it means to be Dixie Fried?"

"What? Where'd that come from?"

"The Carl Perkins song." Doogie put down his beer and played air guitar as he sang, "Rave on, children, I'm with you, rave on, cats, he cried. It's almost dawn and the cops ain't gone, and I've been Dixie fried."

Sandra gave a polite clap from behind the bar.

Doogie bowed and grabbed his beer. "So?"

"I don't know what it means. Fucked up maybe? Dead maybe?"

"Dixie Fried," Doogie mused. "I like that."

Hemmo grabbed the front of Doogie's shirt and lifted him until he was on his toes. "Enough of this shit. You're drawing out the story just to irritate me. What did the damn fish say? And if you say Dixie Fried I'm going to punch you."

"Okay, okay. Put me down. It delivered a message."

Hemmo released him. "Who sent the message?"

"The talking fish said Musma sent it."

"What the hell is a Musma?"

"From what I gather it's a sentient sturgeon living near the Columbia Bar."

Hemmo's mouth opened and shut in exasperation. His hand went into a fist, making Doogie back away. "Did you say a sentient sturgeon living near the Columbia Bar?"

Doogie nodded. "I did."

Hemmo shook his head and seemed about to explode, but instead asked in barely controlled exasperation, "And what does Musma want?"

"For us to rescue the two mermaids that the Finns are keeping in Suomi Hall."

Hemmo's face went white. "And you believe the Finns have them?"

"I do now."

"Why is that?"

"I think you know why. Because you didn't question the fact that mermaids exist. Just that the Finns had them in the hall. So give it. What are the Finns doing with mermaids?"

Hemmo glanced around, then elbowed down to the bar. In a low voice, he said, "Doogie, you know I can't tell you about any of that. I'm sworn."

"But they're holding a pair of fucking mermaids?"

"It's not like that."

"Then what's it like?"

Hemmo ordered another beer and didn't even look at Doogie until he'd taken a drink. Then he said, "They have a good life, Doogie. They want to be there."

"Are they free to go?"

"They're being kept safe, and like I said, they want to be there."

"Come on, Hemmo. Remember when we took liberty in Pusan?"

"Yeah, I remember it. But this is different."

"How is it different? What did you help me do when I found that guy renting out all those young kids to GIs?"

Hemmo sighed. "Beat the crap out of him and took him behind the lines to let him get shot as a North Korean spy."

"And did we do it, Hemmo?"

"Yes."

"And were you happy about it?"

"At the time, yes."

"So why not the mermaids?"

"Because they aren't . . . they aren't . . . "

"It's because they aren't human, right?"

Hemmo cocked his head, then eventually nodded. "I suppose."

"What if there were dogs being abused, would you save them?"

Hemmo nodded again.

"So you'd help a dog but not a mermaid." Doogie pounded the bar with his fist.

Hemmo dropped his gaze to the floor.

Doogie punched him in the shoulder. "Then why the hell won't you help me save a pair of mermaids who are being held against their will?"

Hemmo looked away.

"Doing what's right doesn't depend on the species, race, or ethnicity, Hemmo. Right is just right."

"But the Finnish Brotherhood . . . " Hemmo began.

"What about them? Did they have your back in Korea?"

"That's not fair, Doogie."

"Who said life is fair." He reached up and put a hand squarely on Hemmo's shoulder. "We. Have. To. Rescue. The. Mermaids," he said, enunciating every word.

"So says a sentient sturgeon to a mind-speaking salmon that you ate?" Hemmo shook his head and wiped his face with one of his meaty paws. "This whole conversation is insane, you know that."

But Doogie pressed. "Even then. Right is right."

Bo Diddley broke into his refrain from "I'm a Man" and neither of them talked about it anymore.

THE NEXT EVENING found them in Uniontown—the part of Astoria positively run by the Finns who'd come over earlier in the century like a Viking invasion. Normally, Suomi Hall, Home of the Finnish Brotherhood, was closed to only those of Finnish descent. But once a year on Veteran's Day, they allowed non-Finn veterans into the hall for their celebration. Although Hemmo had been inside the hall a hundred times, this was the first time Doogie, or any Japanese-American for that matter, had been in the hall, and they let him know it right at the door.

"Well, I appreciate the hospitality," he said to the hulking Finn guarding the door.

"Just don't touch anything that isn't yours or we'll have to send you back to Korea where you came from," the Finn said.

"I'm Japanese-American, not Korean."

"Whatever the nationality of the squinty-eyed bastard what fathered you, I don't give a shit. You just better behave."

Ten minutes later, after elbowing their way through the throng of perpetually dissatisfied Finns being served warm beer and eating dried salt cod, they were standing by a door guarded by an even bigger Finn than the first.

"No way, Hemmo. Orders are no one goes down there except those with appointments."

"Come on, Peter. We just got back from the war. We need some tension release."

Peter gave Doogie a look much like a man would a rusted broke-down jalopy. "Not him."

Hemmo pressed. "He's a veteran too. Without him, I never would have made it back. Come on, man. Do it for your country. Do it for me."

Peter was Hemmo's cousin and they'd grown up as close as brothers. He seemed to be considering it, but then shook his head. "Sorry, Hemm. No way will Garn allow his type to touch them."

"What if I just watch?" Doogie asked, putting on his best *I'm just a poor Asian who doesn't know any better* face.

That made Peter blink. "You want to watch?"

Doogie grinned sheepishly. "Sure. I mean, who wouldn't. If I can't actually be with them, then watching would be cool." He tapped his head. "I could save it as a memory for later."

Hemmo put a hand on his cousin's shoulder. "Yeah, Peter. What if he watches? I'll make sure he doesn't touch anything."

Peter gave his cousin a pained look, then sighed. "Damn it, Hemm. Fine. Go ahead. But if I get shit over this, you're going to owe me."

Hemmo patted his cousin on the back hard enough to shatter a normal person, but it barely fazed Peter. "Thanks. You're right. I do. I owe you one."

Peter shook his head and stepped aside. He used a metal circle of keys to open an ancient-looking partially-rusted metal door. Hinges creaked with the weight and effort.

The heady scent of water slapped Doogie in the face as he descended, the aroma dark and murky with a hint of salt. Moss and lichen slimed along the concrete walls and stairs, so he held fast to the rail as he took each careful step. Light glowed green from below. The sounds of Bob Doss's "Don't Be Gone Long" rode over the top of people talking. Laughter, low and deep, gurgled from the chest of someone happy.

When they reached the landing, Doogie followed Hemmo, keeping his head and eyes down, trying to seem as insouciance as he could.

A thin help-yourself-bar was affixed to the wall nearest the stairs. The moss motif continued.

Hemmo grabbed two ceramic cups and filled them with beer from a pitcher. He passed one to Doogie and sipped his own, the cup all but disappearing in the hand of the Finn. Hemmo leaned back against the bar and surveyed the room.

Doogie joined him and allowed himself to see the room for the first time.

A half-naked incredibly fat Finn glared at him from a stool on the other side of the room. The hatred poured from his eyes, but that didn't seem to be enough for him to want to get up and do something about it. Beating up Doogie probably seemed too close to exercise.

Five other Finns, all dressed in white robes, sat in metal chairs around a mossy rock that took up the center of the room, chatting and talking amongst themselves. Several glanced their way, but then returned to their muted conversation.

But it was the other side of the room that got his attention. A large circular grate was padlocked in the middle of the wall. Water trickled from the dark mouth behind it. Probably open to the Columbia somehow, Doogie surmised. The green glow he'd noted before came from each of the two pools on either side of the grate, which seemed to be fed by high tide. Underwater lights green-lit the water, letting you see all the way to the bottom. Each pool was roughly a circle and seemed to be carved out of the rock.

The pool on the left held a man who stood, back to them, chest deep in the water, elbows resting on the pool edge.

No one stood in the pool on the left, but something stirred within it. Doogie stared at it until he finally saw the cresting of a length of tail and a shimmering of scales.

That accounted for one of the mermaids, but what of the other?

Doogie returned his gaze to the pool on the right just as the man threw his head back and groaned. A shudder shot through his body, until he was completely locked into a rigid line. Then, as if the air had been let out of him, he sagged, deflated. He stood, staring at the water for a long moment, then turned, and with both hands, levered himself out of the water. His cock fluttered, then hung, worn and getting smaller. Standing tall, he stretched his arms high above his head. He was older than Hemmo by about twenty years, but still had the muscular physique of a working longshoreman. A tattoo of a triple-masted ship covered his chest, faded and blurred from age. The word *LANKMAR* in big blocky letters below the ship. He glanced up, then walked straight toward them. He passed Doogie without a look, then grabbed a cup and poured beer into it.

"Hemmo," he said, taking a long pull of beer.

"Garn," Hemmo replied, nodding.

"You bring a pet in here?"

Hemmo glanced at Doogie. "He's just here to watch."

"Ahh," Garn said, draining his cup. "One of those."

A flash caught the corner of Doogie's vision and he turned back to the pool Garn had just exited. Blue-tinged hands with black nails grabbed the side of the pool and a head appeared. Long black hair streaked with blue hung wet at the sides of a face the color of a noon sky. Liquid yellow eyes slanted on each side of a petite nose. She was all woman until he took in the lips. Rather than the lips of a person, the mermaid had the lips of a bottom feeding fish—a sucker or a Koi. They were pursed and rigid, making it appear as if the mermaid were in a constant state of surprise.

Doogie couldn't help but stare. Then he understood. Garn. His cock. The mermaid. Her lips. He felt a sickness course through his body that he hadn't experienced since Korea when he'd discovered the man renting out young underage girls to horny GIs.

The mermaid locked eyes with him. He felt his sickness wear away as another feeling began to subsume it. Despite his wishes, he felt himself harden. Thoughts of touching her skin, rubbing his hands along her scales invaded his mind. He could see himself and her, entwined.

Then her eyes broke away and the feeling melted.

He watched as the fat man stood, dropped his towel on the stool, and with grunting effort lowered his prodigious body into the pool, belly so large it almost hid his tiny cock.

The mermaid pushed herself away from the side of the pool and floated on her back. Water rolled off perky blue breasts, each topped with a black nipple. She floated until the man seemed ready, then, like a body sinking into the sea, she turned slightly and sunk beneath the surface. Her tail slapped the water as she turned.

Soon the fat man's head lolled back.

And Doogie knew exactly what was happening and he didn't want to.

Garn suddenly erupted in laughter, head back as he bellowed toward the rocky ceiling.

"Your pet has a hard-on, Hemmo. It wants to join in." Then he laughed again, rollicking in his idea of humor.

Doogie felt his bile rise, realizing that his hard-on remained. With a shaking hand, he sat the cup on the bar and pushed away unsteadily. He spun around, getting his bearings, then ran for the stairs. He slipped twice on the moss. When he got to the top, he banged on the door until it opened. He slid through the doorway, pushed his way through the crowd, out the door and into the street, where he fell to his knees, vomit spewing into the street. He stayed there, letting his cock unharden, the sky spitting drizzle on him until Hemmo came, helped him to his feet, and they both slouched away into the Astorian evening.

IT WAS WELL AFTER MIDNIGHT when Doogie directed Hemmo to pull his Jon-boat to the shore. The river was almost four miles across where they were, making it more an ocean than anything else, with waves and currents eager to capsize a vessel their size. But the hundred feet closest to shore was calm and almost flat, so they'd' taken advantage of it, putting in two miles up and rowing down. They were dressed in black watch caps, black jackets, and black pants. They'd covered their faces in wheel grease. Hemmo pulled gently at the oars, while Doogie stood in the prow of the boat, ready to jump to shore.

After they'd left Suomi Hall, they'd gone back to Doogie's place in John Day, where Hemmo had talked him out of stealing dynamite and blowing the fucking place down. They finished a six-pack of Olympia before Doogie had the idea of conducting night reconnaissance. He wanted to see where that grate let out and if he could access it from the outside.

As they neared the shore, Doogie moved to the front, jumped out with a rope in hand, and secured the boat to an old stump.

Hemmo shipped the oars, then slipped out the front more deftly than a big guy should move.

They both knelt in the lee of the bank. To their right was the access canal that would bring the water into the Suomi Hall basement during high tide. Now it was low tide, so only a few stranded puddles remained.

"You didn't have to come with me," Doogie whispered, "but I'm glad you did."

"I'm sure you would have figured out a way to get caught if I hadn't."

A splash sounded from somewhere nearby making both of them jump a little in their skin.

Hemmo glanced toward the sound, while Doogie began moving forward.

"It's a fish," Hemmo whispered.

"What I figured."

"No, it's really a fish."

Doogie glanced back for a brief instance and saw Hemmo staring at the water. "I heard you, now come on."

"But the fish is staring at me—and it's huge."

This gave Doogie pause. He slunk back down the embankment and crouched near Hemmo. Sure enough, an immense hog of a salmon that had to be near forty pounds sat ten feet away from them. Its rainbow colors winked in the starlight as water dripped from its back.

"What does it want?" Hemmo asked.

Doogie remembered the salmon that spoke with him and now regretted eating it. There was a majesty to the fish in their own environment that was unmistakable. If the giant sentient sturgeon was the King of the Columbia, then these salmon were certainly the Dukes and Dames.

"I think it wants to tell us something."

"What do we do?" Hemmo asked.

"I'm not sure." Then he remembered. "I think I have to touch it." He glanced at Hemmo. "Hold my left hand."

Hemmo grasped it and Doogie stepped into the cold dark water. He reached out with his right hand but was still a little short. But the salmon took the initiative and closed the space, placing its head in Doogie's outstretched hand.

She is dying.

"Who is dying?" he said aloud.

An image formed in his mind—a mermaid, slumped in the water, limbs akimbo and adrift, face slack, eyes closed.

Doogie remembered that one of the pools had been all but empty with just a hint of mermaid.

You must save her.

"I want to—*we* want to. But there are too many of them . . . Finns, I mean."

It must be tonight or she will die.

"But we can't. We need the tide. We're not ready. This is reconnaissance only."

The fish backed away, but remained near them.

Doogie retrieved his hand and Hemmo pulled him back.

"It wants us to—"

"I heard it in my head," Hemmo said, voice low and filled with awe. "It must be because I was touching you."

"Well then, you know what it wants us to do."

Despite the glazed look in Hemmo's eyes, he nodded. "I don't see how we can do it."

"Me neither, I—"

Doogie's mouth hung open as he stared at the shape coming at them from across the water.

Hemmo saw Doogie, followed his gaze, and his own mouth gaped open.

Surging toward them like Moby Dick was a giant white whale. Like its namesake, it seemed capable of crashing through ships, tearing apart structures, and devouring men whole. Although they couldn't see the mouth, two glowing great blue orbs seemed to glower at them from just above the water line. This whale wore armor. Instead of the smooth skin of a whale, this aquatic monster had hard rugged squares affixed to its body. Even whiter spikes ran from the front of its head and along its back.

"Call me Ishmael," Doogie rasped.

First it was far away, and then it was on them. The displaced water slammed into them, sending them crashing against the bank. Doogie felt himself tumble, then go under the water, pulling at him as it receded. He tried to stand, but found that he couldn't move his legs. Looking down, he saw with horror that they were held fast by several pairs of hands. Then his world turned upside down as his feet were pulled out from under him.

His head slammed on the rocky bottom of the shore and all went black. He was vaguely aware through the white hot pain that he was being pulled underwater. His ears rang. An avalanche of spots crashed into his eyes. His legs were tugged ... once ... twice ... pulling him deeper. He shook his head to clear it. And realized that he'd been holding his breath. He opened his eyes and knew why. Somehow, somewhere, he'd been pulled beneath the water and was now living in a green universe where mermaids held fast to his feet. To his front floated a sturgeon the size of a whale. A sturgeon that could only be Musma.

The monster's long snout ended in teeth the size of K-Bars. Four whiskers moved like antennae in the water.

Doogie looked down at his feet and saw that four mermaids held his legs. As much as he thought he'd want to, he didn't struggle. But his lungs did burn. He wasn't sure how long he could hold his breath.

He saw movement out of the corner of his eye and saw Hemmo,

struggling against the tentacles of an immense octopus. The Finn was screaming in the water, great bubbles gouting upward. His muscles popped along his arms, as he used them to try and swim upward, straining to be free. Then be breathed in the water and his eyes shot wide. For a brief instant, he stared at Doogie, panic and worry alive in the eyes, then even that melted away and what life had been in him left with the last bit of bubbles.

Doogie felt the last of his own air go. He started to struggle, but realized that without the air, he hadn't any energy. A sob sprung from deep inside him and shot free, his mouth opening, bubbles escaping. He tried not to breathe in water, he told his lungs not to do it, but they were too desperate to listen and fired a single frantic signal to his brain.

And he breathed in water.

His lungs filled with it.

His body convulsed.

And then he died.

For exactly ten seconds, then Musma reached out with one of its whiskers and grabbed him, pulling him into his mouth. Doogie lay in the darkness, his spirit aware of where he was, but only in the vaguest off-handest of ways. A moment, a day, a week, an epoch later, electricity fired through his body. His arms and legs shot rigid. A burning sensation sizzled impossibly along his wet skin, centering on his chest and neck. Then he was spit out, tumbling in the water, aware that he'd just drowned, somehow alive, and about to drown once more.

Doogie jerked his head back and forth and noted that he wasn't held any longer by the mermaids. He could swim for safety. He needed to swim for safety. But his limbs weren't his own yet. Another sob wrenched free and he began to—

Breathe.

He felt the rush of water through his neck and into, then out of, his lungs.

He brought a hand up and felt what could only be gills. He breathed and stared at Musma, then at Hemmo who was floating dead, nearby.

Why?

He wasn't ready.

Doogie mentally scoffed. *And I was. I never asked to be a fish.*

Not a fish. Something else. Merman. Merro. Dogo. The words are those of man. You are now of the sea. You belong to the Columbia. More man words but now powerful.

But why?

Because I called and you came. We need you.

I had a life. Hemmo had a life. You've taken that from us.

Took nothing. Gave everything. Now go. Save her.

Doogie immediately knew whom he was to save. She had a name but it was a piscine thing and unutterable to the human tongue. He felt the urge, the press to free her. Without a second thought, he surged to the surface, grabbing Hemmo as he went. He swam fluidly, his body understanding what he could never know, the way to move that created the easiest motion. When he neared the shore, he let his feet propel him forward. When his head broke the surface, he wretched free the water that was in his lungs and breathed air as if he'd done it a hundred times.

Doogie had never been strong, but he was strong now. He hauled Hemmo from the water and began pumping his chest.

"Come on, Hemmo. Come on, man," he said as he pumped. The sky was lightening which meant that they'd been under for hours. There was little to no chance that his friend could be alive. He was about to give up, when the Finn gagged, then lurched to his side, expelling water and bile onto the rocky shore. He fell to his side, gasping.

Hemmo lay there, chest heaving, his face white, eyes wide. "What . . . what was that?" he stuttered. His eyes were red as tears found their way free. "I died, Doogie. I died."

"You were Dixie Fried, Hemm."

"I was," he said, coughing. "I was fucking Dixie Fried."

Doogie placed his right hand on Hemmo's head. "But now you're back."

Hemmo locked eyes with Doogie, his eyes pleading. "Was it all real?"

"It was all real, Hemm. It was real and we were saved for a purpose."

"Doogs. What's going on? You're talking funny."

Doogie shook his head. "I can't explain it. I'm now tied into things. I can feel the pulse and throb of the river. I can hear movement in the deep. And what about you, Hemm? What do you hear?"

Hemmo levered himself to a sitting position. He seemed about to say something, then closed his mouth and cocked his head. "I can hear ... what is it I hear ... " Then his eyes brightened. "I can hear the trees." His head twisted to the right. "And the birds. I can understand them. Doogie. I can understand the birds. Oh my God, what is going on?" he lurched to his feet. "They're crazy, Doogie. The birds are fucking crazy."

"Never listen to the birds." Doogie stood as well, smiling. "You have responsibility of the land, without it, the Columbia would have nothing to feed it. My responsibility is to the river, without which, the land would die. We're together in this, Hemmo. You and me."

Hemmo nodded. "I feel it too. I haven't felt so part of something since ... since ... "

"We were fighting in Korea."

"Yes!" Hemmo said pounding a fist into his hand. "Then we belonged to the army. We were saving the Korean people."

"Now we're part of a different army, Hemm." Doogie turned to move. "We have a mission—mermaids to save. Won't last until morning." He considered the graying sky. "We haven't much time."

When they reached the canal, they halted. They'd been in the water a long time. Long enough for the tide to shift. Where before it had been all but dry, it was now filled with water the height of a man's shoulders.

"Hemmo, you stay on the land. I'll take this way."

Doogie dove in and inhaled water until his lungs were once again filled. He swam with a grace he'd never had. Around him swam several mermaids and an immense octopus—the same one which had held fast to Hemmo until he died. As it passed, it touched him, and he felt the creature's sadness at having done what it had. When they reached the grate, the octopus wrapped its tentacles around it and strained, but it was pulling the wrong way. Doogie touched it and sent the image of the grate opening into the room. The octopus immediately understood and began to push, as did the mermaids.

Reaching behind him, Doogie pulled out his K-Bar and began to work at the mortar the grate was set in. He began at the top, his head just barely out of the water. He'd been chipping away for several minutes, when he heard a scream from inside and saw a body plummet down the stairs. Hemmo bound down them and over the body, rushing to the grate. He had an old set of keys in his hand on a metal loop. He tried one, then the next. The third key fit the lock. He opened it, then turned and threw both the lock and the key at the Finn who was coming up behind him. The Finn tried to block it and got a boot in the jimmy for his effort.

Doogie pressed inside.

The octopus and the mermaids followed.

At this early hour, the place was empty.

The others led the healthy mermaid out and down the canal.

The sick one floated face down in her pool, unmoving, the skin more green than blue.

Doogie stared for a moment, wondering what it was he could do. Then it came to him. He dove into the water, grabbed her by the arms, and wrestled the body to the bottom of the pool. He knelt beside her, and began to pump her chest, his hands placed just above her breasts. Underwater himself, he breathed water into her lungs then continued pumping. It wasn't long for her eyes to flutter, then open, revealing sickly yellow orbs. She'd needed some of the Columbia. In here, with the vestigial tide, it just wasn't enough. She needed the river. She needed to get home.

He took her into his arms and climbed out of the pool.

Hemmo had worked through two Finns but a third, this one even larger than he was, body slammed him against the far wall.

"You—Jap—put my property down," bellowed Garn.

Hemmo climbed unsteadily to his feet. "Go on," he said, waving a hand like it wasn't hardly anything. "I got this."

Doogie raised an eyebrow, then turned, and ran toward the canal. With the mermaid in tow, he swam exactly twenty feet before he came up against a metal wall someone had slid in place. He felt for a seam, someplace he could put his fingers to lift or push it out of the way. He took precious minutes trying to find a way past, or under, wondering at any second if he might be seen. But try as he might, he couldn't discern a way through.

So, with the mermaid in his arms, he stood and felt hands immediately grab him and jerk him free of the water. Then he was airborne. Still holding the mermaid, he flew through the air. He managed to turn so that he landed on his back to avoid crushing the smaller delicate creature. The water he'd been breathing spewed from his mouth. He gasped at the air. He pushed the mermaid off of him and tried to catch his breath.

He saw the boot coming. He could roll away, but instead, he rolled into it, caught the boot in between his ribs and his arms, then rolled to his right.

The Finn fell like lumber.

It was Peter, and his mouth was twisted fury.

Doogie couldn't let him stand, so as the Finn pulled himself to his knees, Doogie kicked him in the face.

Peter fell back, dazed.

They did this twice, before Peter managed to grab Doogie's leg. He pulled his smaller opponent close and Peter got two fingers in his eye for his effort. He let go of Doogie, who rolled away, scooped the mermaid into his arms, turned, and ran for all he was worth.

The sound of heavy feet slapping the ground behind him came closer and closer. He was out of breath, but he'd been chased before down Old Baldy and Heartbreak Ridge, so he'd become used to running for his life. But that was Korea, not the ass end of Oregon in the old fishing town of Astoria. And he'd been carrying a carbine back then instead of the slippery yet voluptuous body of a mermaid, her lips pressed against his neck sending thoughts that would make an eighty-year-old keel over for the sheer preposterousness of the position. Even now, with the Columbia River within reach, his cock was hard and his body twisted with the need to react to the mermaid's sexual advances, his mind acting out the fantasy until he was left gasping and out of breath and barely running. The only distraction was an odd track from the new Carl Perkins' song, "Dixie Fried," slashing through his head: *Rave on, children, I'm with you, rave on, cats, he cried. It's almost dawn and the cops ain't gone, and I've been Dixie fried.*

A shout from Peter who was chasing him gave him new energy as he surged forward. The Columbia was less than fifty yards away. Hemmo was already halfway there and waiting with a length of two-by-four in each hand. All Doogie had to do was reach the river and they'd all be free.

He could barely speak, but he had to ask Hemmo. "How?" he hollered as he ran past, exhausted shorthand for *how did he get past Garn.* All those minutes he wasted in the canal looking for a way out let Hemmo get ahead of him. Small blessings in strange places.

"He was in the way of me helping my family," Hemmo said, with more than a hint of pleasure.

And that was all he had to say. Hemmo didn't identify as a Finn any longer. He was now a true denizen of the Columbia, just as Doogie was. They'd not only found a home, they'd found a reason to be there. Now, while the other cats back from the war were slouching toward ignobility and possibly prison, Hemmo and Doogie had a mission. They'd become Sea Lords of the Columbia and he could feel every part of it like it was his own body.

"What?" Doogie managed to yell, more shorthand for *what happened to him.*

Hemmo laughed, then shouted, "He got Dixie Fried!"

Then came the sound of two pieces of wood meeting something meaty, a cry of pain, and a body hitting the ground.

Doogie liked that. And he smiled as he dove into the water, mermaid in his arms, hard-on beneath his pants, lungs filling with the joyous water of the Columbia.

WESTON OCHSE is the author of more than twenty books. His work has appeared in various anthologies and magazines, including The Tampa Review, Vol. 1 Brooklyn, Soldier of Fortune, *IDW, and DC Comics. His work has also been a finalist for the Bram Stoker Award five times and he's been honored to have won the Bram Stoker Award for First Novel. He's recently worked on several franchises, including* Aliens, Predator, Hellboy, *Clive Barker's* Midian, V-Wars, Joe Ledger, *and* X-Files. *He splits his time between Arizona and Oregon and absolutely loves the outdoors. When he's not writing, you can find him hiking, running, fly fishing, or just fusting about.*

THEY'VE COME TO SEE ME FOR YEARS, THE real rockabilly fans, most of them not even born when the whole thing was going on, and I've always told them the same old story, about how it ended for Belinda Cane. I mean they interview me for being me, Ronald Wilson, the man who played with the Hurricane Hunters, but it's really Belinda they want to know about.

There was one piece of the story I've always left out. It's a big piece, though, and the truth is, probably not very believable, though over the years there have been folks who have been suspicious. Had I not been there, and you were telling me what I'm about to tell you, I doubt I would accept it as true either.

TREMBLE

BY KASEY LANSDALE AND JOE R. LANSDALE

. . . there was something in her voice, something different from any voice I'd ever heard.

You can believe me or not. I leave that decision to you. Now that I'm near the end of my life, I guess it's time I set the record straight and explain what really happened in that auditorium in East Texas so many years ago, all the death and violence.

Another thing people always ask is why I don't go out much, and why my house is soundproofed, and I always say I like it quiet and private, and that's true, but there's more to it than that, and it all ties in with Belinda and that day all those years back.

It's phobic, and I know it's unnecessary, but I feel peaceful here, and the idea of going into an old folks' home without my soundproofing disturbs me, and the way things are going with my hip, that just might be where I'll end up. My nephew has been eyeing me a room at the facility out west of town. The idea of me going there has even come up in conversation.

But for now, I can get around, and I feel pretty good, and the memory of what happened seems stronger today than it did ten years ago, while other memories have gone the way of the passenger pigeon. Still, memories fade as you age, so I'm recording it all here for you.

Back then the music was new, and no one had ever heard anything like it. Think about that for a moment. You get up one morning and you turn the radio on, and there's this sound coming out of it that has never been heard before, at least not by the general populace. It's not Frank Sinatra or Perry Como, or folk, and it's not exactly blues, it's passion wrapped up in greasy vocals and a hard pounding beat, all of it painted over with adolescent rebellion and too much time on our hands.

And there was this one hip-cat, Elvis Presley, and he's singing in a way that makes you tremble, makes your foot pat, and he doesn't look like anyone you've ever seen before. A god-like young man singing black folk music, bending it, shaping it in a new way, sending out shockwaves that literally changed the world. There were other greats, black artists, but it was Elvis, due to his talent, and due to the restrictions of the time that got him front stage and center, and frankly, no one else has ever quite commanded the stage the way he did.

I was seventeen then, and I could play guitar, though what I'd learned was more along the line of Bill Monroe and Roy Acuff, and in fact Elvis took Monroe's "Blue Moon of Kentucky," twisted it around, pulled it inside out, and made it sound like no one could have imagined just a day before. Made us all wonder, hell, can you do that? Yep. He just did, and when he did, it was like a hole opened up in the creative universe and a lot of us wanted to squirm through, see what was on the other side.

I immediately started trying to play that hip-cat stuff, leaning on the chord of E like it was holding me up.

I REMEMBER WHEN I first paid true attention to her. She had been there all along, hidden behind a bland misfit mask, but now she was taking on a different look, and that's why I noticed her. I had a different look too, and it was the music that changed us, that brought us together like a magnet to steel.

I had on my blue jeans with the big cuffs, deep enough you could have kept your lunch money in them, had on a tee-shirt with the short sleeves rolled up to show what biceps I had. In that area, I needed a little work, but listening to the radio, to that hard-driving music, had turned me bold, made me want to look like my heroes. I had my hair slicked back with enough oil to lube a bone-dry Buick transmission, duck tail lifted up in the back, not to mention some wispy sideburns.

There Belinda was, coming down the hallway in her dark teal, half-sleeve swing dress with white fringe at the bottom and on the collar, her flame-red hair, mounded up and flared out wide, the collar fringe swishing across her sun-kissed collar bones, as she walked in men's lace-up shoes. Instead of a purse, she had a guitar, an old, worn Martin D-45 with a leather strap.

She noticed me staring as she walked by.

"Higher the hair, closer to God," she said. It sounded sassy, but there was something planned about it too, like she might have rehearsed it the night before in the mirror, wearing what she wore today, holding her guitar in her hand.

She floated on, left me standing there, mouth open. As I said, I'd seen her before, but then she'd been in the same kind of dresses and pinned-up hairstyles as the other girls, but now she was different, like a captured mustang set free. I don't think I'd even heard her speak before this moment, and it was a throaty sound, wild and raw, like an animal she only let out of the cage from time to time. It wasn't her beauty that caught my attention, though she was pretty. It was the way she moved, like she had the music already inside of her, and it was boiling and steaming, just ready to burst out.

She passed a crowd of students, the popular boys and girls, and one of them, Chris, he called out, "Hey, Belinda, I thought witches flew on brooms, not guitars."

"Do the world a favor, Chris," Belinda called out as she swung on down the hall, "go kill yourself."

Belinda didn't miss a beat. She neither slowed nor stuttered, and I watched Chris and the group of boys ribbing one another as she disappeared into a classroom. But you know, I got the feeling there was something about all that female sexuality that scared them. It's why we kill a beautiful, poisonous snake even if it's not bothering us. It seems too pretty and deadly to let live.

Well, I started noticing her quite a lot after that, and maybe I had a thing for her because I felt like I'd found a kindred spirit. I would see her at lunch break, out back of the school where some of the kids stole a cigarette break, or some of the girls and boys stole a kiss or two, where a few bullies beat up young kids and took their lunch money as part of what was an almost acceptable ritual. Belinda would lean against the wall, clutching her guitar like it was a child, looking out at the others, enduring their now-and-again snide comments, lashing out with a word or two, but mostly just leaning silently, watching the way a hawk would watch prey.

One day I came up and stood by her as if we did it every day. We were silent for a while. We looked out at the other kids, laughing and grinning, their hair cut short, their clothes looking as if they had just been pressed, and she said, "They look like their mothers hang them in the closet at night, then take them down in the mornings and set them free."

"That don't seem all that free to me," I said.

Belinda laughed a little. "No," she said, "they don't."

"You carry that guitar, but I've never heard you play it."

"Not that good at it. I use it to write songs. Sometimes, out here, I sit and write in my head, picking out a tune, but mostly I just imagine I'm playing and writing."

"I've started to write a little," I said. "Maybe we could do it together. I actually can play."

"I can sing a little."

It was in that moment that I realized Belinda wasn't nearly as bold as she'd let on. We were delicate, retiring souls, all suited up in rebellion clothes.

WE STARTED MEETING UP regularly during lunch out behind the school, and even sometimes after school, and we'd talk music, and in the end, she would give me a ride home.

We didn't write so much as we just talked. Talked about all kinds of things. Our families, or lack thereof, the way things were changing, the way things weren't. Then one winter afternoon after school, as I waited to meet up with her, she didn't show. It was cold as a dead woman's tit in a brass bra, the sun swallowed by clouds, the air so sharp it felt as if you were swallowing razor blades. I waited and waited, rocked back and forth to get warm, waited beyond reason, but she didn't show. I had seen her at lunch, and then everything seemed fine, so I got worried.

I found her in the parking lot, in her old, rust-colored Ford jalopy, a car that almost needed a stick to prop it up. Heard that thing drive off, it was as if a bucket of bolts was being stuck by a hammer.

Belinda was bent forward in the front seat, crying, head and hands on the steering wheel, windows steamed. I tapped on the glass at the driver's side, but she didn't sit up. I tapped again, louder this time. The way her muscles tensed I knew she'd heard me that time, but still, she didn't move. I walked around to the passenger side and tugged the door open gently, slid inside. It closed behind me with a grinding sound.

Now normally in this type of situation, I would find something funny to say, to break the ice, but I could tell by the way she refused to meet her eyes with mine, this was far beyond what a few off-color jokes could cure.

"What's wrong? What Happened?"

She pointed over her shoulder and into the back seat.

There was a mass of splinters and strings in the backseat.

"What is that? Is that your guitar?"

"What's left of it," she said between sniffles. "That was my daddy's, from 1933. The only thing he ever gave me, and now look at it. It ain't worth kindling."

I sat back in the seat and stared ahead. She'd told me all about her daddy, and from what I could tell, he wasn't worth the powder it would take to blow him up, but he was still her father and that was her only piece left of him. One day he got up, said he was going to put gas in the car, did just that, and kept on driving.

"What happened?" I asked.

"Was Chris and those two stupid girls that are always following him around like puppies. Sharon and Dee."

"Damn, them," I said. "How'd it happen?"

"I was going to the car. Sharon and Dee said their usual crap, and I guess I said mine, and then I saw Chris walking back from my car. The guitar was in my car. You know I never lock it. When I got to the car, it was like that. Sharon and Dee distracted me, and Chris did the damage. Goddamn it, Ronald, that guitar made me feel special. Wasn't any call for that."

I sat in the car with her and put my arm around her and held her while she cried. It was a long deep cry, and I tell you, I felt like crying too, but I held it in. Back then, a man tried not to cry, and if you didn't cry, whatever grieved you, coiled up in a knot, way down deep, angry and sad, and lived there.

I don't know exactly how it happened, but our lips touched, and then there was fire inside of us, and we ended up at a parker's lane, and then she said, "Let's go to my house."

I wasn't sure that sounded like such a good idea, but away we went, and when we got there it was a little rattle-trap place near the railroad tracks, and when we pulled up in what passed for a yard, got out and made it to the porch, a train passed by and the whole place shook so hard I thought it might tumble down.

"In this house," she said, "I always tremble when the train goes by."

"How could you not," I said.

It was dark inside, and it had a damp odor, like laundry had been left out, and when she turned on the light, there wasn't much to see. The furniture looked old enough to have been brought over on the Mayflower, in the bottom of the deck where it was damp. Roaches didn't so much scuttle as strolled. They weren't worried.

"No one here?" I said.

"You know about Dad, but last week . . . Last week I came home and there was twenty-five dollars on the table held down with a salt shaker along with a note. Note was from Mama, said, 'I couldn't make it, but maybe you can. I left you what I have, but the rent comes due in a month, and you'll have to figure it out from there. Sorry. All my love.'"

"That was it?"

"Well, she left me a pair of emerald earrings, but yeah, that was it."

That night in her unmade bed, we made love, and from that point on, we were an item.

THOSE KIDS AT SCHOOL, when they saw her now, without her guitar, they held their hands like they were playing an instrument, or made guitar noises, and moved on down the halls with a smile, now and again, throwing back the words, "Be-bop-a-lula, baby."

It wasn't a torment they abandoned or delayed. It was every day, several times a day. I wanted to set them on fire.

That guitar had meant so much to Belinda. Something of her father's, a piece of her dreams, an instrument to carry her high to the moon, but those privileged jackasses were like weights on her rocket, dragging her back to earth, spiraling her down into an explosive crash.

And it didn't get better. Sharon and Dee made special effort, they prodded her daily, made fun of her hair, made fun of her look, laughed at her shoes, even shoved her books. They were like ten-year-olds high on caffeine and too much sugar.

But there was a beam of light, a small one, and I like to think I was the one that found it, pointed it out to Belinda, and said, *look here*. It was the band queers. That was what they called all of us in the band, the ones who didn't fit in, didn't know the right things to say, and saw the world in different colors.

I was a band queer myself, played guitar in a little quartet the bandmaster led. We played at special events. There was Clifton on bass, James on sax, and Mary Sue, a little girl of Asian descent, they called Jap. She played drums.

It was an odd bunch, Clifton with his harelip, James with a face only a dog could love, and Mary Lou, the product of a Japanese war bride and a father who was a Jew. All of them, and me and Belinda for that matter, were as strange to the rest of our world as peanut butter spread on a cloud.

But together, when we played, there was something there, right from the start. I gave Belinda a spare guitar, but she looked better holding it than playing it, but there was something in her voice, something different from any voice I'd ever heard. It was a freight train, swallowing razor blades, coughing and bellowing out smoke and spurts of fire.

At first, she was hesitant, but then she'd let that voice go, and everything that had ever hurt her, disappointed her, saddened her, came out in a beautiful wail from that tiny 4'8" frame that made the air vibrate like a guitar string.

I remember the first time she let it loose. Everyone quit playing, just stood there amazed, Mary Lou with her drum sticks cocked, as if she'd been frozen in time by an icy blast of wind.

Belinda stopped singing, turned red.

I said, "No. It's great. Hit it again."

And we started the music over, one of our own compositions, mostly written by Belinda. A thing called "Tremble," then known as "Tremble to the Moon," and away she went, singing the lyrics, building it up like she was stacking bricks, and then it was like she let loose with a tornado siren, only melodious, and I felt the hair on the back of my neck rise like coffin nails, and the front of my head seemed to swell, and my whole body went weak as wet straw and those bricks she had stacked came apart in a torrent of anger, need, disappointment, and pain.

We worked our way through, the sax calling out like a dying bird, the base thumping along like a pain in the heart, me bending strings, and those drums beating it out to bring down the sky.

And Belinda's voice. My, oh, my . . .

Had this feeling she had touched the sky, but had yet to rip it open wide. But I knew she could. I could feel the muscle in that voice the way you might squeeze the biceps of a weight-lifting man who had only half-flexed.

NOW, I'M GOING TO STOP HERE. I'm going to warn you. This is the odd part, this is where I'll get the look, I know that, and that's all right. Here it is straight as an arrow, bright like the sky. That voice of hers, it came from some place that no one else could go. Not then, not now, and maybe not ever. No one could find the places she found and come back from them with a sound like a banshee's cry.

In Belinda's house, she had a family bible, and in it were lists of ancestors, and they went way back. She said before the bible was even written, things had been collected by her ancestors, and finally they found their place inside that book, written down from notes and memory. On her dad's side were the singers, but all of them women. Her dad, he played guitar, she said. But the women were the singers, none of them ever recorded, singing at fairs and all manner of spots, pulling in crowds. There were rumors of dancing men and crying women, and finally Belinda's ancestors were run out of town, even burned at the stake, and that was long after Salem, after witches were thought to be myth, and those burnings in the thirties didn't make the history books. But the way those women sang, Belinda's ancestors, they cued something reptilian inside of the listeners, something they regretted feeling in the end.

Yeah. Those women went way back. All the way to Greece, and *before* it was Greece, at least according to all the notes Belinda said were in the bible, written in a tight spidery hand. And then before that were other notes, and then things she couldn't understand in shapes that made no sense.

She told me all of this as we lay in bed on a cold, clear night, the trains coming and going, shaking the house.

"I know how this sounds," she told me, but I'm descended from some powerful women on my father's side. That's why he left, I think, because he saw I was unhappy, and angry, and rumor is, that's where the power comes in. Anger fuels it. I try not to be angry, Ronald, but I am. Maybe it's because I don't fit in. Maybe it's because I inherited it, but I boil like a kettle and foam like a rabid dog inside."

"I know," I said. "I can feel it when I hold you. It scares me a little."

"I get those feelings I can't see the sky, but I can feel the dark, even if it's bright as a blue jay outside. That dark is like a shadow, and it climbs up me, from way, way down in my boiling belly, and it comes out of me in a voice like a storm. And here's the thing, Ronald. I know there's more."

As I said earlier, so did I.

I didn't know exactly what to say, but finally I said, "That sounds like a song."

"It's like Armageddon, Ronald. And you know why? Because I am a descendent of those long-ago sirens that tried to lead Odysseus into the rocks . . . I'm feeling your arm go slack. You're not holding me the same way as before. You think I'm crazy."

"No. I just don't know how you mean it."

"I mean that before the Greeks were called Greeks, even before the stories of Jason and his Argonauts, and Odysseus and his crew met the sweet wails of the Sirens, there were stories of them. Women, who by inheritance, or some strangeness no one has ever defined, had a voice that called to those who would listen. Only the deaf or the ones with plugged ears were safe. It was like those Siren voices had hooks in them, and lines, and the voices pulled those who heard them toward their doom, into the rocks. And I know the source of our voice, for in a way, it's all one loud voice. It's rage, Ronald. It's about women made small, pushed down and lost, like my mother. Without her husband, without a man, she couldn't stand it, even abandoned her daughter. Didn't know how to be herself by herself. She knows, too, what I am on my father's side, and maybe that's the real reason she left. She didn't want to be here when it all goes wild."

"Damn, Belinda," I said. "I . . . I don't know what to say."

"Say you believe me," she said.

I tried not to think too long, tried not to mince what I had to say, but right then I told a lie. "Sure, Belinda. I believe you. Why would I not?"

It's all she wanted, even if she might have thought I was lying, and she slept sound, but I didn't. I got up hungry, vastly confused. I thought my girl had more than her heart and guitar broken. I thought her head had a crack, and maybe her soul too.

I looked in the ice box, but there was nothing there, not a crumb, not water, just what looked like in one corner a clump of hair. I closed the door and prowled in the cabinets, assisted by the light of the moon through the window. I found a box of stale crackers, and ate half of what was there, left the rest for Belinda's breakfast.

I sat on the couch with a lukewarm glass of water, next to a shelf of books so old I could smell the past. One was hanging out, and I turned to push it in, and that's when I thought: *Maybe.*

I pulled it out. And that's how I came across the bible she told me about, so ancient perhaps it had been bound and stitched into place by Adam and Eve. I went over to the sink, where the moonlight was strong, and laid it out on the counter, and looked. In the back were pages of what had once been white space, and they were filled with names, and the farther you went back, the stranger those names became. Greek names.

I felt something stir in me, like a creature thought dead shifting its weight, trying to lie down.

Back at the bookshelf I replaced the bible, saw a large roll of what appeared to be leather tucked inside the corner of the shelf, pulled it out, went back to my spot at the sink. It was bound up with a cord made of leather. I removed the cord and smoothed out the leather scroll. Stitched into it, tight and small, were more of what I assumed were names. It was hard to know. It might have been an extensive list of the long, long dead, and it might have been an ancient shopping list, because I was sure it was indeed ancient. There were also symbols and drawings of ships on the sea, of women on the rocks on either side of the ships. They stood with mouths wide open, like little, dark caves, and there were images inside their mouths, and though they were small, I thought they looked like some kind of creatures. Staring at it made me feel uncomfortable.

I thought about what Belinda had told me, the sirens, ancestors burned at the stake. I rolled up the leather text and put it back.

MONDAY MORNING, BACK AT SCHOOL, Clifton came running toward me and Belinda in the lunchroom, nearly skated past us before stopping to catch his breath. When he spoke, that cleft palate voice, excited and strained, wrestled over words like a puppy grappling with a dinosaur bone.

"You won't *belie—fe—it*," he said.

"Believe what, Cliffy, slow down," Belinda said. "Your words are getting all jumbled up. Just calm it down, what's going on?"

"We're *hire . . . hire . . . hired*." Clifton said, then grunted afterward, something he did from time to time when he got too excited and couldn't get the words out. "We have a . . . a *re . . . real* gig."

"What're you talking about, man?" Belinda asked.

"My cousin," he said, and followed it with a growling noise. "My cousin needs a *ba . . . aand* for her *swee . . . sweet . . .* sixteen party this weekend."

"Well I'll be damned," I said.

"What are we supposed to play?" Belinda asked. "We don't even have an hour's worth of music ready.

"Then we'd better hurry," I said. "Or we'd better be able to play the same songs twice with different notes."

BELINDA, CLIFTON, MARY LOU, James, and myself, all met up that afternoon after school in the band hall to formulate a plan.

"What about 'Peggy Sue'? Belinda, you know that one?"

"Blueberry Hill?"

Belinda nodded, and by the time we went down the list we realized that collectively, we had more music than we'd thought, but we still needed something to close out with. Something killer.

"What about the one you wrote, Belinda?" Mary Lou said. "Tremble to the Moon."

"What about it?" Belinda asked.

"We could use that one as our closer. The way you were hitting those notes the other day at practice, well that ought to knock 'em all dead."

"I'm not so sure," Belinda said. "I don't think the song is done and I—"

"Then I guess you better finish it," I said, and smiled at her.

We reconvened at Cliff's home, in his garage, to see what Belinda had come up with and we weren't disappointed.

"It's just called, Tremble now," she said. "Just follow my lead."
Belinda looked at me and said, "It's in E."

Thank God for small favors.

Belinda tossed her head back, opened her mouth, and let out a note so
guttural, it sounded like there was a saxophone stuffed deep inside of her.

It feels just like a hurricane
Blowin' hot wind
It's a cosmic rumble
Your love that makes me tumble

And I tremble.
Tremble, to the moon
Your kisses driving me insane
Tremble

When I think of you, I know just what to do
Look out baby, the storm is passing through
Blowing hot wind
Tremble, to the moon

The heat it's building up inside
Look out baby, gonna blow the world aside
Tremble
Cause there ain't no place for you to hide
Tremble, to the moon.

Hear the Siren song, take you along
Don't fight it baby, you know where you belong
Tremble
Into my arms . . .
And tremble.
Tremble, to the moon.

Belinda stopped singing, looked around at everyone. We had all stopped playing.

"*Shhh . . . shhh . . . it,*" Clifton said.

"Did I do something wrong?" Belinda asked.

"Hardly," I said.

She had no idea what had just happened. The lyrics weren't Shakespeare, by any means, but her voice. She hadn't heard Clifton's water glass shatter or Mary Lou stop the music, nor had she seen us all sag like wet rags, but we all had. It was the first time I realized that what Belinda suspected she could do was merely the tip of the iceberg. Her voice that day was like three hundred gallons of spit and vinegar and rattlesnake venom forced into a two-quart jug.

"I think that's enough rehearsal for one day," I said. "My soul's worn out and my ears hurt some."

WHAT HAPPENED LATER is what everyone is interested in, of course. It's less known than the day the music died, because the Hurricane Hunters became famous by word of mouth. That's what we called ourselves, the Hurricane Hunters. We never recorded but the one song, but if the list of people who claim to have seen us perform was really the number of people who actually saw when we played at all those little small ass gigs, it would have been the entire population of the United States.

I'll come back to that.

We all got crap from the folks, because it was a small town and we were towing a different line than they were. Poor Belinda was tormented by all those high school jerks, day after day. Knocking the tail light out on her car, rubbing dog shit in her locker. Sometimes at night they would knock over her mailbox or throw things at the house, constantly wrapping it with toilet paper.

There was no end to it. Seemed like it was the entire school, with the exception of the band, and a few folks here and there who weren't too popular either, and wanted to keep their head down.

It really got to Belinda. All she wanted to do was make music, but the anger was boiling inside of her, and sometimes in practice I could feel that anger coming out, and we'd have to take her mic away. We could play full on, and even if she sang without one, you could hear her as if she was standing in front of a hot mic belting it out. It was enough to make me think of those sirens and their songs.

Well, we picked up a few gigs here and there, and then we were out of school, and the kind of music we were playing was really catching on, even in our home town, and I'm sure the kids who had given us hell were now wearing their jeans cuffed and their hair longer and slicked down with oil, but that didn't change how we felt about them.

We went for a year on tour, if it's fair to call making the Chitlin' Circuit by car a tour. Went in that ragged car of Belinda's, the bass strapped to the top, and Jap, as everyone called Mary Lou by now, had a station wagon, and that carried the rest of the equipment, along with her at the wheel and one of us in the front passenger seat. We traded riding and driving, though Belinda always drove her own car.

And let me tell you, pretty as Belinda was, she became even more so, right down seductive-looking. And performing brought out an inner-glow. She'd stand on stage and start to sing and start to wiggle, and you'd see the men in the audience drop their jaws, and you'd see the women grow small. And then the songs would keep coming, especially Tremble, because when she sang that one, perhaps because she wrote it, there was something that ran through the notes, like Adam and Eve's serpent squirming all around, and you couldn't help but think when the show was over and everyone left, a lot of cars must have ended up in local passion spots, rocking to a rhythm inherent to men and women since the beginning of time.

It seemed alright to me, the way we were going, making decent money, and the band was loving it, and I wrote a couple of numbers we performed. Silly stuff actually, and I'm glad they didn't survive, at least they weren't recorded, but to hear Belinda sing them . . . Well, she could have sung little Miss Muffet and moved your soul.

By the second year we were out there, riding and performing, living in tourist courts and eating at greasy spoons, the word was out. We even ended up recording for Blue Siren records, just that one song as I said, Tremble, the one that's survived and thrilled audiences for years with its savage performance, but let me tell you, they had to have Belinda stand six feet from the microphone, and as strong a performance as she gave, the way her voice trembled when she said, "Tremble to the moon," well, on the road, she did it better. Her voice got stronger day by day, and at night we'd lie in bed in some roach-infested motel, and we'd talk, and there was good talk, but it always came back to high school. That whole experience was like a bleeding wound to her. You couldn't put enough gauze or pressure on that wound to staunch it.

I remember saying after we recorded Tremble, and it was getting radio play, "We've left that hole in the road. We got a song out there, and it's a hit. We're on our way."

Course, we didn't know then we weren't really going to make any real money off that song, not with the contract we signed. We were a rockabilly group, not a firm of lawyers. So, we weren't that much on our way after all.

But we would have lived and learned from that experience, and we were supposed to record a B side, which is why for a long time Tremble only had radio play, and no record, until someone got wise and just put the song on both sides and released it, making it a unique item; but as I said, it didn't do us much good financially, and in the long run it's made us nothing more than an interesting note in Rockabilly history.

Still, had we continued on, had Belinda not harvested anger from a field fertilized by the bad blood of everyone who had ever treated someone like crap, we'd have done okay, I think. But she couldn't quit farming that field, and when she said she wanted to see if we could go through our home town of Badger Creek, I wasn't so sure. Then I thought: this may be how she's going to reconcile this stuff, how she's going to quit farming that field of hate, and so I worked to set it up.

It was easy. By then we had a certain fame, due to Tremble and word of mouth, so we were set for what would become a cold winter night full of threatening skies. But until that day arrived, we moved on down the road in dry sunshine, doing our gigs.

By this time, Belinda's voice was like a siren, and I mean both kinds. Yet, it was controlled, and it was beautiful. It was so mesmerizing I would almost forget to play, and finally, one night before a gig, she gave us all wax ear plugs, said, "Tonight, you're gonna need these."

Night before we were to play in Badger Creek, we performed in a little town called Gladewater. It was at a rodeo grounds. She went out there and sang, and even with the open air, the seats all around, you could feel her notes as if they were thugs, moving about the crowd, nearly shoving people down.

I was glad for those plugs of wax. I was glad we were in such an open place and the audience wasn't right up in front of us, but was instead in those wrap-around arena seats, because even that far away, Belinda's voice was a mighty rumble. I won't kid you, even with those plugs, on the stage, I felt faint once, and when it was over, there was blood on my wax plugs. Belinda had stood in front of a microphone, but ladies and gents, it wasn't turned on.

I GUESS IT WAS MID-DAY when we rolled into Badger Creek in our two cars, put ourselves up at the Franklin Motor Inn, a little run of shacks on the outskirts of town near a cafe that served what could only be called the worst food in three counties. I had eaten there a few times while growing up in Badger Creek, and it hadn't improved.

Night before, Belinda had been quiet. Usually we talked while we lay in bed, and snuggled close, but that night she lay there and looked at the ceiling, and the times I tried to initiate a conversation, suggest how we might move the band beyond a road group, record some more, but with a better contract next time, she'd grunt and so on, but it was pretty quickly understood that she didn't have any interest in talking. Her world was in her head, everything else was pretty much void.

During the night, after I'd drifted off, I awoke to a strange feeling in my ears. It wasn't a sound, exactly, more of a sensation; a vibration in the head, the kind I used to get when I was at her house in bed and the train rolled by outside.

I sat up, pushed the covers to my knees. There was this little table across the room with a chair in front of it. Belinda was in that chair with the table light on. I watched her place a glass of water on the table. She took a breath so deep it was as if she were trying to suck all the air out of the room, and from the way her head moved and her shoulders rolled, it was as if she was about to belt out something from a song. But no sound came out. As I said, it was a sensation. She was reaching way down inside, and like a silent dog whistle, something was coming out, because that glass of water was rocking on that table like it was about to leap.

And then I saw the water rise up as if by high tide, and the water danced in the air like a water spout, and the glass broke with a sharp crack and collapsed in pieces on the table, followed by the water.

I felt cold. I felt numb.

Belinda turned off the light, and as I eased under the covers again, she came back to bed.

WE GOT TO THE HIGH SCHOOL auditorium late that afternoon, set up. Belinda was still quiet. We did a run-through on the tunes, but she held back, sang on one of them, and sang so soft she needed the mic, but we didn't say anything, just let her go through it. We knew she could belt when she wanted to.

After practice, we were out back of the auditorium, me and Jap. The others were inside doing whatever, and Jap says to me, "Ronald, I'm scared of her."

"That's silly," I said, even though I didn't think it was all that silly.

"We do this run, I think I'm out," Jap said. "It isn't fun anymore."

"We're going to record more," I said.

"Yeah, well, I don't know. I got a feeling we aren't going to record anything."

That night, as the doors were opened and the kids filed in amongst a few older folks in the back to chaperone the event, Belinda looked out through a split in the auditorium curtain, said, "I recognize a lot of them."

I looked out as well. Yep. Lot of kids we had graduated with, and lots more we hadn't. I saw Chris, Sharon, and Dee, a few others that had been in their crowd. As in school, they moved in a pack, but now dressed not too unlike we were dressed. Weekend hip-cats, arriving at the station after the train had left.

Right before time to go on, Belinda gathered us together just off-stage, and handed us all plugs. "These are supposed to be better. Made to mute gunfire. And we need to move the amps from where they are, point them at the crowd. I want you behind them. You can play this stuff in your sleep. Like usual, I'm going to end with Tremble. During that song, when you see me step up and turn on the mic, that's your cue."

"To do ... *do* ... *do* what?" Cliff said.

"To leave," she said. "It'll be cool. Just stop playing and walk off. In fact, leave the building."

I wasn't sure how cool that was, and of course, I had an inkling what was going on, but you know, you can't think of something like that and believe it's real.

You just can't.

CAME THE NIGHT AND THE TIME, and the auditorium was full. We had the plugs in our ears, but truth to tell, she didn't belt it out. She sang gently, but it was still strong for anyone else. That's the thing. Her voice could fill a room and make it feel as if it was coming out of the amps, but it wasn't. No one could do that but her, and people loved it, even if they had no idea what they were really hearing, and had no idea that the microphone wasn't even turned on.

So, away we went, and I tell you, we'd never been better. Maybe it was because of where we were, who was in that crowd. We were showing him we weren't just a bunch of misfits from Badger Creek.

They loved the rocking numbers and the smoother ballads, and they started to stand and dance in front of their seats, and then in the aisle, and as they did, Belinda brought the volume up, and man that dancing increased, became savage and sexy, and in the back, I could see the chaperones were nervous. To try and contain this bunch would be like walking into a den of lions with a switch and an attitude; it wouldn't have gone well.

In the front rows, as was according to custom, were those who had graduated but a year or so ago. For them, all the unkind words, the busted guitar, were forgotten and unimportant. They had a classmate who had scored big in recognition, if not in money, and they felt they were a part of her success, as if they had boosted and encouraged her all along, and that the things they had done had been nothing more than just clean fun.

I watched them smile, and I watched them dance, and I felt an anger in me. Nothing to compare to that wound in Belinda, but it was certainly enough to make me feel their hypocrisy rise up and onto the stage like a living entity.

Belinda was singing one of her new compositions, "I See You On The Street."

I see you on the street.
You always look so fine.
Like there's nothing painful on your mind.
But me, I'm a walking, talking, empty shell.
I'm a ringless bell.
I'm a heart turned cold.
You've left me unhappy on an empty road.

If things had worked out, that would have been the B side to Tremble. It was a kind of ballad, the shelter before the storm.

Belinda wrapped up the song, shouted out at the audience, "Do you want to Tremble?"

As one they shouted they did, and there was near pandemonium. That song was still hot on the radio and hot on the wax, having been released with it on both sides of the .45. Tremble was simple, catchy, and raw. But it was the voice that made it special.

"This'll be our last song for tonight," and she smiled so big the Cheshire cat would have been envious.

She looked back at us, raised her hand, and the crowd became silent. She held it there, teasing them for a moment, dropped it, and we hit it.

Let me tell you. We had never been so on the money. We rode those notes like bucking horses, and we stayed in the saddle. And outside, the cold winter night had turned savage. Through the high auditorium windows I saw the lightning stitching across the sky. And the dark clouds were visible in those flashes, and they rolled with the drums, and they tumbled with the bass, and the wild, wicked clouds began to cry. Rain splattered the windows, struck the roof like pellets of steel, and my guitar screamed, and the drums did bop, and the base did thump, and the sax did wail, driving that music straight to the bone.

As the music rose and Belinda's voice soared, the rafters rattled like old dry bones, the floor bucked up, the walls shimmied and began to moan, the windows cracked, and the air, as if from some deep Arctic tomb, blew in, lifted greasy hair like invisible jacks, made dresses whip like flags.

Even on stage we trembled with the song. It was as if we were standing in electric quicksand.

That's when the song paused and I did my solo, and let me tell you, I was clawing that one out. I was on fire, and when I finished, Belinda looked back at us, and nodded, then stepped up to the microphone and turned it on.

Everyone had a feeling. They just knew. Jap dropped her sticks and made for the exit, followed by everyone else unplugging their instruments, heading for the door. Everyone but me. I kept playing.

Belinda looked back, and the look on her face was both brave and sad and proud and lonely. I know that's a lot to assign to a face, but I assure you, it was all there. All of her generations of wailing women, all of the things they'd suffered as the "fairer sex." All of the calls and whistles and ass pinches and insults and expectations. You could feel and hear what Odysseus heard that time he was strapped to the mast, and his men, with wax in their ears, rowed with all their might to get past the home of the sirens, to move on out into calmer waters.

I nodded at her. She nodded back, turned to the mic, opened her bright red lips—

And out came her voice, a wild, leaping Cerberus escaped through the gates of hell.

That's when the fun went out of everyone's eyes. That's when they rose up like the water in that glass in the motel room, rose up on their toes, and like the song said, they trembled. They trembled so hard, they trembled so fast, the boys' greasy hair stood up on end. The girls were lashed by their own pony tails, and those with high-up hair, well, you saw it collapse; an avalanche of hair-do tumbling down hill. You could see their cheeks swell and you could see the flesh on their faces start to peel. Bones cracked and poked through the jeans, or through the flesh on their knees beneath sweat-wet dresses; legs bent and buckled, and they began to topple, and writhe on the floor like electric eels.

Belinda's voice rose up, dropped down, moved left and right, and all around. Someone screamed and the lights went out. The world inside the auditorium was as black as the dark side of the moon. My ears were bleeding even with the wax in them.

When the lights went out my electric guitar lost its power, and that's when my courage failed me. It was as if the music had sustained me, but then you might say my common sense kicked in. I glanced at Belinda, but the way she was standing, smiling, watching all that mayhem, I knew I was on my own. I dropped the strap over my head and the guitar hit the stage with a ring, and I grappled for a way out, bounced against the wall and eventually found the opening, and then the exit. Right before I was out of there I looked back, and there were bodies still trying to dance, clawing their way onto the stage, clutching at Belinda like a vanilla treat, and then the roof sagged, and I ran for my life.

THE WAY THE PAPER TOLD IT, it was an electrical fire that had caught breath from the storm and lit up the whole auditorium. Made out like the building was unsafe, and just collapsed, that it wasn't up to standards, and you know, maybe it wasn't. The wind and fire tore up the wood and steel like a piece of wet cardboard left out in a rainstorm.

Even the survivors, though few, didn't know what had happened, or they were too in shock to tell the real story, or perhaps they just couldn't understand it. But I knew, and as time passed, suspicions grew. I'd known that first night Belinda and me had laid in bed and she'd told me about her family that there was hell in the making. I'd sensed that anger burning up inside her and growing and twirling for some time now, but I never said a word.

Next day I tried to find the guys, but I didn't. They hid from me, you want to know it true. I didn't blame them. They thought I had been in on it, I guess, and I suppose in a way, I had. I knew what Belinda was capable of, but I just didn't want to believe it. And truth be told, there was a part of me, maybe a part bigger than I'd like to admit, that felt like those people had it coming. That they had brought that doom and destruction down on themselves and deserved every last lick of what had happened to them. Eventually I quit trying to catch up and make nice with the band. I heard Jap died in a car wreck a few years later and Cliffy, well, I didn't know what happened to him.

James looked me up once, some years later, came to see me, but I had stepped out. He left a note, slipped it between the glass and the screen of the metal door where I lived. Didn't say much, and he didn't leave a number. I had a feeling he felt he had tried, and that was enough, and he was done.

Frankly, I don't lose much sleep about the way it all went down, but I think of Belinda and feel a hole in my heart; I miss her. I felt guilty for leaving her there. Even though I knew she'd have never come with me, and had I stuck, there was no way I would have survived.

Here's a curiosity: They never found her body, so I clung to the hope she made it out somehow and would find me. Though if she did make it, she made sure I was none the wiser.

There was an impersonator I'd gone to see once, heard she was the real deal, and if I closed one eye and cocked my head to the side, wished real hard and clicked my heels, it could have been her. She looked like an older version of Belinda, had her moves, had a long, raised scar that ran from her temple to jaw line, and though the voice was reminiscent, it wasn't the same. She was like Belinda with the juice drained out. I never heard anyone hit those notes before or since.

So here I am. Alone in this soundproofed room, which is kind of silly, since I'm still spinning that "Tremble" .45 on an old record player. It took a long time before I could bring myself to listen to it again, but it's all I have left of her, so now and again, no more than three times a day, and sometimes five on Sunday, I play it, and the trick in reverse is that there's no interruption from outside. It's me and the music, me and Belinda, living hot in the tune.

There ain't no place for you to hide
Tremble, to the moon.
Hear the Siren song, take you along
Don't fight it baby, you know where you belong.
Tremble, to the moon.

KASEY LANSDALE, first published at the tender age of eight by Random House, is the author of several short stories and novellas from Harper Collins, Titan Books, and others. She is the editor of assorted anthology collections and in her latest publication, Terror is Our Business, *Publishers Weekly noted, "Lansdale's storytelling delightfully takes on a lighter and sharper edge." She is best known as a country singer/songwriter whose music has been placed on various television and film networks.*

JOE R. LANSDALE is the author of forty-five novels and four hundred shorter works, including stories, essays, reviews, introductions, and magazine articles. His work has been made into films, Bubba Ho-Tep, Cold in July, *as well as the acclaimed TV show,* Hap and Leonard. *He has also had works adapted to* Masters of Horror *on Showtime, and wrote scripts for* Batman: The Animated Series, *and* Superman: The Animated Series. *He scripted a special Jonah Hex animated short, as well as the animated Batman film,* Son of Batman.

He has received numerous recognitions for his work. Among them The Edgar, for his crime novel The Bottoms, *The Spur, for his historical western* Paradise Sky, *as well as ten Bram Stoker Awards for his horror work, and has also received the Grandmaster Award and the Lifetime Achievement Award from the Horror Writers Association. He has been recognized for his contributions to comics and is a member of the Texas Institute of Literature, the Texas Literary Hall of Fame, and is Writer in Residence at Stephen F. Austin State University.*

He is in the International Martial Arts Hall of Fame, as well as the U.S. Martial Arts Hall of Fame, and is the founder of the Shen Chuan martial arts system.

His books and stories appear in twenty-five languages.

ADAM "DEACON" COLES TAPPED THE BRAKES and swung his '41 Willys coupe to the right, his high-beams illuminating the edge and the drop off. The green Mercury with a supercharger scoop sticking out of the hood brushed against the left side of his car. He didn't care about the body; it was full of dents, and the fenders and passenger door were mismatched colors obtained from the salvage yard. But he didn't want the Merc knocking him over the rise as they took the turn. The Mercury was on the inside of the curve, plumes of dirt and loose rocks clouding behind both cars as they sped, their rear ends bumping once, twice together, then apart again. Each car

THE DEMON OF THE TRACK

BY GARY PHILLIPS

"You are a skilled man," she said. Her accent was heavy but her words were clear . . .

had big bore engines in them that were not stock; their mechanic-drivers had cut and welded and pounded to fit them into their respective vehicles. The roar of those engines filled the cabs of each car as their owners sought dominance.

The crowd hooped and hollered and made other joyous noises down where the race started and would end. Behind the gathered rose a wide ramp of the Santa Monica Freeway under construction, a mass of concrete and rebar sticking out of the end as if the ramp had been sawed off by a storm giant, for this was as far as the work had taken the builders. The goal was to build a byway connecting downtown to the coast. In the process, the homes of working class black folk, in what was called the Pico District—people who'd come west in the '30s and '40s to work the then-boom of oil fields and later aircraft—had been snatched up by eminent domain. Those same homes were rented back to them before they were kicked out and the houses torn down to make way for rivers of freeway cement.

The race took place primarily on a snake of land that had been bulldozed to gradually rise nearly a quarter mile up, then took a whip turn around to descend into a flattened, cleared area that once housed a park and an apartment complex. Now there were stands of unfinished pylons and piles of concrete and wood and glass debris from demolished houses to maneuver around, then another turn through a partially fenced-in area where several heavy duty trucks and tractors—and the crowd—were gathered, back to the rise of land again. To add to the difficulty, it was now dusk and the natural light fading, so a driver's vision and reflexes had to be sharp. The improvised race track was a rough oval the racers had to drive around ten times. This was the eighth lap.

They came out of the turn, the Merc taking the lead. Downhill the cars plowed, the Willys running over a chunk of concrete, which Coles prayed didn't blow out his tire. Reaching the flattened area, he swerved around a pylon, the Merc now on his right flank. The other car zigged and zagged between two interspaced pylons and veered back toward Coles' car. Traveling at more than ninety miles an hour, both were homing in on another pylon dead center, piled concrete on either side of the two vehicles. Coles went left and the other car gobbled distance opposite. But the Willys hit a sizable rut in the earth that would have snapped the front axle in half given the speed they were traveling.

Coles smiled ruefully. Fortunately he'd installed hydraulics taken from a junked WWII airplane wing in the front leaf springs connected to the straight axle. These helped absorb the impact. Good thing he'd run into a man he knew, Ron Aguirre at a car show about a year ago, and Aguirre had shown him the hydraulics he'd installed on a custom car he called a *lowrider*. At the flick of a toggle switch, he could lift and lower the car's shell. Now as they reached the other turn, Coles pressed down again on the accelerator, then pulled the handbrake out in a maneuver he'd been practicing. He fishtailed through the turn, forcing the Merc to swing wider to avoid his car. In this way he gained the lead as he straightened out.

They zoomed past the onlookers.

Coles kept in front but the Mercury was tight on his tail. As they again got near the top of the dirt rise, the Merc attempted to gain an advantage by powering through the turn. But the driver miscalculated when to apply the gas and just as he was about to complete the turn, momentum caused the rear end to lose purchase, and the car skidded over the side of the dirt ramp. It rolled twice and landed upright down below. Coles completed the race, then ran from his car once he'd shut it off, to see about his opponent. Someone had already gotten the other driver free from his wrecked vehicle; fortunately both cars had roll bars installed on the interior.

"You okay, Sak?" Coles asked William Sakamoto. The other driver's face was cut and bruised.

"Looks like I'll live, Deac." He took a step but his knee buckled. Coles put a hand under his arm.

"Okay, maybe I'll sit down a minute," he grinned.

Bystanders laughed and clapped the two on their backs. Somebody had a folding beach chair and set it up for Sakamoto to sit. A few kerosene camping lanterns had been brought and these were lit against the oncoming night. Some of the people left and others milled around, talking about the race, or examining the Mercury while drinking beers. The smell of marijuana drifted about, and one beatnick sat on the crinkled fender of the Mercury, wailing on his bongos.

"Good race, Deac," said a blonde in stripped pants and a sweater top. She handed him a can of Hamm's.

"You're the coolest, Dorrie."

"Ain't I?" she said, wandering away.

A tall man in a snap-brim hat and Hawaiian shirt stepped over to Coles. The night was warm.

"Mind if I have a word with you, Mr. Coles?"

They were near the Willys, and Coles leaned against the driver's door. "What can I do for you?" Coles was in rolled-up sleeves, tan chinos, and worn heavy work boots. His hair was close-cropped and a scar ran part of the length of his jaw line.

"My name's Fred Warrens." He was in his late forties, brown hair long at the nape of his neck, and with hazel eyes. He had a trim moustache and knobby knuckles.

Coles showed interest. "You manage the Centinela Speedway, don't you?"

"Yes, sir."

"What can I do for you, Mr. Warrens?"

"I want you to race at our track."

Coles chuckled harshly. "What, you going to have 'Bring a Negro to the Races' night?" He chuckled some more.

Uncomfortable, Warrens frowned. "That's a crude way of putting it, Mr. Coles, but we would like to offer you a featured spot. I know something of your record. Fighter pilot in Korea, flying Mustangs then the F-80 jets. Over seventy-five missions and ten confirmed kills in air combat. The Deacon of the Air they called you."

"Yeah, well," he said dismissively. "You read that old article on me in *Ebony* so I guess that makes you an all-right sort of guy, huh?"

"What wasn't in that article is since the war you've been building and racing hot rods in pick-up contests all over town. A lot of people, black and white, talk you up."

"Yeah, well, it still means me and mine is unwelcome at you all's precious race tracks . . . all over town."

Warrens looked off at a few people dancing and snapping their fingers as the bongo man beat out a frenzied rhythm. He looked back at Coles. "Let me put my cards on the table, okay?"

"Please do."

"It's no secret that Inglewood is changing and, well, we think we need to change with the times too." Centinela Speedway was on a hill overlooking Centinela Avenue in Inglewood.

"Uh-huh." Coles folded his arms. "You mean them colored folk who've been buying homes near the plant since after the Big One has also meant they go to the races and have noticed the lack of shade down on the track."

Looking past Warrens' shoulder, Coles couldn't help but notice a Mexican-American woman he hadn't seen around before. She was dark-haired and copper-hued, wearing black jeans and a black top, lantern light glinting off gold hoop earrings. She was something. She glanced his way then smiled as a man in a T-shirt offered her a toke on the tea, the marijuana. The woman declined.

"The Inglewood chapter of the NAACP has threatened a boycott campaign," Warrens said. "They've been very active when it comes to jobs and promotions at North American Aviation."

Coles smiled bemusedly. "Didn't you tell 'em you had a couple of black fellas working at your track already, Mr. Warrens? Both of them janitors I believe, now ain't that so?"

Warrens spread his hands. "As I said, we want to do things differently."

"Then bring some coloreds onto the pit crews," Coles countered.

"We can't demand that of a racer and his sponsors. That's their decision to make."

"But you want me to shuck and jive at some kind of hopped-up show, that it? Make sure the cameras are there on me after the race and I got this big shit-eatin' grin on my mug thanking you and de Lawd for this special, special day. Maybe take a knee and break into Mammy while I'm at it?"

"You're looking at this all wrong, Mr. Coles."

"Sorry you wasted your time, Mr. Warrens." He took a pull of his beer.

Warrens lingered, taking in a deep breath and letting it out slow. He adjusted his hat and left.

Coles shook his head and finished his beer. Nearby was a mound of junk and, walking toward it, he tossed his can onto the pile. Turning, he encountered the woman in black.

"You are a skilled man," she said. Her accent was heavy but her words were clear. Like they were being tattooed on his spine.

"Maybe it's equal parts stupid sometimes," he countered, careful not to get lost in those depthless eyes of hers. "But winning is good for business."

"How so?"

"I build custom engines and cars so word gets around when you come in first."

"And coming in first matters to you?"

"Better than getting kicked in the teeth."

"Yes, I suppose that is so."

He made a sound. "I wasn't being that serious."

"I see."

"You're new around these parts."

"I'm Ymar, Ymar Montez." She put out her hand. There was a large jade-and-stone ring on her finger.

They shook hands. "Good to meet you."

"The pleasure's all mine, Deacon Coles."

Those eyes.

"Deac," a voice called out.

He turned to see an inebriated Sakamoto holding out a beer to him. "Here you go, daddy-o."

"Yeah, cool, Sak, but I was just talking to Ymar here," hoping he'd get the hint and blow.

"Who?"

She'd slipped away and Coles couldn't spot her beyond the small circles of light the lanterns allowed.

"Never mind," he sighed, taking the beer.

His friend grinned, bobbing his head to the bongo beat.

Two afternoons later Coles was sitting in the Gas House, a coffee, poetry, and jazz joint on Ocean Front Walk in Venice. The inhabitants of the beach community affectionately called the area the "Slum by the Sea" and was recently immortalized in Lawrence Lipton's book, *The Holy Barbarians*.

"Here you go, Deac," Dorrie Muldare said as she placed his burger and fries on the table. She waitressed at the coffee house part-time while attending UCLA.

"Thanks," he said absently as he sketched and made notations on a pad of lined paper. Three other sheets of paper had been torn away and were on the table too, his cup of coffee having formed a brown stained ring on one of them.

She turned her head to check out his work. "That for a new car you're putting together?"

He looked up at her. "Yeah. It's gonna be a killer." He tapped the eraser end of his pencil on the pad. "Well, of course I gotta get a backer first, but more races, more notches to my rep."

"Right. You know, maybe my dad could help."

"No offense, Dorrie, but those egghead buddies of his don't go in for no racing."

"But they're, you know, *with it.*"

"Hip, you mean."

She smiled. "He just got back from another expedition, excited like a kid in a candy store. He's in a good mood, dig?"

"Where'd he go this time?"

"Some jungle deep in the Mexican interior. He found some Aztec artifacts he and his crew are still sorting through. But my point was, his friends at the university are all about equal rights, right? Some of them gave money to that bus boycott they had down south a couple of years ago. He just signed a petition recently about busting up the restrictive housing covenants here in L.A."

She shrugged a shoulder. "I'll mention it to him. Who knows, maybe they'd sponsor you."

Maybe if Warrens had approached him several years ago, he might have gone along with the idea of a "Negro Night" at the race track, Coles reflected. Get some publicity for himself and do something for good intentions. But when he'd come back from Korea, no airplane manufacturer would hire him to pilot their prototype, or airline hire him to be in the cockpit. A couple had offered him a mechanic's spot. But he was vocal in telling them that if a white man showed up with his kind of record, they'd be bending over backward to give him a job flying. And while car craft was all about skill and knowledge, color was still an intractable bar at raceways where you could put your talents on bigger display than at a street race.

He smiled, spreading his hands wide. "I can see it now, 'The professors of archaeology present... the Black Speedster.' And the crowd goes wild." He let his voice echo off.

"Smart ass." They both laughed as she walked away, passing a bulletin board where numerous handbills were tacked up. These included announcements about upcoming events such as Lord Buckley, His Royal Hipness, reciting his ribald recitations with Art Pepper on sax, and one about details for the Miss Beatnik 1959 contest.

When Coles left the coffee house it was getting on in the afternoon. He walked back to his residence on Brooks Avenue, an apartment he rented in a fourplex in Ghost Town, the Oakwood section. There was a four-car garage on the side of the property that let out onto an alleyway. He took the stairs and let himself into his pad. Coles made a sandwich and, taking that and a bottle of beer back downstairs, put on his worn coveralls and got to work tuning up the Willys in his stall in the garage.

The day fell away to night and Coles was about done. He was on a creeper under the car, bolting the starter back in place. He heard her approach, then saw her feet. She wore leather sandals that laced up to her ankles, and around one of those ankles was a thick stone-and-jade bracelet. She spoke his name and gave him a thrill.

"Hello, Deacon Coles."

He rolled out to see Ymar Montez looking down at him. She had on a gathered skirt and beige cardigan. She put a foot on his floor jack, hands on her trim waist.

"Are you looking up my dress, Deacon?"

He hurriedly got to his feet, wiping his hand on a rag left on the car's fender. "Oh, no, ma'am."

"Buy a girl a beer?"

"Sure, sure. Just let me get cleaned up and we can go over to Muldoon's. It's a pretty okay joint on Lincoln."

She jutted her head at the empty Schlitz bottle. "Don't you have more upstairs?"

"Ah, yeah, sure do."

"Go get me a bottle, why don't you?"

"On it."

He tried not to rush out of the garage. *Keep it casual*, he reminded himself. Just this knock-out chick right off the cover of *Stag* who stopped by . . . Be cool, man, be cool.

He opened the fridge, thankful that two more beers were there. He took them by the necks and an opener back downstairs, figuring to pop their tops with flair to impress her.

She was gone; Ymar Montez no longer stood in the garage.

He regarded the two beers and muttered, "Guess I can drown my sorrows."

"Over here, darling," she said.

He came around to the driver's side of the Willys and gulped. There on the backseat, that A-1 gorgeous doll lounged against the passenger side door, her leg propped up on the seat. She'd discarded her skirt and top and shoes, and was in lacy black underwear. She'd hung the mechanic's light he'd been using in such a way that her form was partly illuminated. The light swayed slightly and it was as if she shimmered in and out of existence.

Coles wanted to pinch himself to make sure this was real. Talk about a wet dream out of the pages of a girlie mag.

"You going to keep me waiting?" She stretched languidly like a big cat, rubbing her hand between her legs.

Coles was deliriously light-headed. "Oh, hell no."

"Then come here and be with me, Deacon Coles. Be with me in your machine, your totem of power."

The two made hot, sweaty love. As Coles moaned her name and a rumble rent his shoulders, weird visions popped into his head, making him dizzy: Images of blood running over a carved stone face; brown-skinned people in plumes and gold; a flash of silver symbols and something more within . . . He gasped as he climaxed, and she raked his shoulder with her teeth, nicking him slightly. He sat back trying to catch his breath.

"That was," he began, his chest heaving like he'd just run five miles, " . . . amazing."

"Will you do something for me, my love." She playfully dug her foot on his slick chest.

"Anything."

"I need you to retrieve an item for me. A keepsake you might say."

"Sure, where is it?"

"A kind of bowl. It's at the home of Professor Edmund Muldare."

"Dorrie's father?"

"The same."

"I don't understand."

"He stole this container among other ancient belongings, you see. They call them *artifacts* and put them in museums for the public, as if that makes it all right. But they certainly make sure their names are associated with these supposed artifacts."

"I hear you," he said.

She leaned forward, her hand replacing the foot on his chest. "It's not his, it belongs to my people." She pressed her body to his and he wanted so bad to protect her. "You know what it means to be denied, Deacon. You know what it means to have strangers come into your land and pillage and take and destroy your history. Try to deny your existence and accomplishments. That you were a civilization while they were still in caves."

"Well, yeah, I guess. But Dorrie's dad isn't like that."

"Really? He took what is mine and seeks to profit from it. Is that right?" Her eyes seemed to fill the space in the backseat.

"No, of course not," he said robotically.

"Then help me."

He blinked hard, knowing this was off. Her argument made sense but he felt like he should talk to Professor Muldare about this, man to man. But he couldn't summon the willpower to say different. And anyway, she had his member in her hand, stroking it up and down, and damned if he wasn't rising to the occasion again. If she had asked him to slap the greens out of his grandma's mouth, he would have done it.

And he loved his grandma.

DORRIE AND HER FATHER, a widower, lived not far from Ghost Town. Nothing was that far from each other in Venice.

"He's away at some faculty function," she told him, head on his shoulders as they drove there in the Willys. "Dorrie is with him as he and his colleagues celebrate raping my land."

Getting through a side window of the Muldare's California

Craftsman home wasn't hard after they'd parked and walked over a concrete footbridge. The house was along one of the remaining canals mimicking the original ones in Venice, Italy. Coles knew black workers had helped dig those canals but were forbidden to buy here back then, though they could settle in nearby Oakwood. Homes stretched on either side, where several other canals had been filled in as the automobile become more plentiful since the late 1940s. The sidewalks were in bad shape or non-existent, quacking ducks brazenly walking or roosting about, more on land than in the water.

In the darkened study, Montez pointed to a bookshelf. "There. My prize is in there."

Coles had brought a flashlight, and he shined its beam at a shelf where she pointed. The cone of light revealed a glass-and-wood case about the size of a breadbox, and he walked to it. There were symbols and images in silver embedded in the case. *Like the ones in his vision when he'd made love to Ymar*, he noted, confused.

Taking a moment, he examined the rectangular case, then swung its dual doors open. "It wasn't locked."

"Give it to me," she whispered. Montez stood in the room but not near him.

He turned his head from her to what was inside. The object was gold, oval-shaped, and rested on three stubby legs, not unlike one of those Fabergé eggs he'd seen in a *Look* magazine once. He removed it.

"To me," she repeated sibilantly, her hand extended like a grasping claw. But she made no move to step closer.

He went to her and the lights came on.

"Deacon?" Dorrie Muldare said.

"Oh God, no, it can't be," her father said. "That witchy woman in the village spoke the truth."

He was an older man with a full head of white hair and horn-rimmed glasses, and he moved surprisingly fast for his age when he rushed forward. "We must stop her!"

"Imperious dolt," Montez said, backhanding the elder Muldare and knocking him across the room. He crashed into a wooden globe, sending it rolling off its stand across the floor.

"Dad!" His daughter rushed to help me.

"Ymar, honey baby, what are you doing?" Coles said, disoriented as if in a dream.

"She's a vampire, Deacon," Professor Muldare said, having got himself up on an elbow.

"I am an Aztec queen," Montez said as she snatched the golden vessel from Coles' hand. "And you will lead my army of the undead, my good Deacon." She pulled the vessel apart, tossing the top half away, which, Coles saw, had acted as a lid. Without it, the bottom half, with its three legs, was a kind of chalice, and it held black fluid. "This life essence of Mictlantecuhtli, the lord of the underworld, will give me the power I've craved for centuries!"

She held the chalice aloft, sneering at the older man. "And to think I have a pirate like you to thank for finding that which had been shielded from me for so long."

"Stop her," the archeologist protested. "She will enslave us all!"

His daughter rose, but Coles was closer. Whatever spell Ymar held over him was snapped once he'd seen her treat the older man so harshly and heard him talk about slavery. He left his feet and dove at her as she started to drink from the container.

"No, you fool!" she bellowed as she was taken down. The dark viscous liquid was sloshed onto the drapes and carpet. She shoved Coles away, and he too was thrown back. He collided with the bookshelf, and the silver-inlaid case tumbled to the floor. Inadvertently he stepped on it, splintering the wood and breaking the glass as he got back on his feet.

Montez was on her knees, bent over, her tongue lapping up as much of the ichor as she could from the carpet. She raised her head, fanged teeth now prominent. The thick black fluid dribbled from her mouth, down her chin. She wiped at it, licking the blood stuff off her fingers, eying Coles with evil intent.

The chalice was on the floor on its side. Part of its interior was coated in a tar-like goop that must have been the residue of Mictlantecuhtli's blood as Montez had claimed. Instantly everyone understood this substance was the most potent distillation of the ancient Aztec deity. Montez strode toward this, her body twisting and reshaping itself, like watching a tree grow on a time-elapsed film.

"Not so fast, Vampira." Dorrie Muldare brought a heavy book down on the back of Montez's head; it was an edition of the King James Bible—said to have been in her family since the 1700s. The Aztec queen collapsed to the ground, groaning.

"Time to spilt," Coles said, scooping up the fancy cup.

The three ran from the house. They heard a screech and, looking back, watched in shock as a now airborne Ymar Montez ascended from the house into the moonlit night on large, leathery bat wings.

"Shit." Coles stared open-mouthed as did the others.

"We can't let her eat the... god's jelly," Professor Muldare sputtered.

"Right," Coles said, cradling the golden vessel like a halfback as he ran for the footbridge leaving Dorrie and her father behind. The now-transformed Montez flew after him. She had clawed feet and hands, face elongated and distorted with bat-like features.

"Deacon," the creature cried at as she dive-bombed him. "I will have what is mine."

Before she could latch her claws into him, he turned and swung like Maury Wills at the plate, striking her with the chalice. She went end-over-end backward and dropped into the canal, sending disturbed ducks into the air. Coles kept running and got to his car.

Having been parked facing west, he peeled off on Venice Boulevard, then made a right onto Speedway, which paralleled the ocean. Oddly, it wasn't named that as some believed because racing took place along the street; it was narrow and two-way. He clipped the side of a Woody station wagon coming from the opposite direction, the driver blaring his horn and cursing at him... until that driver saw a flying human-like creature whoosh down from above chasing the Willys.

Coles neared the Pen, the weight area where body builders worked out. His plan was to take a right off the thoroughfare and maybe lose the demon after him in the maze of streets called courts, only accessible by foot. He'd have to abandon the car, but he was too much of a target like this, he reasoned. He whizzed around the corner of the Lido Hotel, a rundown establishment, even by Venice standards. He nearly ran into two winos arguing in the middle of the street. There wasn't enough room to get by them, and his tires smoked as he braked hard.

"Move!" Coles yelled, sticking his head out of the driver's side window.

"Buzz off," one of the winos said.

Coles edged forward but it was too late. With a resounding thud, Montez landed on the roof of the car.

"The angel of death has arrived," one of the winos said. He prostrated himself before her.

Montez screeched and rammed her hand through the window on the driver's side as Coles tried to roll it up. But it was her clawed feet that grabbed at him instead and tore him from the car, the driver's side door ripped off its hinges as she did so. He was carried into the air, then let go to drop hard onto the ground. He landed, the breath knocked out of him. The Willys shuddered and died; the clutch had been engaged but no one was driving to give it gas. Wincing, he tried to rise.

"Oh, you little insignificant man," Montez said hovering, then dropping on him, all four of her clawed appendages digging into this flesh. Saliva dripped from her fanged mouth as she leaned her face close to his, her forked tongue flicking his nose. The chalice with its unholy residue lay nearby.

"How would you like this tongue wrapped around your cock like I did earlier, Deacon?" She laughed at the horror on his face. "What, you recoil at the sight of me, my sweet?" she taunted. Briefly she willed herself to take on her human guise, the naked woman of pin-up delight. Chuckling, she then reverted back to her monstrous form. "Soon, your ardor will be rekindled when I make you mine, now and forever." Her mouth opened wide, and she lunged forward to bite him and make him her vampire slave.

"It's endsville for us, baby," Coles said, burying a piece of jagged wood with its silver inlay inscription into the large vein in her neck.

Her eyes went wide and she reared back in shock. Coles had picked up the piece after he'd stepped on the chalice's case, shattering it back at the house. He'd figured the hieroglyphs, or whatever they were in the silver, combined to create a barrier to her, which was why she couldn't open that case herself. During the fight, he'd wondered, *What would happen if he got the chance to stab her with a piece of the case?*

His answer now was an inhuman wail of anguish as she tried to fly away, but her wings disintegrated, her body self-immolating as she became earthbound.

The professor and Dorrie drove up in their car. Together with the two winos, who were sobered by fear, they witnessed the end of the Aztec queen of the vampires. Montez's charred skeleton caved in on itself as the fire lingered, and her ashes twinkled as they drifted skyward.

"Wow," Dorrie Muldare said.

"Yeah, crazy," Coles seconded.

"Indeed," her dad said.

WHEN DEACON COLES WALKED into Fred Warrens' office at the Centinela Speedway, he said, "I'll compete in your damn show race. But if I win, then you put pressure on them ofays to hire some colored folk in the pits."

"You got a deal, Mr. Coles."

And when Coles raced his souped-up Willys around the track—money to improve her having come from Professor Muldare and some of his colleagues—he could hear the gas churning through the fuel line and the syncopated whine of oil and metal as the pistons screamed in the cylinders.

As Ymar Montez had burned, he'd noticed a smidgen of the Aztec god's blood had gotten on his thumb. He'd licked it off and swallowed Mictlantecuhtli's essence.

His super-charged senses had become knife-edge sharp, and the smell of combustion inflamed him like a beautiful woman's perfume.

He was now the demon of the track.

Son of a mechanic and a librarian, weaned on the images of Kirby and Kane in comics and too many reruns of The Twilight Zone, **GARY PHILLIPS** *and his pops once rebuilt a '58 Ford Fairlane. Since then he has published various novels such as* Violent Spring, *the first such mystery set in post '92 civil unrest L.A.; edited several anthologies including* The Obama Inheritance: Fifteen Stories of Conspiracy Noir; *and published more than sixty short stories. With Christa Faust, he co-wrote a prose adaptation of the classic Batman vs. Joker graphic novel,* The Killing Joke.

WHEN MY COUSIN TAMMY CALLED WITH the news that my father had been killed in a hunting accident, I hated that I started sobbing. Hadn't I cried enough for my old man? Instead of thinking about the hell he'd put me and the rest of our family through, I was feeling sorry for *him*?

"You okay?" Tammy asked.

Wiping the tears away with my sleeve, I said, "Yeah . . . fine."

"You don't sound fine."

I was still sobbing, but I didn't want her to know. I waited a few seconds, getting ahold of myself then said, "I'm okay. Appreciate you letting me know."

OUTLAWED INK

BY JASON STARR

"These aren't any tattoos," Nick said.
"These are different."

I just wanted to hang up the receiver—get on with my life.

"You want to know how it happened?" she asked.

I didn't, but I asked, "What happened?"

"Your dad and my dad were hunting. It was early in the morning, they'd been drinking the night before, probably hungover or still drunk. Your dad was out ahead of my dad, and my dad thought he was a buck and shot him. My dad said your dad didn't die right away. It took about a half hour before he went. You still there, Ray?"

"Yeah."

"You sure you're okay?"

"Yeah, yeah, I'm sure."

"My mom's planning the funeral. I know you and your dad weren't close. Hell, nobody was close with him except my dad. Anyway, the funeral will be in a few days, not sure when yet, but I'll let you know when I know."

"Okay," I said, "thanks."

"You want to tell Nick or should I?"

My twin brother Nick and I weren't close either. I hadn't talked to him in maybe five years.

"I'll tell him," I said.

"All right," Tammy said.

Long after Tammy ended the call, I was still sobbing.

Not for the same reason, though.

"NICK."

"Who's this?"

"It's me . . . your brother, remember?"

Long pause, then, "Dad died, didn't he?"

"Want to know how?"

"I couldn't give a damn."

"There's gonna be a funeral."

"So?"

"You don't wanna go?"

"Hell no. Why? You going?"

"It could be good for us," I said. "I can drive through Albany on my way and pick you up. You still live in Albany, right?"

"You really wanna pay that man *respects*?"

"Not respects," I said. "Could be a way to let go, that's all."

"I don't need to let go," he said. "I let go when I cut him off years ago."

"I thought I did too," I said. "Believe me, going to Dad's funeral was never something I ever planned on doing. But I think it could be helpful to, you know, see them put him in the ground, to know that he's gone for good. But if you don't want to go, I totally get it."

He didn't say anything.

"Well, goodbye then," I said.

I doubted I'd ever have a reason to call Nick again. The last time I'd spoken with him on the phone was when our mother died. Neither of us had gone to that funeral because we didn't want to see our father again. I hadn't seen Nick in ten years, since I left home after graduating high school in '48. It was sad we weren't closer; that was Nick's fault, not mine. While my dad used to beat Nick and me, around the time we turned fifteen and I came out, Nick started abusing me too.

I sobbed for a while longer, then I tried to get on with my life. I did some chores and cooked myself dinner—spaghetti with canned sauce and broccoli. I lived by myself in a one-bedroom apartment in Johnson City, New York. After high school I needed to get away from my father, so I moved to Syracuse with a friend who was going to college there. I shacked up with a guy in Johnson City, telling the landlord and neighbors we were just roomies, until he dumped me for his old boyfriend. I had nowhere else to go so I stayed there and got a job as a bookkeeper at a shoe manufacturer in Endicott. It was boring work, but it paid the bills.

Since I got dumped, I met other guys here and there, sure, usually ones "experimenting" from the University. Otherwise, the gay scene in the tri-cities—Binghamton, Johnson City, and Endicott—wasn't exactly jumping. There was one flamer bar, Harry's over on Clinton Street in Binghamton, where I used to go sometimes. But about a year ago, I had an awful experience: I was leaving, by myself, when a townie attacked me, beat the living crap out of me. He must have been squeezing a roll of nickels because one of his fists felt like steel. When I reported what happened the next day, the detective at the police station knew exactly who the guy was, but he laughed and seemed more keen on arresting me for what *I* was.

I didn't know why I'd expected it to go any other way.

Before bed, I watched some TV—*The Huntley-Brinkley Report*—but I wasn't really paying attention. In my head, I kept replaying the times my dad beat me and Nick up, or verbally abused us. My mom never helped, but I couldn't blame her because my father was beating her too.

As I was falling asleep, my phone rang. I pulled the receiver off the cradle by the cord.

"Hello?"

"Changed my mind," Nick said. "I wanna see them put that old prick in the ground."

A FEW DAYS LATER, on the day of the funeral, I drove over to my brother's small house in Albany in my car, one of those older Plymouth models that steered like a tank. Although we had identical genes, I almost didn't recognize Nick. He had to be about thirty or forty pounds overweight. He was in dirty khakis and had a prominent beer gut pushing out his crew cut T-shirt. Tattoos covered his big, mostly fatty, arms. He'd had one of the tattoos—a snake—since we were teens. The others were all since I'd last seen him: Cartoon tomcats, broken hearts and switchblades, a lot of World War II stuff.

Maybe he didn't recognize me either because I had to honk before he got in the car.

When he got in he said, "Hey," but didn't shake my hand or even look at me.

The funeral was where we grew up, in Pittsfield, Massachusetts, about an hour and a half drive away.

We didn't talk much during the ride. The sky was gray and it was drizzling but not enough to need the wipers. Nick told me about his new job "at the plant," but I didn't ask him what kind of plant it was. He didn't ask me anything about myself. Most of the time, I was focused on driving, and he was staring straight ahead.

Although Nick hadn't said or done anything, or threatened me in any way, I felt uneasy. My instincts told me I was in danger, that my life was in jeopardy. There didn't seem to be any logical reason why I felt this way; it was just a vibe.

We were riding along Route 90, maybe halfway to Pittsfield, when Nick asked, "You still queer?"

"Yeah," I said. "You still straight?"

He waited about a minute then said, "I think that's why you got it worse than me. Dad couldn't handle it."

Thinking that Nick couldn't handle it either, I said, "Yeah, that's true."

"I ever tell you about the time I tried to kill him?" Nick asked.

"No."

"It was when we were sixteen," he said. "Dad finished beating us and went into the backyard to get more drunk. You were upstairs in bed, crying as usual, and a voice said to me, *Kill him.* So I went down to the kitchen, grabbed the biggest knife I could find, and came up behind him. I saw myself doing it—slitting his throat, all the blood spurting out. But when I was a about to move he turned around and grabbed the knife right out of my hand. He started laughing hysterically, then he beat the living shit out of me."

"A voice told you to do it?" I said. "I didn't know you hear voices now."

"There's a lot about me you don't know," he said. After a period of not saying anything, he added, "So you really think Uncle Frank shot Dad by accident?"

"I don't know, what do you think?"

"Thought he was a buck, my ass," Nick said. "How does a man look like a buck? Frank was in the joint for manslaughter. Trust me— nothing would stop him from killing somebody. Everybody hated Dad and wanted him dead. It's a miracle he lived as long as he did. If I slit his throat that night imagine how much pain it would've saved all of us."

We didn't talk anymore until we arrived in downtown Pittsfield and Nick said, "Well, here we are."

I hadn't been to Pittsfield in a while, but it hadn't changed much. Thanks to the GE factory, downtown was hopping as always, and I noticed some new stores, including a soda shop and a luncheonette that looked like it was jumping.

The part of town where we grew up looked as rundown as it always had.

We still had some time to kill so we went to a shabby diner next to a rundown pool hall and had coffee and breakfast. I still felt uneasy around Nick, like I didn't want to turn my back to him. His story about almost killing our father didn't exactly make me more comfortable around him.

At the cemetery, the sky was still gray and bleak. No one was around except a couple of cemetery workers preparing the gravesite.

Then two more arrived. Uncle Frank looked a lot like my dad—so much so that I actually shuddered when I saw him approaching. He had the same dead, empty look in his eyes that my father and Nick had.

Alongside Frank was Tammy in her wheelchair. The family story was she'd had a "freak accident" as a teenager and fell down a flight of stairs and wound up paralyzed from the waist down, but everyone suspected that Frank had pushed her.

What can I say? I came from a family of psychos, and I was lucky that I'd avoided getting that bad gene.

"Nobody else is coming," Frank said. "Let's get him in the hole so we can get outta here."

He didn't exactly sound devastated that his brother was gone. Then again, none of us were.

A hearse pulled up and the cemetery workers slid out the cheapest looking coffin I'd ever seen. It looked like it was made of cardboard.

"Anybody want to speak?" Frank asked.

"Hell no," Nick said.

As the workers lowered the coffin into the grave, I noticed that Frank had a snake tattoo on his arm, just like Nick's. When the coffin was in position, Nick approached the grave.

"Nick, come on, don't," Tammy said.

It was too late—Nick was already pissing all over the coffin.

Frank was laughing.

I thought it was pretty damn funny too.

"Good idea," I said, and joined in.

"What the hell?" Frank said, and he pissed on the coffin too.

Sadly, this might've been the happiest family moment I'd ever had.

"I SAW YOU LOOKING at Frank's tattoo," Nick said.

We'd left the cemetery and were walking toward my car. The sun had come out but it was still chilly.

"Yeah," I said. "I noticed it looks just like yours."

"We got it at the same place. You should get one too."

"I'm not into tattoos," I said.

"These aren't any tattoos," Nick said. "These are different."

"What makes them different?"

"It's hard to explain. Hey, I have an idea, let's get tats right now."

"Now?"

"Why not? We said goodbye to Dad, showed him how pissed off at him we all are, so now it's time to, what's the word I'm looking for? Commiserate?"

"Commemorate," I said.

"Right, commem—? Whatever, I think today's a day we're going to remember, so we should do something to remember it."

I opened the door to the car and got in, then I opened the passenger door for Nick.

As I drove away, Nick said, "Come on, I'm serious, what do you say? We both get the same tattoo to help us forget Dad, move on."

"Freedom," I said.

"Or how about just *Free*?" Nick said. "Come on, let's do it, we'll go to Outlawed Ink over in Pauling. It's about a twenty minute drive, sort of on the way to Albany. You won't regret it, Ray, I promise."

"You know what?" I said. "Why not? Let's just do it."

I knew I was acting impulsive, but I didn't care. The best things had happened to me when I took risks and I hadn't taken a real risk in ages.

We drove along Route 20, over a mountain, toward the Massachusetts-New York border.

When we got close to town, Nick said, "This is it, right here. Right, the dirt road."

We rode along the dirt road for maybe a half hour until we reached a converted garage with a sign on it: *OUTLAWED INK*.

"Doesn't look open," I said.

"It's always open," he said. "Wait here."

He went to the dilapidated house next to the garage and banged on the screen door. An extremely frail, wrinkled man with a very small bald head—he appeared to be at least ninety years old—came to the door. Nick talked to him for a few minutes. A couple of times the man glanced in my direction, but by the way he was squinting I didn't know if he could even see me.

Nick returned to the car and said, "Okay, he can take us."

"*He's* the tattoo artist?"

"Yeah, one of the best."

"I don't know," I said.

"Trust me," Nick said. "I've been coming here for years. You won't be disappointed."

My instincts told me this was a bad idea, but when had I ever listened to my instincts?

"What the hell," I said.

We waited near the garage for about fifteen minutes. Finally, the man exited the house.

He walked slowly with shuffle stops and then we waited until he found the right key on the chain—it seemed like he tried ten—and opened the door.

Was I really going to trust this guy to give me a tattoo? Could he even keep his hands steady?

"He wants to do you first," Nick said.

Nick could tell I was nervous.

"Don't worry," Nick said. "Look at my body. I've got twenty-six tats. I survived."

I sat in a chair while Nick stood over me. The old guy was preparing the inks or whatever. His head seemed even smaller up close—he might've had the smallest head I'd ever seen on a body. He also now seemed been much older than ninety, closer to one hundred.

"I already told him what you want," Nick said. "He'll show you some styles and colors, and you tell him where you want it."

I chose the style and color—a darkish green—and I told him that I wanted it on the inside of my left forearm, about three inches long. He didn't seem to understand me, even though the fourth time I repeated myself I was practically shouting.

"He wants it three inches," Nick said in a normal voice.

The old man nodded.

I considered bailing again, but as the old man prepared to tattoo me he seemed to know what he was doing. He sterilized my arm and the needle, and I saw him open a fresh jar of ink. Rationalizing, I told myself I was better off with a guy who'd probably done this thousands of times in his life, as opposed to some first timer.

He spent about a half hour on me, tattooing *FREE* on my forearm, in the exact style I'd chosen. It was somewhat painful, but not as much as I'd expected. Then he bandaged my arm.

"That was easier than I thought," I said to the old man. "Thank you."

He didn't seem to hear me. He whispered something into Nick's ear, then left the garage.

"Where's he going?" I asked.

"He has a doctor's appointment," Nick said. "Won't have time to do me today."

"I thought the whole point was we'd get them together," I said.

"What can you do?" Nick said. "The guy has to go. I'll come back some other time. Besides, you're the virgin. We had to pop your tattoo cherry and we did it, mission accomplished."

"What about paying him?"

"I already paid him, don't worry about it."

I hadn't seen Nick pay him, but it was possible he'd slipped him some cash at some point.

Back in my car, Nick and I headed to Albany.

"So," Nick asked. "You feel it yet?"

"Feel what?" I asked.

"Something different," he said. "Or maybe something . . . missing."

I didn't know what he was getting at.

"How can I feel something that's not there?" I asked.

"You can't," he said, "but, trust me, you'll know it's gone."

"Seriously," I said, "what're you talking about?"

Nick laughed. "Oh, man, I didn't know how much fun this would be? I mean, I knew it would be fun, but I didn't know it would be the funniest thing ever." He continued laughing.

Driving, focused on the road, I wondered if Nick was just messing with me, like he'd *always* messed with me.

He recovered from laughing, then said, "Didn't you ever wonder why you're different from me, Frank, and Dad?"

"You mean because I'm gay?"

"No, besides that. You know there's something else, right?"

"You mean personality-wise?"

"Yeah, come on. You can say it. What makes us different?"

"You're all crazy."

"Right," Nick said. "Exactly. Actually we're beyond crazy. We're full-blown psychotic."

If Nick had said this to me this morning, I probably would've been terrified. For some reason now it didn't bother me at all.

"I didn't know you were so aware of it," I said.

"Lemme ask you another question," he said. "Did you ever wonder how we got to be this way?"

"I guess it's genetics," I said.

"No," he said, "it's ink. Tattoo ink. The same tattoo ink that's seeping into your body right now, sucking out your conscience."

"Ha ha," I said. "That's funny."

"You think I'm joking?"

"Yeah, I think you're joking."

He started laughing again, so hard he could barely catch his breath.

"Oh, man," he said. "This is . . . " He was still laughing. "This is the funniest thing ever." He calmed down, then said, "Ever notice how I never feel guilty about anything? I mean, going back to when I was sixteen, and I gave you a hard time? That's because that's when Uncle Frank took me to Outlawed Ink to get my first tattoo. See, we have a family tradition of going there. Frank and Dad went there when they were teenagers and that's how they became psychotic. Like I've been telling you, the ink kills your conscience and replaces it with another voice, a voice that lets you do whatever you feel like doing. If you don't have a conscience there's no limit to what you can do. I'm telling you, I can't even remember what guilt feels like, but I don't miss it at all either."

"You really expect me to believe any of this?" I said.

"It's been over a half hour," he said. "It should be kicking in already. Think about something you feel guilty about."

"This is ridic—"

"There must be *something*," he said. "Come on."

I thought about it, then said, "Okay, not visiting mom in the hospital before she died."

"Okay now, do you actually feel bad about that or do you not give a damn?"

I didn't care at all; I felt totally indifferent.

"You don't even have to answer," he said. "I see it in your face."

I didn't believe it. It had to just be in my head; I was psyching myself out.

There was a Dunkin Donuts up ahead. I slowed and pulled into the lot.

"I need some coffee," I said.

We went in. I ordered coffee and Nick ordered hot chocolate and a Boston cream donut.

I thought, *Aren't you too fat to eat that*? Then said it: "Aren't you too fat to eat that?"

I couldn't believe I'd said what I was thinking.

"There you go," Nick said, "another example. When you lose your conscience you lose your filter. You'll find you're much more honest than you used to be. Though there's another word for honesty—it's called cruelty."

The teenage guy at the counter was overhearing all of this.

"I'll pay for his too," I said to the guy.

We returned to the car. Admittedly I felt different—stronger, more confident even—but I still didn't believe that it had anything to do with the tattoo. Ink destroying my conscience? Did Nick really expect me to believe that?

I couldn't deny it though, I felt different. It had to be my imagination; I was playing games with myself.

When we arrived at Nick's house, I said, "Mind if I use your bathroom?"

"Sure thing," he said.

I followed him into the house. It was cramped, messy, smelled like mildew.

"Bathroom's straight ahead to the left," he said.

After I peed, I washed up and looked at myself in the blotchy mirror. Was I imagining it, or did my eyes look different? They were the same pale blue, but there was something emptier about them. Deader. They looked, well, exactly like Nick's eyes.

I left the bathroom and met Nick in the kitchen. He'd poured himself a glass of lemonade.

"Want some?" he asked.

"No, thanks," I said.

I was staring at his arm, at the snake tattoo. I flashed back to the times when he had assaulted me with a broomstick, calling me "homo" and "faggot" and "Gay Ray."

"You okay?" Nick asked. "You look funny."

A voice, a *new* voice, inside me said, *Kill him.*

A moment later I grabbed a large knife and started jamming it into Nick's throat. I felt excited watching the blood spurt from his neck and mouth as he tried to talk. The sounds he was making even sounded funny to me, and I might've laughed.

I removed the knife and backed away as his body fell onto the kitchen floor. He was bleeding out, definitely dead.

Making sure nobody saw me, I left the house and drove away.

BACK IN JOHNSON CITY, I went about my life. I did some food shopping and chores around my apartment. Before bed, I took off the bandage and checked out the tattoo. Nick had been right—the old man knew what he was doing; it had come out swell.

At work the next day people noticed a change in me. A few people asked me if I'd lost weight, another asked me if I'd gotten a haircut. I think they were reacting to my new confidence, though. I noticed other changes in my personality. I was nicer to people, more charming, but I also felt superior to them. In all honesty, I felt like the people I worked with were a bunch of morons, and I knew if I could do everyone's job for them the company would've been run much more efficiently.

Another new thing I noticed about myself: when I was on lunch break at work I passed a playground near my office and saw a kid getting pushed around by two bigger kids. Old Me would've felt sorry for the little kid, and might've even told the bullies to stop. New Me watched for a while and thought the whole scene was kind of funny.

I wasn't surprised when the cops showed up that evening to question me about Nick's death. Nick had probably told people at "the plant" where he worked that he was going to his dad's funeral, and maybe even that I was giving him a lift.

Old Me might've been nervous about the questioning, especially if I knew I was guilty, but New Me was a good actor. New Me acted shocked when he heard the news and even squeezed out some tears. New Me was also a much better liar than Old Me. New Me wasn't even aware that he was lying. New Me believed his lies were the truth.

The police left, seeming satisfied that I had no involvement in the murder. Luckily Nick had lots of enemies and there were many people who could've wanted him dead.

I continued my routine, feeling bored. I had a kid from the University over one night, but I really just wanted to kill again.

Then, one night, I had a great idea. It was so great I wished I'd thought of it sooner.

I took some time off work and began stalking the guy who had assaulted me outside of the bar on Clinton Street. The detective had told me his name, so he was easy to track down in the phone book. I followed him to work, to the grocery store, the hardware store, church, and everywhere else he went, waiting for the perfect time. On the third night, I had my chance.

He was in a liquor store parking lot late at night and there was no one else around. Approaching him from behind, I said, "Hey."

When he turned, he seemed confused, like he knew that he knew me from somewhere, but he wasn't sure where.

"It's me," I said. "The faggot, remember?"

Now he knew who I was. I also saw the fear in his eyes because he knew there was something different about me, something he needed to fear.

"Don't feel so big and strong without your roll of nickels, huh?" I said.

"The hell're *you* doing here?" he asked.

I loved hearing the terror in his voice. It was also great not having a conscience to hold me back from doing whatever I felt like doing. If someone hurt me, I didn't have to waste my life feeling bad about it, cowering in fear. Instead I could fight back.

Kill him, the voice said.

As I bashed his head against the concrete again and again, for the first time in my life I felt truly free.

JASON STARR is the international best-selling author of many crime novels and thrillers. He also writes original graphic novels and superhero comics for Marvel and DC and has contributed to numerous short story anthologies. He has won the Barry Award and is a two-time winner of the Anthony Award. Several of his books are in development for TV, film, and theater. His work has been translated into over a dozen languages. His latest novel is the psychological thriller, Fugitive Red. *Starr was born and raised in Brooklyn and now lives in Manhattan.*

ONE O'CLOCK, TWO O'CLOCK, THREE O'CLOCK...
lookin' good.

Using the shiny grillwork on Mr. Fairfield's Buick Skylark as a mirror, Johnny Morris slicked back his ducktail and gave himself a once-over. White shirt with his name embroidered in red on the pocket, tight black jeans, the cuffs rolled up, socks just a little grease-stained from work, but he figured he needed the sweet scent of motor oil to cover up any lingering traces of Amalia Rodriguez's spitfire perfume. The Buick had been the scene for a little back seat Bingo.

He was a teenager in love, oh yes he was, as hot-blooded as they came.

WE MIGHT BE GIANTS

BY NANCY HOLDER

*"We are in a life-or-death crisis.
Your girlfriends seek revenge on you."*

Amalia rearranged her beehive hairdo and knelt on the ground with her curvy little bottom in the air. Johnny stayed loose as he stood behind her, taking in the scene. She had on black-and-white polka dot capris and a black sleeveless top, bright red kitten heels, and an ankle bracelet that said *Berto*—her boyfriend—but there was no trace of Berto in that *hot-cha-cha* smile she threw at Johnny over her shoulder. She was blindingly beautiful.

"You see? So we fill up five tubs of water. They try to grab an apple with their teeth and if they do, they get a prize!" She gestured to the four other aluminum tubs, just like the one she was kneeling in front of. She bobbed her head up and down. He gulped.

"That's swell," he said. "A prize like what?"

She dimpled. "A homemade cake. We made cakes. All the girls in my family." She pushed against the rim of the tub and got to her feet. "I'll show you mine." She bent her finger in a come-hither gesture and he followed like a puppy.

About a dozen layer cakes were arranged on a picnic table covered with a Halloween cloth. Some were decorated like pumpkins or spiders; there was lots of black frosting and candy corn. "Here it is," she said, proudly indicating a chocolate sheet cake. Little gravestones made from graham crackers sat among tufts of green frosting grass. "Here." She swiped up a glob of green grass with her finger and held it out to him.

Oh, Amalia, sweet Latin mystery train from down Mexico way, daughter of his boss Mr. Rodriguez, who owned Tusker's Garage and Auto Parts. At seventeen, Amalia was his oldest daughter.

I am out of my gourd.

Mr. Rodriguez kept a baseball bat underneath the counter. And speaking of bats, tonight was the powder-puff baseball game, Sidewinders against the Cactus Flowers.

"That is *muy delicioso.*"

"Tonight you could win it," she replied.

"Fingers crossed." Behind his back.

"You're coming to the game, *sí*? We are going to crush the Sidewinders."

A jolt of anxiety zapped through him. "Wouldn't miss it."

"I'll save you a seat behind home plate." She kissed him on the lips. He'd have to be sure to wipe all that bright red lipstick off.

"Right."

He turned and walked away without looking back at her, because that was what cool cats did. But he was worried about that saved seat. Peggy Sue would be saving him a seat, too. Bet on it.

He kicked an empty Schlitz can through the rain gutter. Along the scattered storefronts, scarecrows and painted skeletons dangled in clusters from posts pounded into the sand. Orange light bulbs were draped around the cacti flanking the adobe post office. For such a dinky little dead-end town, Sonrisa threw one hell of a Halloween carnival. It had always been that way, but as of six months ago, some homesick eggheads at some secret nameless upwind government lab had begun to make a habit of spending their paychecks at the Flight Test Bar, the Rocket Drive-In, Keebler's Diner, and Roberto's Taco Shop. There hadn't been much of an increase in business at Fashion Fair—so far all the eggheads were men and none of them seemed interested in wearing those big frilly petticoats that crinkled when the girls sashayed by. So many petticoats.

So little time.

I gotta put on the brakes.

Mildly cursing his all-American red blood, he ambled across the hardscrabble street beneath Sonrisa's only traffic light, kicking up sand in the sizzling afternoon. Sonrisa was a few dusty buildings and the silver cigar of Keebler's Diner. The sun bounced off it like bullets off Superman's chest.

Inside that diner Peggy Sue was zipping around serving burgers and milkshakes on her roller skates. Zip-zip, *unzip*—

"Hey, Johnny," she chirped as she burst through the door in her loafers and bobby socks. She greeted him with a kiss on the cheek. She was still wearing her pink-and-white striped apron over a light pink poodle skirt, and a matching pink scarf was tied around her blonde ponytail pulled up tight on her head.

He managed a pang of guilt over his two-timing with Amalia as Peggy Sue took his hand and started chattering innocently about the dunking booth, which was the diner's contribution to the carnival. You paid for three baseballs and aimed each one in succession at this lever, and if you hit it, the person sitting in the booth fell off their perch into the water. Peggy Sue's boss Peter, the mayor, and the police chief had volunteered to be dunked. And so had all the members of the Sidewinders, rivals of the Cactus Flowers. Amalia was the captain of the Cactus Flowers and guess who was the captain of the Sidewinders?

It's just that they're both so pretty, he thought. *And so different. Amalia is red, black, white, and Peggy Sue is like a tasty little cone of cotton candy. Fire and sugar.*

He realized she'd said something to him that required a response when she stopped talking and looked at him expectantly as they reached the perimeter of the Dunkin' Well. The tank had been assembled, and a water hose running from the spigot in the You-Wash-It was in the tank, filling it up.

"So you can be our water boy tonight," she cooed.

"Uh," he said, and just then, a man in a black suit, thick black glasses, and crew cut—had to be an egghead—stopped on the other side of the dunk tank and looked through its plastic sides at Johnny. The man—Flat-top—kept looking. Staring, even, like a big weirdo.

Johnny lifted a brow and stuck a pose. "Yeah?" he challenged.

Flat-top moved on. Johnny watched him go. There was something strange about that guy.

"He look okay to you?" Johnny murmured.

Peggy Sue smiled up at him. "Who?"

"That cat in the suit. I think he's keeping tabs on me."

Her lashes actually fluttered. "I only have eyes for you, Johnny. I'll see you later. I have to warm up for tonight." She moved her shoulders in an exaggerated shiver. "I have to be on my game. Amalia Rodriguez is so *aggressive*."

Oh, baby. Baby, baby, baby.

"Later, gator," he said, tugging on her ponytail.

HOW HAD HE EVER DREAMED he could make time with the two most beautiful girls in a tiny town like Sonrisa? Same way he had run through the others, he supposed—by being cagey. Mainly he didn't get why he didn't have a terrible reputation. If a girl acted like him, she'd be labeled faster than a drag race down by the power plant. Gina, Doreen, Thomasina, Louanne, Amalia, Peggy Sue. Long, long list.

I am cruisin' for a bruisin'.

He combed his hair for the walk home, using the Fashion Fair window as a mirror. His pompadour was a thing of beauty. Guys around here were stupid not to work on their looks. The ladies appreciated it when you made efforts.

As he slipped his comb back in his pocket, a figure blurred behind him, reflected in the glass. Two round discs caught the still-brilliant sunlight. Glasses. Was it that egghead again? By the time he turned, there was no one there.

He shrugged and ambled on home, turning over his predicament in his mind: the Halloween carnival, the baseball game, the two beautiful captains. Halloween was only three days away; could he wear some kind of costume or a mask tonight, hire someone to dress up just like him, be in two places at once . . . that might work on a TV show like *I Love Lucy* or *Buck Rogers*, but no one was going to buy that in real life. Besides, who was he going to ask? When it came to guys, Johnny was a lone wolf. Why hang out with your competition?

Home sweet home was little and dusty but it was just his ma, him, his kid brother Stan, and his little sister Jackie. His dad's picture was on the mantle. Young Richard Morris was all dolled up in his sailor suit, with the white hat and all. His ma said it was the sailor uniform that did it, that if she'd met Richard in his civvies, she would never have eloped. A weakness for good-lookers ran in their family.

He continued to consider his predicament as he helped Jackie cut and paste her alphabet letters in her first grade workbook and then put away the dishes for his ma. He figured his best choice was not to go to the game or the carnival. He could say he'd gotten sick. That was smart; he might get cut some slack that way. Unless the two girls talked to each other. But they wouldn't, would they? They came from different sides of town.

He went out back to have a smoke and think things over. He kept returning to the costume idea. He could be Ro-Man the Robot Monster. Yeah, if he had two gorilla suits, two skull masks, two goldfish bowls, and an accomplice. Which he didn't. Besides, would other nineteen-year-old guys be wearing costumes to a girls' baseball game? Not on your life.

He sighed and tamped out his cigarette. Maybe it was time to beat feet. Peel out of this tiny pueblo and go to Albuquerque.

There was a rustling in the scrubby bushes by the laundry line. He walked over to investigate, parting the gray-green leaves.

Crouched down was the same egghead who had wandered past the dunk tank about an hour ago. The man's glasses slipped off and he pushed them back on his face as he straightened up, dusting the sand from the knees of his black suit.

"Hey, kid," he said, as if there was nothing unusual about hiding in somebody's bushes.

"Hey, yourself," Johnny retorted, balling up his fists. "What the heck, man?"

"I mean no harm. Really." The guy put his hands in his pockets. He gave the sky a glance and blew air out of his cheeks. "Here's the thing. There's going to be a bomb test in a little while."

Johnny shrugged. "You guys have had a million of those things."

"Yeah, but this one's . . . "

The guy's eyes ticked past Johnny and widened. Huge. As if he'd seen Ro-Man. "Damn it," he muttered. He plopped down in the bushes.

Johnny turned around to see what had scared him. The horizon was the horizon—fence, a saguaro cactus, more scrub, the power plant in the distance, the blazing sun. But no, there was some kind of shimmer in the air—like a big soap bubble or something, and—

A sharp *clang* rang out behind him. Johnny whirled back around.

Flat-top was *gone*. As in *vanished*.

He beat the bushes looking for the man. There, at the base of the scrub, gleamed a metal panel. He touched it. There was a *fwooomm* and then the thing slid open with the exact same clang. In the sunlight Johnny saw what appeared to be a metal playground slide canted at an angle. He reached down to touch it, and the dang thing slid open right under him.

He fell downward like a rocket as the panel banged shut above. He managed to cover his face with his hands as he flew along like he was in some race going for pinks. Then smacked *wham!* into something soft and bouncy.

Hands grabbed him and hoisted him to his feet. And what he saw—

Great balls of fire!

Men with heads as big as jack-o'-lanterns, all big eyes and grins, except their skin was green. They were wearing silvery suits like long johns, and one of them shouted at another one, "Agent XYX! See what you've done!"

Johnny was so stunned he fell backward, only one of the—what, spacemen? *Spacemen?*—caught him and kept him upright.

"Superior Agent QQ2, I apologize, deeply," said one of the spacemen. Had to be Agent XYX. He looked at Johnny and then pressed a button on a big bulbous metal bracelet on his wrist. The button glowed with an eerie blue light that bathed the spaceman. Then his appearance transformed into the egghead Johnny had seen squatting in the bushes.

"Greetings, Earthman Johnny," Flat-top said. "Please don't be alarmed. You are safe here." He cleared his throat. "Safer than any of those poor other Earthlings above us."

"What? What are you talking about? What the heck is going on?" Johnny whirled in a circle. "You're Russians, right? Stay back, you damn Commies!"

Flat-top shook his head. "We come from the planet Altara-Z. We landed here many of your Earth years ago, when your civilization began experimenting with dangerous weapons."

"What? *What? Under my house?*" Johnny doubled up his fists and started swinging at the spacemen. At the aliens. The aliens from another world. They winked in and out of existence, as if to dodge Johnny's blows. Exhausted, he stopped and stood surrounded, panting.

"Six months ago, your 'eggheads' had a breakthrough, and we determined that we must act to stop your people from destroying this planet. We built this lonely outpost to monitor your progress and report back to our leaders on Altara-Z."

What the actual heck? Johnny's heart was jumping. His all-American blood sizzled in his veins. Dots danced before his eyes. Then everything went hazy.

"*Mzaabbeeht!*" cried Flat-top.

And Johnny went down for the count.

WHEN JOHNNY WOKE UP, he raised his head to discover that he was lying off to one side on a soft silvery mattress in a vast cavern filled with pipes and whirling fans. Spacemen were racing around, shouting at each other; purple steam hissed and swooshed out of pipes. The aliens jabbered wildly.

With their attention elsewhere, Johnny seized the moment. He inched his way to the edge of the mattress. Then he slowly planted his leg on the floor and half-rolled off. No one noticed. Crouching down, he snaked away from the gang, completely unsure if he was sneaking toward or away from more danger.

Stay cool, he told himself.

He kept going, weaving around more pipes and a strange object that floated in the air, spinning and hissing. He crept farther. His hands trembled; bands of terror bound his chest.

The floor rumbled again. And then as he crept forward, the slide he had originally fallen down shot up from the floor at an angle. He hurried toward it, planning to crawl up it if he had to. But the moment he touched it, he was hurtled upward as if he had been shot from a cannon.

The panel was still closed at the other end! He was going to slam right into it!

He braced for impact—

—and found himself flying into the air and landing in a heap at the feet of Flat-top Agent-in-the-Nick. Johnny tumbled and rolled. The alien-in-disguise held out a hand and when Johnny hesitated, let out an impatient grunt, wrapped his hand around Johnny's wrist, and hauled him to his feet. Johnny took a swing at him, but the guy ducked. Johnny tried again and the monster let go.

"Listen, Johnny, we don't have much time," Flat-top said. "As we feared, your people have exploded their weapon. Your atmosphere will soon grow too toxic for us. We are departing."

"Okay, so, that's good, right? For us? That you're beating feet?"

"I can offer you sanctuary, but you must come back inside our vessel *now*."

He reached for Johnny's arm, but Johnny turned and—

His house—

It had grown, it had to be at least sixty feet high. It reached into the cloudless sky like something from Jack and the Beanstalk. His knees buckled and Flat-top grabbed at him as if to drag him back to the panel.

The porch door swung open with a mighty *crash* and there stood his own mother, now massive, terrifying, at least fifty feet tall! She scanned the horizon.

"*Johnny!*" she shouted, and the force of her voice knocked him flat on his back.

"Oh, my gosh, oh, gosh," Johnny blubbered. "Ma! Ma, down here!" He waved his arms.

She froze and cocked her head. Then she bent over and stared down at him. The pores in her skin were like craters; her eyes were as big as the high school gymnasium.

"Johnny? Oh, honey, oh! What's happened to you?"

His eardrums pounded. She reached out a hand as big as a car, about to pluck him up. About to squash him. Johnny scrabbled away from her enormous fingers. In a frenzy of horror, he got to his feet and began to run.

"Johnny!" Flat-top cried.

"Johnny!" Ma shouted.

He clapped his hands over his agonized ears and ran blindly. Around tumbleweeds, through tumbleweeds, over tumbleweeds. Kicking up sand. Lots of sand. Sand, sand, sand.

Losing his human appearance, the spaceman caught up to him, jogging alongside. Flat-top was panting hard.

"Earthman," he said between gasps. "I must return to the mothership. We offer you a home—"

"*He is mine!*" a familiar but very, very, very loud voice reverberated across the landscape.

Johnny froze. Stared. Stared hard . . .

. . . and could not fathom what he was seeing.

Two titans were locked in battle—smacking, slapping, and batting at one another. It was Amalia and Peggy Sue, their shrieks echoing across what he realized had once been the town's baseball field. Dozens of giants—Johnny recognized his fellow Sonrisans—were yelling, trying to break up the fight, panicking, running. The ground shook. Their faces were so *huge*! Their eyes *blazed*.

Something caromed through the air like a flying saucer—it was a gigantic cake pan, loaded with an avalanche of chocolate.

"Mewheebit!" the alien cried. He grabbed Johnny's arm, pushed down on his bracelet, and unbelievable heat enveloped Johnny's entire body.

I'm burning up!

Then he and the spaceman were back inside what had to be a flying saucer, a real honest-to-god spaceship, and he was surrounded by spacemen and, outside, his girlfriends were as big as dinosaurs. The cabin he stood in was vibrating like a huge purring cat.

Spacemen were strapping into seats and putting on cylindrical helmets. Johnny's rescuer threw him into an empty chair, lashed him in, and slammed a helmet over his head. The aliens jabbered at Flat-top and he jabbered back.

What the heck, what the holy heck?

Whoosh whoosh whoosh, they blasted upward. Window panels flashed open as they somersaulted into the heavens. Then they whirled past the tubs of apples, as big as lakes, and the dunk tank, now the size of an oil rig.

And then Amalia caught sight of the saucer. Her eyes glinted through the windows, then narrowed. She stared straight at Johnny, who was strapped into his seat. He flailed, trying to free himself. The spacemen were going wild, jabbering and shouting at each other.

"*He is in there!*" the spitfire bellowed. The saucer dipped and wobbled. Amalia raised a hand to grab it. Johnny struggled. Her hand came closer. Flat-top began yelling louder.

"Let me loose, Agent Guy!" Johnny shouted.

Then suddenly the saucer zipped backward out of Amalia's reach. Johnny heaved a sigh. But in the next moment, something massive crashed into the spaceship and sent it tumbling end over end over end. The view in the window blurred in a crazy-quilt. Then Johnny watched in horror as an enormous baseball mitt filled the panels. It was going to catch the spaceship!

But just in time, the craft zipped sideways, out of reach. A massive roar shook the walls. Spacemen who were not strapped down went flying.

Flat-top leaned over Johnny, a hundred percent pure green-blooded (probably) alien creature, and declared, "We have to stop them!"

"Let me up," Johnny insisted. "Take me to your leader."

"That would be Ultra Supreme Leader XQC," Flat-top replied.

In short order, the spaceman unstrapped Johnny, took off his helmet, and hurried him past the windows. The ship was flying backward, out of range of Peggy Sue, who had hunkered into position with a Louisville Slugger over her shoulder and an expression of pure venom on her face. The girls were playing ball with the saucer!

Flat-top had Johnny by the arm and was hustling him toward a space creature sitting in a large padded chair. The alien jabbered at Flat-top, and Flat-top jabbered back.

"Ultra Supreme Leader XQC says that we do not wish to jettison you," Flat-top said, "but we must break the atmosphere soon or we will not have sufficient fuel to make it back to Altara-Z."

"How did this happen?" Johnny demanded. "Was it something we did? The weapons test?"

Jabber-jabber-jabber.

"That is a topic for another time," Flat-top said. "We are in a life-or-death crisis. Your girlfriends seek revenge on you."

"We gotta stop 'em," Johnny concurred. He thought a moment and then he snapped his fingers. "The power plant. They'll be zapped." Guilt and sorrow panged through him. This was all his fault. This was happening because he was so irresistible to girls. "See, electricity will kill them. It kills humans, even giants!" He wondered for the flash of an instant if it killed space aliens. He was dazzled by stupefaction.

Flat-top and his leader spoke in Alienese back and forth, back and forth, in bursts, and then Flat-top said, "We have decided on a plan. You stand in view so that your girlfriends can see you. We will lure them to the power plant. They will then be . . . zapped."

"Yeah, that could work." He pulled out his comb. "I gotta look as good as possible to make sure they follow us. Do you have a mirror?"

PEGGY SUE GOT ELECTROCUTED.

Once she hit the transformers she danced and shuddered and when she fell over, the saucer bounced on the shock waves. Amalia saw what was going on. She could have saved herself, she could have, but she stared up into the window of the saucer, where Johnny stood, tears gushing down her cheeks. Geysers of tears. A flash-flood. He reached out a hand and murmured, "Oh, baby. Baby, I'm sorry."

And then *she* reached out a hand and gripped one of the transformers. *Zzz-zzzl-zzz!* And the mystery train of sweet backseat love stopped dead in her tracks.

Free from threats, the saucer soared into the stratosphere.

JOHNNY SIPPED WHAT TASTED LIKE pineapple juice in a shimmering glass as Flat-top said gently, "Don't blame yourself." Around them, the aliens were repairing the ship. Outside the window, there was a black sky and zillions of stars.

"I got questions," Johnny said. "Lots of them. So how did everybody get bigger except me? What weapon was *that*?"

Flat-top cleared his throat. "The timing was a bit . . . off. There were errors. But you were secured."

"I was *what*?"

"Rescued. Drink your nutrient beverage," Flat-top urged. Johnny took a sip. Then, almost to himself, Flat-top said, "I panicked. I almost ruined everything. Your courage . . . it was everything." The alien smiled at Johnny. "Of course."

Johnny raised a brow. Flat-top blinked and raised his chin as if listening to words that Johnny could not hear. Then he took the shimmering glass from Johnny and held it between his own hands. "Ultra Supreme Leader QXC has ordered me to reveal everything to you."

Johnny wasn't sure he liked the sound of that, but he stayed loose. Flat-top set down the pineapple-nutrient-thing and took a deep breath.

"Your people were not turned into giants. They are the same size they've always been."

Johnny reeled. He blinked. "Then that means that, what? That we *shrank*?"

"Yes. We of Altara-Z are able to manipulate matter in that way."

"But why? Why did you do that to me?"

Agent Traitor hung his head. "Because we needed to find a way to make you less irresistible to your females. We overshot. We apologize."

"You made me little?" Johnny stared at Flat-top. "You made me little so Amalia and Peggy Sue—"

"—and all the other human girls, yes." Flat-top nodded.

"*Why?*"

"So that you would come with us willingly. The mission was bungled—"

"But *why*?"

Flat-top began to pace. "Because I was nervous. I couldn't think straight." The spaceman turned away, turned back. Then he raised his hand and pressed the buttons on the metallic bracelet on his wrist. Gone was Flat-top, gone was the green spaceman, and in his place, there was a *her*—a va-va-va-voom girl. Curvy like Amalia and blonde like Peggy Sue. With freckles like his first kiss, Gina Sanatello, and lips like Doreen McKenney, his first trip to second base.

"*Flat-top?*" Johnny cried.

"You see me in my true form," Flat-top said softly. "We have maintained disguises until we were given the all-clear signal by the homeworld. We Altara-Zians are a race of females. Females devoted to *you*."

The gorgeous babe lifted up her chin and closed her eyes. All around her, the spacemen stopped what they were doing and gazed at Johnny. Then in a split-second, they transformed into beautiful, beautiful girls of all shapes, shades, and sizes.

"While monitoring your world, we found you," Flat-top said in a come-hither voice. "We formed a daring plan. And now, here you are."

"Wow," Johnny said huskily.

A tall redhead approached. "We had to move up our timetable. Not only because of the weapons test, but because Amalia and Peggy Sue posed real danger. We didn't know what would happen once they realized that they were rivals."

"Yeah, about that," he began. But what could he say? His two best girls had been fried to a crisp because of him.

"It wasn't your fault," Flat-top interjected. "Your civilization has not yet learned to share, as we of Altara-Z have learned to do." Beside her, the redheaded nodded. "And you are, after all, completely irresistible to women."

Johnny looked around the room at the spacemen—correction, space*women*. At all of them—dozens of them. Also nodding.

"Yeah," he said, "I am."

He pulled out his comb. The spacegirls sucked in a collective breath. In the gleam from Flat-top's bracelet—whoa, he had to change that nickname *for sure*—he pumped up his pompadour. As one, all they all sighed.

One o'clock, two o'clock, three o'clock rock . . .

"Well, there's plenty of me to go around."

"Yes, oh, yes," the spacegirls said in one happy voice.

In a blaze of glory, the spaceship shot toward home on a bruise-free cruise starring dreamboat Johnny Morris, red-blooded American teenager in love.

NANCY HOLDER is the New York Times bestselling author (the *Wicked* series, with Debbie Viguié) of over 80 novels and 200 short stories. She has received five Bram Stoker awards, a Scribe award, and a Young Adult Fiction Pioneer Award. She is the former vice president of the Horror Writers Association and currently sits on the HWA board of trustees. A recent work was the novelization of Crimson Peak, the classic gothic film by Guillermo del Toro. Her current ongoing project is the comic book series "Mary Shelley Presents" for Kymera Press, adapting the work of women writers of the supernatural from all over the world. She presents lectures and presentations on Mary Shelley whenever possible. She is on Facebook and Twitter @nancyholder. She lives in Washington state and travels to Italy whenever possible.

"TAKE MY CAR. THE REELS ARE ALREADY IN the trunk. Bring the new girl—she'll help. Get going now. We ain't got much time."

This is what my boss, Robert "Bobby" Fordyce told me the moment I stepped onto the lot this morning. I hadn't slept much last night. None of us had, I'm sure. I didn't know what I'd expected, but it sure wasn't this.

"Get going where?"

"Jesus, Tommy. What we talked about."

"I thought you were joking."

UNIVERSAL MONSTER

BY DUANE SWIERCZYNSKI

When you're desperate, you turn to desperate people. People like Marvel Whitehead.

"No, I was not joking. I just got off the phone with my guy in Defense. We're all set. All you have to do is drive. Get it out there, get it underground. Not too deep." He gestured to the new girl. "She'll give you a hand."

The new girl blinked. I didn't know her name. I'm not sure Fordyce did, either. She was deathly pale and wearing white. Bad combination, honey.

I extended a hand. "Tom Parks."

She stared at my hand, unsure of what this was all about. Steaming mug of coffee in one hand, steno pad in the other, as if she were an extra who had been suddenly nudged into a speaking role. And already she'd forgotten her line.

"Explain it to her on the way," Fordyce said. "I'm late for a production meeting. C'mon, get going already."

"Okay. Follow me, new girl." She'd get around to telling me her name eventually.

Fordyce's car was parked in his usual spot. It was a '58 Lincoln Continental convertible, Mark III, just a few weeks old. A gorgeous bombastic machine. Ordinarily, I'd be thrilled to sit behind the wheel for a while. But now my stomach was already churning; this always happens when I don't sleep. I was glad he'd had some lackey shove the reels into the trunk—I didn't want to touch them.

New girl stood by the car door, staring at it, mug of coffee still in her hand. The poor dear. I took the mug from her hand, whip-dumped the java into the nearest bush, then placed the mug on the curb. Somebody would return it to Fordyce's office. He counted the fucking things, I swear.

I opened the big slab of a door, guided new girl into the plush mint green seat, then walked around and took my place behind the wheel. I'll admit it; I was a little intimidated. I'd spent the last five years knocking around Burbank in a second-hand Nash. This was like being in charge of a Navy destroyer.

On the way out of the lot I waved hello to Benny, head of security. I used to have his job. And someday, he would have mine. This is how it worked in Hollywood.

I hung a right and drove up Lankershim, which was a diagonal slash mark across the floor of the valley. After a while I stole a glance at my companion for the day. The new girl had a large head resting atop a tiny body. Pretty, of course; Fordyce doesn't go for any other kind. But not exactly my type.

"Bobby tell you what this is all about?" I asked, mostly to get a conversation going. If I was going to spend most of the day with this girl, I'd like to know what I was up against.

She held my gaze for the longest time before shaking her head.

"You don't know what's in the trunk?"

There was another awkward, long pause before she twitched her oversized head, indicating no.

"Well, honey, you're in for one hell of a story."

IN THE TRUNK of the Lincoln were five reels of a new movie. My job was to take these reels deep into the Nevada Test Site—Fordyce apparently called in a favor with an old war buddy—and bury them. There was an A-bomb test scheduled for this coming weekend. The moment the count reached zero the reels would be blasted from the face of the Earth forever.

I'd certainly rest easier when that happened. Fordyce, too. We all would.

But I didn't start there. What kind of storyteller would I be if I skipped right to the end?

"You know Marvel Whitehead, the director?"

The word "director" seemed to spark her interest. But again, she gave me a little head shake. No.

"Marvel Whitehead is a nut case. Don't let anyone tell you otherwise. Not that he's ever going to work in this town again—Bobby will see to that. But if he ever approaches you, wanting to lure you into one of his celluloid abominations, you run the other way. You got me?"

If she did, she gave no indication. She just stared at me.

"Anyway, Bobby hired him because he needed another monster picture. He always needs monsters. The studio hasn't had a bona fide hit since the green guy with the gills. When you're desperate, you turn to desperate people. People like Marvel Whitehead. Goddamn weirdo."

We were headed up into the mountains by this point, on our way to the desert. I wondered if I should put the top up. It was already oven-hot.

"I was in the office when Bobby brought him in to pitch. He tried a bunch of bullshit on us. Rampaging insects made of human body parts. A country full of witches. Ghosts who weren't really dead, and so on. Nothing clicked with Bobby. And then Marvel pulled the old, 'Well, I do have one more thing, but I don't know if it would interest you, people have never seen anything like it, I don't know if audiences could stand it, blah blah blah.' We both realized all that other bullshit had been a set-up for this big idea he obviously wanted to pitch. So Bobby says, 'Come on, let's hear it, already.'"

I side-eyed new girl to see if the warm air had made her drift off to sleep. But no. She was paying close attention to me, hanging on my every word.

"Marvel had an idea for a new kind of monster. One that people in the audience can't escape, he says. That's because it actually comes to life and crawls off the screen, he says.

"Bobby says, 'So you're saying this is some 3-D thing? C'mon, Marvel, that shit ain't been new since *Bwana Devil.*'

"Marvel goes, 'No, I'm not talking about 3-D. I'm talking about an entirely new film process that brings screen images to actual, pulsating, tangible life.'"

I struggled to remember the exact phrase he used. You'd think it'd be burned into my memory by this point, but scientific mumbo-jumbo wasn't my thing. I searched the big blue sky as if the words might be floating around up there. "Silver . . . crystals or something."

New girl sat up in her seat. "Silver halide crystals," she said. "Suspended in gelatin on a film base. This is how images are recorded on film."

Cut to me: *gobsmacked.* "How did you know that?"

She smiled, which is the first one I've seen sneak onto her face. It was utterly disarming. Suddenly I wasn't thinking about her big head or her waifish body. I was halfway to falling in love.

"Why, I'm a chemist," she said. "Specifically, an expert in the photochemical process."

"Then what the hell are you doing working as a D-girl for Bobby Fordyce?"

To that, she had no response. She looked at me blankly for a minute, then returned her gaze to the horizon.

WE WERE OUT in the blazing wasteland of the Antelope Valley by this point. Sweat ran down my neck and past my collar and into my undershirt. Meanwhile new girl looked as if she had just stepped out of an icebox.

I thought maybe we could stop at a diner out in Pearblossom, grab a sandwich and a soda pop before hitting the road for the long haul out to the test site. But when I asked new girl if she was hungry, she acted as if she didn't even hear me.

Maybe she was right. Better to drive these infernal reels out to the desert and bury them as quick as possible. The sooner I was done with this little errand, the sooner I'd be back in my stuffy apartment in North Hollywood, drinking rail bourbon and fooling myself into thinking I was just doing this crap until somebody bought my heist picture.

"So anyway," I continued, "Marvel says he has this test reel he wants to show us. And he happens to have it on him. Of course. Bobby books a screening room on the lot, and we head off to watch it.

"And you know what? The damned thing *was* impressive."

I didn't get into it with new girl, but if I'm being perfectly honest: it was the most startling thing I've ever seen in my thirty-four years on this planet.

THE LIGHTS GO OUT. The projector clacks and settles into a steady hum. The screen glows. And then . . . picture.

We're looking at a yard—somewhere out in the Valley. There are orange groves nearby. We don't see them on screen. But my nostrils fill with the stench of citrus.

There's a blonde standing in front of the yard. She's holding a gardening pail, drizzling her sad little flower bed. She's wearing nothing but an Oxford tied up in front and a pair of short-shorts terminating about mid-thigh.

I think this is going to be a crude little strip tease act for Bobby. Plenty of directors have tried it before, skipping the pitch and plot and going right to casting.

But I'm wrong.

The cute blonde gardener notices us. Places her pail down on the neatly-trimmed grass. Walks toward the camera. She's cat-like and knows some moves. Nothing we haven't seen before.

What we haven't seen before happens next. I'm trying to describe it now, and still having trouble wrapping my head around it.

The blonde gardener is almost at the camera, which is the point when you'd expect her shape to overwhelm the lens and the image to blur.

But she never blurs. She continues walking straight toward us.

There's the screen. And there's the screening room. The screen is part of the screening room, but they're still two separate things, right?

Not anymore. I can't tell where one stops and the other begins—because it's all the same.

Fordyce stands up in his seat, mouth hanging open. I follow his lead. Marvel chuckles softly to himself. The blonde steps closer, and closer.

"What's the gag here, Marvel?" Fordyce asks. "How are you doing this?"

And closer . . .

"You snuck the actress in here," I say, then turn toward Fordyce. "He snuck the actress in here and did some editing trick. Like an optical illusion."

And closer . . .

"This is no illusion, my friends," Marvel says. "Film is emulsion. And emulsion is life."

The blonde is standing right in front of Fordyce now, reaching up to touch his face. He flinches. She laughs. He relaxes. Her fingertips graze his cheek. Fordyce closes his eyes; he shudders in delight. I've never been more jealous of anything in life.

The reel ends; a harsh white light blinds us.

A blink later, the blonde is gone.

"YOU LIKE THE GIRL, eh, Bobby? How about I make you monster, same."

That was Marvel's entire pitch. Brilliant, right?

I make you monster, same.

Fordyce hired him right on the spot, gave him four weeks to shoot. He tapped me to oversee production, make sure things didn't get out of hand. But really, my mission was to spy on Marvel's secret process. This thing was poised to become the next big thing in motion picture history, and Fordyce wanted to make sure he had iron-clad control over it.

But Marvel kept me away from the set at all times, despite my best efforts. Fordyce gave me endless shit about this. I was supposed to be his security guy/fixer—yet I couldn't force my way onto a goddamned soundstage on our own lot?

That was exactly right. I couldn't force my way onto a goddamned soundstage on our own lot.

For one thing, the red "filming" light was always on. Always. That was the first lesson I'd learned at the studio. If you were to dare open a door when that red light was on, then you should fully expect to be forcibly ejected from the lot—first, your decapitated head, followed by the rest of your body.

But then I got wise to that trick. There was no possible way Marvel was burning through celluloid non-stop.

One day I tried to get in at 4 a.m. The door was open, but within seconds two swarthy men in out-of-date suits with fezzes on their slicked-back heads intercepted me. They hooked my arms and carried me back outside. Their skin was oily. Their bodies gave off a dank, musky odor. They didn't speak English; they spoke *Grunt*. Where Marvel found these guys, I have no idea. But they were there when I tried to breach the soundstage three more times over the next two days. I reported all of this to Fordyce.

"Tommy," he pleaded. "At *least* get me a good look at the monster. We gotta get guys working on the poster!"

"I can't even get into the soundstage."

Fordyce paced. "And who the hell has Marvel put in this thing? Is he paying them out of his own pocket? Because casting tells me they're in the dark."

It was a good point. I didn't have an answer for that one, either. But I did have a solution in mind.

"Here's what we do," I said. "Let me gather some of my old pals from security. We kick in some doors, we storm the place, and we shut down the film until Marvel does some explaining."

The notion truly appealed to Fordyce. I could tell by the cruel little gleam in his eye. But then he listened to the accountant on his right shoulder. He grimaced like he had a hot tooth.

"Ugh," Fordyce said, wearily. "I can't afford to shut him down now. We're opening in Texas in three weeks."

WE WERE CROSSING OVER into Nevada now. I was sitting in a pool of my own bodily fluids, while new girl was still alpine fresh. Someday she'd have to tell me her secret.

"Finally, after all of this hassle, he turns in this thing he called *Summus*. Nobody knew what the hell it meant. Fordyce said screw that—we're calling it *The Crawling Shadow*."

"Summus," new girl says. "A Latin word meaning the greatest, the most exalted."

"Just like Marvel's ego." Again, though, I'm surprised. New girl chimes in at the damndest moments. Where did Fordyce find her?

Right about then I heard this horrible wrenching sound of twisted steel. I checked the rear view. The trunk lid was popped up and hanging by a couple of crooked hinges.

"What the hell?"

"Nitrate film stock is combustible," new girl says. "It's been cooking in the trunk for hours!"

"What are you talking about? I'm pulling over . . . "

"No, keep driving!"

Something grabbed my left wrist from behind and squeezed hard. I looked down and—okay, I'll admit it, I lost my mind a little. Because I didn't know what I was looking at: part squid tentacle, if squid tentacles had tiny razor-sharp bones and spikes running up and down them. Its color was nothing out of our world. The slimiest gray you can imagine, outlined by the deepest blacks and shimmering with these tiny white sparks that hurt your eyes.

Whatever it was lifted my hand high off the wheel. Except for the blood trickling down my arm from my wrist, I probably looked like I was raising my hand to answer a teacher's question in class.

Oh—and I screamed my face off.

New girl told me, "Try to stay calm!"

I wanted to tell the new girl where she could stick her calm, but then the thing grabbed hold of my right wrist too and yanked it off the wheel. I had both hands in the air like this was a stick-up. New girl was digging in her purse for something. What, was she going to reapply a coat of lipstick before we crashed?

And then the damned thing lifted me out of the driver's seat.

By some miracle I hooked my right shoe under the bottom of the steering wheel, so I was able to keep the Lincoln on the road and me from flinging up into the air. With my foot off the accelerator, however, the car was slowing down. Which was a good thing, since I didn't want to be ripped apart by some tentacle monster at high speed.

Tentacle monster—that's when it came back to me. I'd seen these things before.

Just last night.

Sort of.

MARVEL WHITEHEAD INSISTED on a preview audience first—even before Fordyce was allowed to screen it.

Fordyce cried horseshit—this was still *his* picture, this was still *his* studio, and so on. Marvel was able to work his mystical voodoo on him, though, telling Fordyce he wanted him to hear the delighted screams of the audience before seeing a single frame of the film himself. I could tell this secretly appealed to Fordyce. He *hated* horror movies, so to be able to skip out of actually having to watch one of the damned things?

"This is a bad idea, Bobby," I told him. "Don't you want to see this thing before we unleash it on John and Mary Q. Public?"

"Let him have his preview," Fordyce replied. "Get me a bunch of rubes from out in the Valley. Fill the seats with flotsam. Nobody under 18. Nobody who knows anybody, you got me?"

I got him. But I also went to my old buddies in lot security and told them to be ready.

Cut to preview night, and Fordyce was nervous-pacing outside the screening room. It was a crowded house; everybody loves a horror picture. Our usual projectionist, Terry, was bent out of shape because

Marvel insisted on using his own guy—one of those Fedora-wearing tough guys. Fordyce calmed Terry down with a belt or two from his flask, told him he'd make it up to him.

And then—about twenty minutes in—the screaming started.

Not delighted screams from a well-planned jump scare. These were *help me, I'm going to die kind of screams.*

Fordyce looked like he was about to vomit. He knew the mistake he'd made right away. I told him not to worry, and got my security buddies in there. I told them to come loaded for bear, and they did, kicking down the doors and taking out anybody in a Fez. I made a beeline for the projection room and almost dislocated my shoulder breaking down the door. The projectionist pulled a roscoe on me. I slapped it out of his hand then punched him in the face until my knuckles throbbed.

The room was full of a loud whirring sound. The machine didn't sound right, and I knew I had to turn it off. I didn't know how film projectors worked, so I went looking for a plug. But I happened to steal a glance through the port, and I wish I hadn't. Because all I saw, under the flickering lights, were scenes out of a butcher's worst nightmare. I couldn't tell the quivering body parts from the quivering people hiding *under* the body parts. The blood all over them glowed.

On the lower left hand corner of the screen, a slimy little rope pulled itself up into the screen and disappeared, leaving a glowing slug trail behind.

The next day, I would realize what it was: a tentacle.

ANOTHER TENTACLE SQUIRMED its way along the body of the Lincoln and down into the floor of the car. I thought it was going for new girl, because that's what monsters do. But then we started to accelerate, and I realized what had happened. *It found the goddamned gas pedal.*

I turned my right foot this way and that, still trying to stay on the road. The little bones and spikes dug deep into my wrists, so there was no way I could pull my hands loose. What was this thing trying to do?

I turned my head around and saw that another tentacle was headed straight for my kisser. Yeah, I screamed again. (Wouldn't you?) My wailing, though, was cut short by the sharp pangs of metal through metal—in this case, bullets through the trunk lid.

Something in the trunk yelled—and I say *something*, because that sound couldn't have possibly come out of a human being.

The thing released my wrists. I dropped back into the seat next to new girl, who was holding a small silver pistol that almost looked like a prop.

"Take the wheel!" she said, then fired four more times into the trunk. I wanted to cover my ears so I didn't have to listen to that unholy caterwauling, but I had to keep steering, even as the blood gushed down my arms. Something slid by my left leg. The third tentacle, retracting.

She kept firing and I kept driving but soon I realized something was wrong. (Well, aside from the obvious.) Her cute little pistol wouldn't have been able to fire all of those shots. It had to be a prop gun . . .

Prop or not, it was hurting the thing in the trunk.

The third tentacle lifted itself up until it was eye-level with me. The damned thing twitched, and then whipped toward my face. I ducked just in time.

New girl didn't.

FORDYCE RAN UP TO THE BOOTH a second later and went right for the projector. Rumor was, his first job in the industry was running the reels in some backwater down South. True or not, he knew what he was doing. The awful whirring of the machine died.

My job is to fix situations like these. Well, nobody in my position has *ever* had to fix something as awful as this. But I was ready to do whatever it took.

"We go with a mad killer story," I told him. "He snuck onto the lot. I don't know how many dead we got down there, but I'm sure the survivors can be bought off. Maybe throw in a studio tour or something, too . . ."

But Fordyce wasn't really listening to me. He was busy gathering up the reels of his movie, the one he'd greenlit, the one he'd paid for, the one he'd have to deal with.

"Bobby?" I said. "You listening to me?"

"We're going to have to nuke this fucking thing."

I KEPT DRIVING, too afraid to stop.

As long as I kept driving, I told myself, that thing wouldn't come out of the trunk again and try to tear me apart like a French baguette. After all, it had only attacked when I said we were pulling over.

New girl was unconscious in the passenger seat. The tentacle had clocked her in the head pretty good, but I didn't see any bruising or blood. This didn't surprise me. You couldn't bleed if you weren't real.

She had come out of Marvel's movie, too, just like the monster in the trunk.

Part of me wished she'd wake up so I could ask her a few questions, but the other part knew it was better if she stayed asleep. This had been Fordyce's plan all along. Take the reels of film and the new girl to the test site and ... *blammo*. He didn't tell me because he thought I wouldn't believe him.

And you know what? He was probably right.

The sun fried the top of my head, and I was covered in blood and hyperventilating every couple of minutes, but otherwise it was a pleasant ride. I reached the security gate at the test site. They let me through, despite the unconscious girl next to me and the popped-up trunk lid riddled with bullet holes. They even gave me a handy paper map, showing me the route to take to the burial place. Guess Fordyce had called in a lulu of a favor.

Predictably, the X on the map was a fake town that looked like a movie set. I pulled up in front of a "general store" and took a long breath. I wanted to stay in that moment forever.

But a job was a job, and my job was to bury those reels.

I slowly made my way around to the trunk, expecting the worst. But all I saw were those five metal cans, looking all innocent. *What did we do, Tommy?*

I dropped to my hands and knees and started digging with my fingers. My wrists felt like they had razor blades inside them. Fortunately, the reels didn't have go six feet under, just covered up.

"What is this place?"

I looked up to see new girl, hugging herself as if cold, stumbling away from the Lincoln. Oh great. Now I was going to have to kill and bury a fictional character, too. The things I do for the studio.

"Nuclear test site," I told her. "Tomorrow morning, whatever's here won't be."

Her eyes widened in horror. "You're burying the film here!?"

"Yeah. Unless you know of a better nuclear test site nearby."

"You can't! You'll destroy the world!"

"No, just this abomination of a movie," I said. "No offense. I'm sure you were great in it."

"You don't understand, you simpleton!" she cried. "I told you, I'm a chemist. Specifically, an expert in the photochemical process."

"And?"

"The creature is made of silver halide crystals. When exposed to heat and light, it manifests itself in our reality."

"So?"

"You idiot—what greater source of heat and light is there in the world than a nuclear explosion?"

Okay, new girl had a point there. I thought she was incapable of speaking lines that hadn't been in Marvel's script, but apparently she was slowly adjusting to our world, improvising. Good for her. Unfortunately, I'm also fairly confident that Marvel's monster was telepathic. Because the moment I realized I was making the biggest mistake in all of human history, tentacles started popping up out of the film cans, immobilizing me and new girl, too. *It wanted this to happen.* And maybe Fordyce did, too. Maybe Marvel had gotten to him, told him it would be the biggest opening ever. And who could resist something like that?

Fade to credits

DUANE SWIERCZYNSKI is the Edgar-nominated author of ten *novels including* Revolver, Canary, *and the Shamus Award-winning Charlie Hardie series, many of which are in development for film/TV. Duane has also written over 250 comics for Marvel, DC, Dark Horse, Valiant, IDW, and Archie, and collaborated with James Patterson on* The House Husband, The Shut-In, *and* Stingrays, *as well as CSI creator Anthony E. Zuiker on the bestselling* Level 26 *series. Earlier in his career, Duane worked as an editor and writer for* Details, Men's Health, *and* Philadelphia *magazines, and was the editor-in-chief of the* Philadelphia City Paper. *He now lives in Los Angeles with his wife and children.*

VIOLET CUPP WAS THE FLAG GIRL. THAT always brought the hound dogs out.

Before Violet, the most important draw was the rods. Fully two-thirds were not even street legal, but you could see the sheer love in every turn of polished chrome, every carefully-Bondo'ed curve of bodywork (Bondo was newly popular with enthusiasts, having been invented the previous year by a World War II veteran to replace automotive filler putty, which was loaded with toxic lead—the source of the growingly unfashionable term "lead sled"). Each spark plug—the visible ones—looked brand new, without a hint of grit. All pipes,

DRAGGERS

BY DAVID J. SCHOW

*It was track law among Faults, like a
commandment: You die, you lose.*

shined to mirror brilliance and then buffed again. And again. The sensuous tuck and roll; each Brodie knob as ostentatious as a vulgar engagement diamond. The rubber met the road in contact patches the width of a dictionary; huge rear tires were commonly called "balonies," for reasons obvious to everybody except squares.

After the blown gassers, your notice went next to the drivers, but the people everyone was really waiting to see were the "faults," from "asphalt surfers." But those mysterious individuals stayed out of sight and kept to themselves until rally time—anticipation was the name of their game. Until then, there was alcohol (whatever wasn't being used by specialty cars), sex (hookups for later), dick-measuring (all varieties)... and rumor. The very air seemed flammable and demanding, tuning up onlookers like Benzedrine.

Hearsay had it that a Fault named Rodrigo was coming back for his first local competition in several months. His anonymity was god-like; barely anyone knew anything about him beyond whispers.

Violet Cupp had legs up to *there*, an ass beyond *here*, tits out to *there*, eyes of straight razor blue, and about three feet of raven hair down to, yup, the very same *here* as her butt. She had vigorously fornicated with many of the drivers—she loved guys with hot cars— with the exception of a newcomer to the heats named Breezer something-or-other. She wanted to pick him out of the throng and proposition him sometime between midnight tonight and dawn tomorrow, executing her patented cat-stretch designed to thrust her ample bosom forward so she could deliver her favorite line: "Will *these* change your mind?"

Violet used what she had. Most of the mob losers took one gawp at Violet and concluded she was brainless, which was not true. She was a prize, a piece, rowdy as hell and ready to party... and four years from now, she would lock down a Masters in engineering and applied science, at a time when less than six percent of women in the United States possessed a college degree; when female students seemed doomed to post-grad trade-work as stenographers, nurses, dental assistants, social workers, or legal secretaries. Liberal Arts were the focus of the onrushing future. Violet recognized this and saw the coming wave. She was practical, goal-oriented, and logical. She saw little logic in denying herself a good time. In fact, she used men the way most men used most women, these days. She remained hopeful that the species might eventually evolve a bit more. Just a bit.

Presently held spellbound in her thrall was a road jockey named DeCampo, a hard-on with a blond flattop who had taken to the fashion of wearing his belt buckle off to one side in the belief that it lent a slimming effect. He was another one of those brand loyalty rodders, a guy who believed that you should only have an Olds engine in an Olds body, for example.

"Did you ever notice that when cops harass you, they always tell you what you want to do?" Violet said. "*What you wanna do* is step out of that car. *What you wanna do* is dig out some ID I can believe . . . "

DeCampo caught on, still staring at her chest. "What you wanna do is raise your hands over your head and lace your fingers." Distantly, somebody else's radio played "Hound Dog."

"Elvis got in trouble," said DeCampo. "For singing that very song, and wiggling around on that Milton Berle show a couple of weeks ago." He fired up a Chesterfield, cupping his hand around the flame from a book of matches. On a windy day like this one, out here far from the world of nowhere-daddys in general, he liked to make a game of lighting so skillfully that he only wasted one paper match per smoke. No second chances.

"It's harmless," said Violet. "The wiggling. The gyrations. The contortions."

"They're calling him the nation's only atomic-powered singer." He snorted as though he did not believe it, or simply hated any competition.

"Doctors have already said the music isn't harmful." She looked wistful as she watched DeCampo's smoke dissipate on the breeze. "Better to pay attention to a gummy blower. *That* will mess you up, in real life." She didn't need to say that she would rather eat the gluey deposits off said carburetor than ever consider disrobing in the same time-zone as DeCampo, who was just too nakedly hungry.

Bakehurst Field was a defunct private airstrip exactly one-and-a-half miles outside the technical city limit. The mid-sized municipal field had shut down in 1951 when the owner/manager, Big Ben "Airdog" Moran, had succumbed to a sledgehammer heart attack at age thirty-six, having survived being shot down in a bomber by the Nazis, a bullet hole in his left lung, a hardpan parachute landing in hostile territory, and over a year spent in a German prison camp. The runway and taxiway remained unpaved until 1947, when they gained bituminous asphalt tarmac and landing chevrons (for such things as touch-down zones and fixed distance marks). There was a ramp and a little half-assed crosswind runway (never completed), and two out of three hangars (one had caved in due to a hurricane two summers back); the office and air traffic control bungalow had been annexed by transients and assorted small, gnawing critters until the Draggers claimed the space a few months after the hurricane. Prior to that, their events had been held at what was once a rodeo stadium, where there had been no paving at all on the track inside the dilapidated grandstands. Having actual pavement still seemed luxurious.

The Bakehurst main runway was dead flat with nearly zero gradient. It ran 35 feet wide and 2,500 feet from threshold to threshold—a smidge less than half a mile—mostly because old man Moran had built it right up to the edge of his property line. Weather and stress had taken their toll on the surface, which was now weed-ridden and disrupted by cracks that resembled deep cuts with elevated flaps. Past the far end was a flattened dirt strip that extended about another hundred feet, which was "level" only insofar as it could be compacted by cars skidding to a halt and turning around on it. It was strewn with clods, rocks, gravel, and dig-outs like horizontal dirt graffiti.

This was important, because a race rarely if ever stopped at the terminus of the landing strip. And nobody ever swept up the runway.

Semi-permanent residence of the defrocked office building had been assumed by a rodental dropout named Lonnie Lacks, who sort of camped out there without running water or electricity, awaiting the bidding of the Draggers, who tolerated and occasionally fed him. Lonnie most often wore Army surplus pull-overs and sandals he had fabricated from blown Dragger tires. If you let him corner you, he'd give you an earful about how Allan Ginsberg had been railroaded into Bellevue on a trumped-up insanity plea, and how some guy named Kerouac was practically the Second Coming as far as philosophical literature was concerned. Lonnie also ran a still out of his squat, and would happily dispense his rotgut moonshine to everybody who attended the Dragger heats, at five bucks a pint—outrageous, considering a sixer of Rheingold cost $1.20.

The crowd was never that big. This wasn't your usual barely-legal dragstrip hoedown. Again—not for squares.

"That guy has green on his rod," muttered DeCampo, still trying to keep Violet's attention even though she had turned to move away. He pointed out a newcomer who was tinkering on his engine. "Bad luck, man."

"Ancient history, *man*," she shot back. "That was almost forty years ago. Fifty, if you count Lee Oldfield." The source of the persistent superstition that green was an unlucky color for racers rooted all the way back to two deadly crashes, first in 1910, then 1920, the latter occurring on a board track in California infamously known as a "Murderdome."

The litany of hot-rod superstitions ran with the weight of the best Egyptian curses: Don't race during a full moon; fuzzy dice were de rigueur ever since pilots sought their mojo during the war (the acknowledgement was that drivers knew they were "dicing with death"); eating peanuts in the pits was just pissing in the face of fate, daring something bad to happen. And at big Number One on the hit parade—no women in the pits, ever.

All reasons the Draggers flaunted their illegitimacy.

"Besides," Violet told DeCampo, "you've got green piping on your shirt, champ. Don't be so oogly-boogly."

Actually, the car they were looking at was predominantly black with spiderweb-like green pinstriping. The guy working on it was more concerned with rotating his distributor cap *just so*, to ensure better timing. Most of the rods here ran on high-octane "av-gas"—basically jet fuel—to belay engine pinging and knocking, more gruesomely referred to as "pre-detonation." It could eat rubber hoses fast if you weren't diligent; the high lead content meant you had to be extra-obsessive about making sure your carbs were firing correctly.

Others checked their tire pressure, over and over, with the surety of religious ceremony. Others siphoned gas out of their tanks, to decrease their total racing weight. The mantra was always: *You need the rubber to go and the gas to flow.*

Violet zeroed in on the new meat, the guy fussing with his rotor button.

Chuck Detweiler—"Breezer" to his tribe back in Philly—had never fully recovered from his first look at James Dean in *Rebel Without a*

Cause a mere nine months earlier, also the celebratory date of his second life-experience with oral sex, courtesy of a Williamson High School junior named Molly Patterson. This had transpired—but of course—at the Big Chief Drive-In. Molly had surfaced (just after the scene where Jim Stark asks Plato about the "chickie run"), wiped her lips with the back of her wrist, kissed Chuck deeply and fully, and summed the whole experience up as "a breeze," thus casting the die. Not a bad deal overall, for an admission price of two bits.

Molly had also encouraged Chuck to compete amongst the Draggers, back around the time of the last New Year's Eve run. Molly was . . . dark. That was the word. Her expression, her hunger played as borderline evil. Tasty, seductive badness. She chaperoned Breezer to his first Dragger event. Then Molly's family had moved out of town, her father chasing some government sinecure. Breezer would always wonder what had become of Molly.

But the drive-ins, man, those would *never* fade away, not as long as citizens drove cars. Not ever.

Instead of affecting a look he knew would be judged as Dean-manqué, Breezer limited his adornment to pegged jeans, motorcycle boots, the red windbreaker (a compromise) and Dax pomade, which could hold your hair in shape for a solid week. He also knew how to stovetop-cook the stuff up on his own, adding petrolatum and hair grease to customize the effect, the same way he calculated the most strategic fuel mixtures for the powerhouse in his very choosy, one-and-only, called the Beast with the kind of affection only Dr. Frankenstein could have felt.

Like the patchwork man of fiction and film, the Beast had begun as a '35 Ford Phaeton convertible sedan. Breezer had dropped in a 283 Chevy engine with a Duntov cam and an Edelbrock manifold with three carbs; the rest was a mélange of Ford bits: front suspension (from a '32), transmission (from a '39), brakes ('40), rear end ('40, with 4.44 gears), and steering (from a '53 Ford pickup). The profile from dropped front axle to rear deck was sultry, pure California rake. Breezer had hit an easy 130 on the flats in ordinary competition.

But once Breezer had seen the Draggers in action, he felt the call of mainline dope the same way he had cottoned to James Dean's studied alienation. To become a Dragger took the biggest balls and rawest guts—as the faithful had witnessed—and Breezer felt the call, just like many others, outwardly-ordinary yet craving deeper accomplishment and credibility. It was akin to a secret cult, a private society; a scream against the norms. No gang embroidery or weird handshakes.

The excitement really started to cook around midnight. Everybody up past bedtime, sneaking out of the house, far from parents and police and prying eyes. Only about fifty or so "members" in a club that had no name, and no badge except exclusivity; their gaze a pinpoint chromium, caffeinated on amphetamines and fuel-injected with Lonnie's homebrewed swill. A blood rite, to be sure.

As a first-timer, Breezer and his Beast were in harness for the opening heat.

On standby was a fellow introduced to Breezer as Duane, who had a Polish last name with too many consonants rear-ending each other into a three-car pileup, totally unpronounceable. Duane drove a steel-bodied "step-down" woody wagon that combined a '48 Hudson Commodore four-door sedan with the rear roof section of a '54 Hudson with completely hand-built ash and mahogany veneer. The "step-down" aspect was its low center of gravity; the ride served as the de facto ambulance when things got wet. The by-rote cover story was always that someone had fallen out of a car while joyriding. *These darned kids today . . .*

Breezer's opponent for the first heat was Tool Stokes, a Negro wrench who held forth from a still-vital soybean farm not far from the ex-airstrip. He had an amazing retinue of relatives and pets, including Grampaw Stokes (who maintained a very profitable apiary full of honeybees) and a one-eared, mean-tempered bloodhound named Griswold (who could actually sniff out lost jewelry, no lie). Tool was behind the wheel of his pride and joy, Matilda—a channeled bronze '32 Ford Roadster with Edelbrock heads. Tool liked to chain-smoke Luckies and tell people different stories about how he had lost his left fuck-finger (infection, following a mishap with a band saw . . . but Tool loved the art of salty embellishment).

Standing immediately behind the Beast was a Fault named Harry (or Henry) Coggins, suited up in a steerhide motorcycle jacket (police issue) and his lucky football helmet. He liked the green spiderweb pinstripe job and told Breezer so.

Tool's rearview remained vacant ... until Rodrigo, the most feared Fault of all, revealed himself. Except for Rodrigo, no Fault had ever attempted two heats in one night; the crosstalk suggested that Rodrigo had boasted about "just warming up." It wasn't rumor; it was legend already.

Both Rodrigo and Harry-or-Henry refused the usual offer of handcuffs. Rodrigo didn't even glance toward his competition. All that bullshit about gentleman rogues and honor on the battlefield had no place here. He strapped his own crash helmet tight.

Violet Cupp stood between the cars, her legs spread wide, exuding a come-on so primal and practiced that it almost counted as an attack. She stretched to give the male contingent the cleavage they wanted. She paused with a naughty sneer, then made a silent-movie bad-girl kissy-face ... and dropped the checkered flag.

Breezer put his pedal down smoothly. Parallel to him, Tool kept his eyes locked full forward, relentlessly accelerating. Their beloved and pampered engines roared approval and demanded more. Tool's ever-present Lucky dangled from his dry lips, its cherry hot, its ash disintegrating on the wind.

And behind them, Rodrigo and Harry-or-Henry hung on to the specially-reinforced rear bumpers, intentionally designed not to wrench free when held by a screaming human being dragged behind an automobile at zero-to-sixty in seven seconds or thereabouts, depending on the supercharger, horsepower, overdrive options, shifting strategies, and so on. They had to hang on, or lose—they had both refused the cuffs which would have secured them to their hangs.

At about ten elapsed seconds they would tear past the quarter-mile marker. Ten seconds after that, maximum, they would run out of road. Four to eight seconds for a full stop, from speeds up to eighty miles per hour.

Then they would see what was left of their passengers, their Faults.

Except something happened that Breezer could *not* see. Tool's car veered off-track at high speed, taking Rodrigo with it. The Beast blew onto the finish dirt alone.

Far behind him, Harry-or-Henry was still rolling on the tarmac, broken arms flopping like tentacles, blood already starting to fly. Breezer still couldn't hear any of the sounds the guy or his bones were making.

Back at the starting line, blond-boy DeCampo attempted a lame joke: "So where do you think the 'roll' in 'rock 'n roll' *came* from, anyhow?!" Nobody laughed.

Violet rolled her eyes. *Nope.* Never would she cozy down on DeCampo's little red wiener, no day, no way, no how. Not now. Never.

Tool's heap shambled to a halt in a storm front of track-shoulder dust, but Rodrigo was nowhere to be seen . . . until Breezer saw the big guy filling up the Beast's driver's side window, heard him yanking open the door, felt him rousting Breezer out of his ride with one fisted glove.

"You cut Tool off! You cut me off! That fucker had better *die*, and I mean it!"

It was track law among Faults, like a commandment: *You die, you lose.*

Rodrigo's voice was hot tar and broken glass. He was strong enough and mad enough to hold Breezer aloft one-handed. Breezer's boots dangled a foot off the ground. Rodrigo's breath would haze your eyes to tears and make you regret thinking of roadkill. His teeth ran in irregular crags that looked sharpened, maybe filed. One eye was fused almost shut by an old injury. The more visible eye had a huge black iris, like a dog's. His shredded leathers were smoldering and Breezer could see him bleeding from a dozen fresh wounds. Rodrigo tore off his helmet with his other hand and smashed it down to spin in the gravel with that abrasive bucket sound helmets make. Close-up, Rodrigo's exposed head seemed twice the size of Breezer's own, upholstered in thick features, scar tissue, and crimson rage. His hair hadn't grown back on one side after a previous race. His features had caught a lot of flak, and his skin looked like rubber bacon.

"*Fucker!*" A fist the size of a six-pack plowed into Breezer's face and flattened his nose to tomato pulp. Then Rodrigo dropped him and stalked away.

Rodrigo was not a brute, nor a subhuman, Breezer thought as his brain popped a fuse. Rodrigo was barely an Earthling.

Then, nothing. *Nada.*

WHEN BREEZER AWOKE, Violet was leaning over him, so guess what he was staring at. Distantly, somebody else's radio was playing "The Great Pretender" by the Platters, which would eventually chart at number one on both the pop and R&B hit list.

Breezer mangled a few sounds by way of inquiry. He gathered that Violet was patching up his nose. It felt as though a divot of bone and bad choices had been gouged out of the front of his skull with a pickaxe.

"Near as we can figure, Henry must've let go of your bumper. I knew he should have used the cuffs; he was too green."

So the guy's name had *been "Henry" after all.*

"...he rolled right in front of Tool, and Tool had to swerve, and that swung Rodrigo offsides, y'know, his center of gravity? Which messed up Rodrigo's grip... and *bam*, here you are. Your nose is definitely busted."

Breezer struggled to ask the obvious, a backwash of blood bubbling in his throat.

"Henry's not dead yet, but soon. Then maybe Rodrigo will calm down. And it'll be Ray's problem."

Ray was another individual with peculiar but specific responsibilities here, very similar to Duane the meatwagon pilot, except in Ray's case the by-rote cover story was *I'm afraid your kid has blown town with no forwarding address... run away from home...*

(In actuality, casualties got dumped off Beaudine Bridge after midnight with full quasi-military honors—also Ray's idea, which was why he was nicknamed the Undertaker.)

"Except now Rodrigo is hollering for *your* blood, too. Screaming foul. He'll never forfeit, and he'll be wanting payback—just so you know." She tried to be gentle with the tape on Breezer's face. "That's a headache you can't take a pill for."

It was exactly the same as dreading the reigning bully with an after-school vendetta against you. It didn't have to make sense. It just *was*. Past a certain point of being terrorized, you heard the bell and walked out onto the playground with a new mindset. All chips in. No more running or hiding; no more excuses or prevarications.

"I'm ready." Breezer still wasn't ready, but he said the words anyway. His vision seemed shrouded in a sodium-yellow fog that softened things at the edges.

"Tell me something, while you're looking."

He finally met her eyes. "Sorry."

"Don't be. What is it with you guys and breasts? Call me curious."

Breezer didn't hesitate to respond. It took his immediate attention off his throbbing face. "It's the most obvious visual way you're different," he said quietly. "Everything else is hidden away. They're not like eyes or lips, which men have, which can be highlighted with paint, kinda like pinstriping. We can't help but be attracted to the difference. Just like we can't help being attracted to this event, right here. It's different. It's something more. It's like you can't *not* look. Maybe it's part of the reason I decided to come here and get my face broken."

"Good answer," she said. "You're definitely worth sleeping with."

That made his heart give an off-time thud.

The dragway had tasted its preferred refreshment—blood, leaked motor oil, flung droplets of human sweat. Its appetite had been whetted. It was now awake, alive, and ready for another round.

Breezer's vision remained fuzzy and unreliable. He barely registered the second heat.

Lily P. (for Price) dropped down at the helm of her own Roadster, which she'd discovered rotting behind a Texaco station in 1954 and rebuilt from the ground up with a '52 Olds engine connected to a '39 Ford tranny using a Cregar adapter—her idea. Channeled body, sculpted nose, custom hood and fadeaways—all her. A dyke as tough as a cement nail, Lily was never without a cigarette dangling from her bee-stung, pinup lips, or her scarf, which she wore like a World War I ace.

DeCampo had once seen her loop that scarf around the neck of a cat-caller and nearly break the idiot's spine. She existed, and competed, in complete defiance of the norm superstition about no women in the pits. The same basic sufferance extended to Tool Stokes, as well.

Dragger heats were not where conventional rodders congregated.

Lily's opponent was the locally infamous Speed-Shift Madison, at the helm of his chop-top '32 three-window Ford Coupe, running a supercharged flathead Mercury with Evans speed equipment. Canary yellow with "69er" painted on both doors.

Behind Lily was a Fault named Lloyd Farewell (no kidding, that was his real name—"farewell") versus "Jerky" McDonagh (former real-world name, Jerry, who had survived at least two previous events with a wealth of dislocations, burns, abrasions and scar tissue, hence "jerky"). Both opted for the handcuffs after seeing what had happened to Henry Coggins.

Lily prevailed, and Lloyd Farewell did not die. By much.

"Oh, shit," said Violet to Breezer. "Here he comes."

Rodrigo filled up Breezer's vision. Dear Lord, but he was ugly to behold. The flesh occluding Rodrigo's damaged eye was like a bad weld, but worse, that eye still moved around, not tracking with its brother, but cognizant in a totally different way. You could make out the man's skull in his expression, the clenched and off-center jaw, scraped bone itching to burst free of the last scraps of baked brown flesh, especially on the side where his hair had been sandblasted away long ago.

"Challenge," Rodrigo said in his cemetery voice. "I challenge you."

Breezer was struggling to focus, his right eye still blurred. *An eye for an eye*, he thought.

For a challenge, drivers had to be picked, or volunteer. Challenge was a right reserved to any Dragger, any Fault who felt cheated. Rude payback, in the most direct and painful way possible, the law of the asphalt jungle.

"I don't think I can drive," said Breezer, hopelessly knowing what came next.

"You don't drive. Not against me, *puto*. You *compete*. Or I'll break your fucking neck right here."

The crowd, the watchers, the observers, had gathered around them. Tool Stokes and Lily P.; Henry Coggins (bleeding, bandaged, wobbly, but still breathing); Undertaker Ray and Ambulance Duane; Lonnie Lacks (swigging his home-brew, as his own best advertisement); DeCampo (who looked as though he'd just wolfed bad pork down the wrong tube); Lloyd Farewell and Jerky McDonagh (whose own wear and tear made him look like a bathing beauty next to Rodrigo); Violet and all the others. A jury, mulling a verdict. In the center, facing his foe, was the guy formerly known as Chuck Detweiler, now just Breezer, being judged, all around.

Nearby, somebody's radio was playing "Honey, Don't" by Carl Perkins. The B-side of "Blue Suede Shoes," on Sun Records, a rockabilly classic in its own right.

In his entire life, Breezer had never reacted favorably to someone—anyone—telling him *no*. Or *don't*. Sudden rage blindsided him.

"You name it," he said, staring directly into Rodrigo's good eye, the one with the dog-pupil. "If you've got the sack to game it. Except... lose the leathers. Show everybody how fucking hideous you really are."

The color actually drained from Violet's complexion. Her half-smoked Kool nearly plummeted from her mouth.

Rodrigo seemed to swell bigger, to engorge like a boner, as he smirked and peeled off his shredded Perfecto, which had once resembled the one worn by Brando in *The Wild One*, if you could imagine that garment barbecued until its surface was more like pemmican. He was bare-chested beneath.

Everybody gasped, or held their breath.

Rodrigo's torso was leanly muscled, ridged and scarred in the manner of golem or gargoyle skin. Crimson droplets dappled him in aerosol; he appeared to be sweating blood, not losing it deleteriously. Not a hair to be seen anywhere, and his nipples were long gone. But the most spellbinding thing were his tattoos. Dozens of them. All calendar dates. Up one side and down the other, on his shoulder blades, on his biceps, on his backs. Every victory. *5/22/51. 7/13/55. 12/24/54.* Some mottled and faded blue, the way old military tats turned to mud. *2/2/53. 2/15/53. 2/28/53.* Some unreadable, like hieroglyphics. Some blackened, like burns or blood-patch or road rash. Over fifty of them.

Henry Coggins came unhinged at the knees and collapsed. Duane rolled him over. Henry was husking air like a gut-shot antelope. "He's in bad shape," said Duane. "We'd better—"

"Better nothing," said Rodrigo, turning to nail Breezer with his hot, canine gaze. "Let me show you how this works."

Rodrigo shoved Duane to one side—impressive, because Duane was a big guy—and straddled Henry Coggins, grabbing his head in both hands, bringing his face so close their foreheads were touching. "Told you I meant it," he whispered. "Time to let go."

What happened next could have been a hallucination or mass hypnosis, but Breezer sensed it was neither. This was as real as it got.

Plenty of Henry's blood had gone from inside to outside. Even through his field dressings, new blood seemed to flow, in defiance of gravity or common sense, toward Rodrigo's grasping fingers. Past his wrists. Up his arms. And *into* Rodrigo's own new cuts and scrapes and shreds, which buttoned themselves up, fading into the bas-relief of his ruined flesh.

Henry Coggins sagged into death without so much as a rattle.

"And no helmets," Rodrigo said unnecessarily to Breezer.

"YOU DON'T HAVE to do this," Violet told Breezer.

Lily P. had stepped up to drive Rodrigo. The glint in her eyes suggested that perhaps she had a plan to merely back over the son of a bitch. Then forward. Then back, then repeat, until he was macerated to a stain. Unless that would not work against a monster.

Tool Stokes, egged on by Rodrigo over the first heat, volunteered to drive Breezer. Tool thought of pulling the Army .45 from his glove box and putting a slug into Rodrigo's brain pan ... but what if that didn't work, either?

"He'll beat you," Violet said.

"He might beat me, but he won't win," said Breezer. "I've got a magic talisman." He pulled a furry piece of paper from the fob pocket of his Levi's. It was folded into a tight little square about the size of a Chiclet, yellowed and worn. "You hold onto it for me."

"I don't get it," said Violet.

"I came here for *him*," Breezer said levelly. "This was all supposed to happen exactly this way. Don't worry about me."

"You're gone all the way nuts," shrugged Violet. But she stashed the folded paper, which felt like very ancient newsprint. Stashed it in the best possible place, too—under one bra strap. "Tell me something: Have you ever done this before?"

"Nope."

She sighed. "Nice knowin' ya."

He couldn't breathe through his busted nose. He stepped up behind Tool's '32. *No helmets. No handcuffs. No nancy-boy stuff.* He rucked off his jacket, still zipped, leaving his very un-Dean-like tank top.

"You can keep the wife-beater, snowflake," Rodrigo rasped from about ten feet away, positioned behind Lily's Roadster. "All that pink meat is sweet, but nobody needs to see your titties."

Breezer gave him the finger without looking at him.

Both Roadsters—Tool's and Lily's—grumbled contentedly as they guzzled fuel from custom-built, mild-steel tanks.

Rodrigo took to one knee and grasped the rear drag bumper. Breezer did likewise.

And Violet dropped the flag.

Tool's balonies spewed a double helping of takeoff smoke right into Breezer's eyes as the rear of the car dropped down and dug out. The roar of the engine obliterated everything else.

Everything else. Rodrigo didn't exist anymore, nor did Lily, the track, the onlookers. All Breezer could feel as his scrotum was abraded by the runway was the sensation of both arms trying to rip free of their sockets.

With friction came heat. Breezer's face wasn't on the pavement—yet—but it felt the same as hovering over a lit burner on a stove, his sweat evaporating as soon as it popped. From the waist down, his brain had decided on a brand new definition for Hell.

Then, pain. Elapsed time could not have been more than a second and a half. Breezer knew he was already bleeding, fresh rips in his skin now ripping wider, his jeans sanding away to dandelion fluff. His feet felt afire in their motorcycle boots.

Something inside him *broke* like fruit dropped from a great height. Fuck it all, he was starting to roll laterally, the same as a crippled ship listing to port.

Velocity and new damage tore his right-hand grip free, and he pawed to regain it. He glimpsed his own blood lubricating the insides of his knuckles.

Then Tool soared over the first genuine bump in the roadway. Breezer nearly screamed, but that was not possible; his teeth were clenched and would permit no sound to escape, save the desperate, almost sobbing pant of each superheated breath. The whole universe smelled like burning rubber and scorched bone.

Bam! His broken nose hit the bumper, one, two, three times. He could not swallow his own blood fast enough.

Bam! They were off the runway and onto the dirt, pluming up their own fogbank of brown dust. Breezer could not hold on any longer. His hands were dumb grasping tools, shellacked in blood. *Bam!* they hit the end of the track, and *bam!* Breezer was free of the car, and rolling helplessly.

His left ankle snapped inside his boot. His right elbow similarly snapped, before he stopped tumbling sidewise over burrs and weeds and broken bottles and discarded lug nuts and pointed rocks and junk wood with nails sticking out of it and . . .

Rodrigo was not really dusting himself off, merely pretending to. Bloody, sliced to ribbons, still standing, still aware in his inhuman, reptilian way, thinking about new scar tissue and a new tattoo. Breezer, barely able to do anything except remain on his back, exsanguinating, took a microscopic amount of pleasure in noting that Rodrigo was limping. Slightly, but still.

Rodrigo's shadow blocked out the moon as he squatted over Breezer.

"Losers lose," he said, his voice more clotted than before. "Losers die."

Everybody from the track had caught up with them, surrounded them again, to witness the payoff to the drama.

Breezer felt a broken front tooth with his tongue. A bubble of blood formed between his lips, abruptly popped, and sprinkled blood on Rodrigo's face, where it was absorbed.

"That's not the rule," Breezer said. "The rule is you lose, you die."

"You lost. You let go."

"I made it past the finish line before I let go."

Rodrigo stared for a moment, then smiled horribly, airing out his bloodstained, sharpened dentition. "My hero," he said. "Sudden death. *We go again.*"

"You go," said Breezer. "I might could use a little nap. Tell him, Violet."

The group parted for her. She couldn't pretend not to know what Breezer was talking about, but the look of wolfish hesitation that broke Rodrigo's smug expression was almost worth the wait.

"Tell him. You read it, right? Tell him."

"How about I tell you to shut up?" said Rodrigo, as Breezer's blood continued to flow toward the larger man's open wounds.

"Rodrigo Castelnuevo Santiago," Violet recited from the much-folded scrap of newspaper entrusted to her care. Of course she had peeked. "Pronounced dead at the scene of a vehicular collision in Triple Pines, no known relatives, buried at city expense last April fourth... just about three weeks after the last time he competed here."

"You can't win if you're already dead," said Breezer. "That's not the Dragger way. *Tú muere, tú pierde ... puto.*"

"I'll be damned," muttered Tool, in slow, whistling amazement.

The blood-flow had already reversed, channeling now toward Breezer. In the instant of revelation and exposure, Rodrigo was trying to see the world through eyes that had scabbed to dishwater gray; to speak without vocal cords or saliva. His choke-hold on Breezer became vague, slipped, and disengaged.

You die, you lose.

Breezer thumbed his Italian stiletto switch and the blade telescoped out with a *snick*. He carved *LOSER* into the available area on Rodrigo's chest as the corpus literally caved in.

Pretty soon there was nothing left to make anybody a liar.

The Draggers all looked at each other and nobody spoke a word. A prime commandment had been violated—by Rodrigo—and they all seemed to know that they might not be meeting up at Bakehurst Field, ever again. It was the sort of terminative moment one feels when your time, your era, is suddenly behind you.

Later, after they had finally managed to have sex—post-healing, except for one memorably clumsy hospital-bed event that had helped him forget all about Molly Patterson, just for a while—Breezer told Violet a story about how Rodrigo had been involved in the deaths of some friends, in another time and place, including the former owner of the switchblade. Violet was kind enough not to tell Breezer that the whole damned story sounded lame and made up on the spot. And later still, before college, with Lily's help, she eventually built her own rod and competed—but not as a Dragger—after Breezer moved on, or changed nicknames, or rode into the sunset—it didn't matter.

Breezer had never wanted merely to win, without competing.

On the same day that the Dragger event had transpired, a military C-118 transport bound for Europe from McGuire Air Force Base hit an air pocket and crashed in a New Jersey swamp, killing forty-five aboard and grievously injuring twenty-one more. It barely made the news, while Violet was helping Breezer to stand on his good foot, and Ambulance Duane was preparing to spackle him up. In the distance, somebody else's radio was playing "Que Sera, Sera" by Doris Day.

DAVID J. SCHOW is an award-winning writer who lives in Los Angeles.

His novels include The Kill Riff, The Shaft, Rock Breaks Scissors Cut, Bullets of Rain, Gun Work, Hunt Among the Killers of Men *(part of Hard Case Crime's "Gabriel Hunt" series),* Internecine, Upgunned, *and the forthcoming* The Big Crush *(2019).*

His short stories have been regularly selected for over thirty volumes of "Year's Best" anthologies across three decades and have won the World Fantasy Award, the ultra-rare Dimension Award from Twilight Zone *magazine, plus a 2002 International Horror Guild Award for* Wild Hairs, *his compendium of justly provocative "Raving & Drooling" columns written for* Fangoria. *The newest of his ten short story collections is a greatest hits anniversary compendium titled* DJStories *(2018).*

He has been a contributor to Storm King Comics' John Carpenter's Tales for a Halloween Night *since its very first issue. Storm King has just released the first in his five-issue series for* John Carpenter's Tales of Science Fiction—"The Standoff."

Schow is also the editor of the landmark horror anthology Silver Scream *(1988), the three-volume* Lost Bloch *series (reprinting Robert Bloch obscuria) for Subterranean Press, and* Elvisland *by John Farris (Babbage, 2004).*

*DJS has written extensively for film (*The Crow, Leatherface: Texas Chainsaw Massacre III, The Hills Run Red*) and television (*Masters of Horror, Mob City*). His nonfiction works include* The Art of Drew Struzan *(2010) and* The Outer Limits *at 50 (2014). He can be seen on various DVDs as expert witness or documentarian on everything from* Creature from the Black Lagoon *to* Psycho *to* I, Robot. *Thanks to him, the word "splatterpunk" has been in the Oxford English Dictionary since 2002.*

BILL FOLEY STRETCHED OUT ON THE beach chair, eyes closed and thoughts drifting. He could hear the whisper of the surf, the calling of tropical birds, the rattle of palm fronds overhead. He also heard the soft swish of footsteps approaching through the sand, and felt the coolness of his friend's shadow as she leaned over him with another mango daiquiri and said—

"Sheriff?"

Foley snapped his eyes open. He looked up into the worried face of Deputy Katie Burns.

Katie? Suddenly the palm tree became a coat-rack, his chair felt

THE STARLITE DRIVE-IN

BY JOHN M. FLOYD

*"It headed toward the Starlite, didn't it," Katie said.
"The old drive-in theater."*

hard and creaky, and instead of bare toes he saw his booted feet propped up on the desktop in his office.

"Wake up," Katie said. "They found another body."

WIDE AWAKE NOW, the third-term sheriff óf Terry County, Mississippi, steered his cruiser into the gravel lot of the Deer Lick Mobile Home Park. Above the fence in the distance he could see the once-white wooden screen of the abandoned drive-in movie theater that had been such a part of his teenage years. Old but still standing, after all this time. Like Sheriff Bill Foley.

He and Deputy Burns climbed out into the chilly November morning, crossed a muddy yard littered with cinderblocks and bald tires, and banged on the door of one of the double-wides. The woman who answered the knock looked like Willie Nelson in a Dolly Parton wig. She said, without bothering to remove her bent cigarette, "They're all out back."

"They" turned out to be Elmer Higby, his twin sister Elmira, and their cousin and his wife, Doogie and Lucille Sistrunk. Like most everyone in town, Sheriff Foley had known them all his life. When he and Katie showed up in the Higbys' backyard, Doogie's broad bottom was perched on the rusted hood of a '58 Thunderbird, Lucille was sipping a Bud Lite on the front fender, Elmer was leaning against a sad-looking pecan tree, and Elmira, who'd been puffing on something suspiciously smaller and more fragrant than a Virginia Slim, quickly stuffed the still-smoking butt into the pocket of her sweatsuit.

Nobody said a word. Doogie spat a stream of tobacco juice into the dirt and pointed to a clump of brush twenty yards away.

Behind it was a pile of red guts that had once been Darryl Wayne Goodman. Foley knew this because of the orange gator-skin boots on one end of the body and the turkey-feathered cowboy hat lying near the other. On the off-chance that there were two people in the county with that kind of taste in head-and-footwear, Foley eased a wallet from the pocket of the victim's bloodied and muddied jeans and checked the driver's license. It was Darryl, all right.

"Where's the rest of him?" Foley asked.

"Ain't sure," Doogie said. "One of his arms is downair by the creek."

The coroner—actually her assistant, since she was out of town for the day—arrived soon afterward to load up the parts and pieces of Darryl Goodman and cart him away. Neither the Higbys nor the Sistrunks knew what might've happened to their neighbor, but it didn't take a genius to figure it was the same thing that had killed Booger Ray Willis the night before last, less than half a mile west. Mangled corpse, nothing stolen from the body, no footprints or other evidence left at the scene.

"What done this to him, Billy?" Lucille Sistrunk asked.

Foley shook his head. He had no answers to offer.

KATIE BURNS DIDN'T EITHER—but she'd never been shy about voicing her thoughts.

"A seriously big-ass animal of some kind," she said, when they'd returned to the sheriff's office. "Has to be."

Foley slumped into his desk chair. He wished he were still dreaming. "Didn't see any paw prints. Just like the other night. And that ground's been wet for two weeks."

"I know it has."

He sighed and rubbed his eyes. "Prints or not, what kind of critter could *do* that? Black bear? Panther? Unless something's escaped from a zoo someplace, them's the only options I know of, around here. Besides, neither one a them's apt to tear a man up that way, for sure not twice in two nights." He looked up at her. "You listening to me?"

Katie was reading a note that had been left on her desk. "It doesn't just do it to *people*, apparently."

"What?"

She held up the note. "This says Ethel Boggins called in while we were gone. Said something killed her dog last night. German shepherd."

"I know Ethel—she lives near Higby's trailer park. Killed the dog how?"

"Slashed him to pieces. Greg took the call—says he's driving out to take a look."

"Good," Foley said. Gregory Waszewski was the other deputy, a pleasant but lazy psychology graduate that Foley had hired last year when no one else would take the job. And since the office dispatcher was on maternity leave, Deputy Waszewski had been handling most of the phone calls. He liked doing that, and paperwork, and interviews too, as long as they were done in the office. He wasn't fond of guns or confrontations. *Smart man*, Foley thought.

But investigations also involved getting out in the real world now and then, and Foley had been encouraging Greg to do more of that. Maybe it was working.

Katie tossed the note onto her desktop. "So what do we do?"

"We see what Doc Green says, when she gets back and looks at Goodman's body. And since all this seems to be happening around Deer Lick Road, we have to keep asking residents there if they've seen anyone or anything strange lately." He paused. "We got one of three things, here—a bear, a big cat of some kind, or a psycho with a butcher knife. And none of 'em's good."

Katie nodded, looking thoughtful.

"Oh, one more thing," he said. "Call Greg on his cell phone."

"And?"

"Tell him to be careful."

THE NEXT TWO DAYS were the most hectic—and frustrating—the Terry County Sheriff could remember. He and his two deputies questioned a dozen families in the square-mile section where the two mutilated bodies (three, counting that of Ethel Boggins's dog) had been found. Foley had also recruited several local hunters to scour the area, although so far he'd sent them out in daylight hours only. He figured anything nocturnal could also be tracked in the daytime, and he wasn't eager to add any more citizens to the death toll. It wouldn't be long, he knew, before the state police got involved, and he honestly wasn't sure if he dreaded that or welcomed it. He knew how to issue speeding tickets and defuse domestic arguments; murders and/or animal attacks were a different matter.

As it turned out, no confirmed sightings of large predators were made during that time by the three law officers, their hunting parties, or the interviewed residents. But a teenager did report a glimpse of a giant "ape-like" creature in his grandma's back yard one night, and an elderly guy with binoculars said he'd spotted two men entering a small building on the premises of the old drive-in theater at dawn. One of the men was tall, he said, with a long black overcoat that billowed behind him like a sail, and the other wore what looked like an old-timey high-school football jacket. Dark with white stripes on the collar, waist, and sleeves.

Odd information, but not earthshaking or case-changing. For the tenth time, Foley and Katie studied the map of the area in question;

they'd already trudged over most of its woods and pastures these past couple days, alert and armed to the teeth. All they'd seen, except for their fellow trackers, were trees, grass, a shallow creek, the trailer park, a few wood-frame houses, the weedy expanse of the deserted drive-in, and the vast construction site next to it. An outfit called Merrillton Development was planning a shopping center there, although the project had been delayed because of recent rains. Bulldozers and backhoes were parked onsite and waiting for clearer skies.

Regarding their witness reports, Foley was understandably skeptical of the ape-man sighting, but the fact that two strangers were seen roaming the grounds of the drive-in this morning—the only logical-sounding lead so far—convinced him it was time to look closer there.

Which he did, late that afternoon. The sheriff and Katie left Deputy Waszewski to watch the phones, drove out to the old open-air theater on Deer Lick Road, and parked beside the low wooden building that had once housed the projection room/office/concession stand.

It was a cold day, but cloudless for the first time in weeks. Rows of short poles—in the sheriff's high-school years they'd held little metal speakers that moviegoers unclipped and hung on their car windows—stretched into the distance. Bordering the south side of the property was the highway; to the north, behind the looming wooden "screen," was a stretch of woods and a cotton field; and to the east and west were the trailer park on one side and the construction site on the other. A lone sign, faded and weather-worn, stood beside the road: STARLITE DRIVE-IN.

Foley got out, popped the trunk, and dug a heavy flashlight out of a box that also held various other items he'd purchased to use on the secondhand boat he kept at a friend's marina on the Gulf Coast. He reminded himself to take those out soon; if higher authorities did get involved in this case, he didn't want to have to explain the presence of fishing tackle, life jackets, flare guns, and bait buckets in a county patrol car. At the moment, though, he found himself wishing that was his only problem.

He slammed the trunk and walked with Katie to the building. It was long and windowless and shaped like a shoebox, half of it enclosed and the other half an open-fronted shed. Underneath the shed roof were two shiny rows of fifty-five-gallon drums. When Katie asked about them, Foley said, "Gas containers for all the trucks and digging equipment next door. The construction folks probably leased this property so they'd have a place nearby to store their fuel." But his attention was on the other half of the building. With one hand on his holstered revolver Foley turned the doorknob, pushed the front door open, and stepped inside.

The office was empty but for a chair and an ancient two-foot-square TV set. On the far wall was the door to a second room, one that had obviously been locked at one time; a broken latch hung from the half-open door and a padlock lay on the floor in one corner.

That second room was empty too, except for the wall shelves. Stacked there were dozens of big reels of film, some in cases, others lying overturned with their black and shiny innards spilling out. Katie used Foley's flashlight to examine several of the reels. "Old movies," she said to him, then smirked and added, "Real gems, too. From the fifties and sixties, looks like." She read off a few titles: "*Mothra. Killer Shrews. Day of the Triffids. Rodan. Son of Godzilla. The Horror of Dracula. The Blob. The Creature From—*"

"I get the idea. In fact, I'd heard about it."

"Heard about what?"

"Delbert Turner, the guy who owned this place forever, died a while back. When he had to close down, years before, and sell all his projection equipment—well, some said he couldn't make himself get rid of the old movies. Or at least the scary ones."

Katie narrowed her eyes. "What are you talking about, Billy?"

He let out a sigh. "It was a crazy thing. Notice I didn't say he closed down—I said he *had* to close down. From everything I've heard, there was a rash of unexplained murders around here, along with . . . well . . . sightings."

"What?"

"Sightings," Foley said. "People said they saw things, in the woods near the crime scenes."

"What kind of things?"

"Nobody was ever sure. *Creatures*, some witnesses said—like those from old horror stories, spider-people, aliens, mummies."

"You gotta be kidding."

"I'm telling you what I was told. And a few folks, religious nuts mostly, started saying all this was happening because of the otherworldly movies Turner was showing—this was the fifties, remember—and things got ugly. Vandalism, threats, demonstrations, boycotts, you get the idea. Anyhow, Turner wound up having to shut down." Foley waved a hand at the shelves. "But apparently he kept the films. Just locked 'em up and left 'em here all this time. When the Merrillton Development people bought the site from Turner's kids this year, probably to use, like I said, as a fuel-storage depot during the building of their project, I guess the construction team must've busted the locks, looked around, and decided to leave it as is."

"What about the murders? I mean, after the drive-in closed . . . "

"They stopped," he said.

Both of them stayed quiet for a minute, thinking about that.

"That *is* a crazy story," Katie said, wiping her dusty hands on her jeans. "But back to our current problem—looks like this place isn't big enough for two men to hide out in. Do you agree?"

"I agree."

She seemed about to say something else when her cell phone buzzed. She answered the call, listened a while, said "Thanks, Doc—good to have you back," and disconnected. "That was Dr. Green," she said. "Called to tell you she's examining the second body."

"Why'd she call you and not me?" Foley asked.

"She says you're always grumpy on the phone."

"Yeah, well, I'll be bright and cheerful when I retire."

He saw something flicker in Katie's face. Sadness? She said, "Two more months, right?"

"Counting the days."

She studied him a moment. "What'll you do, when you leave?"

"Where'll I go, you mean? The Caribbean. White beaches and blue lagoons."

"Seriously?"

Foley pushed back his hat and scratched his forehead. "There's something I been meaning to tell you." He paused, then said, "You know the name Sywell Burdette?"

"Sure. Oil tycoon. Houston, right?"

"He was my mother's brother. Her only sibling. She died when I was born."

Katie blinked. "Your uncle's a billionaire... and you never mentioned it to me?"

"Never told *any*body. Dad and me moved here from Texas when I was two years old—he and Uncle Sy didn't get along. I don't even remember him." He shrugged. "Sy never married, never had kids, never contacted us here. Then, when he died last year, his lawyers called me."

She narrowed her eyes. "Are you telling me you inherited the Burdette fortune?"

Foley chuckled. "No. Almost everything went to charities. But he left me his beach house and a passel of land in Jamaica."

Her mouth dropped open. "My God, Billy. And you're really moving there?"

"Yep. That's where I was this summer, on vacation."

"You told me you went to New Orleans."

"I did, to catch the plane."

She gave him an odd look. "You sly devil. You have a sweetie down there?"

"No, I'll need to find one of those to take with me," he said. "I'm accepting applications."

For several seconds both of them stayed quiet, their eyes locked.

Katie's cell buzzed again. She fumbled the phone from her pocket, took the call, listened for a beat, and replied, "Okay. We're on our way." When she disconnected she said, "The coroner again. She wants to talk to us."

Foley squared his hat and nodded, all business again. "Let's go. Nothing more to see here."

"Good." Katie, looking preoccupied, paused at the splintered door and took a final glance at the gloomy room, at the stacked reels of film. "This place gives me the creeps."

They were outside and headed for the car when Foley stopped in his tracks. In fact he was looking down *at* his tracks. "Well, I be damn," he said.

"What is it?"

"The guy with the binoculars. Where was it he said he saw them two men, this morning?"

"Right here," she said. "Walking across the lot toward this building."

Foley looked up at her. He didn't say more. He didn't need to.

The only footprints leading to or from the building—or anywhere—were his and Katie's.

AN HOUR LATER they were back at the office, Bill Foley with the same mixed feelings that had plagued him for three days. On the one hand, he felt he should do something—shoot somebody, catch somebody, *something*—to stop all this. On the other hand, he knew he had to keep thinking straight or they would accomplish nothing. There were just too many unknowns. And their visit to the coroner half an hour ago had added yet another.

"Fang marks?" Foley had repeated, when Dr. Green told him what she'd found.

"That's right. Like a snake would make, though these were bigger. As I said, most of the wounds indicate an animal attack, or feeding on a corpse that was already dead. The other damage was so extensive my assistant must've missed those two punctures."

"So what are you saying, Sally?"

Dr. Green shrugged. "I'm saying something with long teeth bit him. Bit him in the neck."

Now, alone in the sheriff's office, Foley and Katie dropped into their desk chairs. This was getting weirder and weirder; visions of Transylvania and Boris Karloff were dancing in his head. After five minutes or more, Foley blinked, looked around, and said, "Where's Greg?"

"Gone home, probably. He's not one for staying late."

"No, but he does when I ask him to. He agreed to work tonight."

Katie stood, crossed the room, and sat down in front of Deputy Waszewski's computer.

"What are you doing?" Foley asked.

"Checking the call log. If he went someplace, he'd note it on here."

"We actually do that?"

"Greg and I do. If you ever learn anything about technology, you can too." She clicked a few keys, studied the screen, and added, "Here it is. He's gone to see Ethel Boggins. The lady whose dog was killed."

"Why'd he go out there again?"

"She called at 5:40, it says here, about the time you and I were headed to the coroner's. Greg says Ethel told him she saw something in the field behind her house. Said she couldn't tell much about its size because of the distance, but that it was big, and gray, and looked like . . . "

Katie stopped, staring at the report.

"Looked like what?"

"A lizard. She told him it looked like a big lizard, walking on its hind legs."

They turned to each other. Foley could hear the clock ticking on the office wall.

And suddenly Katie's eyes widened.

She focused again on Greg Waszewski's computer, typed something in, waited, studied the result, and fell backward in her chair as if slapped. "Michael Landon," she murmured. "I *thought* I remembered that."

"What?"

"Michael Landon. From *Bonanza*. And he was Charles Ingalls, in *Little House on—*"

"I know, Katie. I'm even older than you are. What about him?"

She turned to face him. She still looked stunned.

"The bite marks in Darryl Goodman's neck," she said. "The giant ape. The fact that we saw no footprints anywhere around the bodies— *or* where those two strangers were sighted. The big lizard, walking upright. The guy in a long black overcoat, flapping in the wind." She leaned forward, holding his gaze. "Think about it, Billy."

Foley shook his head. "I don't know what you're—"

"Internet Movie Data Base." She pointed to the computer. "*I Was a Teenage Werewolf.*"

"You were what?"

She swiveled the monitor around so Foley could see it. "Not me," she said. "Him."

On the screen was a movie poster of a young Michael Landon, wearing a grin and an old-fashioned high-school varsity jacket. Also shown was a hairy monster in the same coat: dark, with white stripes along the bottom, and around the cuffs and collar. At the top of the poster were the words *I Was a Teenage Werewolf.*

Sheriff Foley felt his mouth go dry. "The football jacket. The one the old man saw."

For a long time neither of them said a word. Finally he looked at her.

"It wasn't a black overcoat, on the other guy," he mumbled. "It was a cape. Wasn't it."

"I bet it was," she said.

A silence passed.

"This is insane," Foley said. "A werewolf and a vampire? Even *thinking* it is insane."

"I know." Her voice was barely a whisper. "But it adds up. All those things people are seeing. Put that together with the unsolved murders you told me about from years ago, and what folks said they saw *then*— and the fact that the killings stopped when the drive-in closed—and those reels of film in that room . . . "

Foley could hear himself breathing.

"Creatures from old horror movies," he said. "But—how can that be?"

Her eyes drifted back to him. He'd never seen her so pale.

"What if they're going in and out of there?" she said. "That construction work—the moving in of all the heavy machinery next door to the drive-in—what if that woke 'em up? I can't believe I'm saying this, but—maybe these things have been locked in that room all these years, and it's like a pressure building up. In those reels." She paused. "And then, when whoever it was—the Merrillton people, I guess—pried the lock off the door, it . . . "

"It freed them," Foley said.

She nodded.

He fell backward in his chair, mirroring Katie, and gazed sightlessly out the window. He felt weak, as if gut-punched. "We could be wrong. This could all be as ridiculous as it sounds."

"I hope it is. But I don't think so."

"So what do we do?" he asked. "Tell somebody?"

"Tell somebody what? Tell the state cops we've decided Little Joe Cartwright is out there killing people? That King Kong and Godzilla and things that don't leave footprints because they aren't *real* are sneaking through people's yards, and Count Dracula's drinking their blood?"

"Isn't that exactly what you're saying happened?" he said. "My God, Katie, if what we're talking about is true—"

He stopped, feeling his stomach turn over as a thought hit him.

Greg Waszewski.

"Greg's out there," Foley said. "Get him on the radio. Hurry. I'll try his cell phone."

Katie dashed for the dispatch room while he phoned Waszewski's cell. He got no answer. "He's not in his car," Katie said, coming back. She looked on the log to find the home number of the lady who'd called, punched it in, and hit the speakerphone button.

"Ms. Boggins?" she blurted. "This is the Sheriff's office. Is Deputy Waszewski there?"

He wasn't, Ethel said. He'd left there thirty minutes ago. No, she didn't know where he'd gone. But he'd asked her a strange question, just before he left. Something about that huge reptile-looking thing she'd seen, in the field behind her house.

"What question?" Katie said.

"He asked if I saw where it went."

"Did you?"

"Sure did," Ethel said. "And I told him."

Foley saw Katie go rigid, and felt his insides turn to ice. Because both of them knew what bordered the cotton field behind Ethel Boggins's house.

"It headed toward the Starlite, didn't it?" Katie said to her. "The old drive-in theater."

"Yes. How did you kn—"

Katie hung up. For a moment she and Foley sat motionless in their seats.

"Greg wouldn't go poking around there," she said. "Not alone, without telling us. Would he?"

Foley swallowed. "He might. If he thought I wanted him to."

Both of them jumped to their feet and headed for the door.

AS SOON AS FOLEY'S PATROL CAR turned off the highway into the darkened lot of the drive-in, its headlights found what he'd feared he would see. Deputy Waszewski's cruiser was parked beside the shoebox-looking building, nosed in at a slant. The deputy himself was nowhere in sight. A round object about the size of a volleyball lay in the mud between the car and the open front door; otherwise there was nothing else besides the rows of short speaker-poles and the wooden rectangle of the movie screen standing dirty-white in the light of the rising moon. The place was as silent as a tomb.

Foley stopped the car sixty feet away, leaving his headlights on and aimed at the scene. Quietly he and Katie climbed out, guns drawn. As an afterthought he holstered his pistol, walked to the rear of his car, opened the trunk, pushed aside the box of boating gear, and took out a twelve-gauge pump shotgun. He eased the trunk-lid down without slamming it. Then they crept toward the long building, their shadows stretching eerily out in front of them.

The only sound was their footsteps. The long rows of fuel drums under the open-fronted shed gleamed red in the car's headlights. They were still twenty feet from the building when they recognized the round object in the mud beside the deputy's cruiser.

It was Greg Waszewski's head.

Foley froze. Katie, her trembling left hand clapped over her mouth, was already backing up. But the raised pistol in her other hand looked steady enough, and he felt an odd surge of pride for her. *Stay focused*, he told himself. Together they backed up, inching toward the safety of their patrol car. He knew he'd have to check the building later—but with Greg's death and what else they suspected, he wanted some reinforcements first.

Slowly they retreated, trying to watch everything at once. Foley's hands were sweaty; his heart hammered in his ears. Thirty feet to their waiting cruiser. Twenty feet. Ten. Five . . .

Then he heard a sound behind them. Together they whirled, guns pointed, to squint into the headlights. Suddenly their vehicle jolted back and forth on its shocks, and something woofed and grunted in the darkness.

Whatever these creatures were, they were here. Now.

Foley felt his knees go weak. He glimpsed something, a shape of some kind, several yards away on his left, and fired a blast into it from the shotgun. It had no effect. Katie did the same at a shape in the other direction, aiming and firing twice.

"I hit something," she hissed, her breath rasping in her throat, "but it's still standing."

"I did too."

She sidestepped toward him. "We know they're not real, right? If they don't leave footprints, and if our shots don't hurt 'em—maybe they can't hurt *us*."

Something sure hurt Willis and Goodman and Waszewski, Foley thought, but before he could reply, fingerlike claws two feet long slammed onto the top of the cruiser from behind it, and then clenched to shatter the windshield and crumple the roof in a screaming of metal. The front of the car tilted backward onto its end and was raised clear of the ground. It hung suspended above them, the contents of the unlatched trunk spilling out onto the dirt at their feet. The headlights, still on, stabbed up into the sky for an instant, illuminating a horned, oblong head as big as a Volkswagen, with giant yellow eyes and rows of ragged teeth—and then the police car was flung aside. It sailed ten yards or more and landed with a crunching *thud* in a tangle of speaker-posts. The lights winked out.

"Okay, so maybe they *can* hurt us," Katie whispered.

She and Foley stood back-to-back, leaning against each other. He could hear more wheezing and growling, getting louder. But his vision was adjusting to the absence of the headlights, and, true to its name, the drive-in was bathed in the glow of the stars and the rising moon. Whatever had destroyed his car had turned away for the moment, but a dozen other shapes were weaving and advancing, each of them horribly disfigured or of unnatural size. He fired another blast into one of the monsters—*Reptilicus?*—and it accomplished nothing. They were closing in.

It occurred to Foley that he could run and try to distract them long enough for Katie to reach Greg's cruiser. But it was too far away, and he doubted she'd leave him anyway.

Off to his right, something roared. Something else howled. He saw Wasp Woman, her eyes bulging and her razor-sharp appendages reaching and scraping; the Fly, with its paper-thin wings and monstrous eyes; and several sickly pale creatures with oversized hands that had to be the Mole People. Towering above them all was the scaly, dinosaur-like sea monster Gorgo. Foley could smell their zoo-like stench, could hear them muttering and snarling.

Then he saw it.

Right there on the ground beside him, in the moonlit clutter that had poured out of the open trunk when his patrol car was lifted . . . And he knew what he had to do.

"Quick," he said. He handed Katie the shotgun. "When I tell you to, start firing—first your pistol, then this. I'll be kneeling, so shoot in all directions. Understand?"

"What're you gonna do?"

"Just trust me. I only need ten seconds."

The creatures were very close now, on all sides. From the corner of his eye, Foley saw the snapping, doglike snout of a Killer Shrew, and ducked just as the huge stinger of the Black Scorpion scythed past his ear. Behind him he heard Katie curse and use the shotgun to club away the nearest of the Giant Leeches.

With a murmured prayer Foley drew his revolver, aimed it carefully at one end of the low building fifty feet away, and shouted, "*Now!*"

As she started shooting, he fired six times, *pow-pow-pow-pow-pow-pow*, then dropped to his knees and grabbed a black plastic case from the items he'd seen on the ground beside him. He opened it, fitted its contents together, and looked up again at the building. He saw that the fuel drums at the end of the open shed were now leaking gasoline through the six holes he'd shot into them a moment ago. As Katie blazed away behind him, Foley aimed again, past the surrounding creatures, and this time what he fired was a magnesium flare that traced a bright orange arc through the night and into the shed.

He saw it hit home, shouted for Katie to get down, and threw himself over her in the dirt and wrapped her in his arms and squeezed his eyes shut while the world turned red and the air caught fire and the ground heaved underneath them.

FOLEY LOOKED AROUND at the rising water, at the circling sharks. The tide was coming in, and the rock he was standing on would soon be submerged. He'd tied his orange T-shirt to one end of a long, jagged board from his sunken boat's hull and planted the board upright in a crevice of his tiny rock-island. The shirt flapped gaily in the morning wind. Having done all he could, he sat down, pulled his feet in close and away from the water, shut his eyes, and waited.

And the impossible happened. Twenty minutes later he heard someone calling. A boat was headed toward him, two men rowing, another standing in the bow. A long white yacht sat at anchor a hundred yards away. When the boat bumped against his rock, and the standing man helped him aboard, Foley almost asked, *How could you see my signal when I couldn't see your ship?* Instead he just said, "You saved me."

"It was you who saved *me*," the man replied. But it was a female voice.

Foley opened his eyes and saw Katie. She was sitting at his bedside. Smiling.

He tried to turn his head to look around—then winced and raised a hand to touch the bandage above his ear.

"Take it easy," she said. "The doctor'll be glad to see you're awake."

Foley moved his eyes, took in the bright window, the bouquet of flowers on the sill, the small TV hanging in the corner.

He drew a shaky breath and exhaled. "How long have I been out?"

"It's Friday morning," Katie said.

Friday... He tried to remember. The otherworldly battle at the drive-in had been what? Wednesday night?

Then he had another thought.

"You were in my dream," he said.

Her eyes twinkled. "The one where I saved you?"

"No, a different dream. The other day, when I was sleeping at my desk in the office—"

"That's because I was the one who woke you up."

"No. Someone walked to me through the sand, to my beach chair." He paused, and swallowed. He hadn't realized it, until now. "It was you. You were there with me."

Blushing, she said, "Billy, I think you're still a little groggy—"

He shook his head. "I'm fine. Just thinking out loud." *Wishing out loud*, he thought. But there was something else they needed to discuss. "Are we alone?" he asked.

She looked at the door. "Right now we are."

"Tell me what happened."

Katie let out one of those it's-a-long-story sighs. "You did it," she said. "That's what happened. You killed them, Billy. You killed all of them, at once."

"No—I mean, what happened, *exactly*."

She leaned forward and gently squeezed his hand. "Well... I saw you fire the flare gun, heard you yell at me to duck. I did, and you landed on top of me, and just as one of those things leaped at us—it all stopped."

"Stopped?"

"They disappeared. All of them. I heard—felt—the blast, and they just vanished. Like you must've thought they would. When the building blew up, with the film reels—so did they."

He nodded, thinking about that. His last-ditch gamble had worked. "Were you hurt?"

"No. You shielded me. You're burned pretty bad, but they say you'll be okay. Your shirt was on fire, and it took me a minute to realize it, and when I did I rolled us over and put it out. Before that, though, you got hit, and passed out."

"Hit with what?"

"You won't believe it. When the fuel cans blew, they took out not just the building but the car parked next to it. You were struck in the head by a lug wrench from Greg's trunk." She looked as if she might cry. "Could've been worse. His cruiser's hood landed two feet from us, and I heard that old TV set we saw in one of the rooms was blown right through the middle of the movie screen, seventy-five yards away. Went through it like a slug through a bullseye."

A silence passed. He thought for awhile, then focused on her. "They're really gone?"

"They really are. You destroyed their source," she said. "Bill Foley, monster hunter."

He broke out a smile. "We ain't 'fraida no ghosts."

"No, we ain't."

Another silence. "What about our story?"

"Good point," she said. "We need to make sure we agree."

"What's your version?"

"A mix of truth and lies. I told them a guy smoking a cigarette in a long black coat came out as we approached the building, we shouted a warning, he shot at us, we returned fire, some of our rounds probably hit the stored fuel drums, and his cigarette must've blown the place up."

Foley thought that over, and nodded. "That's good. I'll say the same."

"At first I worried because they'll only find Greg's remains, not my made-up villain's—but the state experts say the temperature in there was hot enough to melt bones. Our story should work. I told them we might never know whether this man committed all three murders or only that of our deputy."

Both of them fell silent. In a hushed voice he said, "I still can't believe Greg's dead." *And that I was the one who suggested he get out in the field more.* Foley wished he'd told his deputy never to leave the office again.

She nodded, tears shining in her eyes. "But we also know—you and I, at least—that there'll be no more killings."

After a moment Foley asked, "What about our mashed-up car?"

"It was inside what they're calling 'the blast radius.' Its gas tank exploded. Nothing left."

"And the guy the old man saw, in the football jacket?"

"I didn't mention that to 'em," she said, "but it's in our earlier notes. They'll probably be searching for him."

"I've heard teenage werewolves are hard to find."

Katie sniffled, smiled, and then turned serious. "It's a shame, in a way. We know what really happened, you and I, and even though it's the truth ... we'll never be able to tell anyone."

He smiled too. "Never say never. It could be a horror novel. Change the names, different city and state, different people, use a pseudonym ... "

"You really *are* delirious," she said. "Who would write this masterpiece? You?"

"Why not? I even have a title: *The Starlite Drive-In*."

She barked a laugh. "Fine. But I think I should be co-author."

"That makes sense. Both of us'll need something to do down there."

Her face changed, and went very still. "Sheriff Foley," she said. "Are you asking me to go with you? To Jamaica?"

He looked into her eyes. "That depends."

"On what?"

He grinned. "Can you make a mango daiquiri?"

JOHN M. FLOYD's work has appeared in more than 250 different publications, including Alfred Hitchcock's Mystery Magazine, Ellery Queen's Mystery Magazine, The Strand Magazine, Woman's World, The Saturday Evening Post, Mississippi Noir, *and* The Best American Mystery Stories. *A former Air Force captain and IBM systems engineer, John is also an Edgar Award nominee, a three-time Derringer Award winner, and a three-time Pushcart Prize nominee. His seventh book,* The Barrens, *is scheduled for release in fall 2018.*

THE TRUCK COVERED IN COLORFUL SIGNS touting, *Dr. Morbismo's InsaniTERRORium Horror Show!* pulled up at 11:20 a.m. before the Rialto Theatre in Ginmill, Texas. They'd made the drive from the motel in San Antonio in three hours, expecting to find a dusty, dying small town with a ramshackle theater that held maybe two hundred. But Ginmill seemed active, and the Rialto was, surprisingly, an honest-to-Abe old-fashioned movie palace, complete with a long, ornate marquee, glass displays on either side of the six-door entrance, and a ticket booth outside.

There were three people in the cab of the truck; all three stared out

DR. MORBISMO'S INSANITERRORIUM HORROR SHOW

BY LISA MORTON

This new era wanted thrills, not gentle wonder . . .

at the Rialto as if they'd just seen snow in a Panhandle summer. The older man on the passenger side asked, "Jean, are you sure this is the right theater?"

The woman who rode in the center of the truck, one skirted thigh pressed up against the gear shift, pulled a lined notebook out of a case on her lap. She read notes scribbled down on a page and then looked out the window. "No, this is it—the Rialto at 120 Main Street in Ginmill."

The driver, a tall thirty-year-old named Sam with a flop of auburn hair that a lot of women liked, said, "Why, hell, Doc, this might be the biggest joint we ever played!"

"Don't swear in front of Jean," the older man grumbled.

"Papa," Jean said, addressing Doc, "I may only be twenty, but I've already heard plenty of swearing."

Doc glowered at nothing in particular before turning away to step down from the cab. The other two followed as Doc examined the ticket booth and tiled entryway.

"I'll tell ya one thing," Sam said, "this theater's been out of commission for a while." Doc turned to the other man, who was pointing at a poster in one of the glass displays. In vivid green and black, a woman screamed beneath the title, *The Thing from Another World.* "That picture came out two years ago. Even the drive-ins haven't had it for at least a year."

Doc swiped a finger through dust on the box office counter and said over his shoulder, "Jean, tell me again how you found this joint."

Jean shrugged. "They were in my booking guide."

"And how old's your booking guide?"

Jean muttered something neither of them heard.

A car pulled up and parked behind their truck. An enthusiastic young man leapt out, whistling as he examined the lurid signs covering the truck. "Dr. Morbismo's InsaniTERRORium Horror Show—ain't that somethin'?" He paused before a part of the banner that advertised: *Mutilo the Giant Bloodthirsty Beast!* "Is this Mutilo really a giant?"

Sam—who donned the sweaty, threadbare Mutilo costume for every performance, and who stood 5'11" in stocking feet—snickered, but was silenced by a glare from Doc. The skinny, enthusiastic new arrival turned away from the truck and approached with one hand thrust out. "Oh, sorry, forgettin' my manners. I'm Ronnie Harwood. Are you Doctor Morbismo?"

As he pumped Doc's hand, Doc replied, "Actually I'm Fred Knox from Columbus, Ohio, but you can call me Doc."

Ronnie moved onto Jean. "And you must be Mrs. Knox, the one I made the arrangements with. You're the doc's wife?"

Jean shook his hand, her lips curled in amusement. "Daughter and assistant."

Ronnie didn't release her hand, but added, "Gosh, you're 'bout as pretty as a movie star!"

Sam stepped forward to grab Ronnie's hand, pulling his attention away from Jean. "And I'm Doctor Morbismo's other assistant, Sam. So you manage the Rialto?"

"Oh, no—I *own* it. I inherited it from my pa when he passed on six months back, God rest his soul. Hey, I reckon y'all wanna see the inside, right?"

"We'd like to see the stage, yes," Doc said.

Ronnie rushed forward with keys to unlock one of the doors opening into the lobby. "If you folks'll just wait right here, I'll turn on the lights." He vanished into the dark space.

Sam conferred softly with Doc and Jean. "Well, I guess a recent inheritance explains why it hasn't been used."

Doc looked around, unconvinced. "I dunno, Sam . . . it looks like it's been out of commission for longer than six months. Who lets a beautiful space like this just sit?"

The lights in the lobby went on, and the trio gaped.

The interior of the Rialto was an art deco masterpiece. A glass snack counter stretched fifty feet, while on either side of the lobby, wide, winding staircases were flanked by intricate gold columns. The carpet featured a complex geometric pattern in red and black, the mosaic behind the snack counter (showing cowboys and Indians sharing a meal together) was worthy of a museum. Despite light wear and a layer of dust, the Rialto was a well-preserved tribute to an era when style mattered as much as functionality.

"Wow," Sam said. "This one's a beauty."

After a few seconds, Ronnie reappeared. "I got the house lights on inside the theater, so we can take a look."

"Mr. Harwood," Jean asked, gazing around in astonishment, "when was the Rialto built?"

"Oh, ain't she sweet? Built in 1910 as a vaudeville theater, then converted to moving pictures in 1925. My daddy bought her twenty years ago, just about the time the movies got sound. She seats a thousand. Wasn't that long ago that this place was packed every weekend. Folks would come from as far away as Nacogdoches."

Ronnie pushed open leather-upholstered padded double doors, and they stepped into the theater.

The cavernous space was even more impressive than the lobby. Above and on the side, balconies overlooked the main floor. The seats were carved wood, upholstered in more of the geometric-patterned cloth. The ceiling featured intricate wood designs painted in contrasting colors and punctuated with huge wrought-iron chandeliers. The screen was hidden behind a curtain that showed a picturesque vista of the sun setting over the Texas prairie.

"Holy cow," Jean breathed out.

Doc, though, was already making his way to the stage. He stopped at a waist-high lip just before the raised stage, looking down. "It's got an orchestra pit. And a proscenium arch with real wings—hallelujah!"

Ronnie scratched his dirty blond hair in perplexity but said, "I told ya it was nice!"

Doc climbed the steps at one side of the stage, paced it back and forth, peeked behind the curtains and then strode to center stage. "Well, this'll do just fine!"

Even without amplification, his voice boomed out across the seats.

The Rialto took him back to the great theaters he'd played in his youth, when he'd been a young magician (*The Great Knox!*) touring the East Coast. Jean's mother, Ethel, had been his assistant then; they'd both been young—he was dashing, with his pencil-thin mustache and piercing eyes, she glamorous, with her perfect figure clad in sequins and stockings—and he'd loved every minute of it. They'd thrilled audiences nightly, becoming successful enough to need two trucks and a permanent company of six assistants. There'd been nothing brilliant about The Great Knox—he possessed neither Keller's genius for creating new illusions nor Houdini's charisma—but he knew that some of his audience left in wonder, lifted from mundane existence for a few precious hours. He liked to say that as a magician his greatest trick was making memories appear.

But then audiences had grown weary of magic, the motion pictures had captured hearts with larger-than-life glowing (and talking and singing) images, and Ethel had died of pneumonia somewhere east of Oklahoma City, leaving Fred with mounting bills and a two-year-old daughter. Wonder was harder to find; memories weren't enough.

One day Fred heard that a former magician named El-Wyn was wowing audiences and box offices with something new called a "spook show." Fred attended a performance and was simultaneously amused by its simplicity and astonished by the viewers' colossal response. Most of the show could have been Fred's—it consisted of standard routines like a Spirit Cabinet, the Dancing Handkerchief, the Floating Light Bulb, with accompanying patter about ghosts and The Great Beyond. It was the grand finale, however, that had the audience screaming: a three-minute blackout as El-Wyn's assistants, invisible in black clothing, flew ghosts made of cloth coated with radium paint through the theater. The spectators screamed, hooted, and howled laughter at the greenish, glowing specters soaring over their heads. This new era wanted thrills, not gentle wonder.

On the way out of the theater, The Great Knox had the same thought that so many other failing magicians had: *I could do that.* He didn't completely like it, but there were bills to pay and Jean to look after.

So he *did* do it. That had been eighteen years ago.

It hadn't been a bad living. Doc regretted missing so much of Jean's growing up (she'd been raised by his sister), but as soon as she'd graduated high school she'd come to work for him. Along with Sam, they made a great team.

And playing a gorgeous old palace like the Rialto nearly made Doc's eyes moist.

"Excuse me, Ronnie . . . ?" That was Sam. Doc turned away from examining the backstage area to see his assistant flagging down the eager young owner.

"Yes, sir?"

With one eyebrow cocked, Sam asked, "Level with me: Why are you renting to us?"

A flicker of panic raced across Ronnie's face before his smile returned. "I love spook shows! We haven't had one at the Rialto in a long time, and I—"

Sam cut him off. "Looks to me like you haven't had *anything* at the Rialto in a long time."

Ronnie looked down and shuffled one foot like a kid caught stealing a nickel. "Well, sir, that's my fault. I'm just not the businessman my daddy was. *Heck fire*, a year ago I was working in a gas station."

Doc knew the kid was fudging, and from the look on Sam's face, Sam saw it, too. It was a worthy question, but Doc loved the Rialto and wanted to play here. Before Sam could continue the interrogation, Doc intervened. "Ronnie, can you show us the dressing rooms, please?"

Sam thankfully took the hint and shut up.

Ronnie led the way into the right side of the backstage area. Down a short hall was a row of doors. Ronnie opened one, reached in, flicked on lights. Doc was pleased to see a small, clean room with chairs, mirrors, and vanity. "Thank you for keeping it nice."

Ronnie glowed. "You bet, Doc."

Sam began going over details with Ronnie about getting their equipment in place for tonight's late show.

"Are there gonna be ghosts?" Ronnie asked.

"Oh, there are gonna be *plenty*," Sam answered. "We've even got ghost *spiders*."

Jean interrupted the startled look on Ronnie's face to ask, "You got the movie we asked for, right?"

Ronnie's eyes darted nervously. "I . . . uh . . . was going to tell you about that. I couldn't get *I Walked With a Zombie*, but I got somethin' just as good."

"And what's that?" Sam asked.

"*Bela Lugosi Meets a Brooklyn Gorilla*. Oh, and which one of y'all runs the projector?"

Jean stepped forward, shoving a sheaf of papers under Ronnie's twitching nose. "Mr. Harwood, I've got a signed agreement here that states quite plainly that it's up to *you* to provide the projectionist."

"Well," Ronnie said, looking anywhere but at Jean, "it's just that our old projectionist moved to Houston a few months back, and I don't know of anyone else in Ginmill who can run one of these things . . . "

"Oh hell," Sam said, before turning to Doc with up-held hands. "Sorry. I know—swearing."

Doc waved it all off. "Never mind. We'll do the show without a movie."

Jean asked, "What about all the ads that have already gone out? They mention the movie."

Doc asked Ronnie, "You got a mimeograph machine?"

"Yes, sir! Got one in Daddy's old office. Works just fine."

Turning to Jean, Doc said, "Jean, we'll need to run off flyers to pass out around town."

"I'm on it."

To Sam and Ronnie, Doc said, "Good. Now let's get that truck unloaded."

Leaving Jean to grab some clip art and make a new flyer, the men walked out of the theater. Ronnie directed Sam to bring the truck around to the back, where the Rialto had a loading dock. As they began to unpack, moving in the huge haunted cemetery backdrop, the Asa levitation equipment, and the trunks and boxes of equipment, Doc went inside to the stage to start arranging.

When he walked back into the dressing room, Jean was pale, clutching herself, mouth still open in shock.

Doc rushed forward. "What's wrong—?"

"I . . . Daddy, I . . ." Jean dropped into the old wooden chair at the vanity. "Something *very* strange just happened."

Jean wasn't prone to either exaggeration or hallucination. Doc pulled up another chair and sat by her side. "Tell me."

"Well, I was standing there, pasting together the new flyer, and the lights started to dim. I looked up, thinking there must be a problem with the power in here, and then something touched me."

"Like what?"

"It felt for all the world like a hand stroking my head. I glanced in the mirror and thought I saw someone behind me, but when I turned— *no one was there.*"

"Jean Marie Knox, are you trying to tell me that you saw a *ghost?*" Doc tried to keep his tone even—his only child had mastered bookkeeping in three weeks when she was still a teenager, she was the most level-headed soul he'd ever known—but magicians were among the most skeptical folks on earth.

"I know how it sounds, but . . . well, doggone it, I've had this feeling like I was being watched ever since we got here."

Doc turned his eye on the room, looking for stray spider webs, air vents, anything like the tricks they used every night to tease audiences, but there was nothing. With a sigh, he turned back to his daughter, placing a comforting hand on her shoulder. "Honey, why don't you go outside and find us a place for lunch. Sam and I will finish unpacking, then meet you out on the front sidewalk."

Jean was plainly relieved. "Okay." She tidied up her papers and left.

Ronnie watched her go before asking, "Everything okay, Doc?"

"I'm sure it'll be fine," Doc answered.

But he wondered what could possibly have gotten into his daughter.

IT WAS NEARLY 1 P.M. BEFORE they were seated in a worn leatherette booth in Pokey's Diner, a block from the Rialto. A middle-aged waitress with a massively-teased hairdo and a tired smile handed them menus. "Got a special today on fried chicken, comes with mashed potatoes and green beans. Best in the county."

Sam immediately returned his menu. "Good enough for me . . ." He squinted at her name tag before adding, " . . . Babe."

They all ordered the lunch special, and though they hadn't sampled all the other fried chicken in the county, they agreed that Babe had told the truth. They discussed details for the night's show—the foot controls on the Asa Levitation needed some adjustment, they needed to mix up more fake blood for the jigsaw dismemberment effect—but broke off when their check appeared. Sam pulled out his wallet, removed a twenty—a great deal more than the cost of the three lunch specials—and handed it to Babe with the check and a question. "So, have you been around this town long?"

"Sweetie," she said, deliberately accentuating her drawl as she thrust one bony hip out, "I was born in this heap and ain't never got out."

"Then maybe you can tell us why the Rialto Theater looks like nobody's used it for two years."

Babe didn't answer, but her eyes darted to the next booth over, where a young man sat with his back to them. Without turning, the man said, "*I* can tell you all about that."

Looking vaguely disgusted, Babe snatched the money and check and headed over to the register. The young man turned to face them, and Doc saw that he was good-looking, maybe Jean's age, with jet black hair and skin the color of caramel candy. "The good people of Ginmill think it's my fault, after all."

Sam swigged his coffee before asking, "And why's that?"

"Because the Rialto is haunted, and they think I murdered the fella who's now the ghost."

The diner fell completely silent. Doc looked around and saw that it wasn't just his table—every other conversation had died, with all eyes on the man who'd just spoken. After a few seconds, a middle-aged couple sitting a few booths down slapped bills on the table, glared in their direction, and walked out without another word.

The young man sagged in resignation. "See? They hate me."

Doc turned to look the man in the eye. "Well, I don't. Would you care to join us and tell us your side of the story?"

"Where you folks from? And why do you care?"

"We care," Sam said, "because we rented the Rialto to perform in tonight. See, we got a ghost show to put on."

"You got problems, then," the young man said as he pulled up a chair. "They think the Rialto's already got ghosts. Ain't nobody gonna set foot in there now."

Doc and Sam exchanged a worried look, but Jean thrust a hand out to the man. "My name's Jean Knox, this is my dad Fred, and this is his assistant Sam."

The young man shook hands, relaxing as he realized they were friendly. "Billy Crockett."

Jean turned a smile on Billy, and Doc wasn't sure how he felt when he saw it returned. "Like Davey?"

"He was supposedly a great uncle on my pa's side. My mom, though, she's from Juarez."

"So, Billy," Doc said, anxious to break up the lingering smile being shared by his daughter and this town boy, "tell us what happened."

Billy's smile fell. He looked down, shrugging. "Ain't much to tell. Jim Black was my best friend. We grew up together, played music together, eventually got jobs together at the Rialto. Back then it pulled in hundreds every night. Jim and I worked there as ushers. At the end of every show, we'd go in and clean up all the popcorn buckets and candy wrappers.

"One night we were working up in the balcony and we got into a fight—nothing major, just a silly thing about a scene in the movie. We yelled at each other, but we did that all the time, didn't mean nothin' by it. But that one night Jim backed up hard, hit the balcony railing, and flipped over it. He broke his neck, was dead by the time I got down there to him."

Jean asked, "So folks thought you pushed him?"

"Yeah. In court, Beau Harwood, the Rialto's owner, testified that he'd heard us fighting up there. And Jim's folks refused to believe that their son could've just slipped, so they really blamed me. My mom bein' Mexican didn't help any."

Billy looked away, and Doc felt for the young man when he saw his eyes glinting.

Billy gulped once and went on. "Lucky for me, the jury agreed with my defense that there was a 'reasonable doubt'. But the Rialto just wasn't the same after that. As if it wasn't bad enough that some folks believed a murder had happened there, others started reporting weird goings-on."

"Like what?" Sam asked.

"Like spots that suddenly got cold for no reason, or seeing somebody out of the corner of their eye, but when they turned nobody was there. A lot of girls came out saying somebody had touched them."

Doc glanced at his daughter and saw her shiver.

"My mom has an aunt who's a *curandera*—you know, like a healer—and she says that spirit won't leave 'til it's good 'n' ready. Anyway, the Rialto couldn't hardly sell a ticket. Then Beau got sick and just let it go. I think his son Ronnie would like to get it going again, so he brought in you folks."

"What do you think?" Jean asked.

Billy clutched himself tight. "All I know is I wouldn't go in there."

Silence descended on the group for a few seconds. Finally Doc leaned forward, rubbing his chin thoughtfully. "Billy, what if you had the chance to prove to everyone that you're innocent?"

"Sure, but . . . how?"

"You be a part of our show tonight. We'll stage a séance to contact Jim. And then we relay the message to everyone that Jim says you didn't do it."

Billy looked perplexed for a second before realization crossed his face. "You mean you'd . . . *lie?*"

Jean jumped in. "It's not a lie, Billy—you *didn't* do it."

"I don't know . . . I think folks around here just *want* to believe I did it."

"We'd pay you," Sam said, as he opened his wallet.

"I was supposed to practice with my band tonight," Billy added.

"You've got a band?" Jean asked.

"Yeah—Billy and the Blue Burners. Jim used to be our drummer. We'd just cut a record when he . . . when *it* happened."

Jean shot her dad a look, and Doc asked, "You any good?"

Billy didn't answer. Instead he walked to a juke box in the corner of the diner, fed a coin in, punched a number, and returned to the table. After a few seconds the diner filled with the joyous racket of drums, twangy guitar, boogie woogie piano, and a high young voice singing about "dancin' in the barnyard."

"That's you?" Jean asked.

"Yeah. I'm amazed they haven't yanked our record out of this juke box yet. Probably the only one that's left."

Jean listened for a few seconds, smiling and bobbing her head. Even Sam tapped a foot as he noted, "That's pretty good stuff."

"I thought so. Now nobody wants to hire us, though. We're that band with the Mexican who killed his best friend."

Jean looked at Doc, her eyebrows raised, and Doc understood her question. "Go ahead," he said.

"Billy," Jean asked, "how about if you and your band open our show tonight? The movie we usually show first fell through, so you'd be doing us a favor. Your band plays for a while, then you join us for our show. We all make money, and maybe folks in this town get reminded how good you are."

Billy stared for a second in disbelief before barking a short, incredulous laugh. "Thanks, but I really don't think—"

He broke off as Sam pulled a wad of bills out of his wallet, peeled off five twenties, and set them on the table. "Now that's just an advance against the full payment. You'd get the same amount that would've gone to renting the movie."

"And the projectionist," Doc grumbled.

Billy's fingers began to walk across the table toward the cash. "What would I have to do in the show?"

Doc said, "We announce you during the Spirit Slates. You come on stage. I'll pretend to be in contact with the spirit of Jim, we'll ask him if you killed him, then we show the audience a message written on the slates that says you're innocent."

"That's it?"

Doc nodded. "That's it. You don't have to say anything if you don't want to. It'll just take a couple of minutes."

Billy slapped a hand down on the greenery and pulled it toward him. "Not like anybody else in this town is handing out jobs." He inhaled deeply before saying, "Okay, just tell me what time we should be at the theater."

AT 6:03 P.M., DOC WAS ONSTAGE checking out the placement of his equipment when he heard a loud clatter. He looked around and saw that the two Spirit Slates had fallen from their usual spot on a table next to the Spirit Cabinet. They'd never fallen like that before; as he walked to them he glanced around but saw no one.

He picked up the slate that normally held the "ghostly" message behind a fake insert; tonight the message should have read, *BILLY IS INNOCENT*. Instead, the message said, *YOUR GENE IS PRETTY*.

Doc gaped for a second before looking up, anger simmering. He called out, "Who wrote this?"

After a moment Sam emerged from the wings. "Sorry, Doc, did you say something? I was working back in the dressing room."

Doc held up the slate. "Got any ideas?"

Sam laughed. "No, but whoever it is needs to learn how to spell 'Jean'."

"You didn't write this?"

Sam's laughter shut off instantly. "No, Doc, 'course not. Looks like somebody's having some fun with you."

"Fun. Sure."

Doc ground his teeth as he grabbed the slate with the message and went in search of Ronnie Harwood.

"'COURSE I DIDN'T TOUCH your equipment, Doc—heck, that stuff scares me too much!"

Doc held up the slate so Ronnie, who he'd found getting concessions ready in the lobby, could read the message. Ronnie took one look and went pale.

"That's Jim's writing."

"So you're trying to tell me a ghost *really* wrote this?"

Ronnie looked at Doc with guilt plastered over his freckles. "I'm sorry, Doc, I know I shoulda told you about the ghost before you signed the rental papers..."

Doc sighed as he lowered the slate. "Ronnie, look: I don't believe in ghosts. I make fake ghosts for a living. I know every trick in the book. And believe me, when I find who wrote this message, I'm going to throw that book right at them!"

Doc turned and left, already rubbing the message from beyond off the slate.

BILLY AND HIS BAND ARRIVED at 8 p.m. As they began setting up their instruments in front of the curtain (being careful to avoid Doc's equipment just on the other side), Doc noticed that Billy seemed especially anxious, his eyes darting, fingers trembling.

"You going to be able to do this?"

Billy gulped and looked around. "First time I been back in this place. I can just *feel* him here. Makes me edgy, you know?"

Doc almost answered, "No, I *don't* know," but turned and left instead.

AT 9:18 P.M., BILLY AND the Blue Burners finished their sound check. The new flyers Jean had created and run off on the Rialto's mimeo machine had stated that the doors opened at 9:30.

Doc was in the dressing room, relaxing for a few moments with a paper cup of bourbon. He figured he'd need it to get through this show.

Sam poked his head in. "Good news—the flyers worked, because the line to get in is around the block!"

"That's good. Thanks, Sam."

Sam ducked back out, leaving Doc alone. He sipped his bourbon, enjoying the few moments of peace before what he thought would be an unusually raucous show. As the ghostmaster, he always tried to stir up belief with an opening speech about "contact from the Great Beyond," and "we cannot always control the spirits, so don't be surprised if you feel a tap on your shoulder and there's no one there." But like nearly all professional magicians, Doc was a lifelong skeptic. He knew other folks wanted—no, *needed*—to believe in things like magic and ghosts, and he was happy to fulfill that need even if he'd never shared it.

That's what he was thinking when the lights went out.

"Oh, for God's sake," Doc grumbled, figuring that the old Rialto's wiring hadn't been checked in a long time.

Something vaguely iridescent appeared at the corner of his vision. He turned to look, could just make out a glowing mass floating near the ceiling in one corner. As he watched, the wavering, oblong shape began to move slowly across the room.

"Oh, haha, Sam, very funny. Now turn the damn lights back on!"

There was no response. The unformed glow reached the far corner of the room and seemed to pass through the wall.

The lights went back on.

Doc was alone in the room.

He cursed as he slopped some of the bourbon onto his shirt, then he rose from his chair, went to the door of the dressing room, opened it, looked in both directions but saw no one.

He returned to his dressing room table, grabbed the bourbon bottle and swigged directly from it, trying to dispel the chill that had grabbed onto him.

AT 9:32, THE RIALTO'S DOORS opened and the crowd started filing in. Peering out from behind the curtains, Doc saw an excited mob, with boys grabbing their girls to elicit shrieks while others shouted, "Hey, Jim!"

He knew that this was a dangerous stunt; this whole evening could boil over into a riot. But he liked Billy and thought the poor kid had been dealt a bad hand. If he could correct that *and* make a little money, he'd consider it a great night. It was worth the risk.

At least he *hoped* it was.

AT 10:05, BILLY AND the Blue Burners came out on stage.

The crowd started to jeer. Somebody near the front yelled, "Dirty killer!"

Billy ignored it. He kept his head down and went straight to his guitar. Watching from backstage, Doc had to admire Billy's courage . . . but he thought Jean, standing next to him, might be admiring something more about the handsome musician.

Billy turned to his band—three boys whose flannel shirts matched Billy's, and who looked nervous as hell—and counted off a beat.

Within ten seconds of the first song, the crowd had shut up. By the second song they were clapping and hooting with the rhythm. By the fourth song, a few couples were jitterbugging in the aisles.

Doc thought maybe Billy might be the *real* possessor of magic here.

AT 10:53, BILLY AND the Blue Burners finished their set to a round of applause. They made their way off the stage, and Doc watched as Jean gave Billy a hug that he returned with gratitude and relief. Sam and Ronnie cleared the stage of the band's amps, the upright piano, and the drum kit, leaving one mike on a stand.

At 11:01, the curtain came up, and the crowd gasped as they saw Doc and his equipment revealed against the cemetery backdrop.

Doc stepped up to the remaining mike, his expression somber, even menacing. "Good evening," he intoned, deepening his voice. "My name is Doctor Morbismo, and I welcome you to my InsaniTERRORium."

The crowd laughed—as Doc knew they would—until he silenced them with a simple production of flash paper that shot a startling light right from his fingers. The onlookers went silent. Doc continued. "Tonight you will experience things that are far outside of your normal day-to-day existence. You will be here, participating, as together we open the door to the spirit world. I will be your guide for this strange and eerie journey, and although I will be in control, the forces from beyond death cannot always be commanded. We will venture far into those frightening realms, and you will see and hear many things you cannot explain. You will see objects move on their own, messages written by the spirits, and possibly even various ghostly creatures. We will meet the very ghosts who inhabit this theater, and attempt to converse with them. And now ... prepare for the InsaniTERRORium!"

Doc bowed to applause and whistles, then a recording of Saint-Saëns' "Danse Macabre" began to play as Sam pulled the Asa Levitation table forward. Jean entered from stage left, her low-cut evening gown drawing catcalls from the audience. Doc ignored them to focus on the performance: first, he mimed placing his daughter into a hypnotic trance and then he helped her onto the table before taking his place behind it. He placed one foot on the secret hydraulic lift button in the floor as he lifted a hoop that he moved carefully around the table, following the twists and turns in the table's hidden supporting arm. Finally he set the hoop aside, moved his foot to the "down" button, and lowered the table to floor height. As Jean appeared to reawaken from her trance and step from the table, Doc was pleased to hear the music drowned out by applause.

Then someone shouted out, "Show us the *real* ghost!" The call was swiftly accompanied by a murmur of agreement.

Doc knew this crowd wasn't going to settle for a standard evening of classic illusions followed by a staged séance and the black-out. He had to improvise.

"Very well," he said into the stage mic, "let us speak to the spirits. Mr. Crockett, will you please join me on stage?"

Jean gave her father an inquisitive look, but understood when Doc whispered to her, "*Slates.*"

The audience began to mutter and hiss as Billy stepped hesitantly onto the stage, looking far less confident now than he had when singing about girls in twirling skirts who break boys' hearts. He let Jean help him to center stage, where Doc now held the two slates.

A voice shouted, "Here's your chance for revenge, Jimbo!"

The audience howled laughter. Doc palmed another piece of flash paper from a pocket, calling out, "The spirits require *silence*," as the paper ignited in a fiery flame.

It worked; the Rialto went quiet as a tomb.

Doc held up the two slates as he spoke into the mic. "What you see here are two ordinary slates, the kind you might find used to teach children ... but tonight we won't be teaching children, but reaching spirits." Doc handed the slates to Jean, who walked to the lip of the stage, turning the slates end over end. "As you can see, both sides of the slates are empty."

Jean finished showing off the slates, and returned them to Doc, who produced a piece of chalk he'd fished from a pocket as Jean had shown the slates. "Now, here we have a regular piece of chalk. I'm going to place this piece of chalk between these slates, and then I'm going to request that Mr. Crockett ask a question of the spirits who haunt this place."

Doc made a show of placing the chalk between the slates and tying them together with a length of velvet cord. Jean took the mic to Billy, and Doc felt a pang of guilt when he heard how the boy's voice was choked with genuine emotion. "Jim, if you're out there—and I think you are, because I always knew when you were around—I want you to tell everyone here what happened. Tell 'em that we were just horsing around like we always did, that you fell when I was nowhere near you, that I've thought about you *every day since* and wondered if I could've done something to save you. Tell 'em, Jim. *Tell 'em.*"

The next part should've been Jean taking the microphone over to where Doc held the slates out before him, holding it to the slates so the audience could plainly hear the sound of the chalk scratching (really Doc's thumb hidden on the back side). The trick should've ended then with pulling the slates apart to reveal, *I AM JIM*, written on one, and, *BILLY IS INNOCENT*, on the other.

Instead, the slates were suddenly ripped from Doc's two hands by some unseen force.

He gaped with the rest of the audience as they flew across the stage, where one was cast aside violently. The chalk squealed as it was pulled across the surface of the slate. After a few seconds, the chalk dropped and the slate turned to face the audience, who saw these words written on its black surface:

LEAVE
BILLY ALONE.
I JUST FELL.

The lights went out.

Doc almost called out to Sam and Jean to get the ghosts and run through the audience with them, but then a different glow caught his eye. There was another loud noise as the slate fell to the stage, but what the audience was screaming at was the figure forming there, a shimmering blue haze congealing and focusing until it was a boy of maybe seventeen, tall and lanky, with a narrow face and an usher's uniform.

In the audience, people began shouting, "Jim!"

Doc watched, too stunned to move, as the apparition began to glide across the stage, stopping only when its own glow revealed Billy, standing, shaking, with Jean half-crouched in terror behind him. Billy stood his ground, though, as the ghost of his friend came to him, slowly, floating... and then raised its right hand to waist level. Billy didn't try to stifle a sob as he reached out for the hand. At the moment the two hands—one alive, one dead—would have touched, the ghost disappeared and the theater lights came back on.

For a second, no one knew what to do. The audience was frozen. Billy cried. Sam and Jean stared in disbelief.

After a few seconds, Doc stepped forward, grabbed the mic, and said, "And that's our show, folks. Good night!"

WHEN THE TRUCK EMBLAZONED with gaudy banners for *Dr. Morbismo's InsaniTERRORium Horror Show!* pulled out of Ginmill, Texas the next morning at 9:04, it was accompanied by a second truck carrying Billy Crockett and his Blue Burners, who had accepted Doc's invitation the previous night to tour with them as the permanent opening act.

But there was also a fourth passenger on Doc's truck. Neither Doc, Jean, or Sam were quite sure where he rode, but they knew Jim Black was with them. He'd appeared again last night after the show, backstage, and Doc—now a believer—had offered him an afterlife in the ghost show biz. As far as they knew, Jim had accepted.

Dr. Morbismo's InsaniTERRORium Horror Show! would be the only ghost show in the world with the real thing.

LISA MORTON is a screenwriter, author of non-fiction books, and award-winning prose writer whose work was described by the American Library Association's Readers' Advisory Guide to Horror as "consistently dark, unsettling, and frightening". She is the author of four novels and more than 130 short stories, a six-time winner of the Bram Stoker Award, and a world-class Halloween expert. She co-edited (with Ellen Datlow) the anthology Haunted Nights; other recent releases include Ghosts: A Haunted History and the collection The Samhanach and Other Halloween Treats. Lisa lives in Los Angeles.

S HE WAS THE HOTTEST BABE FLINT HAD EVER seen. Flaming red hair, juicy red lips, black eyes full of smoky heat with a voice to match, a body that would make a priest drool. She was with Bruno Gianetti when he first set eyes on her in Sparkie's Tavern, but she wouldn't be for long.

Sparkie's was where a lot of the guys from the Speedway hung out, and Flint was there that day sipping suds and listening to Rick Neale and Sam Clements bull about the hundred-lap main event on Saturday afternoon. He had a table all to himself, like always except when he was with a chick. The other drivers didn't want anything to do with him.

HOT BABE

BY BILL PRONZINI

"Drive all out today, Jack," she said.
"Faster than ever before. Fast, fast, fast."

They all thought he was too reckless on the track, that he'd deliberately caused the last-lap spin-out up north that had killed the kid leading the pack so he could win the race himself.

Well, he had, but so what?

It wasn't the first time he'd gotten away with that kind of tactic. Jockeying claimers and hardtops at the state tracks was dog-eat-dog— you did what you had to do to collect a purse, and to hell with anybody who got in your way.

Saturday's main was the top event in the local racing season. It wasn't official from the Speedway promoters yet, but rumor had it that the purse for the winner would be five percent of the gate. Any way you hashed that out, it came to two grand or better if there was a full house, and there always was whenever they had a hundred-lapper.

Flint and his Deuce had won two mains already this season, and he intended to win this one too. But it wouldn't be easy. There were a lot of good drivers entered, Neale and Clements among them, but the stiffest competition was likely to come from Bruno Gianetti.

Gianetti was real good, drove hard and played almost as rough as Flint. Flint had been racing against him off and on for two years now and knew the Deuce was faster than Gianetti's Dodge on the straightaways if he played it smart; he'd taken him more times than he'd been taken by hanging back, not letting the bugger nose him toward the wall or the infield, then punching out in the stretches. Gianetti was good, all right. But Flint was better. He'd win that two grand prize on Saturday one way or another.

That's what he was thinking, sitting there with his Lucky Lager, when Gianetti came waltzing in with Brenda on his arm and started showing her off, calling her his woman, acting the big-stud role. He'd picked her up at a track down in the Central Valley after winning a $500 purse in what he claimed was a record time. She dug speed, he said, the faster the better, the more hard-nose driving the better.

She didn't deny it.

Flint knew he had to have her as soon as he saw her. Yeah, and she knew it too. The first time their eyes met, sparks crackled between them. Gianetti saw the sparks fly—hell, they probably singed him on the way by—but there wasn't anything he could do about it. He'd been stupid-lucky to get his mitts on her in the first place. He was no prize to look at—big, but with plenty of fat mixed in with the meat, and ugly as sin. Maybe it was the ugliness that had turned her on. Flint was no James Dean himself, but his looks had a hard-ass smolder to them that Gianetti's lacked. He'd never had any trouble getting chicks to drop their pants for him. But none he'd ever had looked half as hot as Brenda. The two of them were made for each other.

Flint figured it would take a little time to yank her away from Gianetti, maybe not until after he won the Speedway main, and that he'd have to maneuver some to do it. But he was wrong. She showed up at his pad that night, wearing the same tight green dress she'd had on at Sparkie's, the flaming red hair hanging low over shoulders, and those juicy lips licked wet.

He said, grinning, "How'd you find me so quick?"

"It wasn't hard. Everybody on the circuit knows Jack Flint."

"Yeah, and the jealous bastards are all afraid of me. But not you, huh?"

"No. Not me."

"You have any trouble getting away from Gianetti?"

"Never mind him," she said. "It's you I want and me you want. I knew it as soon as I saw you this afternoon."

"Baby, so did I."

Two minutes after she came inside, they were going at it hot and heavy. *Man, oh man!* He'd known she'd be a pistol in the sack, but not one as scorching as this. Best he'd ever had by a mile. And she couldn't get enough, wore him out all through the night and part of the morning.

In between times he tried to get her to tell him where she'd been and what she'd been doing before Gianetti got hold of her, but she wouldn't talk about herself. Okay with him. He didn't like talking about his past, either. The present and the future were all that mattered.

"You're mine now," Flint said just before she left. "Not Gianetti's or anybody else's, now or ever."

"And you're mine."

"A hell of a team, you and me. After I win the main on Saturday, we'll take the two grand and head for Vegas, have ourselves a ball before I start burning up the tracks again."

FLINT SPENT THAT AFTERNOON at the Speedway, working on the Deuce's mill, getting the timing right. He'd offered to go with Brenda to collect her stuff in case Gianetti gave her any crap, but she said no, she could handle him and there wouldn't be any hassle. And there wasn't. She was in Flint's pad when he got home, already moved in and waiting in bed for him. She really couldn't get enough. Well, neither could he.

They went out to dinner, and afterward to Sparkie's so this time Flint could be the one to show her off. Gianetti was there, hanging onto the bar next to Rick Neale, pie-eyed drunk. His fat face got even uglier when he saw them.

"Hey, look who's here! The bitch and the son of a bitch."

Flint glared at him. "Shut up, Bruno."

"Yeah? Why don't you come over here and make me?"

Neale said something to him and put a hand on his arm, but Gianetti threw it off. He lurched away from the bar, knocking over his stool, and staggered to the table Flint and Brenda were about to claim, spilling beer from his mug on the way.

"Goddamn woman stealer." Then, with one bleary eye on Brenda, "Goddamn *whore* stealer."

The crowd in there got real quiet.

"You want a piece of me, fat-stuff?" Flint said. "One more crack like that and you'll get more than you can handle."

Gianetti raised the mug threateningly. "How'd you like this shoved up your ass?"

The table hadn't been cleaned off yet; Flint grabbed an empty beer glass, cracked it against the table edge. The top shattered, leaving him with the jagged-edged lower half.

"Hey," Sparkie yelled, "none of that crap in here!"

Flint paid no attention to him. Out of the tail of his eye he could see Brenda standing tense, expectant, her face flushed with excitement. Speed and sex weren't the only things she dug.

"Go ahead, try it," he said to Gianetti. "I'll slice you to ribbons."

Gianetti stayed where he was, breathing like an ox, the mug still raised.

"That's enough!" Sparkie came out from behind the bar, the marlin spike he kept under it clenched in one big hand. "Both of you cool it now, or take it outside."

Gianetti broke the stare-down first. He lowered the mug, backed off a step as Sparkie ran up. "This isn't the end of it, man," he said in slurred tones.

"You got that right."

Sparkie snapped, "Flint, put that glass down and haul your ass out of here. And take her with you."

Flint didn't argue. He set the broken glass on the table, grabbed Brenda's arm, swaggered out with her.

In the parking lot he said, "I saw the way you looked in there. You wanted to see me cut Gianetti, didn't you? Slice him up."

"No. Hurt him, yes, but not like that, with broken glass."

"How then?"

"On the track tomorrow. Find a way to hurt him there."

Flint laughed. "I'll do just that. Count on it, baby."

THE STANDS WERE ALREADY two-thirds full when Flint rolled into the Speedway pit area on Saturday afternoon. It was a little past one o'clock; the first time trials wouldn't start until two. There'd be a packed house, all right.

Brenda was already there, in Section A right behind the starter's flag, the best seating at the track. The promoters gave each of the drivers tickets for two seats there, no charge. Flint backed the trailer into his spot and then went up for a few last words with her.

"Drive all out today, Jack," she said. The feverish excitement was in her eyes again. "Faster than ever before. Fast, fast, fast."

"Pedal to the metal all the way until I'm first past the checkered flag, babe."

Larry Timkins, the fish-faced grease monkey Flint had hired as his pit man, helped him jockey the Deuce off the trailer, gassed her from the five-gallon drum wired to the roll bars inside. Then Flint fired her up. The carbs were running a little rough, so he told Timkins to work on the idling jets.

The time trials started. But when it was time for Flint to make his run around the oval track, he discovered that Timkins had done a piss-poor job adjusting the carbs. His time was good, but not good enough as it turned out. He would have the outside pole in the main.

Gianetti would have the inside.

FLINT STOOD WITH SOME of the other drivers to watch the start of the semi-main—a 35-lapper made up of the twenty-five slowest qualifiers. There wouldn't be any heat races today.

Gianetti was over in the pits with his Dodge. Flint had seen him briefly during the trials, and they'd exchanged glares but that was all. For once Gianetti had kept his fat mouth shut.

The public address announcer called the main event, giving the cars plenty of time to line up on the track in front of the starter's flag. You could feel the tension in the air; the overflow crowd was buzzing. Flint glanced up at Section A. He couldn't see Brenda in the throng, but he knew she'd be on her feet yelling once the race started.

When the announcer finished introducing the drivers, Flint and the others revved up, and then the opening flag dropped. There was plenty of jockeying for position on the first lap, Gianetti hunched over the wheel of his Dodge casting hate-filled side glances in Flint's direction. Then they reached the starter again, got the green flag, and the race was on.

Gianetti was after him right away. Instead of keeping to the outside, he edged over and bumped fenders hard, trying to make Flint lose control and spin out. Flint weaved to avoid him, straightened and floored the Deuce. But Gianetti didn't let him get in front, cutting over just in time. Their fenders grazed again. Flint pulled back, let Clements in Car 12N take the north turn before he did. If he hadn't, Gianetti would have forced him into the wall.

Lap after lap they played hardball dodge-'em, throttles wide open. The other drivers couldn't keep up, or dropped back a notch on purpose so they wouldn't get caught in the grudge duel. The crowd loved the action, making so much noise you could hear them shouting over the roar of the engines. Brenda'd be hollering loudest of all, that frenzied look on her face, urging Flint to make good on his promise, which he damned well would.

The opportunity came on the seventy-sixth lap. Gianetti, his patience gone, pressed him hard and recklessly toward the wall. At the speeds they were traveling it would have been impossible to overtake him. Flint didn't even try. He eased off the gas, letting Gianetti prod him even closer to the wall, their fenders scraping and raising sparks, then he double-clutched into second, trusting the gears to hold, and shoved the accelerator pedal to the floor. A sharp wheel flip to the left caught Gianetti unprepared, made him lose control. The Dodge bounced back, spun, narrowly missed two other cars before it skidded off into the infield.

The yellow caution flag was out when Flint came back around the north turn, well in the lead now. None of the other drivers could overtake him. He had the race won.

Except that he didn't. Without warning, that crazy bastard Gianetti floored his Dodge out of the infield and back onto the track, right in front of the Deuce on the straightaway.

There should have been just enough time to avoid a collision. Flint yanked the wheel hard right, or tried to, but it seemed to lock up in his hands. And then it was too late.

The Dodge fishtailed sideways and the Deuce smacked the driver's side head on.

Crash of rending mental, burst of searing heat and flame—

—and then somehow Flint and the Deuce were out of it, still upright on all four wheels, still moving fast with the track clear ahead. He couldn't believe the Deuce had come through with no visible damage, that he wasn't hurt, not even a scratch. He tried to hit the brakes and gear down, but the impact must have screwed up the hydraulics and the gearbox. The accelerator linkage, too—he couldn't slow down. He could still steer some, but not enough to pull off the track.

The Deuce went hurtling around again, Flint fighting the half-locked wheel to get past cars that had slowed for the red flag. When he came through the south turn he saw the fire truck and the ambulance rushing across the infield, people running toward the two flaming wrecks melded together ahead—*two* wrecks, *two* drivers trapped inside. But that couldn't be, one car was Gianetti's Dodge and the other looked like the Deuce—

Then he was past them and rocketing around the oval again, and when he barreled through the south turn this time the wrecks weren't there, the ambulance and fire truck and running people and other cars and drivers were all gone, nobody was there but him and the Deuce. And the track ahead . . . the track had become an inferno.

"Faster! Faster!"

He heard Brenda's voice shrieking inside his head, only it wasn't inside his head, it was coming from the stands . . . but the stands weren't there anymore either. Where they'd been was a massive wall of flame, Brenda towering in the middle of it, screaming in a voice loud as thunder, "Faster, faster, faster!"

Flint started screaming too. Because now he knew who the hot babe really was, and what she'd meant when she said, "You're mine," and that he'd never stop driving this oval of fire.

A full-time professional writer since 1969, **BILL PRONZINI** *has published more than 80 novels, four nonfiction books, and 350 short stories in a variety of genres; he has also edited or co-edited numerous anthologies. His collection of horror and dark suspense stories,* Night Freight *(Leisure, 2000), was nominated for a Bram Stoker Award by the Horror Writers Association. In 2008 he was honored as a Grand Master by the Mystery Writers of America, their highest award.*

KATIE SITS ON THE EDGE OF MELISSA
Richardson's bed, secretly picking at the satin bedspread. Or maybe, she thinks vaguely, it's silk, or something so expensive she's never heard of it.

"What do you think of this one?"

Katie looks up to see Melissa holding a pink chiffon dress even with her shoulders. The dress has white ribbons running every couple of inches from top to hem; a pretty double wide ribbon serves as a belt. Before Katie can answer, Melissa spins away to show it to the other two girls in the room, practically skipping to where they've emptied

---

THE PROM TREE

BY YVONNE NAVARRO

*"You don't really believe that nonsense
about The Prom Tree, do you?"*

Melissa's jewelry box on the floor and are poking through its contents. The girls look up and squeal appropriately at the same time Katie grimaces to herself and hopes Melissa doesn't pick that one. The color makes her skin look mottled, as though she's spent the last couple of hours dipping into Daddy's rec room bar. Melissa is new in town and her father is a colonel on Post. Sally and Belinda have been best friends since Belinda's family arrived in town a year and a half ago, and Katie wouldn't put it past them to intentionally convince Melissa to wear the most hideous dress possible. Sally is a shuckster—a word she heard her father use when he was talking about someone dishonest—and Katie has known her since her father was stationed here on Fort Huachuca almost four years ago.

Katie slides off the bed and walks over to where all three girls are cooing over the pink dress, then drops to the floor next to Sally and Belinda, ignoring the annoyed look Sally shoots her.

"Let's get this stuff back into the box before something gets lost," Katie says evenly. She also knows Sally sometimes has sticky fingers, so she leans forward before anyone can react and quickly scoops up the jewelry—rings that are no doubt real, a pair of diamond studs, and more. Little things that individually are worth more than her mother earns in months as a secretary at the furniture store off Fry Boulevard. If Sally wants to sacrifice something to The Prom Tree, she needs to look closer to home.

It's funny—but not in a good way—how one of the circles of the most popular girls in Carmichael School always pulls Katie in with them for a school year. The next year, it's a different circle... but again, a popular one. It's like she's the token townie. For the millionth time Katie wishes she had a real best friend, a girl she could talk about boys with, share secrets with, borrow clothes from, who would sit with on her own worn, comfortable couch and eat popcorn while watching *The Millionaire* every Wednesday night. Do these girls hang out with each other? Of course they do... but they never invite Katie. They include Katie now and then because her family's been here for six years; her dad has managed to guarantee his billet for another two, until she can graduate high school and get settled into college. So she *is* a townie—there aren't that many people who remember Sierra Vista when it was Fry, Arizona—and they exclude her for the very same reason: she's old news, boring as reruns of *My Little Margie* and the dust that hangs in the air for most of the school year. As for Katie herself, she continues to let it happen, always in search of that elusive true best friend.

"Definitely the pink one," declares Belinda. Katie cringes inside but knows better than to protest. One more year, she tells herself. Then she'll be out of this town and away from these shallow, spoiled girls. Maybe at college in Flagstaff she'll find the friend she's always wanted.

"Let's head to the soda shop," Melissa says. Her tone is bright but with a hint of a question; she's only been in town a month, so she knows her place—and it's not at the top. Not yet.

"Cool," Sally says, and Belinda nods in agreement.

"I have to pass," Katie says. She has zero money right now, and her small allowance is a long way off. Her dad is a staff sergeant, and her parents' combined salaries aren't bad, but they don't support a lot of extras. "I need to get home and help Mom with stuff."

All three girls make sounds of disappointment as she follows them out of Melissa's house, but there's a tone in there that only Katie catches: the one that makes her realize they don't care, and it hits her in the heart.

Katie heads home on her bike, wheeling easily along the relatively well-maintained roads on Post, then getting her teeth jarred as she comes out of Fort Huachuca and bumps along the poorer streets of downtown Sierra Vista. She goes down Fry but makes sure to turn north on one of the side streets so she won't pass her mom's workplace and run into her boss, Mr. Wright. Her mom is home by now, but Mr. Wright looks at Katie longingly every time he sees her, letting his eyes study parts of her body that he shouldn't—never in front of Mom, of course. Katie doesn't say anything because her mom has what her dad calls "that damned Irish temper that's gonna get you in trouble someday." Katie thinks her mom would probably pick up the heavy Underwood typewriter on her desk and throw it at her boss's head if she saw him licking her daughter up and down with his eyes.

The Arizona sun is high and hot and Katie's sweating by the time she turns into the driveway of their rental house, skidding to a stop just like she did when she was a kid. She drops the old bike in the middle of the driveway and goes around to the back, where the windows are open and she can smell fresh apple pie.

"Hey, Mom," she says as she bangs through the screen door.

"Hay comes from a barn," her mother says. Gloria Morgan is elbow-deep in dirty dishes. She wipes the back of her hand across her forehead. "You're late. I told you to be home by three to put the pie in."

Katie glances at the clock above the cabinets—dancing chickens, how stylish—and sees with a start that it's almost five-thirty. How times flies when you're with your *friends*. "Sorry."

"I got the pie in the oven so that it'll be done by the end of dinner, but the house is going to be hot. I don't want to hear any complaints about it."

"I won't," Katie tells her. "I promise." What her mom doesn't say is that Dad is going to be ticked off. He's been out on the Fort Huachuca rifle range all day, working what her mom affectionately calls baby soldiers until they can actually hit something—hopefully not one another—they shoot at. He'll like the pie but not the heat bleeding from the kitchen into the dining room. And Staff Sergeant Frank Morgan could complain all he wanted, thank you very much.

Katie turns toward the hallway with her mind already wandering back to the three girls she was with after school. She hears her mom say something almost as an afterthought before she stops and goes back. "What?"

"I asked if you would please dry these so I have more room." Gloria inclines her head toward the mound of mixing bowls and plates next to the single metal sink. From the looks of it, her mom had been cooking since she'd gotten home from work.

Katie takes a spot on her mom's left and starts wiping the dishes, something she has never understood in the Arizona climate. In mid-May, when it was already blistering outside, they'd dry on their own in no time if they were just spread on the counter for a little while. "Are you sure you don't want to—"

"No," Gloria says firmly. "Your dad will want to see a clean kitchen when he comes home, not a mess."

"Okay." There's no point in arguing.

"Besides," her mom adds as she puts another clean dish on the stack, "it'll also mean fewer dishes to wash after dinner."

Katie nods although she thinks to herself that the only reason that's true is that every dish in the house is either in the sink or on the counter.

"So how did school go today?"

Katie shrugs. "Same old thing."

Gloria smiles slightly. "Same teachers, same classes?"

"Sure."

Gloria looks at her out of the corner of her eye. "Boys?"

Katie feels her face turn red, the heat going quickly up from her jawline to the tops of her cheekbones. "Mom!"

Gloria's small smile widens into a grin. "You think I don't know about boys, hon? It wasn't so long ago that I was sixteen, too."

Katie shakes her head. "Well, no boys."

Gloria rinses another couple of dishes in silence, then swishes a handful of silverware around in the dishpan. "Prom's next week."

"I know that," she says sharply.

"Tone, please."

"Sorry, Mom." Katie waits for her mother to drop the small bundle of spoons into the towel. "I just ... no one's asked me," she finally admits. Her hands are a little too tight around the towel and she forces her fingers to relax before her mom notices. The look Gloria gives her conveys that her mother is sorry; still, there's no pity in her eyes, and for that Katie's grateful.

"Is there a girlfriend you can go with?"

Katie bites back a sarcastic reply and instead simply says, "No."

Gloria's face falls. "Oh." For a moment she doesn't say anything. "I suppose it's hard to find a friend when the adults are always PCSing."

PCSing—*Permanent Change of Station*. Katie knows the military term well, although it hasn't applied to their family for some time. Most military brats like her move with their parents after four years. Katie doesn't know how her dad had managed it—something to do with Post being unable to fill the Range Master billet—but he'd gone to his Commander and gotten held over for a second term. Her mom told Katie they wanted her to be able to go to high school with her middle grade friends.

If only they'd just let things be.

"That's not the problem," Katie mutters before she can stop herself. Maybe her mother doesn't hear her, but no—the shocked look on the older woman's face as she glances at Katie says otherwise. Katie is finished with the drying and now she just stands there, caught, her eyes suddenly stinging with tears she doesn't want her mom to see. It's too late, of course. Moms are like that.

Gloria's arms are around her in an instant. "Oh, honey." She nudges Katie toward the table and fishes a tissue out of her apron pocket. "How can I help?"

Now Katie's leaning on the battered Formica table, unconsciously adjusting when one edge lists a little. It's funny that she flips between loving and hating its pale pink color. Right now it looks familiar and comforting—how many nights has she sat here and done her homework?—but she will *always* despise the nasty aqua-colored metal cabinets.

"Katie?"

She blinks at her mom, surprised at how wet her eyelashes feel. "Huh?"

"How can I help?" her mom asks again.

Katie gives the barest of a shrug. "You can't, really. It is what it is."

"Which is what, exactly?"

"Just popular girls and their pettiness. It's no big deal, really." Katie straightens and realizes she's clutching the wet dish towel. She turns back to the sink and folds it, then drapes it over the edge.

Her mom guides her back to a kitchen chair and Katie lowers herself onto it as her mother sits across from her. "I know you're not being bullied," she said. "So what else?"

"Just the same old shit."

Instead of saying something about the swear word, her mother rolls with it. "And that shit would be . . . " Gloria pauses, thinking it over when Katie stays silent. "Ah." She leans back. "Not fitting in."

Katie stares at her. How does she always seem to know what's happening in Katie's head? She's spooky that way.

Her mother sighs. "Katie, why do you always try to socialize with those uppity girls? You're way too good for them. Put two or three of them together and they still don't make a complete brain."

Despite her misery, Katie can't help giggling. Sometimes her mom can really fling the insults. She sucks in a breath, then blurts out what's really making her heart slam.

"It's a leap year."

Gloria does her best to keep her expression blank, but Katie sees it—that darkening in her mom's sea green eyes, the way her lips tighten—both mean she knows more about something than she's letting on. "You don't really believe that nonsense about The Prom Tree, do you?"

"I—I'm not sure. A lot of people believe it. They say someone stacks up and dies every leap year on prom night, and the only way to keep it from happening is to put something personal—something really *meaningful*—on The Prom Tree."

Her mother actually laughs. "Sounds like a great way for a person to go to the tree and collect all the valuables."

Katie shakes her head. "No. Once something is hung there, it won't come off. Ever."

"And you've seen this tree in person?"

Another shake of her head. "No."

"I honestly think it's just an old superstition grown into some scary Halloween-in-May story." Now her mom's gaze is steady. What she says next is painful. "Honestly, honey. I thought you were smart enough not to believe stuff like that." She gets up and goes to the oven and opens the door, checking on the pie. "Looking good."

"What are we having for dinner?" Katie asks, not because she's hungry but because it's expected.

"Liver loaf sandwiches. I made a Jell-O mold salad this morning. The goal was not to heat up the house." Katie tenses at the barb, then her mother continues. "Maybe I can talk your dad into waiting a bit for dinner, then we can eat on the patio. It'll be in the shade, and remember I found that electric fan at the thrift store last weekend. I tried it and it works. If we use the extension cord, it'll just reach outside."

Katie doesn't know whether it's a silent apology for the dig or the liver loaf sandwiches—*ugh*—but it soothes nonetheless. "Sounds good." She's shaking inside and sick to her stomach, but she manages to keep her voice level. All she wants right now is to flee to her room. Before she can escape, Gloria glances at her a final time. "By the way, have you seen my silver bracelet? I thought I left it on top of my dresser but now I can't find it."

"Nope."

"Go start your homework," Gloria says with a sigh of disappointment. "I'll call if I need your help with anything else."

"Okay." Katie slips out of the kitchen and heads to her room, but she has to stop in the bathroom and throw up.

And you've seen this tree in person?

No.

She's never lied to her mother before.

IT'S THREE DAYS BEFORE the prom.

"Hi, Daddy."

Frank Morgan looks up from his newspaper and gazes at his daughter. "What do you want?" he asks, but there's a smile in his brown eyes and his face softens.

Katie wants to slap herself. He's right, of course, though he doesn't have to say it. She never calls him *Daddy* unless she wants something, not since her early teens when she decided the word was too babyish. She feels an embarrassed blush creep across her cheeks, but she can't chicken out now, she just *can't*. She forces out the words, hoping she sounds normal. "Can I borrow the car after dinner?"

"*May* I borrow the car after dinner," her dad corrects. He's still holding his paper but his eyes are focused on her.

"May I borrow the car after dinner?" Katie dutifully repeats.

"Why?"

"I need to go to Willcox—"

"Long way," he interjects, but Katie keeps going.

"—and pick up a history book from the library." Her throat wants to hitch but she won't let it. "It's for a paper due Monday. I tried to get it here but they don't have it. The librarian called over to Willcox and they're holding it for me."

Her dad lowers the newspaper and runs one hand over the fresh, high-and-tight cut he got this morning at the fort's Post Exchange. "You're saying they're going to be open that late." A statement, not a question.

"The Willcox Women's Club has a quilting bee tonight." The

longer this goes on, the stronger Katie's heart is slamming inside her chest. A delicate line of perspiration breaks out high on her forehead. She hopes her bangs will hide it. "The library's in the Women's Club, so one of the quilting ladies has it for me."

"Ah." This seems to satisfy him. "Keys are on the table by the front door and I filled the tank this morning. Tell your mother where you're going." Her father picks up his paper again, then adds, "Be careful, Katie."

She swallows. "I will." Katie does what she's told and her mother echoes her dad's cautionary words before filling an empty milk bottle with water and handing it to her. In the front hall, her fingers are shaking so much that she almost drops the keys to the old Chevy Fleetline. On those rare occasions when she's allowed to use the car—unlike the richer kids, the Morgans have only this vehicle—she usually stands in the hot desert air for a moment before she gets in, wishing it would magically change into a rag-top Thunderbird, or maybe a cherry red Buick Roadmaster with a souped-up engine.

Not this afternoon, though. As she climbs in and starts the engine, all Katie can think about is what her dad said—"*Be careful, Katie.*" The words flip in her mind, back and forth, because she can't decide if they mean exactly what they seem, or if they apply to something else, something so much darker.

Lying, for instance.

The first lie, the one to her mother, had been hard. Katie had always heard that the next one, and the next one after that, were easier. In her admittedly limited experience this is *not* true. The lies she'd just told to her father—one layered upon another, and another—had been *awful*. Something else the kids at school are fond of insisting is that a lie told so as not to hurt someone's feelings is a "white lie" and thus doesn't count. Does that include lies told to protect someone? *No,* Katie thinks. A lie is just a lie, a deception, no matter the reason behind it. If she is caught—if she gets into an accident, the car breaks down or someone sees her and sings to her parents—Katie will have to bear her mom and dad's disappointment. And that will hurt more than anything else in the world.

Even so, Katie throws her book bag on the passenger seat, then rolls down the window and pulls out of the driveway. On the road it's too hot to keep the windows up so she drives slowly, holding back so the tires don't kick up too much dirt. Once she gets to State Route 90, which is paved, driving will go a lot faster, and the same is true for Benson Highway. That will take her all the way to Willcox, quite a ways up the road.

But Katie isn't going to Willcox.

On the surface, that feels like a good thing. Willcox is nearly two hours away, while she will make her real destination in about an hour and a quarter. The roundtrip could be a problem; it leaves ninety minutes free, but what she has to do won't take long at all. She can't very well go back to Sierra Vista and hang out at the new DQ—she might as well put a sign on the car that reads *Don't Tell My Parents I'm Here!*

Well, she'll figure it out as she goes.

KATIE'S TRAVEL TIME ESTIMATE is a little off and by the time she steers to the side of the highway, she's drenched in sweat, but at least the car is still going strong. She's drunk half the water and knows she has to ration it to make it all the way back home. She checks for cars behind her, then gets out and closes the door. There's a sluggish breeze outside, just enough to ruffle her blouse, although her rolled-up dungarees are so damp they feel like they weigh twice as much as she does. She needs to get this done before she can head home, so she sucks in an uncomfortable lungful of hot air, then makes herself look across the highway.

Texas Canyon.

Katie has been here twice before, the first time on a road trip with her parents to Lordsburg, New Mexico. She'd been young, probably around eleven, and the only two things she can remember about the trip are how long it took—*forever*—and Texas Canyon. She doesn't know what other people think of it, but Katie thinks it's wonderful, a fantasy land of enormous rocks rounded by the weather until they look like huge pebbles scattered as far as the eye can see on both sides of the road. They look, she thinks, like God decided to make marbles to play with, but got bored before he finished the task. Some are so precariously balanced atop others that she's sure they'll topple. But they never do.

The second time she'd gotten sucked into a Saturday drive with Melissa. She'd thought it would be just the two of them, a nice long trip to get to know one another and maybe come out the other end real friends. When Melissa had stopped to pick up Sally and Belinda, Katie realized that once again she was the token townie. Melissa was going on hallway gossip as she headed out to Texas Canyon, and Katie wasn't sure they'd find their goal.

She'd been wrong.

The Prom Tree had been there in all its junk-laden glory, and the other three girls giggled and made fun of it while Katie had sat in the back of the brand new ragtop and stared at the tree and its ravaged reminders of years previous. When Melissa and Belinda had started throwing condoms at it while Sally laughed until tears ran down her face, Katie had scrunched down as far as she could in the back seat. She'd had the sickening sensation that The Prom Tree could *see* her, that it would remember and somehow take revenge.

Now she turns slowly and looks behind her. Her pulse increases and Katie closes her eyes for a moment, trying to calm herself. She has heard about it so many times. The kids at school laugh about it; the old folks at the VFW whisper tales of it on the occasional Friday nights she and her parents go to dinner there. Katie doesn't think she's smarter than the average Joe, but anyone with half a brain—one side of her mouth lifts as she remembers what her mom said about her cliquish friends—would realize one group was retelling and exaggerating rumors while the other was passing frightening old truths to the next generation... truths that should *not* be ignored. The thought brings Katie back to the present and what she needs to do, so she finally opens her eyes.

The Prom Tree.

It stands in front of a trio of alter-like boulders, hundreds of gnarled, dead branches reaching skyward like paralyzed, white spider legs. Katie stares at it, her impression that it isn't a tree at all. It's a bush, withered by drought until it's nothing but a skeleton of itself. She imagines the biggest branches being hollow, dry wooden veins parched and still somehow searching for life. The idea is terrifying but Katie still takes a step forward, then another. She stops just short of the branches that stab the air, realizing they are actually more black than white. Their ends are agonized kinks that protect the heart of the tree, despite that same essence having abandoned it long ago.

But there is more to protect here. Much more.

Under the relentless Arizona sun, the things hanging on the tree glint. The breeze has disappeared and there are no cars as far as she can see in either direction. The silence is heavy, the air suffocating. Katie wants to do what she has to, but she forces herself to stay put, makes her gaze examine each and every offering in front of her. A frayed Christmas rope, threadbare from the elements, twines through the lower limbs, and there are a lot of timeworn holiday ornaments on it: red, green, gold, silver balls, all in varying shades of faded color. Equally prominent are the children's stuffed animals, weather-beaten and shabby with dirt but still adding flashes of dull color. There's a Humpty Dumpty with dirty yellow hair wearing a plaid suit; a pink-eared lamb whose formerly white fur is now permanently gray—its stuffing is gone so it hangs like a limp, morbid skin of itself. More things are tangled in The Prom Tree's grip—baby toys, a red wooden apple, a few bells that might have once hung on someone's front door. On one of the highest braches is a pair of boy's shoes tied together by the laces. The scariest of all the sacrifices is a dirty pink pacifier that's cracked on one side.

Other tidbits also hang on it, a few small, twinkling pieces that pull the eye away from the pathetic display of old toys and ornaments. As Katie dares to move closer, she sees them for what they truly are: pieces of jewelry, a mixed bag of cheap drugstore finds stuck on the branches like the afterthoughts of an inexpensive party. The condom packs that Melissa and Belinda threw lie at the tree's base; already covered with Arizona dust, they might've been there for months. Shoddy gifts, indeed, to an unnamed entity that might enfold the life or death of someone within the claws of its dead, wooden embrace.

Katie steps carefully between the outstretched talons, swallowing as she twists and sidesteps until she has come as far as she's able, nearly touching the bone-white trunk and narrowly avoiding getting stabbed in one eye. Despite the broiling spring sun, in here she feels as though she's stepped into a gloomy space custom-fit to her body. A chill startles her and the hairs on the back of her neck and arms rise, as though someone is running fingers over her flesh. There are valuables—a chain with a small diamond pendant, a ruby ring, a strand of rose-colored pearls, a pair of gold earrings—hung on the branches that no one dares take for fear The Prom Tree's spiked limbs will capture them forever. Katie's hand slides into the side pocket of her pants and she pulls out her mom's treasured silver bracelet. In her palm it looks like a tiny, shining snake, and when her quaking fingers drape it carefully in the middle of a high, dense patch of branches and hook it securely to a deadly-looking thorn, she exhales the breath she hadn't realized she was holding. She backs out without looking but no branch pulls at her and none of the two- and three-inch thorns pierce her skin.

Then Katie is free of the tree's insidious power; her reward is the oppressive Arizona heat that suddenly enfolds her. She can breathe again and she welcomes the heated air, the sting of the car's fabric seat through her clothes as she climbs into the car and starts the engine.

Safe, she thinks. *It's all good.*

The Prom Tree is satisfied.

KATIE GOES TO THE PROM by herself because her mom will not take no for an answer. She surprises Katie with a new dress in a subdued purple floral pattern, and while Katie thinks purple is not her best color, she does appreciate the time her mother put into making it. While Katie is two thumbs and eight more, Gloria takes after her own mother and is an excellent seamstress. She also has a better than average sense of design; thus the dress has a bit of fullness and goes to mid-calf, but none of the ridiculous tulle ruffles or clouds of lace. Best of all, one of those stupid crinoline petticoats can't fit under it.

Katie's mom drops her off at the dance. After Gloria pulls away, Katie walks over and finds a spot to sit on the low concrete wall that fronts the school. It's crowded, with girls giggling as they huddle together and eyeball the guys who've come solo... and some who haven't. There's enough organza, ruffles, and just plain *poofyness* to fill the baseball diamond at the back of the school. Most of the young men are dressed in tuxes, others in dinner jackets above smartly creased dress pants. Some of the girls are wearing corsages pinned to their dresses or on their wrists; most of the guys have boutonnieres on their jackets.

Katie's gaze is drawn more to the cars, the biggest, the shiniest, the loudest. And, God, how she loves the shine of the chrome—the more, the better. A ragtop Cadillac, cherry red with white seats, cruises past; it's obviously borrowed from Daddy. In fact, most of the vehicles in the long line in front of the school are Daddy-owned, although there are a few shows of true money like the sleek black Thunderbird that seems to glide more than drive, the crazy-looking Ford Sunliner that's overfilled with guys and a couple of dollies who've already exercised their illegal right to sample liquor. More than a few cars are stuffed with people who yell and hoot from windows as their cars pass. Is it to get attention? Or just a display of thumbing their noses at discipline? As one of the school's recognized nerds, Katie doesn't understand. She watches a Crown Victoria ease to a stop on the road and wonders if all four guys in the car will survive the night, or if one—or all—will die in a stack-up because of booze or drag racing or both. The car's radio is blasting and Katie recognizes the song: "Heartbreak Hotel" by that new singer, Elvis Presley. The two-door car is beautiful, white over turquoise with chrome swooping down its sides; below the Ford's hood ornament, its grill and bumper blaze with the surrounding reflected lights. What would it be like to ride in a car like that? Or better, drive it? When the guy behind the wheel revs the engine, Katie can't help smiling.

The boy in the passenger seat sees her and leans out the window. He grins around a wad of gum. "Hey kitten, wanna take a ride with me and my pals?"

Katie stares at him in surprise. "W-What?"

He motions for her to come to the car. "C'mon."

She tries to image how the Crown Vic's interior looks, what it would feel like to cruise down the road in a car that doesn't bounce and bottom out because the struts have been bad for years. She almost stands up, then it sinks in how the boy is already slurring his words. Instead, Katie shakes her head. "No, thank you."

Instantly his face turns mean. "Stuck up *bitch*," he snarls. His mouth works and suddenly he spits at her. She jerks back, but his aim is short. A good thing; the mass at her feet is green and slimy with saliva—that nasty chlorophyll stuff. The Ford roars away, the guys inside laughing and jeering.

"Don't let those germs get you down," a deep voice says. Katie looks up and sees a guy wearing a dark gray jacket over black pants. Only his shirt and crisp bowtie are white; to Katie he looks like the one sane guy among all the stiff, white-suited teenagers. There's a space on the wall next to her and he sits without asking. "My name's Marty."

After a second's hesitation, she says, "I'm Katie."

"Nice name." He leans forward and rests his elbows on his knees.

"It's really Kay, after my grandmother, but everyone calls me Katie." She has no idea why she said all that. Marty is tall and good-looking, way out of her league. While he seems completely at ease, she's suddenly nervous. She fights the urge to twist her fingers. He turns his head to look at her, and butterflies zip around her stomach; beneath light brown hair he has sky blue eyes. He's crazy handsome and she doesn't know why he's talking to her.

"Are you by yourself?"

Embarrassed, all Katie can do is nod.

"Me, too."

"Why?" Katie blurts. Appalled at herself, she feels her cheeks turn red. "I-I'm sorry—"

Marty laughs. "Don't be. I like people who say what they mean." He looks thoughtful for a moment, then one corner of his mouth lifts. "Honestly? I just can't stomach all these giddy girls. I'd rather not have a girlfriend at all than settle for someone like that."

Katie does her best not to gape at him as her stomach flips. He doesn't have a girlfriend? "Are you a junior?" she asks. "I am, but I haven't seen you around."

He shakes his head. "Senior. I'll start college in the fall." Another little smile tugs at his mouth. "I've seen you in the halls now and then, but now I know why we don't have any classes together. So you graduate next year? What then?"

Katie looks down at her lap, absently smoothing the fabric. "I don't know," she admits. "My parents want me to go to college but I kind of want to get a job and help them out."

Marty's gaze is steady. "You should go to college," he tells her. "If you want to help them with finances, that'll be better in the long run. You'll make a better living. And you can always get a part-time gig somewhere."

She's thought about that, too, but it seems too personal to discuss with a stranger. Behind them, music suddenly spills from the open double doors of the school. When Katie turns to look, Marty touches her lightly on the hand. "I think that means prom night has officially started. Will you be my date?"

There's a lump in her throat that's keeping her from speaking, so she only nods. They stand at the same time, and when he offers her his arm, she feels like Cinderella going to the fantasy ball.

And for a while, Katie forgets about The Prom Tree.

THE NEXT MORNING Gloria surprises Katie and her dad by putting together a breakfast of pork links and pancakes topped with fresh strawberries. After that, they all change into their Sunday best and climb into the car. As her dad heads to the First Baptist Church, Katie sits quietly in the back seat. She's so deep into her own thoughts that she starts when her dad speaks.

"Your mom told me you were smiling when she picked you up last night." Katie looks up and sees her dad watching her from the rearview mirror. "I take it you had a good time."

It isn't a question but Katie knows he expects an answer. "I guess so."

Gloria turns around on the seat so she can see Katie. "Our girl here was talking to a very tall young man when I pulled up." When Katie gawks at her, her mom laughs. "Didn't think I saw, did you?"

"He's just a friend," she mumbles.

Her mother makes a noise, and this time it's Frank who laughs. "About time you had a boyfriend," he says. "Just make sure you two keep it respectful."

"We just met last night," Katie protests. "It's not—"

Still looking at her, Gloria's raised hand cuts her off. "A beautiful, smart girl like you? It will be."

Katie blushes but doesn't argue, because yes, she wants it to be... something. She's relieved when her mom turns back to the front. She considers herself fairly smart, at least compared to a lot of the girls at school, but beautiful? Unfashionably long brown hair, green eyes from her mother, and plain clothes—she prefers white blouses and solid-colored skirts—that her mother makes at home. No, Katie would never believe 'beautiful' applied to her. Right now she's just happy to be in the car with her parents. Just like she'd been last night, when her mom came to get her.

Marty walks Katy out to just before the wall and stays with her as she waits for her mom. Laughter is everywhere as the teenagers spill from Carmichael. Most of the guys have Daddy's car so they can drive home. There are a good number of girls like Katy who are waiting to be picked up. Most are still joking around and giggling, but a few, like Katy, stare anxiously at the oncoming line of cars, looking for Mom or Dad. When the old Fleetline stops at the curb, Katie has never been more grateful to see her mom driving it.

Nothing is far away in Sierra Vista and her dad is pulling the dusty old car into the dirt parking lot within minutes. As her mother opens the door and climbs out, Katie hears her tell Frank, "I still can't find my bracelet. I must have lost it." Her dad says something in response but Katie can't hear it over the sudden, guilty pulse in her temples. She's grateful that neither parent turns to look at her as she follows them into the church.

They find a bench where they can sit together and Katie watches people as they come in. The town isn't big, twenty-five hundred people tops, but Sunday services are always crowded. Today, however, it's standing room only. Her dad leans over and murmurs in Gloria ear, "I don't see the colonel."

"I don't see how you can pick anyone out of this crowd," her mom replies. There's an edge to her voice that makes Katie realize it's not just herself who's suffering in the heat.

The service feels extra long to Katie, but she supposes it always does. By the time it's over, she feels like a dish of ice cream forgotten on the table, melted and sticky. Since they're so far in the back, her dad nudges her and they all slip out the door instead of waiting for everyone in the pews ahead to go first. Outside there's a small breeze, barely enough to cool them off. It's better than nothing because Katy knows her dad won't leave until he's shaken the preacher's hand.

It's an eternity before the congregation thins enough so that her parents can reach Preacher Abernathy. Normally smiling, today the elderly man's expression is solemn. "Good morning, sir," her dad says. "Very nice sermon today."

"Thank you, Frank," the preacher says. He nods toward Gloria and Katie. "Ladies."

Her dad tilts his head. "Is everything all right? You seem . . . "

"Troubled," Abernathy fills in for him. His voice is grave. "I'm assuming you haven't heard."

Frank and Gloria glance at each other. "Bad news?" her mom finally asks. Katie can hear the reluctance in her mother's voice and she tenses. *Oh, yeah*, she thinks. *Here it comes.*

"Mrs. Richardson was killed in an automobile accident last night," the preacher tells her parents. "She was on her way to pick up her daughter after the prom and lost control of her car. She . . . " He glances at Katie, then decides to continue. "She went through the windshield but the sheriff can't determine exactly what she hit."

Her dad's mouth drops open and her mother gasps. "The colonel's *wife*? Melissa's mother?"

Abernathy nods. "Services will be on Wednesday morning at Fry Cemetery."

They talk for a few more minutes and no one notices Katie standing like a statue a few feet off to the side.

THE RIDE HOME is mostly silent, with only Katie's mom breaking the quiet now and then with, "I just can't believe it."

Frank Morgan says nothing and Katie wonders what he's thinking, if he's wondering how he would've felt if the sheriff had knocked on their door with such horrible news. Katie says nothing, knowing there's nothing she can do to lessen the shock. As they get out of the Chevy and head into the house, Katie sees her mom's shoulders shaking; when her dad closes the door behind them and heads to the bedroom to get out of his Sunday clothes, Katie turns and wraps her mother in a hug. For a long second her mother doesn't move, then she lowers her face to Katie's shoulder and sobs quietly.

"I'm sorry, Mom," Katie whispers, holding her tightly. "I'm so sorry."

A minute passes, no more, then Gloria raises her head. Her eyes are red, the light powder on her face streaked with wetness. "It's so awful," she says, wiping at her cheeks with the back of one hand. "I talked to her at the grocery a couple of days ago. We talked about planning a family picnic after school lets out. I can't even think how heartbroken her daughter must feel."

Katie makes a comforting sound and steers her mom down the hall. "Go change your clothes," Katie says in a soothing voice. "Then maybe you should take a nap." Gloria raises her eyes, but Katie shakes her head. "Don't worry about lunch. I'll fix something for all of us." Her mother sniffles, then lets Katie push her toward the closed door at the end of the hall. "You'll feel better after a little sleep."

Her mom finally pulls the door open and disappears inside her bedroom, where Katie knows her dad will be waiting to hold her. She turns around and goes into the kitchen, and for a long while she stands in front of the familiar Formica table. Katie thinks about the family breakfast this morning and how different it is in here now, with no one in the kitchen but herself, how it's so quiet and . . . empty. And she's so glad the emptiness is temporary rather than permanent.

Had Melissa been as close to her mother as Katy is to hers? Will she miss her? A silly thought—of course she will. But had she been *friends* with her mom, friends like Katie was with Gloria? Because there is no one in Katie's life she's closer to, no one else she can confide in and trust to not repeat something, even if it's something Katie's father shouldn't know. And Katie finally realizes . . .

Her mother has always been her best friend.

And Katie will do anything, lie, steal, even sacrifice to The Prom Tree, to keep her safe.

YVONNE NAVARRO is the author of twenty-three published novels and a lot of short stories, articles, and a reference dictionary. Her most recent published book is Supernatural: The Usual Sacrifices *(based in the* Supernatural Universe*). Her writing has won a bunch of awards and stuff. Lately she's been really getting into painting and artwork. She lives way down in the southeastern corner of Arizona, about twenty miles from the Mexican border, is married to author Weston Ochse, and dotes on their rescued Great Danes, Ghoulie, The Grimmy Beast, and I Am Groot. They also have a talking, people-loving parakeet named BirdZilla. Instead of a To Do list, she has an I Want To Do list. It has about 4,274 projects on it and won't stop growing.*

"VITALIS," JIM BOB SAID.

"Bull fuckin' shit. Brylcreem." And since that was Dwayne sayin' it, that shoulda been the final word, 'cause it was Dwayne's band, he was the lead singer, he ran the show, but Jim Bob had drunk too much or smoked some reefer or something, and he didn't let it go.

"Naw, man, Vitalis gives you the *dry* look, and you don't get grease all over your pillow or your girl's hands and shit. Brylcreem makes you look like you dipped your head in old motor oil."

Maybe he was joking, trying to play it like the radio commercials,

I'M WITH THE BAND

BY STEVE PERRY

*He had some serious and weird shit
going on inside his brain, too . . .*

but it was a stupid fucking thing for Jim Bob to say, really stupid. It was, after all, "Dwayne Bogan and the Blades," so *his* band, plus Dwayne was six inches taller than Jim Bob, thirty pounds heavier, and at age twenty, two years older—three over me—and meaner than a stepped-on cottonmouth moccasin. Dwayne did *not* like anybody to argue with him, and certainly *no fucking way* the double bass player!

"So, you're sayin' I look like I use thirty-weight Bardahl on my hair?"

You could have cut the rage in the room with a switchblade, but Jim Bob didn't notice.

Dwayne's jacket creaked as he stepped off the shitty stage. Place was a no-class juke joint somewhere between Centreville and Liberty, stunk of stale beer and peanut shells, both of which spotted the floor, and also smelled a little bit of his leather, which was still pretty new. First thing Dwayne had done when he got some money was buy a Langlitz motorcycle jacket; it was top of the line, cost a shitload, and it fit him like skin. I think maybe some of the girls went with him just to watch him peel that jacket off.

He swaggered to where Jim Bob was uncasing his stand-up bass.

Jim Bob all of a sudden came to Jesus, and out of whatever trance he was in: "Oh, wait, hold on, I wasn't talking about *you*, Dwayne! I was just, you know, sayin'—"

Dwayne's jeans, rolled up high-waters, unwashed for a few weeks, creaked like the stage as he thumped Jim Bob in the chest with the heel of his right hand, knocking him back a couple steps. Not really a hit, but more than a push.

"Yeah, well, you don't fuckin' say *anything* about my hair!"

Dwayne had the best DA of anybody in the band, that was pure fact: long, crow-black, and tight, and if it was slicked down with motor oil or Brylcreen or whale blubber, it didn't keep the girls off him. He got more pussy than the rest of the band combined. He didn't have a regular girl, so he always got first choice, always picked the hottest tomato, and didn't matter if she was old enough to be legally-ripe yet.

I was careful to turn my back while I ran the cable to the vocal mic, so Dwayne wouldn't see me smile. He was just as likely to come back on the shitty stage and backhand me for the hell of it as not. Yeah, I'm with the band, but I'm just the road crew and back-up guitar player, if Dwayne hurts his hand fighting, or doesn't feel like playing any particular night. Most nights, I just stand offstage and watch.

He couldn't see my smile, but he must have sensed it. "You got somethin' to say there, Cecil?"

I shook my head. "Not me, boss. I'm just stringing my cable here."

His voice rose. "*My* cable, you mean. You get my amp fixed right this time, too. And make sure the Tele is fucking tuned. That high E was flat last night, it threw me off. "

First off, he was full of shit, because I always had the axe tuned so it was dead-on; second off, he could have turned the tuning peg an eighth and fixed it if it had been flat, but he wasn't a real musician. Oh, he could sing okay, mostly on-key, honkin' Elvis or Buddy Holly just fine, but I can out-sing and play circles around him, that's a fact, too.

"Yessir."

Roy came in, carrying his sax case. "What a rathole."

Roy's face had a fresh set of zits he tried to keep covered with Clearasil, but looked like a bunch of pale blotches on his red face, uglier than the zits. He just turned nineteen, which he celebrated by catching the clap after a gig in Jackson.

"It'll look better once we get the joint hoppin'," Dwayne said. "Where the fuck is Bonehead?"

We looked at each other. His kit was there and all set up, but no sign of our drummer. Not unusual, Bonehead lived in his own reality. He somehow always managed to show up before a gig, but sometimes it was like he had disappeared off the face of the Earth. We'd be at some juke like this one, middle of fucking nowhere, no place else Bonehead could even be, and we couldn't find him.

He had some serious and weird shit going on inside his brain, too. Talked religiously about seeing flying saucers, being able to control the weather, and how what we thought was reality was actually just some South American butterfly's dream.

Strange cat, Bonehead. Hell of a bad-ass drummer, though. He could lay down a beat and keep time like nobody's business.

"You do the set list?"

I nodded at Dwayne. "Scotch-taped to the back of *your* Telecaster, like always."

"You write it big enough?"

"Yessir."

Dwayne needed eyeglasses, he couldn't see for shit up close, but it'd be a cold day in Hell before he would wear specs. First person who called him four-eyes would probably wind up in the hospital; Dwayne was quick to double his fists when he got pissed off, and he'd done some boxing before dropping out of high school. He could punch.

"Run 'em down," he said.

I knew the list by heart, but I picked up the Fender Tele and pretended to read:

"*Little Darlin', All Shook Up, Young Love, Bye-Bye Love.*" I paused. "*Party Doll, Jailhouse Rock. You Send Me—*"

"Wait. Stop. Didn't I tell you we ain't doin' nigger shit? Scratch it off!"

I nodded. Took my pencil from behind my ear and lined through Sam Cooke's "You Send Me." I'd tried sneaking it into the middle of the set a couple times before, maybe it would skate, but, no. Dwayne wouldn't let us cover a lot of the *Hit Parade*, though some we did do was race record stuff that had been covered by white singers. Elvis doing Big Mama Thornton. Tab Hunter covering Sonny James. The white guys always sounded like shit compared to the Negroes, but I was careful not to say so to Dwayne. Or that the black guys had done it first. If he wanted to think Pat-Fucking-Boone had come up with Little Richard's "Tutti Frutti"? Let him.

I ran through the rest of the set list as Dwayne lit up a Kool and inhaled the mentholated tobacco deep into his lungs. Kools were good for the voice, he said.

"You got it wrong. *Whole Lotta Shakin'* is ahead of *That'll Be the Day*." He blew smoke in my direction.

"Yessir."

He did this every other place we played in, changed those two around. I thought maybe he did it just to fuck with me in particular.

"And add *Searchin'* to the end."

Before I could stop myself, I said, "You got the chords to that?"

If looks coulda killed, I'd have gone down in flames and burned right through the plywood stage floor.

"I got the fuckin' chords."

I nodded. "Yeah. Sorry." He'd have to play it in C-major, only four chords, and no way could he do it in a horn key. Leiber and Stoller had written it in B-flat, which he couldn't play. He didn't have the words memorized, and even in C-major, I wouldn't bet a plugged nickel against a silver dollar he could get through it without screwing up.

Of course, by that late, most of the crowd would be sloshing-drunk, and probably only the band would notice, not including Dwayne, of course.

I also didn't mention that the Coasters, who sang the song, were Negroes. He didn't know that. In fact, he didn't know much about anything.

Sometimes, Dwayne made a brick look smart.

Bonehead just suddenly appeared, as if he'd come through the wall.

"Where the fuck you been?"

Bonehead smiled at Dwayne, eyes hidden behind his shades. "Valhalla, man."

Dwayne shook his head. "Crazier than a shithouse rat. All of you."

HALFWAY THROUGH "WAKE UP Little Susie," sixty, seventy people stomping along, it started to rain.

That naturally happened a lot in the summer in Mississippi, frog-drowning downpours hitting all of a sudden . . .

The low tin roof, not two feet above Dwayne's head, rattled and shook, the sound of little wet hammers loud enough to halfway drown out the band. I hauled ass from behind the curtain to adjust Dwayne's amp before he yelled at me. He was already dialed at eight, so I upped it to ten. Twenty watts, it wasn't gonna get much louder. It was already fuzzing, but if the crowd of locals noticed or gave a crap, I couldn't tell.

The smell inside the bar was bad enough—sweat and spilled beer and peanut shells—but the hot and damp air got damper and made the smell worse, and now there was a little leak over the bandstand that dribbled just enough to make a tiny puddle on the wood stage, a couple feet to the left of where Dwayne mangled the Everly Brothers' hit 45-record.

I looked at Bonehead, who smiled at me.

Crowded up against the stage were the local girls who thought Dwayne was the coolest, and I knew he was deciding which one he'd screw later.

Halfway through the set, we took our fifteen. The rain slacked some, but it was still coming down in a steady beat.

We stood at the bar, drinking our cans of Jax, and Dwayne sniggered and said, "I'mon punch that little blonde with the pony tail."

Bonehead and I looked at each other. Fifteen, maybe sixteen, that one; they didn't check IDs much out here in the sticks, and Dwayne didn't care. If they were big enough, they were old enough.

Not like we hadn't seen it before. Rock 'n' Roll had its privileges. Drummer got some, if he wanted; the sax guy, even the bass player. Not so much the crew. Not that I was bad-looking, but I wasn't on the stage, except for the nights when Dwayne was too drunk, hurt, or lazy to play, and even then, I had to be careful not to show him up. He was fixin' to fire me half the time, usually after I'd covered for him, and I knew a small part of him resented what I could do. So gettin' laid was at the bottom of my list of worries, though I wouldn't have minded moving it up.

It was hard, knowing I was a better player and a better singer and not looking to hop into the sack with jailbait, like Dwayne, but that's how it was. His band, and the truth of it was, we were afraid of him.

Besides, nobody was twistin' my arm keepin' me here, were they?

I put my empty on the bar and started for the stage.

"Where you going, dickhead? Break ain't over."

"That amp is fuzzing pretty bad. I'm gonna wiggle a couple tubes, see if I can fix it. And that puddle is getting close to the mic stand. I need to move you a couple feet to the side."

"So I'm standing behind fucking Jim Bob? I don't think so. Leave it, it won't hurt nothing."

I shrugged. "You're the boss."

"Fuckin' right about that. Hey, darlin', why don't you get me another beer? Can't sing dry." He patted the waitress on her ass.

She gave him a tired smile and walked toward the end of the bar.

I PULLED THE WALL PLUG, reached into the amp's back, wiggled a couple of the tubes out, blew on the connector pins, put them back. Plugged the amp in again, and as I started to step off the stage, bumped into the mic stand and knocked it over.

Made some noise.

Dwayne yelled, "Way to go, retard! That stuff costs money, be careful!" He laughed, and the crowd laughed with him.

I set the mic stand back up.

DURING THE SOLO in Ricky Nelson's "A Teenager's Romance," Dwayne's treble E-string snapped. He glared at me, nodded at Roy, who took the lead on sax.

Any guitarist worth a shit could finish the solo with five strings, but Dwayne only knew how to do it one way, and adjusting on the fly wasn't in his bag. So he let the Telecaster hang on its strap, and when Roy finished the solo, Dwayne leaned back toward the microphone to start the next verse. He grabbed the mic stand with both hands, like he always did when he wasn't playing the guitar.

That's when he started shaking more than Jerry Lee Lewis on speed, vibrating so hard the sweat flew off him.

The crowd thought it was part of the act, and it seemed to go on for a long time, but it was only about five or six seconds. He couldn't let go, and then he collapsed, taking the stand down with him.

I ran out, pulled the amp's plug, and dropped to my knees to examine Dwayne.

He was deader than black plastic, and even if he hadn't been, he wouldn't have made it to the nearest hospital, because it would have been me driving him there, wasn't no place close, and the juke joint couldn't call for an ambulance, because *some*body had cut the wire on the pay phone outside earlier in the day . . .

EVENTUALLY, SOMEBODY WENT and got a couple deputies, and they came out and saw Dwayne was sure-enough dead. They asked me about the amp and the puddle and all, and I told them I wanted to move the mic but Dwayne wouldn't have it. The waitress backed me up, so did Roy and Jim Bob and Bonehead.

Terrible accident, electricity and water and all, but hey, shit happens. They shook their heads, hauled the body off, and that was the end of that.

They didn't say anything about the fact that Mississippi was a dry state as they left the juke, no alcohol allowed, neither.

AS WE WERE LOADING the old panel truck with our gear, I found myself alone with Bonehead. "Nice work. On the weather."

He smiled, nodded. "I wasn't sure I could actually do it, make it rain like that. And it helped you put the hole in the right place."

I shrugged. "Big deal. Sharp screwdriver."

"And the string."

"Easy. Just a nick, right by the nut. Figured he'd break it on the solo, that being the only string he knew how to use."

That, with the plug flipped and its polarity reversed when I plugged it back in, and the mic stand set up just a bit into the puddle after I knocked it down? Exactly as I figured it would go.

Adiós, Dwayne.

We smiled at each other.

SO NOW IT'S JUST The Blades, and we're doing all right. Added a piano player, got a deal workin' with Sam Phillips, over at Sun Records, in Memphis. I sing the lead and play the guitar, we cover a lot of race record music, and we're working better places now. Opened for Carl Perkins last month, be opening for Elvis in two weeks at the state fair.

And when we play outdoor gigs at the state fairs?

We never get rained out, neither, because our drummer?

He is *way* beyond badass . . .

STEVE PERRY has sold dozens of stories to magazines and anthologies, as well as a considerable number of novels, animated teleplays, non-fiction articles, reviews, and essays, along with a couple of unproduced movie scripts. He wrote for Batman: The Animated Series *during its first Emmy-award winning season, and during the second season, one of his scripts was nominated for an Emmy for Outstanding Writing—which no doubt caused the subsequent loss of that award. His novelization of* Star Wars: Shadows of the Empire *spent ten weeks on* The New York Times Bestseller List. *He also did the bestselling novelization for the summer blockbuster movie* Men in Black, *and all of his collaborative novels for* Tom Clancy's Net Force *series have made the NY Times Bestseller list. He is a recipient of the Willamette Writers Lifetime Achievement Award.*

He lives in Oregon with his wife, two Cardigan Corgis, and one ornery cat.

Somewhere in the Florida Everglades, 1959 . . .

HOWIE AND THE HOWLERS HAD THE SMALL crowd at Waldrop's General Store jumpin' and jivin'. In the 'glades, there weren't a lot of places a man could get a cold draft and a hot band, but Waldrop's was one. On the grocery side were bread and milk and the like, but also an aisle of packaged cookies, canned foods, and even some dry goods and hardware items—a little of everything and not a lot of anything. Hell, big Dan Waldrop even had a gas pump out front.

The other side was a café, but on weekend nights, tables got pushed

MYSTERY TRAIN: AN ARCANE INVESTIGATION

BY MAX ALLAN COLLINS AND MATTHEW V. CLEMENS

"Sometimes Alexander's investigations can be quite dangerous . . . "

to the walls, a band would play, and the swampers would mosey in to kick up their heels. A few locals would strum guitars or play a washboard with spoons, singing songs everyone knew. Occasionally, a road band would get lost and play Waldrop's for gas money.

Like tonight.

The band had taken a wrong turn and, running low on both gas and money, had struck a deal with big Dan to play for a couple of hours in exchange for a full tank and directions—the paying gig was a few days off.

Howie and the Howlers were a young rockabilly band from upstate, with the expected leather jackets and greased-back hair. Now they broke into a cover of Sid King's "Shake This Shack Tonight"— given their volume, they seemed to be trying their best to do exactly that.

A friend might have described owner Dan Waldrop as portly, but there were damned few friends in the 'glades. Dan knew most of the guys, especially the five habitually congregating beside the cracker barrel, thought of him as just plain fat.

A man of property, Dan liked to convey his position by what he wore, clothes making the man—open-collared white shirt, black pants and vest, big white plantation-owner hat. He did, after all, own a damn sight more than the whole cracker barrel bunch put together. So, he really didn't care what they thought about his size. It was the same attire he'd worn to woo and win the heart of his wife, Liz. No reason to go changing up now.

As if on cue, his wife slinked into the café from their bedroom in back and instantly commanded every eye in the room. The petite brick-house blonde wore a skirt that showed a lot of leg, and a sheer white blouse that did nothing to hide her thin black bra's efforts to restrain breasts threatening to escape and leave the swamp behind. She brushed against Dan, her skin not quite as hot as the surface of the sun.

She leaned in, her voice husky in his ear. "Gimme a beer."

Dan went dutifully over, raised the lid on the cooler, pulled a Schlitz out of the icy water, and used the attached opener. When he turned, every man in the place, and even a couple women, were watching Liz dance all by herself.

Didn't bother Dan that other men wanted what he had. In a way, he kind of liked it. But he didn't like how much Liz relished teasing them.

When the song ended, he strolled over and handed her the cold bottle. She leaned her back against the wall, thrust her breasts out like a dare, really giving the café crowd a show as she took a long pull on the cold beer, leaving her lips all moist and glisteny.

She was already pretty well lit, Dan knew. Since they got married, she split her time between that and completely shit-faced. Her party girl attitude had been a big plus to Dan once upon a time. But now they were married, and as he watched her drink the beer, he said, "Jesus, Liz, give it a rest, willya?"

Her lush lips smiled, but her eyes flashed nasty, then she ran her tongue around the neck of the bottle before taking another long pull.

Even as he watched the muscles of her throat work as she swallowed, Dan knew he would do anything to keep her. In the corner, the band broke into a cover of Don Woody's "Barking Up the Wrong Tree."

Howie, the lead singer, compact, sinewy, blue eyes shining, white teeth flashing, sang, "You're barking up the wrong tree, that's what she said to me," eyes glued to Liz and her swaying hips. She moved toward the screen door to the railed porch that ran around three sides of the building.

As the tall, skinny Howlers bass player did his last "woof woof," into the microphone, Howie was already announcing the band would be taking a ten-minute smoke-'em-if-you-got-'em break.

Dan went over to the band bringing a tray with bottles of cold Coke. If the Howlers wanted beer, they could pay like everybody else.

Howie grabbed a Coke and kept right on past Dan and out the same door as Liz. Dan wanted to follow the singer, but the other Howlers and the small crowd hemmed him in.

Outside, the air was hot and thick—to Liz, it was like breathing water. Damned humidity never let up, and tonight a cloud of green fog rolled toward the back of the store from the swamp.

Somewhere a train whistle called—some lucky fool was leaving this damn place. Steamy or not, this was better than being inside. That singer was cute, she thought, and, 'less she missed her guess, would be out here any second, sniffing around like a hound dog. They all wanted a piece of her—Dan, the cracker-barrel bunch, the guys who brought their girlfriends and wives to hear the rockabilly band, every damn one of 'em—but all Liz wanted was *out* of this swamp.

The screen door squeaked open and Howie strutted onto the porch like she'd willed it. Swigging his Coke, he looked more like an excited boy than the kind of man she needed to make her escape from this swampy hellhole. She knew at once he was just another wolf howling at her door.

"Pretty hot night," Howie said, with a lascivious grin.

"Hot enough, I guess," Liz said.

"I bet you like it that way," he said, easing closer to her, grin growing as fast as the bulge in his jeans.

Losing interest already, she took another long pull on her beer. The weird green fog was inching closer to the porch. Fog in the Everglades was nothing new, Liz thought, but *green* fog?

Howie said, "You look like could use a really good time, baby. Kind these hicks don't know how to show you."

She gave him an *are-you-still-here-?* look. "You said it for me in the microphone—you're barkin' up the wrong tree."

As the green mist enveloped them, Liz thought she heard Howie bark a harsh laugh, but then it was more than that. *Hell! He was howling!* And it wasn't like his howling inside. Doubled over, barely visible in the damned fog, he writhed, the noises he was making sounding more like an animal than a man.

She backed away, terrified, but there was nowhere to go. The swamp nearly surrounded the store, the railed porch ended behind her, and Howie was between her and the door. If she went over or under the rail, this time of night, she was as likely to run into a gator or cottonmouth as not.

The howl turned into a shriek, Howie contorting, shrouded by the fog, and Liz shivered as she backed up against the porch rail.

"*Dan!*"

She had no idea if her husband or anybody else heard her scream. Fear froze her in place, as Howie emerged from the mist and filled her wide eyes—except it wasn't Howie, but some hideous beast, fur sprouting from its face like a wolf's, fangs bared, but in Howie's clothes.

"*Dan!*" she cried again, but her husband and everyone else inside failed to appear. The creature Howie had become moved menacingly toward her, growling, spittle flying from his gaping, fang-filled mouth.

When he was close enough for the stench of his breath to nearly overwhelm her, she brought the beer bottle down onto his skull with a satisfying crack.

The beast snarled, bent slightly, shaking it off, and as he did, she kneed him hard in the balls. Falling back, the wolf howled in pain as Liz slipped under the rail of the porch and ran around behind the store, gators be damned.

Running as best she could in the dark, in her sandal-type heels, she tried to keep an eye peeled for stray reptiles and that fucking wolf, who, by the splashing sound of it, was now pursuing her. Where the hell was Dan, or anyone else for that matter?

She kicked out of her shoes and flew barefoot over the swampy ground, the back door with the single light bulb dangling over seeming miles away, not thirty yards. The harder she ran, lungs burning, pain searing her bare feet, the louder the growl of her pursuer grew. She didn't dare risk a look back.

Only ten yards to go. She just might make it—unless tonight was the night Dan finally remembered to lock up the damned back door. But she was so close, the glow of the dim bulb calling to her . . .

Then the monster's hot breath touched her neck. She looked at that door just a few steps—and a lifetime—away. Her step faltered, yet she pressed forward. The animal's claws grazed her shoulder, the pain like someone held a torch to her skin.

She stumbled, the beast about to take her down, so close to the door but even if she got there, she'd never get it open in time. Then that door swung open and light poured out, an answered prayer.

Only a few more feet.

Diving through and in was an option, but how to get the door closed before the monster got inside with her?

Then, as suddenly as the door had opened, the space was all but blotted by the shape of big Dan Waldrop, rifle in his hands.

The first shot went into the air. Liz never stopped sprinting, and the creature must have stopped in its tracks, its breath no longer on her.

"Down, Liz," Dan roared, the butt of the rifle jumping to his shoulder.

She dove, landing in the muck.

Dan fired.

The animal howled. When Liz looked up, it had disappeared into the fog and swamp, just a hint of that green fog still drifting.

"What in the goddamn hell was that?" Dan asked.

"Howie," she managed.

"Howie . . . the *singer*? That was a damn animal, some kind of wolf! Jesus, Liz, how much did you have to drink tonight?"

"I'm telling you, Dan," she said, near hysteria. "That green fog rolled in and he turned into a wolf or whatever the hell."

Dan knelt down to her. Her dress was ripped from her shoulders, blood trickled from where the beast had scratched her, and her breasts were nearly bare as she folded herself into her husband's arms and wept.

Looking out into the swamp, Dan said, "I don't what the hell that was, but I'm gonna find out . . . and I reckon I know a man can help me do just that."

BEVERLY RAITH WAS RIDING through the Everglades in the backseat of a Jeep, sitting next to a blonde in a white dress showing more skin than it covered, behind a fat driver who looked like a plantation boss; her own new boss sat in the front passenger seat. Beverly couldn't help but reflect on what had turned into the most surreal twenty-four hours of her life—had it really only been one day since her desperation for a job had led her to this godforsaken place?

She'd been about out of options. Stranded in Salem, Massachusetts, she couldn't even raise the bus fare to get back to her mom and dad in the Midwest. A registered nurse, the petite blue-eyed blonde had worked at Salem General, only making it through the winter there because the hospital didn't want the bad press that would come from laying off staff in the winter.

She was drawing unemployment benefits of not quite forty dollars a week, but that would hardly keep the wolf from the door. That need had brought her to this neighborhood known as the Point, and the ghostly mansion on the corner of Congress and Leavitt Streets. While most of the dwellings in the block were either apartments or row houses, the corner house stood alone amid the shadows of two big trees in the yard—a long-in-the-tooth Victorian mansion, complete with widow's walk.

Myrtle in pediatrics had told her the Arcanes were weird, but they had money. Beverly went up the walk past grass that still contained hints of snow. She knocked on the heavy wooden door and waited, and when it finally swung open, a slender woman answered who might have been only a few years older than Beverly's twenty-eight. Where Beverly had a blonde pageboy, the woman had raven hair that hung nearly to her waist, and wore a black dress that made her porcelain skin practically glow.

"Mrs. Arcane?" Beverly asked.

The woman smiled, her teeth even whiter than her pale skin, and extended a frigid-looking hand. "I'm Alicia Arcane. You must be Mrs. Raith."

"Beverly, please," she said, shaking the woman's hand, which proved surprisingly warm.

Alicia waved her inside. "I've got tea set up for us in the dining room. Thank you for being punctual."

The foyer, with its wide second-floor staircase and crystal chandelier, was larger than Beverly's living room. At right, next to the open doorway to the living room, stood a full suit of armor with the dings and scratches of ancient use. Double doors at the left were closed, likely leading to a music room or library.

Her hostess led Beverly past the stairs and into a formal dining room where windows lined one wall; even though the morning was sunny, the space seemed somehow overcast. The table was a long, ornate thing with one chair at each end and seven on either side. The centerpiece appeared to be black roses in a black vase, two red roses extending just above them, a circle of shrunken skulls around the base of the vase.

Oh-kay, she thought.

Alicia said, "A little something Alexander picked up in his travels. He gets called upon to investigate some rather... unusual cases. The centerpiece was a gift from a tribe of pygmies in Madagascar... Tea?"

Still looking at the shrunken heads, Beverly managed a nod.

They sat at the near end of the table with Alicia at its head. Pouring, Alicia asked, "Sugar? Milk?"

"Sugar, please."

They each took a sip, Alicia offered lemon cookies from a waiting plate, and Beverly politely took one. Then they finally got down to business.

Alicia said, "I suppose we should discuss your duties as a... well..."

"Your advertisement said 'nurse,'" Beverly said.

"That covers the lion's share of the work—but not all of it."

"My understanding was that—"

"Alexander suffers from a rare mental disorder, Cotard's Delusion—do you know it?"

Beverly shook her head. "I don't usually deal with patients who suffer mental problems. What exactly is—"

"Alexander believes he is dead."

Agape, Beverly considered simply fleeing, but there was something about Alicia's violet eyes that drew her in. Plus, she still needed the job...

"Alexander still moves among the living, and he of course continues to conduct his occult investigations."

"But believes he's *dead*?"

"Yes. He firmly believes he is a spirit who only remains on this plane for the time being. He has seen the best doctors, but no one has been able to make any progress."

"How long has he been this way?"

Sadness encroached on the hostess's placidity. "Over twenty years," she said. "Since an early case, in Haiti. Alexander believes he was killed by zombies there, but since he wasn't killed by a living human, he believes his spirit is doomed to walk the planet until God decides to free him."

"How do you think I can possibly help him?"

"The duties, as I said, are not normal nursing. In order to help Alexander cope, you would be in charge of making sure that he eats, sleeps, and maintains a relatively normal pattern. When he does not, he lapses into something near psychosis."

"Perhaps you need a psychiatric nurse . . . "

Alicia shrugged. "Let me be frank, Beverly—I am asking you to masquerade as Alexander's 'secretary,' not just to the world at large, but to Alexander himself . . . medical personnel tend to upset him."

Beverly rose. "I'm sorry, Mrs. Arcane, I thought this was a normal nursing job, and—"

Patting the air in front of her, Alicia said, "Please, Mrs. Raith—hear me out. I am quite desperate."

"I'm sorry . . . "

"And *you* are desperate, too, aren't you, Beverly? Desperate to hold onto the house that you and your late husband bought and filled with so many unrealized dreams."

Beverly sat back down, stunned. "How did you know that?"

"After our mutual friend Myrtle paired us up, I did some checking on you. I know you're a very good nurse and out of work. I know your husband died in Korea and you have been holding on by your bootlaces ever since."

Beverly's outrage was tempered by the truth of what the woman said. "What did you do—hire *detectives*, or . . . ?"

"The Arcane family has been in Salem for a very long time, Beverly . . . I have many contacts."

Shaking her head, Beverly said, "I don't know if I can do what you ask."

Alicia reached out, put a hand on hers. "I think you can. I'm sure of it, in fact. But to be utterly honest, there is one other thing I feel I must mention."

"Yes?" As if this weren't demented enough already.

"Three other of Alexander's 'secretaries' have met with . . . untimely demises."

The words hit her like a physical blow. "Would you mind defining 'untimely demise'?"

Alicia nodded solemnly. "Sometimes Alexander's investigations can be quite dangerous. Two of the deaths were accidental, one a murder. These things happen."

"Not to me," Beverly said, rising again. "I'm just a nurse, that's all. And that should be enough for me to find conventional employment."

"I understand your trepidation, but I believe you are much more than 'just a nurse.' You have been on your own for over five years and not given up or given in. You have real spine—and I'm quite sure you can be beneficial for Alexander."

"I'm sorry, I just . . ."

Interrupting her, Alicia said, "Stay one month and I will bring your mortgage up to date and, in addition, pay one hundred dollars a week."

That was more than she'd made at Salem General, and would get her out of debt!

"Stay six months," Alicia went on, "and I will pay your mortgage off—*plus* the hundred dollars a week."

The house was all that was left of Jack and her life with him—but was that enough to take a crazy job with a lunatic? She wanted to walk out, wanted to say no, but instead found herself saying, "All right. One month and we'll see."

Alicia clapped. "Wonderful. Let me call Alexander down and you can meet him."

Sitting again, Beverly watched as Alicia rose, went to a side table, wrote a note, then inserted the paper into a metal cylinder. She put that into a wall-mounted vacuum tube that carried the note up and away.

Alicia returned to the table, sat again. "He should only be a minute—he was expecting to meet you today."

"He will be able to . . . 'see' me?"

"I'm sorry," Alicia said with a little laugh. "Yes, Alexander's aware that he can interact with living people. The biggest issue you will have is getting him to eat and sleep. He believes he does not require these things and it will take outsmarting him to get him to comply."

That much didn't worry Beverly—she'd had plenty of fussy patients over the years.

"Don't underestimate Alexander, Beverly. He's ill, but extremely smart, even brilliant, though quite disturbed."

Abruptly, the hostess rose, and Beverly followed without thinking. Seconds later, a tall, slender man descended the stairs, wearing a black suit that might have been stylish half a century ago—Edwardian coat, frilly white shirt, black looped bow tie. Dark hair swept back, tiny wisps of gray at his ears, he sported a Van Dyke beard neatly trimmed with salt among the pepper there, as well.

She had to admit, for an older gentleman, he was handsome enough. But she wondered if a side effect of Cotard's Delusion was an inability to smile.

When he reached the bottom, Beverly extended her hand to him, but he said, "Dr. Alexander Arcane. I'm sorry, I don't shake hands."

The phone rang, distant but distinct, and Arcane excused himself, leaving Beverly standing there, hand out, feeling the fool.

Alicia said, "It's nothing personal. I should have warned you."

"I understand," Beverly said, dropping her hand.

Arcane came back, steel gray eyes boring into Beverly. "How soon can you be packed and ready?"

"I beg your pardon?"

"We must depart as soon as possible—we're needed in Florida." He turned to Alicia. "Do you remember Daniel Waldrop?"

"That crude fellow in the Everglades? The giant leeches?"

"Exactly right," Arcane said. "Fellow's just had an encounter with what he takes for a werewolf."

First pygmies, now werewolves! It was all moving too fast for Beverly. Involuntarily, she took a step back. "Perhaps this isn't the right position for me."

"No," Alicia said, the word at once a plea and a demand.

"Excuse me?" Beverly said—was she a prisoner of these very odd people?

Arcane said to Alicia, "I have to phone and have the plane fueled, then I must alert the I.N. If you'll excuse me, Mother will fill you in on the details."

Mother? Beverly had taken the woman for Arcane's sister. Or perhaps his wife, but how could so young-looking a woman be . . . ?

Arcane vanished back up the stairs.

When they were alone, Alicia gripped Beverly's arm, violet eyes imploring. "Mrs. Raith, Beverly . . . accompany Alexander this one time and I will bring your mortgage up to date and pay you *two* hundred dollars a week, plus expenses. On your return, if you wish to walk away, I won't try to stop you."

She knew she should run from the house this instant, get as far away from these nutso people as possible. But the money, the chance of owning her house (her and Jack's house), kept her rooted to the spot.

She heard herself saying, "This one time."

Alicia, suddenly all business, said, "Go home, pack a bag. The Everglades are humid and hot, so bring bug spray, if you have any, buy some if you don't, and meet Alexander at the Arcane hangar at the airport. There are signs—you'll find it. Do you need money for cab fare?"

Beverly shook her head, but Alicia was already pressing two twenty dollar bills into her hand.

"Hurry. With a werewolf, Alexander will be in a real rush to see it."

Before she knew it, Beverly was hustling breathlessly up the stairs of a DC-3, an airplane bigger than she'd ever been on, the word *ARCANE* painted on its side in gothic script.

Alexander Arcane had been waiting for her, but did not bother to introduce her to the pilot and co-pilot. The passenger compartment held eight seats, the rear of the plane completely revamped. Behind the four rows of seats, a ham radio setup reminded her of her dad's rig back in Indiana. The starboard side was lined with bookshelves with netting to keep the volumes secure.

Arcane waved her to a seat. "If you need anything, you'll have to fend for yourself. I will be doing research with the I.N."

"The I.N.? That's the second time you've mentioned it." She sat and tugged her seatbelt into place.

He loomed over her now. "The International Network. Something of my own design—experts worldwide, sharing information on their chosen fields through the use of . . . "

"Ham radios," she finished. "That's quite brilliant."

He bestowed a smile on her. "I know."

So he *could* smile. What some might call arrogance seemed to her confidence. Something about him, whether the Edwardian suit or the wounded aura his illness gave him, charmed her.

He moved to the back and it wasn't long before they were soaring above Massachusetts, the sunset turning the sky red outside her window as the plane rattled south.

Behind her, she heard Arcane saying, "So, Joaquin, you had a werewolf in Peru—how did the man get infected?"

Arcane listened, throwing in an occasional, "I see," and soon Beverly found herself drifting. As night closed in, the adrenaline of the day fading as Beverly found herself slipping into a restless sleep in her seat.

NOW BEVERLY WAS CLATTERING over a dirt road in the back of a Jeep, with a blonde floozy bouncing against her. Up front, Arcane was talking to an obese character called Waldrop, and she had to strain to hear over the racket of the Jeep.

"So," Arcane was saying, "this vocalist appears to be the only one infected?"

The big man shrugged. "Near as we can tell."

Turning to the blonde, Arcane asked, "Young lady, you were the only one on the porch with this musician when he transformed?"

The blonde, named Liz, nodded, the Jeep hitting a pothole and tossing the woman practically onto Beverly's lap.

"Sorry," Liz said, but made it sound like the fault had somehow been Beverly's.

Arcane asked, "If he was transformed into a werewolf, and we think the green fog played a part . . . why didn't you, my dear?"

Judging by the blonde's expression, her mouth an almost perfect red O of lipstick, the thought had not once entered that pretty head. She shrugged.

Arcane said, "Tell me more about the green fog."

"Started out as a sort of . . . haze. Then it built, like smoke, like something was burnin' in the swamp, but then it was fog all right, but not like the usual garden variety . . . like Dan said, it was green, and kind of glowin'."

Beverly wondered if maybe she had judged the woman a bit too harshly—Liz had recounted the experience well.

"If Dan hadn't been there..." Then Liz, shivering, leaned into Beverly, who hugged her close.

Arcane just frowned at the blonde, as if her fear didn't register on him. "Can you provide any more details, Mrs. Waldrop?"

"Like ... like what?"

Arcane considered that for a couple of bounces of the Jeep, then asked, "The two of you were alone on the porch?"

"That's what I said."

"Why were you the only two out there?"

Liz sat up a little straighter, her posture defensive. "How should I know?"

"Surely you know why *you* were outside?"

"It was a steamy hot night. I took my beer and went out on the porch, lookin' for a breeze."

"And this singer—what was his name?"

"Howie. The leader of the band."

"Howie followed you out?"

She nodded.

"And you have no idea why?"

Waldrop spoke up. "Same as all men! Wanted to make time with my little Liz."

Arcane raised an eyebrow at Liz and she shrugged, wiggled her eyebrows, nodded. Beverly watched as Arcane, still turned in his seat to look back at them, digested that.

As the vehicle jostled him, he asked, "Did Howie have a beer, too?"

Liz gave an indifferent shrug.

Waldrop had an answer, though: "I didn't serve them boys anything but Coca-Colas. They was all underage."

Nodding as if he'd already known this, Arcane said, "I believe we have our first clue."

How could that be a clue? Beverly wondered. Since when did a Coca-Cola turn a man into a wolf? It usually took liquor to do that.

She noticed the overhanging trees shading the road ahead, almost as if they were driving into a tunnel. When she was a teenager back in

Indiana, she'd always enjoyed the outdoors, but this swamp was giving her the heebie-jeebies.

As they entered the corridor of shadows, the sun practically disappeared, and Beverly could barely make out the dirt road ahead of them.

They were maybe a hundred yards into the tunnel of trees when something swooped down next to Beverly. She lurched back, but Liz screamed, and Beverly watched helplessly as the woman was lifted out of the Jeep by something Beverly couldn't quite discern.

Waldrop hit the brakes, but it was too late. When Beverly turned, Liz was hanging from the arms of a hairy humanoid creature that had been suspended upside-down from a tree limb, and had grabbed her when the Jeep rolled beneath. It was Howie, all right, a werewolf now in the remnants of the singer's tattered clothes.

But it was daylight! What about the moon, and how it turned a man into a wolf?

Beverly watched in mute horror as the werewolf swung Liz out and dropped himself to the road with her, then took off across the swamp with her draped in his arms as if a groom taking a bride across the threshold.

Arcane was already jumping out of the front seat. From his Gladstone bag, he pulled a pistol that looked like something out of the Old West and also, of all things, a flask. Then he lit out after the wolf and its prisoner, while the woman's husband stared in woeful disbelief. Beverly got out and followed Arcane, heeding an instinct she didn't understand.

The wolf, still lugging the blonde, veered off the road into the swamp, Arcane rushing to close the distance, Beverly sprinting just to try to keep them in sight.

She followed them off the road, the muck practically swallowing her feet, then she was falling even farther behind.

The fetid stench of the swamp nearly overwhelmed her as she stumbled through the knee-deep stagnant water, branches and brush clawing at her as she pushed through, the werewolf somewhere nearby...

Was she stalking it or was it stalking her?

She forced herself to keep moving—as in the operating room, *don't think, just react.* She slogged forward. She could hear the wolf and Arcane still struggling through the muck ahead of her, but she'd lost sight of them among the shadowy trees of the Everglades.

Struggling against the water, vines drooping down to tickle and torture her, she kept forcing herself forward, then something slithered past her ankle and she stifled a scream. No good would come from giving away her position. The swamp had gone silent up ahead, then she heard a very unstifled scream, a gunshot, and a long, low moan.

She broke through a thick growth of trees and saw Arcane in front of her, slumped against a tree, seemingly passed out—or worse. Was that blood on his face or just a shadow? From here she couldn't tell.

And Liz was on the ground, also out cold, though she was obviously breathing, the largely exposed breasts heaving as she lay sprawled in the weeds, a pin-up for a pervert.

Beverly took one tentative step forward, then the water exploded as the werewolf rose before her, water cascading off it, as if its whole body dripped drool, teeth bared, its arms raised, razor-sharp claws ready to rip down through her.

Three secretaries had died before her.

Ducking, she felt the wind of the werewolf's swipe, but the claws flashed past her without inflicting injury. She came up kicking, catching the beast in the stomach and knocking it off balance.

Arcane must have been playing possum, because suddenly he jumped on the wolf from behind, wrestled the animal to the soggy ground, Beverly jumping into the fray with him, to hold the creature down as the doctor shoved the flask into the wolf's open mouth and poured the contents down its throat.

The wolf coughed, fought, kicked them off, then rose, peered down at Beverly like it was about to rip out her throat, then suddenly its eyes rolled back into its head and the wolf shuddered head to foot, before falling backward, out cold.

Looking to Arcane, she said, "Did you *poison* it?"

Rising, brushing the swamp grime off his Edwardian coat as best he could, Arcane said, "Better—I got him dead drunk."

"What?" she asked, incredulous.

They watched as, gradually, the supine lupine figure transformed back into Howie—albeit, a nearly naked Howie. Covering the passed-out man's shivering torso with his jacket, Arcane said, "The fog, I finally determined, came from Cape Canaveral."

"That's so far away!" Beverly said.

Arcane nodded. "But they send waste through the swamp on trains, and one of them derailed yesterday. It must have leaked and caused the fog that turned Howie here into a human throwback who resembled what we think of as a werewolf."

Her mind was reeling. "Why didn't it do the same to Liz?"

"Because she had alcohol in her system. Somehow that counteracted the effects of the fog on her. I'll have to do more testing later, but to put it in layman's terms, the alcohol turned him back."

"Amazing. I was worried . . . so worried . . ."

"Well, anyone would worry facing a beast like Howie here."

"No, I mean . . . I thought you were dead."

"Well, I *am* dead. Didn't Mother tell you?"

Arcane and Waldrop loaded the unconscious Howie in back of the Jeep, and Arcane sat back there with him, pistol in hand, just in case. Up front, Liz sat in Beverly's lap, on purpose this time, but the blonde's eyes were on her husband, adoringly.

Back at the General Store, Liz clung to Waldrop like he might disappear if she let go. When night had fallen, Howie and the band howled at the moon, with no chance of transforming, at least not into werewolves. The owner served them beer on break now, not Coke.

Beverly found Arcane sulking in a corner as the band rocked the house.

"Have you eaten anything?" she asked. "The barbecue here's really something."

He frowned at her. "I thought Mother had explained! The dead don't eat."

"Oh, I know. She told me all about it. Quite well-preserved, your mother."

"She does look good, for her age."

"Which is?"

"Oh, I don't know. One-hundred-something?"

She decided to let that pass. "You should eat, and drink. You don't want to be impolite, do you? You want to stay on Waldrop's good side, after all—who knows when the next swamp thing will crop up."

Arcane nodded at this sage advice. "Well-reasoned. I believe you will make an excellent secretary."

Surprisingly, she agreed.

He ate a full rack of ribs and had several beers—so did she, just in the case that green fog rolled back in. Then she said to him, "You cured your patient, Doctor—why aren't you smiling?"

He gave her a sour look.

Hoping to cheer him up, Beverly asked, "You want to dance?"

"To this noise?" he asked, and shivered. "Honestly, Mrs. Raith, I believe I liked him better as a werewolf."

MAX ALLAN COLLINS received the 2017 Grand Master "Edgar" by Mystery Writers of America. The MWA's Grand Master Award represents the pinnacle of achievement in mystery writing and was established to acknowledge important contributions to this genre, as well as for a body of work that is both significant and of consistent high quality.

*He is the author of the Shamus-winning Nathan Heller historical thrillers (*Better Dead*) and the graphic novel* Road to Perdition, *basis for the Academy Award-winning film. His innovative '70s series,* Quarry, *has been revived by Hard Case Crime (*Quarry's Climax*) and became a Cinemax TV series. He has completed ten posthumous Mickey Spillane novels (*Killing Town*) and is the co-author (with his wife Barbara Collins) of the award-winning Trash 'n' Treasures comic cozy mystery series, beginning with* Antiques Roadkill *through the current* Antiques Wanted.

MATTHEW V. CLEMENS—A frequent co-conspirator with Max Allan Collins, they have collaborated on twenty-four novels. The pair has also written comic books, graphic novels, jigsaw puzzles, and their short stories were collected in My Lolita Complex and Other Tales of Sex and Violence. *They have also appeared in numerous anthologies including* Hardboiled Horror, Hollywood & Crime, *and* Worlds of Edgar Rice Burroughs.

Their latest Thomas & Mercer thriller, Executive Order, *was released in April, 2017.*

Clemens has also had short stories published in the anthologies Occupied Earth *and* Killing Malmon. *With Pat Gipple, he co-authored the true crime book* Dead Water: The Klindt Affair.

You can learn more at www.matthewclemens.com.

"**W**HAT DO YOU THINK YOU'RE DOING?" asked the teenager with a high crewcut and grasshopper arms. "This is Doctor Baleful's territory!"

The kid with the cigarette dangling from his mouth and leaking pustules sneered as the two gangs faced off against each other in the middle of a hot sidewalk. "Says who?"

"What do you mean, 'says who'?" asked Grasshopper Boy, who'd tried desperately but unsuccessfully to acquire the nickname 'Grasshopper Man' instead. "Everybody knows this is Baleful turf. If I were you, I'd take my buddies and scram."

Lab Experiment Turf War

BY JEFF STRAND

"You gonna step aside and let us pass,
or is there gonna be trouble?"

The three other lab experiments (Coyote Kid, Joey Dead-No-More, and Wally Two-Head) behind Grasshopper Boy stepped forward in a group display of leather-jacketed menace.

"I don't see Baleful's name on this street," said the kid with the oozing pustules. "You see his name, Danny?"

"Nope," said a kid with seven eyes, three of which were on his face, hidden behind dark sunglasses. (He'd added the extra lens himself.)

"You see his name, Alan?"

"Nope," said a kid who would have been short even if his body wasn't missing from the waist down.

"You see his name, Harold?"

"Nope," said a kid with the arms of a praying mantis coming through his sleeveless letterman jacket.

"Gee, none of my associates see Doctor Baleful's name on this street," said the kid with the pustules. "As far as I'm concerned, that makes this Doctor Awry's turf."

Joey Dead-No-More groaned, and it wasn't in disbelief at what he'd heard.

"What's wrong with *him*?" asked the kid with the pustules.

"Aw, he used to be dead." Grasshopper Boy spat at the ground and ran one appendage through his greased pompadour.

"I can see that. What made him dead?"

"Car wreck."

"Looks like it was a car explosion."

"Yeah," Grasshopper Boy said. "And *that's* why Doctor Baleful is the best mad scientist in this part of the city. Let's see Doctor Awry put somebody back together when they look like Joey did after he got pulled from the wreckage."

"Can he even talk?"

"Well, no. He barely had any neck left."

The kid with the flowing pustules snorted.

"Hey, he walks just fine though," Grasshopper Boy insisted. "Doctor Awry couldn't have pulled that off."

"If he was one of Doctor Awry's experiments, he'd be singin' and lindy hoppin' like Bill Haley!" The kid hopped a couple times in what was apparently supposed to be a dance move, causing several of his pustules to spurt even more freely.

"Ha!" said Grasshopper Boy. Chrome chains clinked as Coyote Kid and one of Wally Two-Head's heads also laughed. "Doctor Awry ain't even a real mad scientist. Everybody knows he's just as sane as can be!"

"You take that back!"

"You guys don't even have nicknames. What kind of unholy experiments don't have nicknames? Danny, Alan, Harold ... there's no menace! What's your name?"

"Frank."

"Not even Oozing Frank?"

"Just Frank."

"What a joke," Grasshopper Boy said.

Frank flicked his cigarette into the middle of the contested sidewalk, where it landed at Grasshopper Boy's motorcycle-booted feet. Then he pointed to Wally Two-Head. "If Doctor Baleful is so amazing, how come only one of his heads is alive?"

"I'm a work in progress," Wally's good head said.

"That other head is dead and rotting. Looks like it's gonna fall right off. Even the stitching ain't any good. What's the point of that surgery if the other head isn't going to do anything? Any seamstress can sew a severed head onto somebody's shoulder."

"Oh yeah?" Frank asked. "But would any seamstress cut off an *innocent* victim's head to use in the experiment? You think Doctor Baleful just happened to find a head lying around on the street?"

"So he's a serial killer. My great-uncle was a serial killer. That's nothing special."

"Well, look at you and look at Harold."

"I'm looking," Grasshopper Boy said.

"It's the same work, but you've got the arms of a grasshopper and he's got the arms of a praying mantis. Which is more impressive?"

"Grasshopper by far."

Harold gaped at Grasshopper Boy. "You're nuts! Nobody's scared of lousy grasshoppers! Praying mantises are fearsome insects that brutally murder their spouses!"

"But were they a biblical plague?"

"You're thinking of locusts."

"Same thing."

"No they're not."

"Enough of this," Frank said, raising a class-ringed fist. "You gonna step aside and let us pass, or is there gonna be trouble?"

"I already told you, this is Baleful turf. You got someplace to go, you can take the long way around. You ain't passin' through here."

"Your grasshopper arms don't even move that well," Harold went on, gloating. "Look how articulated my praying mantis arms are. I could play a guitar if I wanted. I bet you couldn't even play a tambourine."

"I could play six tambourines at once if I wanted!"

Wally's second head fell off. It lay there at his high top sneakers, unmoving.

Everyone stared at it for a couple moments until Frank asked, "Are you going to put it back on?"

"I don't really like to touch it," Wally admitted.

"Well, you'd better pick it up or there'll be trouble. Nobody litters on Baleful turf."

Wally hesitated, then picked the head up by its duck's ass hair and held it at arm's length.

"I'm going to count to three," Grasshopper Boy said. "If you're still here when I'm done, it'll be messy. One . . . "

"You might as well not waste time counting the last two numbers," Frank interrupted. "We're not going anywhere."

"Fine!" Grasshopper Boy said.

Coyote Kid took out a switchblade from his pressed jeans and snapped it open. Wally did the same with the hand that wasn't holding a head. Joey Dead-No-More just groaned and stumbled a bit. Grasshopper Boy, who had a switchblade in his pocket but couldn't actually hold it with his grasshopper appendages, did nothing.

On the other side, Frank took out his own switchblade. Danny took out a switchblade and glared with all seven of his eyes, even the ones that were under his cuffed tee-shirt. Alan had no pockets since his half-body didn't allow him to wear pants, so he just held out his hand as if a switchblade were in it. Harold removed a switchblade from his pocket with his fully articulated praying mantis hands, spun it around, tossed it in the air and caught it, then snapped open the blade with dramatic flourish.

Then they all stepped forward, except Alan.

"*Stop!*" a voice cried out.

Everybody turned to look, except Joey Dead-No-More.

It was Sue, her red neck scarf fluttering behind as she ran between the two gangs. "Stop this right now! You don't have to fight!"

"Sue, what are you doing here?" Frank asked.

"You know her?" asked Grasshopper Boy.

"Know her? Why, she's only the most beautiful girl in the neighborhood. We'll be married someday."

"Married?" Grasshopper Boy scrunched up his face in disgust. "Sue, you're going to marry that oozing freak?"

Sue looked at the ground. "The pustules came after we started going steady, but I refuse to let them get in the way of our love."

"No way! I won't let you marry an Awry!"

"Who are you to say?" Frank demanded.

"I'm her brother!"

Frank turned to Sue, aghast. "Your brother's a Baleful?"

A tear ran down Sue's face. She wiped it away, smearing her blue mascara. "I wanted to tell you, but I just couldn't . . . I know how you get!"

"How about how *I* get?" Grasshopper Boy asked. "You can't go steady with an Awry! I forbid it!"

"It's too late," Sue said.

"It's never too late to break up with a filthy Awry!"

"I'm . . . I'm . . . I'm carrying his baby!"

"You're . . . *what*?"

"I'm going to be a mother, and he's going to be a father, and together we're going to be parents and get out of this place!"

"Whoa, hold on, wait a minute," Frank said, taking a step back. "Are you, uh, are you sure it's mine?"

Sue nodded, patting fondly at the bottom of her cropped cardigan sweater. "I'm sure. You're my one and only true love."

"You're positive? I mean, think hard. What about that one night we were drinking after the sock hop? There were a couple of minutes when we weren't together. What about when you went out into the woods? Anything could have happened, right?"

"It's yours, Frank. There's nobody else."

Frank wiped some perspiration and pus from his forehead. "Okay, well, that's interesting news."

"It can't be true!" Grasshopper Boy shouted. "I can't have a boil-covered nephew!"

"They aren't boils, they're pustules," Sue explained. "And that's not how science works. Our baby will be beautiful if it's a girl or handsome if it's a boy!"

"You two seem like you have a lot to talk about," Frank said, edging away. "My buddies and I were just passing through, and we don't want to interrupt an important discussion between siblings, so we'll be on our way."

"You're not going anywhere," Grasshopper Boy said. "No Awry impregnates my sister and gets away with it!"

"Please, Kingsley—"

"Don't call me Kingsley! I'm Grasshopper Man now!"

"Grasshopper *Boy*," Coyote Kid corrected.

Grasshopper Boy pointed at Frank, as well as he could. "You'll pay for what you've done."

"I know," Frank said, sadly. He stared at his class ring. "I'm not ready to be a father. I'm gonna have to drop out of school, and get a job, and I'll never have time to hang out with my friends anymore. I was going to make something of my life, you know? I was going to be a famous stuntman. That dream is over."

"How could you be a stuntman?" Grasshopper Boy asked. "You'd leak all over the floor where you're doing a dangerous stunt and break your neck."

"I'd wrap myself in absorbent cloth first. Jeez."

"Stop it, you two!" Sue shouted. "This has gone far enough. The Awrys and the Balefuls need to stop this ridiculous turf war!"

"It's not ridiculous," said Grasshopper Boy. "I don't like the implication that we're here goofing off. This is serious stuff. We have to protect what's ours."

Sue shook her head. "You're all grotesque lab experiments. There's no reason to fight. Think what you could accomplish if you joined forces."

"That'll never happen! I'd never join forces with an Awry! Never!"

"But *I'm* an Awry!"

"Not if you don't marry him."

"You don't understand." Sue wiped away more tears as she unbuttoned her cardigan. "Do you remember that time doctors told me I had a bad heart and only six weeks to live?"

"Of course. You said you got better."

"I lied." Sue ripped open her shirt underneath, revealing a grisly scar on her chest. "Doctor Awry gave me a goat heart!"

Grasshopper Boy gasped. "Close your shirt! I can see part of your bra lace!"

"I'm a deranged Doctor Awry experiment just like them!"

"*Noooooooooooo!*"

The other experiments all looked down at the sidewalk, awkwardly trying to avoid eye contact.

"I'm sorry!" Sue wailed.

"If you needed a heart transplant, why didn't you go to Doctor Baleful?"

"I did! He wanted to stick a *monkey* heart in me. I'm no monkey!"

Grasshopper Boy turned to Frank. "Did you know about this?"

"No. I saw the gnarly scar, obviously, but I never really asked about it."

"I'm a Baleful by blood," Sue said. "But I'm an Awry by love and surgery. And I just know that you can work out your differences. It doesn't have to be the Awrys versus the Balefuls! Together, you can be the Awfuls."

Everybody looked around, considering the idea.

"Nope," Grasshopper Boy said. "Balefuls forever!"

The rival gangs rushed at each other. Switchblades slashed across body parts. Danny bellowed in pain as two of his seven eyes were punctured. Wally took a blade to both his original head and the one he was carrying. Joey Dead-No-More fell over without being stabbed. Coyote Kid went full feral with the smell of blood in the air and tore off Harold's praying mantis arms with his teeth, right at their delicately articulated joints.

Grasshopper Boy and Frank rushed at each other. They fell to the curb, pus spraying everywhere as they engaged in furious battle.

"Stop it!" Sue screamed. "Stop it! Please!"

Grasshopper Boy punched Frank in the face. More fluids spewed forth, but it really hadn't been much of a punch, considering certain limitations regarding Grasshopper Boy's arms.

The leaders of the two rival gangs stood up.

Frank lunged at Grasshopper Boy, switchblade extended.

Grasshopper Boy moved out of the way at the last second.

Sue let out a gasp of pain.

"Oh no," said Frank, staring at the blade imbedded deep in her chest scar. "No, no, no . . ."

Everybody else stopped killing each other.

"You stabbed her!" Grasshopper Boy said.

"I didn't mean to! I was trying to stab you!"

Sue dropped to her knees and let out a gurgle. "*Goat . . . heart . . . not designed . . . to have . . . a knife in it . . .*"

And then she died.

For a very long moment, nobody spoke.

"We did this," Alan said, raising himself to the full height of his half-body. "We all did this. We couldn't put our rivalry behind us, and it cost Sue her life. Why are we enemies? What's the point? This senseless tragedy could have been so easily avoided, but we were blinded by hatred. Sue was right. We should be one gang. Maybe not the Awfuls—that's a terrible name—but why not the Balerys?"

"He's right," said Grasshopper Boy, weeping. "And I vow that this will be Sue's legacy. She brought us together."

"Also, half of us are dead," Frank said, "so it makes sense to join together from a numbers perspective."

Coyote Kid pounced upon Frank and ripped out his throat.

"Sorry," he said, licking the blood from his muzzle. "I'm in favor of ending the turf war, but he *did* kill your pregnant sister."

Grasshopper Boy nodded. "I'm okay with that. But *now* Sue's legacy begins. Now we are one."

As police sirens sounded in the distance, they all knew it was time to flee, even if that meant leaving friends and loved ones dead on the sidewalk. And though they accidentally left Alan behind, and Joey Dead-No-More just sort of writhed around on the cement, the rest of the members of the two former rival gangs ran away . . . together.

JEFF STRAND is the author of over forty books, including Pressure, Dweller, *and* Wolf Hunt. *He has never participated in a street race to impress the girl of his dreams, nor has he ever said "Daddy-O" except in an ironic manner, nor has he ever worn a black leather jacket, even that one year at Halloween when he went as a '50s greaser. All he really did was roll up a pack of cigarettes in the shoulder of a white t-shirt. You can visit his website at* www.jeffstrand.com, *but he doesn't even own a switchblade so it's okay if you don't.*

WE WERE DOWN AT THE DRIVE-IN WHEN I saw this girl, and something inside me melted. The girl wore a white collared shirt, clearly borrowed from her dad, and rolled-up jeans. Her hair was flapper short, like Amelia Earhart. She looked to be about my age, as far as I could tell in the flickering light from the movie screen and the street lights. She was the most wonderful thing I'd ever seen. I burned with shame. Girls weren't supposed to have those feelings for other girls.

She saw me looking at her, and I guess she wasn't mad because she smiled at me. We had something in common, anyway, which was that

THE SHE-CREATURE

BY AMELIA BEAMER

A single loud laugh came from the shadows,
as bold as the She-Creature in the movie . . .

we weren't in our cars with our families watching the movie. She was by herself on the sidewalk, singing "Duck and cover, duck and cover," only she was grinning like it was the biggest joke ever. "Kneel and kiss your ass goodbye," she sang, and I wanted to laugh out loud. I'd seen that video of kids hiding from the atom bomb, and it was so scary. But it was hardly scary at all with this girl singing it.

Because she was looking at me, and because she was by herself, I went up to her. The sidewalk next to the drive-in belonged to everybody, I told myself. I had every right to be here, although I didn't know what I would say. My heart pounded. I had all of these fluttery feelings inside my chest and my belly, which I was not supposed to have.

My mom said that I would have opportunities she didn't get, I would go to college and get a husband and have a good life, but I didn't want a husband and I wasn't sure I wanted college. What I wanted, I didn't have words for, but it was hard to know what to say now that she was here. I heard a tinny scream, from the movie. I'd seen this one already, *The She-Creature*. A pretty secretary gets turned into a prehistoric monster, all green limbs and fangs and muscles. Nothing's that scary when all you can hear are tinny voices cackling from the speakers in people's car windows.

"What's your name?" the girl asked me. "I'm Gayle."

"Joy," I said, and blushed. I was the unhappiest girl ever named Joy, and I'm sure everyone could take one look at me and know I shouldn't have been named that. I pulled my skirt, trying to cover my knobbly knees. "I like your jeans," I said.

She nodded. "How old are you?"

"Sixteen," I said, and tried to think of something clever to say. "Almost seventeen." I wanted desperately just to be near her, to make her laugh, to have her smile at me again. I might as well have been trying to climb to the moon using a rope. Everything I could think of to say sounded awkward in my mind. "Which high school do you go to?"

"It's summer," she reminded me. "I guess I'll start at Castlemont in the fall. I'm a senior." She crossed her arms, and I felt bad for bringing it up. She was a transfer student, then. Probably someone who was used to moving around, because she didn't seem worried about it.

But if she was going to be at Castlemont, I could be useful to her. "I'll be a junior," I said. "I'll show you around, make sure you get your books and everything. There's some nice people there, although it's a lot of bossy kids, and mean kids too."

She smiled, but it was only with her lips. Her eyes were flat. "Schools are all the same," she said. "When I'm done with high school, I'm going to move to San Francisco and be an artist."

San Francisco was only twelve miles away, but she might as well have said she was going to Mars. She was so bold. If I said something like that to my parents, they'd spank me and tell me I was ungrateful, and that they deserved better.

"I paint," she said, answering the question I hadn't asked. "I'm going to be a famous artist, and live the way I choose." She looked at me then, and it was so intense I felt she'd see all of my secrets, but it wasn't the way the girls at school looked at me, like they were cats and I was a half-dead mouse to play with. Gayle had a question in her mind, and maybe she answered it because the next thing she said was, "I'm going to break into Children's Fairyland at midnight. You should come with me."

"I'd love to." My heart pounded harder. I shouldn't have said yes. Good girls didn't do things like that. I'd have to lie to my parents, and I wasn't good at lying. Gayle might have cigarettes, or liquor, and she might want me to try them, which I was scared of but I knew I'd say yes because I'd do anything to make her like me.

"Good," she said. She didn't seem scared.

I WENT HOME WITH MY FAMILY in our Cadillac, after *The She-Creature* was over, and I guess Gayle went home too, and then I told my parents I was staying at Judy's, from school. We have a telephone, but my parents don't like talking on it, so I thought I'd be safe. I took my bicycle downtown to Children's Fairyland, and I hoped Gayle would be there. The summer air was cool, and I wished I'd brought a sweater; Oakland was cold at night, but it had taken all my nerve to leave and there was no going back now. I'd have to stay out all night. Which I'd never done before, but I was growing up and that meant that I didn't fit into who I used to be, and I didn't fit the grown-up everyone expected me to be either. So I was going to have to try things.

I put down my bicycle at the gate to Children's Fairyland. Gayle was there already, and she smiled when she saw me. She wore a leather jacket now, like Elvis, on top of her jeans and collared shirt, and I felt that I might die right there from happiness. The idea of getting closer to her flitted through my mind, but it seemed so impossibly rich, like eating a whole cake to myself. Surely I'd get sick if I did that.

Looking at her was enough.

"Come on," she said. The gate to Children's Fairyland was locked; it was purple and had two golden silhouettes of fairies facing each other, about to hold hands. One looked like a boy, and one a girl, and I wished for a moment that they could both be girls, as shameful as that was. I thought I must be the only person who felt like this, and there must be something wrong with me.

I followed Gayle around the side of the amusement park, where there was a hole in the fence. She held the fence up for me, and I got under it without ripping my shirt. I brushed dirt off my legs and pulled up my socks for warmth.

We were inside Children's Fairyland, and I couldn't see anything but lumpy figures in the distance. It was so dark here, no streetlights, and I could feel Gayle more than I could see her. In the distance I heard an occasional car passing, and somewhere a cricket singing, but it was quiet. So quiet it almost felt like we shouldn't talk. I had the sense we shouldn't be here. That we were disturbing something.

"You must be cold," she said. "Want my jacket?"

I wanted nothing more in the whole world. Before I could stammer out a reply, I felt her jacket around my shoulders. The inside lining was warm from her skin. I felt that feeling again, like I could have died from happiness. The leather smelled rich and it was soft. "Thanks. Won't you be cold, though?"

She shrugged. "I'm used to it." She gave me that look again, as if she was trying to look through my eyes to see the contents of my soul. My heart beat fast. I wanted to be good enough. I wanted to be whatever it was she was looking for. And there was no way I could say any of what I felt.

"Come on, let's walk around," she said.

It occurred to me, I would have been excited to be in Children's Fairyland, if I wasn't so excited to be here with Gayle. "I've always wanted to come here," I said. "But I can't see anything. I should have brought a flashlight."

She took my hand. "It's okay, I know the way around."

The logical part of me wanted to know how she knew the way around, when she was clearly the new kid in town. Maybe this was a trap, and some boys would spring out from the darkness and laugh at me, or worse. Surely we would get caught, and then my parents would be angry with me. But I had a girl holding my hand, and I couldn't think about anything else.

"You grew up in Oakland," she said. "You'll remember. See, the puppet stage is off to the right. The Ferris Wheel for the little kids is over there." She pointed, but I felt more than saw the direction she meant. "A lot of the figures, the Three Men in a Tub, the Alice in Wonderland stuff, are all around here. The chapel's farther back that way. The Wild West is in the back."

It all sounded wonderful, although I'd have to take her word for it that the darkness contained such things. "I've never been here."

"Really? I thought you grew up in Oakland."

I felt emboldened by the darkness. This girl didn't know my last name. She couldn't run and tell my parents, or my teachers, or the ladies at church. I could say anything. "I did. Grow up here, I mean. I was ten when Children's Fairyland opened, I'd never heard of an amusement park before, and I wanted to go more than anything. But my parents never took my brother and me because they thought it wasn't Christian. And I don't know if that's true, because all the kids I go to school with had been when they were kids, and they still say 'Under God' during the Pledge of Allegiance."

She squeezed my hand. "You are so cute, do you know that?"

And my heart flipped inside my chest because I realized that maybe, just maybe, she felt the same way I did about girls. But that couldn't be true, because I was the only one. And I knew it was wrong to feel like this. Maybe I just wanted her to feel the same way I did, so I wasn't alone. She was so close, a breathing, living, wonderful-smelling she-creature right next to me, holding my hand. We were alone, here, where nobody would see and nobody would care, if we kissed. I wanted to, but I swallowed it down. If she got mad, and left me, I wasn't sure how to get back to the hole in the fence by myself. By the time I'd had all of these thoughts I realized she'd asked a question, and she was waiting for me to say something. "I, uh, nobody ever says that."

"Well, that's their fault. You're super cute." She walked slowly, and the ground was paved so I could find my way easily enough, but now I felt like I didn't even touch the ground at all. Somewhere I heard a cricket sing.

"Can I tell you something?" I said. I didn't know this girl, but I felt like this was my chance. I had to admit who I was.

"Anything," she said. "I'm not like those girls at your school."

"I think I might be a Communist."

She burst out laughing. "Do you even know what a Communist is?"

The feelings I kept bottled up rushed out then, and I probably sounded angry although I didn't mean to. "I know that they're bad, and that they go against the American way. And I don't want the American way. My mom always talks about how I'll have a better life than she did. I'll get to go to college and find a husband who's educated, and I won't have to go work in a factory like she did when I was a baby, and I feel so ashamed because I wish that we could have another World War, not a bomb war, but an old fashioned war like my dad fought in, so I could wear pants and work in a factory. I could make bombers, like the old posters."

She was laughing again, and the warm sound filled the darkness, and she squeezed my hand. I felt like even the shadows were laughing. And I was embarrassed, but I also felt better for saying it aloud. "Isn't that a Communist?" I hadn't even said the part where I wanted to kiss girls. I wasn't brave enough. That really *was* against the American way.

"You're not a Communist," she said. "There's nothing wrong with you. It's them that are wrong."

Something creaked, like metal. Maybe a Ferris Wheel got rocked by a breeze. Only there was hardly any wind tonight. We stepped deeper into the darkness. I felt there was something watching us, curious about us, maybe. But I was having such a good time with Gayle, I didn't want to say anything about the noise. Surely it was the wind.

"I always thought I was a Communist," I said. "I guess it's silly, now that I say it out loud." And then I gathered my courage and leaned over and kissed her on the cheek. Girls did that, with other girls, it wouldn't be a big deal. She could think it was me saying thank you, and nothing more. Except when I felt her skin against my lips, I felt a burst of emotion, deep down in my belly and in between my legs, and I wanted something very much, I just didn't know what it was. My heart pounded.

She stopped walking, and as I was starting to feel scared she would be upset, she put her arms on my shoulders, and kissed me full on the mouth. I'd never kissed anyone like this before, it wasn't a closed-mouth peck, and for a moment there were noses everywhere, but then I got the hang of it, and it was wonderful. She tasted of horehound drops. My She-Creature, she was something more than human to me. She had power. She was natural, and no rules could control her.

I could have stood there all night, drinking her in, but then we heard a cackle in the distance ... We weren't alone.

"There's someone here." I grabbed her hand. Fear made me bolder. "Did you invite someone else tonight?"

I'd adjusted enough to the darkness that I saw her lip tremble in the moonlight. "No." She paused. "But I heard it." She whispered now. "We should go back."

We'd been walking for a while, and we'd stopped, and my heart beat fast to think about what we'd done when we stopped. I felt so special, so lucky, and at the same time so scared that someone had seen us. God Himself might decide to come down and show me who's boss. "Which way back?"

Gayle faced one way, and then another, spinning on her heel. Even in my fear I thought her movements were beautiful. "I have a secret," she said. "I haven't been here before. I don't know the way back."

"I thought—" I started to say, and then shut my mouth. She had pretended to know her way around, I guess to impress me, only she'd thought I'd know my way around, so I'd let her down. "Never mind, let's just get out of here. Calm down for a second and think." I looked up at the sky. "When we came here, the moon was over there," I struggled to remember.

I heard peals of childish laughter coming from somewhere. No way were there children out there at midnight. So whoever it was could fake children's laughter. I guess they wanted to scare us. It was working. Whispers circulated, only I couldn't understand anything they were saying or even if it was English. "Just stay calm. It's probably some boys who don't have anything better to do."

A single loud laugh came from the shadows, as bold as the She-Creature in the movie, regressed into her past life as a sea monster.

I looked up at the sky, trying to remember where the moon had been. "It was," I pointed, "that way when we got here. So we need to go that way."

"We just have to go back the way we came," Gayle said. She seemed like she was close to tears. "I'm sorry, I just wanted you to think I was cool."

I held tight to her hand. "You are cool. You're so cool. You can be my best friend, if you want to. I like you." I wanted to say she was the best thing that had ever happened to me, and that I wanted nothing more than to kiss her again, but we were in the middle of a strange place, in the dark, and it felt like the whispers were getting closer to us.

Another creak, in the distance, and then a splash. A sound like something heavy was Army-crawling over the sidewalk toward us. I heard a grunt.

I pulled us back in the direction I thought we had come. "All we have to do is get back to the fence," I reasoned, "and then we can trace it back, and find the hole." I put as much confidence as I could into my voice, because Gayle was starting to whimper.

"It's all my fault," she said.

"No, it's not," I said, and pulled her along as fast as I dared. "I wanted an adventure, too. I wanted to impress you. And it'll be a fun story, once we're out. We just won't tell anyone about you-know-what."

She pulled my hand to her mouth and kissed it, and inside my chest my heart melted. We weren't safe yet, we might not even be going in the right direction, but it was worth it to be here with her.

A line of figures ran past us, zigzagging like soccer players after a ball. They seemed about our height, only they were very fat, and the speed at which they ran reminded me of the sound of a pack of cards being shuffled. Because, I saw in the moonlight, they *were* a pack of cards, with arms and legs and faces. Like in *Alice in Wonderland*. Only real.

And all at once, I forgot to be scared. Because what sixteen-year-old could really be scared of fairy tales?

"Rub-a-dub-dub," called a voice in the distance. Then came a hefty splash of water in a bucket, and then what I could only imagine was the watery sound of a whale exhaling. The park was alive, all around us, with a mix of chirps and whispers and giggles and animal noises. In the distance I heard an elephant's trumpet.

"*You kids get off my lawn,*" an old woman called out. "*It's my shoe, and I'll live in it if I want to.*"

"*Meet you at the top, Jill,*" a boy yelled. "*Last one there's a rotten egg!*"

Then a grown man's voice. "*You have to come down off that wall, Mr. Dumpty.*" And a grumpy man's voice, a little slurred. "*No, I do not! Who are you to tell me where to sit?*"

The grown man was patient. "*I'm one of the king's men.*"

I pulled us to a stop. "Listen," I said. "It's the fairy tales come to life. I don't think we're in any danger."

And I knew from the way Gayle looked at me then, like she pitied me, that a gulf had suddenly developed between us. Even in the darkness, her eyes had gone flat, like she'd retreated inside herself. "Fairy tales aren't real," she said, slowly and deliberately.

But I could hear them all around us. I could see them out of the corners of my eyes, and more than anything I could feel them, and they were playful. Curious. These stories had been around for centuries, some of them. It made sense that at some point they'd been told enough times, they'd frightened and thrilled enough children, that they'd become real, here in the darkness with no grown-ups around. Especially now that they were made into physical objects, here at Children's Fairyland. Daily they were worshipped, in a sense, by what must be hundreds of children *oohing* and *aahing* and running around. Perhaps my dad was right in thinking Children's Fairyland wasn't Christian. But it wasn't dangerous. I felt like I'd know if something was dangerous, and these creatures just weren't.

But I didn't argue with Gayle. "It was just a joke," I said. I could still hear the cackles and whispers and animal calls, and part of me wanted to run back and play with them. The fairy creatures were real; they knew it, and I knew it, and they clearly didn't need for her to believe in them.

"I think I see the hole in the fence," I said. "This way." I went to take her hand, but she pulled away from me.

"I can see it, it's all right," she said. Her voice was flat and she wasn't looking at me but I think she was angry.

My heart broke. Somehow I'd done this to her. Made her get small and hard. It hurt worse than I ever knew how to hurt. I didn't know what it was I had done that was so bad she had to pull away from me, but I thought it was because I could still feel the fairy tale creatures, and she must've too, but she couldn't accept it.

But my life had prepared me for keeping inside what I really felt. There were some secrets that people just couldn't handle. So I wouldn't let her know how much she had hurt me, when she pulled away like that. Of course she thinks fairy tales aren't real.

I kept putting one foot in front of the other, without crying. I found the fence, and I held it up so she could crawl through, and then I took off her jacket and passed it underneath the fence. The air was cold against my arms, but I didn't mind. The hairs on my arms raised up, and I could feel the creatures coming closer, wanting to check me out. I thought of Shakespeare, of the Scottish play, that people don't use its real name because they think it has magic in it. The magic of witches. The magic of women. Because it wasn't only children who had access to magic. Surely it wasn't just fairy tales that were real.

Gayle reached through the fence to hold open the gap. "Come on," she said. She was annoyed now, I could hear it in her voice, and it made me want to disobey. Because what was it that was so important about being on the far side of the fence, anyway? I wasn't scared of the creatures at all now. I felt like I was safe here. I remembered a story about a boy who was turned into a tree because of a magical spell, and I wondered if that would really be so bad. Because I knew how fairy tales worked. If you stepped into the woods, into the realm of the fairy tales, you were under their rules.

"What are you waiting for?"

I didn't answer. I knew what would happen if I crawled under the fence after her. I'd go home, and do what my parents wanted me to do, I'd get married and have children and take them to church. The same way my parents had done these things to make their parents happy. I'd probably never kiss a girl again.

Behind me the animal calls grew stronger.

I felt like, to Gayle, I was still a child, someone who believed in fairy creatures, while she had already crossed the gulf between childhood and being a grown-up. Because my parents had that same flat look as her in their eyes sometimes, and so did the church ladies, and my teachers, and everyone who said I was lucky and I would have a better life than they had. I knew I wasn't a child anymore. Children didn't have the feelings I had. I knew this because when I had kissed Gayle, I felt magic, and I couldn't go back to a world where that kind of magic was forbidden.

"Come on already," Gayle said on the other side of the fence. She sounded really scared now.

But I didn't. I felt something old and powerful coming up inside me, and I savored it. If *The She-Creature* was based on a true story like it said it was, I might have a past life as a monster that I could call up. After all, if I could feel the fairy creatures, and hear them, I must belong with them. I must be one of them. If I stayed here with them, I'd be free. Free from a world that had no place for me.

I squatted down so I was eye level with Gayle. A fence separated us, and she looked uncomfortable reaching through the fence to hold open the gap. I puckered my lips, and moved toward her, expecting that she would pull away, but she didn't.

I kissed her goodbye through the fence. Just a little smacker, on the lips, with my nose and cheeks against the cold metal. Already my teeth were changing, so I kept my mouth closed. I felt muscles coming to the surface, and wings sprouting from my back.

She must have called out, when I leapt up and ran back into the park, but I didn't hear her. I was the She-Creature now.

AMELIA BEAMER is a lifelong reader and writer. When she was a child, she wanted to grow up to be a writer, or maybe a Muppet. Her publications include the queer zombie novel The Loving Dead, *as well as short fiction and nonfiction about literature and pop culture.*

For over a decade, she's worked as a book and magazine editor, doing work she loves. These days she focuses mostly on novels by independent writers of SFF/H who want to level up their writing chops and bring their best work to market. For fun she likes to run around on playgrounds with her niece and nephew, and she is a great lava monster. Her nephew says she's the most fun person ever, except for maybe Jim Henson. Her website: ameliabeamer.com.

Seattle, 1958

THE BIG MAN WEARING A TRENCH COAT OVER his hulking body and a Fedora on his domed skull avoided all eye contact as he navigated the bustling crowds at Pike Place Market, hoping no one noticed his pants were shredded to tatters, or that his shoes had been stretched and torn to try and cover large deformed feet.

His face of course was even worse, and why he kept his head down, hidden in the collar of the coat. Passersby would dismiss him as a vagrant...

Hopefully.

FISH OUT OF WATER

BY WILL VIHARO

She reminded him of the girl he'd first seen swimming along the surface of the Amazon River...

Sinatra was singing "Witchcraft" from the radio of a brand new Ford Thunderbird parked near the fish market, where the big man loitered, attracted by the scent of fresh seafood. This festive, colorful environment was completely foreign to his sensibilities and understanding, though one thing he did know from experience: He had no money.

Around him, merchants were tossing fish as part of some entertainment for a crowd of tourists. First a snapper flew past, then a great cod. No longer able to withstand his gnawing hunger pangs, the big man leapt and intercepted a large tuna being flung through the air that seemed to hang, leering, right before his eyes. He caught it, but when he landed, his hat flew off, fully revealing his horrible face.

A woman screamed. The crowd scattered. A nearby police car sped forward, sirens wailing.

The big man picked up his fedora and ran with the tuna under one arm, fleeing up Pike Street and knocking people over like they were bowling pins, until finally making a right on Third Avenue to duck behind trash cans. The police raced past; he'd escaped for now.

Little did he know, a citywide bulletin had already been issued. The authorities were on the lookout for a hideous fish-stealing giant.

THE BIG MAN MOVED on to a dark and deserted alley in Pioneer Square. Enveloped in the shadows of dusk, he felt safer and began devouring his stolen catch.

He'd only finished one mouthful when he heard a woman's sudden cry of terror and assumed someone had spotted him again. But when he turned to locate the source of the scream, farther down the alley, he saw instead a young woman being viciously assaulted by a gang of leather-jacketed thugs with greasy hair, three with their jeans pulled down around their ankles, another already on top of her.

Instinctively, the man lumbered toward them and began tossing the four assailants aside as the girl, shivering in the cold, misty air, tried covering her violated body with the remnants of her bloodied clothes.

The teenage rapists jumped on the man, cussing and stabbing him with switchblades, but his prowess was overwhelming. Their punches bounced off Phinn's face like pennies off a brick wall. His blows landed with far more efficiency, but seemingly less effort, as he pummeled the punks with a mixture of ferocity and ennui, as if he'd been in this type of battle many times before, against far more powerful adversaries. This was amateur hour for a veteran warrior like himself.

Bones cracked loudly and flesh bled profusely as the big man fought off the gang, swatting them like bugs, and soon they were limping away in painful retreat, bruised by the humiliation as much as the beating.

The big man carried the nearly nude girl, now passed out from shock, up the alley and into an abandoned warehouse nearby.

She was about twenty, with long, wavy, brunette hair, ivory smooth skin, and a taut, curvaceous figure that was bruised and sullied with street grime and bodily fluids, little of which were her own. She also had track marks on her arm, but he didn't know what that meant.

Despite the experiments, human beings were still an alien species to him.

The big man set her down gently on the dusty floor. He hadn't even a chance to finish his first meal in two days, having dropped the tuna during the struggle. But he didn't care. At least he wasn't alone anymore.

As he sat beside her, contemplating her broken beauty with sadness, his mind wandered back to his place of origin, his memories as murky as the lagoon that spawned him, so many, many years ago, and so very, very far away from here . . .

SHE REMINDED HIM OF THE GIRL he'd first seen swimming along the surface of the Amazon River as he glided deep below her on a parallel path. Even though his brain had been chemically altered, he recalled her angelic visage, and the primitively erotic sensation of her soft skin against his scales, which had been shed due to the scientifically-engineered transformation, forcibly induced while he was in captivity for the *second* time.

Why couldn't they have just let him alone?

The expedition that first disrupted his tranquil, solitary existence in his natural habitat was not even the first. That one had left him for dead. The second, commissioned by an aquarium in Florida, drugged and kidnapped him from his home and put him on public display as a source of amusement for gawking tourists, chained and humiliated, his resistance kept in check by an electronic prod.

Until he escaped and wreaked havoc in this so-called civilized society. Until he was again shot, and again mistaken for deceased.

The third time he was discovered, a team of scientists took him captive and transported him from the Florida Everglades to the San Francisco Bay Area, where he was caged at a private Marin County residence. There, murky medical operations were conducted, removing much of his original identity, converting him from a humanoid amphibian to something closer to a human being, essentially manipulating the process of evolution by accelerating a mutation that might've otherwise taken centuries.

Once again, he escaped captivity, wounded and near death, returning to the only sanctuary he knew: the nearest large body of water, which happened to be the Pacific Ocean.

But his gunshot wounds, along with the fact his gills had been surgically removed, disallowing his ability to breathe underwater, would've proven fatal had the sole passenger of a passing yacht not found him floundering near the shore, gasping for air.

The boat's occupant, a retired medical doctor on vacation, rescued the drowning mutant and assumed he was either a disfigured burn victim or a poor soul suffering from a progressively degenerative disease like acromegaly.

The doctor treated the mutant's wounds and fed him life-saving nutrients intravenously. The mutant was touched by the doctor's kindness, since it was an unprecedented attribute in his experience with humans thus far.

By the time the yacht returned to its homeport off Bainbridge Island, just across Puget Sound from Seattle, the doctor and the mutant had become friends, communicating through hand gestures.

Two years later, the doctor and the mutant—now dubbed "Phinn," after the doctor's late wife's maiden name—were close friends, though no one knew of this secret relationship. Phinn was kept hidden away in the doctor's remote residence, where he was taught the English language and some rudimentary skills of social function.

Then one day the doctor died suddenly of a heart attack while they were sharing a meal in the dining room. Phinn was confused and devastated. Grief-stricken, he wandered out into the night.

Though he knew he could no longer swim underwater due to his altered physique, Phinn realized he could still swim above the surface. Given his immense strength and stamina, he was able to cross Puget Sound and come ashore on a secluded section of the harbor, where he rolled a bum for his clothes and crusty fedora, and then let him go. His urge to kill had greatly diminished over the past two years.

But his primitive instincts had not been completely mollified by the hormonal injections.

After hiding out in the shadows of society for two days, Phinn decided to try roaming amongst the humans in his "disguise," driven by hunger...

THE GIRL WOKE SUDDENLY, saw Phinn's face, and screamed.

Phinn winced at the sound, and a tear rolled down one of his greenish cheeks. Tear ducts were one of several involuntarily triggered biological by-products of the transformation that still surprised him.

Her screams ceased, and she sat up, assessing the situation. Her exposed flesh was covered by old newspapers that formed a makeshift blanket.

Phinn had found some old newspapers and covered her exposed flesh with a makeshift blanket. She realized it was Phinn who'd covered her, and asked in a hoarse whisper, "Who are you?"

"I am... Phinn," he responded in his halting, gravelly voice, still adjusting to the development of biologically synthesized vocal cords. "I... saved you from... the... the... "

"Thank you," she said as tears escaped her eyes. "Thank you. My name is Julie."

Phinn nodded, then bowed his head, no longer able to sustain direct eye contact, suddenly ashamed of his wretched countenance.

Julie reached out with a trembling hand and wiped the tear from his cheek. "You saved me. No one else has ever lifted a finger to help me. Ever."

"Someone saved *me*... once," Phinn said, his normally slow speech pattern accelerating with emotional momentum. "So now... I save you. Can you also save me? I need... to hide... "

"What's wrong with you?" Julie asked abruptly, letting her internal thoughts slip through her restrained façade. Despite her gratitude, she found Phinn's appearance unsettling. But she didn't want to alienate her savior with an outward expression of revulsion. So she instantly recalibrated her reaction, and said, "I mean... are you sick or something?"

"I'm... just... this is just who I am," he said. "I am sorry. Should I leave you now?"

"No!" Julie said, grabbing hold of his cold hand. "Please. Come with me. I don't live far."

Julie stood unsteadily, still holding Phinn's hand. She gestured for him to rise with her, and the newspaper blanket fell away, exposing her breasts.

Phinn removed his trench coat and put it around her, revealing his misshapen and scarred torso.

Julie touched one of his massive pectoral muscles. "You're so strong," she said in a whisper.

Phinn nodded humbly. "We should be careful, so no one sees me... like this."

"I'll protect you," Julie said, leading him out the warehouse and back into the alley, then quickly through strolling pedestrians toward her apartment a few blocks away. Phinn kept the Fedora over his face, shielding the most alarming aspect of his appearance.

HER STUDIO APARTMENT was sparsely furnished, equipped with a kitchenette, a tiny bathroom, and a Murphy bed she usually kept pulled out, since it was where she spent much of her time, working for Frank.

In fact, the boys that had raped her were initially "customers," but when she rejected a gang-bang, even for cash, they decided to make it a gang rape, without charge. They'd chased her out of the apartment and to that alley, where Phinn had rescued her.

She considered it kismet, despite the expense of her pride.

"I'm sorry I can't offer you some place more comfortable," Julie said.

"I am very comfortable," Phinn said, smiling inwardly, since his mouth retained too much of its original composition for him to actually do so.

She pulled up one of the cheap wooden chairs from her Formica dining table and sat on it, offering the bed to Phinn.

"You'd only break the chair," she said with a grin.

Phinn agreed and sat on the bed's edge, which creaked under his weight.

"Where do you come from?" she asked.

"That is a long story," he said.

"I have time," she replied. "I don't have to work until late tonight."

So he told her everything. And she accepted it.

Then she told him all about herself.

"I ran away from home when I was only sixteen," she said. "So I know what it's like to be homeless, like you. My father was ... like this man, Frank, who owns the bar I work at, though he's nothing more than a gangster. My father treated me like Frank treats me. Even ... *you know*. I loved my mother, but she died a long time ago. So finally I couldn't take it anymore and I ran away. I'd rather be alone than living with a monster." Her eyes widened. "Oh, I didn't mean—"

"I understand," Phinn said. "Please continue."

"Well, Frank found me one night and at first he was real kind. He offered me food and shelter and a job dancing in his club. And that's all I did for awhile. Then at a party upstairs one night he asked me if I wanted to try some, you know, drugs, and I was already drunk, so I did, and next thing I know, I was under his thumb. He made me do other things too, that I don't want to talk about. I've been thinking lately I need to get away."

She paused, eyeing his reaction, hesitant to continue. But Phinn nodded, so she went on. "Maybe ... maybe we can go away together. I've been thinking of escaping to the San Juan Islands, far up north, and hiding away in a cabin in the woods that my mother once owned. My father never goes there anymore, but if he did ... well, I have you now, don't I?"

Phinn nodded.

"So I've made up my mind," she said.

THE NAUGHTY NAUTICAL'S blue neon sign was a bright mermaid, beaming through the darkness and light rain as Phinn and Julie cautiously approached the nightclub's rear entrance and snuck in.

The place was dark and small and loud, over-decorated with "exotic" décor, dangling fishnets and tiki statues and fish float lamps.

A West Coast Jazz quartet performed on stage in between the burlesque acts, the saxophone player and drummer staying to provide backup music for the dancers while the guitar player and flutist took a break. Frank was hanging out behind the bar with a bartender she recognized as Jimmy Siu. Frank was a real man of talents, Julie thought, watching him snap his fingers to the beat, as besides fronting the club, he also played resident pimp and drug dealer.

Three years earlier, and taking full advantage of her gullibility and vulnerability, he'd got her hooked on heroin when she was only seventeen. Then he forced her to work the streets.

All that was about to change, Julie decided. The rape, as physically abusive and psychologically traumatic as it had been, finally gave her the inner strength to stand up to the bastard, especially now that she had Phinn for both emotional and physical support.

She led Phinn quickly through the club, guiding him as he kept that hat over his face. They made their way past a few patrons sitting at tables watching the voluptuous dancer that had just taken the stage, went up the dark stairs, and into Frank's office.

"Wait for me here," Julie said after she let Phinn inside. He nodded.

Then she went back downstairs and to the bar, where she confronted Frank, as he sipped a martini, a triple from the looks of it. Jimmy Siu the bartender scowled at Julie and looked to say something, glanced at Frank, then decided to keep his mouth shut and suddenly got busy wiping down tumblers.

"Hey, you're up next!" Frank waved a menacing finger at her. "Get into costume, so you can get back out of it!"

Him and Jimmy shared a real hearty laugh over that.

Frank was a large man, though not nearly as large as Phinn, with slick black hair and a gut like a wine barrel. He had a greasy, pockmarked face and cold eyes as dark as coal, and he seemed to perpetually drool from the left side of his mouth. Everything about him disgusted her, and yet she'd allowed him to have his way with her more times than she liked to count, in exchange for drugs.

But never again.

"I'm quitting," she said resolutely. "We can talk in your office if you want. But I want my pay, then I'm gone. For good."

Frank laughed harder till he realized she was serious. "You know what this means?" he said, pantomiming a hypodermic needle shot into the right sleeve of his shiny silk suit.

"I'm done with that too," she said. "All of it."

Jimmy snorted, trying to suppress his amusement, but when Frank began chuckling, they both shared another laugh.

"Sure toots," Frank said. "Like you said, let's go upstairs and work this out ... "

Julie couldn't miss the big wink Frank gave Jimmy before he followed her up to his office.

Before Frank noticed someone else was in the room, he'd shoved Julie to the ground and slammed the door behind.

"What the hell do you think—" he began, then stopped short when he saw Phinn rise behind the desk, bristling and clenching his giant hands into fists.

Frank's jaw fell open. A little gasp escaped, before he composed himself enough to demand, "Who the hell are you?"

"This is my friend, Phinn," Julie said confidently, standing back up. "I brought him along to make sure you don't try any funny business. Not that I'm joking, either. Now give me my money, we'll leave, and you'll never see us again."

"'Zat so?" Frank said, his gaze still deadlocked with Phinn's, even as his knees knocked.

"Yeah," Julie responded resolutely.

Frank seemed to strain in his efforts not to break, but he lost that brief showdown of wills fast enough against Phinn. Frank went to the wall safe, spun the knob, opened it, and removed a stack of bills, tossing it at Julie with contempt.

"Lucky you caught me in a good mood," Frank said.

"Yeah, you're a real jovial Gus."

"Take your pet monster and that smart mouth and get the hell out of my sight."

With a triumphant smile, Julie nodded, gestured at Phinn, and they left.

BACK AT HER APARTMENT, Julie celebrated by making Phinn a seafood dinner and drinks. She mixed her own Mai Tais, using the same recipe she'd learned from The Naughty Nautical, and they sat listening to her transistor radio, without speaking, just comfortable in companionship. Phinn had drank plenty of wine and bourbon when living with the doctor, so alcohol was not unfamiliar. Fact was, he rather enjoyed its intoxicating effects.

Finally, as Bobby Darin was singing "Dream Lover," Julie stood up, went over to Phinn, and kissed him passionately on the lips until the song's final crescendo. Phinn lifted her and carried her to bed, following his own primeval mating instincts.

After they made love, Phinn held Julie in his arms and fell asleep, dreaming of a lonely, prehistoric place that was growing dimmer and dimmer in his memory. He'd never known such peace.

She made him breakfast the next morning, a shrimp and crab omelet that he consumed with relish, and they sat and talked about their future together, perhaps in the San Juan Islands, or even farther north.

"Have you ever been to Vancouver?" she asked. "My mother is from there and took me to visit her parents when I was a child. We grew up in Tacoma, which isn't far from here. Anyway, Vancouver is very nice too, but there are a lot of people there, and it's cold. You probably prefer someplace warm and tropical, right?"

Phinn shrugged. "Anyplace with you will be . . . paradise," he said.

She smiled. "Maybe Hawaii. It's going to be an official state soon!"

For once, the possibilities seemed limitless. She could relate so much to Phinn's isolation from the rest of her own race. She'd always felt like she belonged to a different species, undefined, but distinct from everyone else she ever knew. Until now.

LATER THAT EVENING she took him to a drive-in where they watched a double bill: Elvis Presley's latest movie, his last before being inducted into the Army, *King Creole*, plus *I Married a Monster from Outer Space*, though the two of their lips didn't pay much attention to either one.

By the time they got home, Julie was getting ill, feeling the withdrawals of quitting her addiction so suddenly. She writhed on the floor, sweating and coughing and crying, finally vomiting in the kitchen sink.

Phinn took her in his arms, rocking her until the convulsions passed. He tucked her into bed and they lay together until she finally fell asleep. Hours passed, and then—

THE DOOR TO HER APARTMENT burst open and Frank barreled in, his face showing matched parts fury and disgust at the sight of them in bed together. Beside him were two henchmen who grabbed Julie while training their guns on Phinn.

"I'll take care of you later, freak," Frank said as he yanked Julie out by the hair.

Phinn knew they were going back to the nightclub, and once they left, he raced after them hoping to intercept.

He got to the club fast enough, but outside were two ugly mugs guarding the door, both big and looking anxious. Phinn quickly disposed of them, fatally but quietly, before sneaking past the other henchmen inside and up to Frank's office.

Phinn broke through Frank's door, just as Frank had earlier broke through his own, only here the results were grimmer: Frank sat on top of Julie, pummeling her face with his fat fists. Phinn rushed Frank and quickly subdued him.

Frank was accustomed to imposing his will via intimidation rather than direct violence, since most of the time, his flunkies did his fighting for him, if it came to that, and it rarely did, since they carried guns that warded off physical interaction. Most of the time. Now Frank was experiencing exactly the type of painful punishment he once promised to inflict on his enemies if they didn't obey his whims. Now he understood why they chose compliance over conflict.

Phinn didn't offer that option, though. It was too late to negotiate.

Lifting Frank high above his head, Phinn threw the gangster through the window, spectacularly smashing the panes. Frank fell with brutal force into the alley below, where his screaming body bounced off of a fire escape before landing with a loud thud on the edge of an open garbage dumpster, then falling to the wet ground like a broken doll.

Phinn turned to see Julie lying dead on the ground from Frank's vicious beating. He'd been too late to save her. After Phinn kneeled and lifted her up, she dangled limp and lifeless in his powerful arms. He wept for a moment, then roared with all the primeval anger left him before setting her back down gently on the floor.

PHINN WENT BACK DOWN and rampaged through the nightclub, ripping chairs, tables, and bodies into pieces. Blood splattered, bones and wood splintered, bottles of booze shattered.

Frank's two henchmen opened fire with machine guns, riddling Phinn's bodies with bullets. The barrage slowed him down, but did not stop him. He ran toward them and ripped each of their heads off, keeping both of his slightly webbed hands busy, tossing their decapitated craniums aside like softballs.

Jimmy Siu was not an enforcer, just a bartender, so his only defense was to throw bottles of precious booze at Phinn. Drenched in premium alcohol, Phinn picked up Jimmy and shook him like he was mixing a human cocktail. Jimmy's guts splashed around like the ingredients of a complex recipe inside a fragile cocktail shaker. The liquid blend burst through its fleshy container and spilled all over the bar. Phinn tasted some of his unique creation, the "Jimmy Siu." *Not bad.*

Wracked with pain and weak from blood loss, Phinn staggered out into the night, heading toward the Sound and its soothing waves.

HE WAS ABOUT TO WADE into the water and just let himself drown. But then he remembered Julie's face, her touch, the short ray of hope she had given him, and the alleviation of his lifelong loneliness, if only briefly.

The image of her smile made him stop short. He decided to swim along the surface, despite his badly leaking torso, north to the San Juan Islands, the place his Julie had called a future home for them both.

Now he'd just live there alone, like he was back in the Amazon's lagoon. At least in the wilderness no one could hurt him anymore. He'd get there, he resolved, or die trying.

A honking sound followed by wild whooping noises broke the somber contemplation of his future life.

The truck pulling up fast behind him was full of the same delinquents that had gang-raped Julie. Phinn recognized them right away, but in his weakened, injured state, he was in no position to fight them all over. As the truck careened to a stop, he recognized the song blaring on the radio, "Be-Bop-a-Lula" by Gene Vincent. It was something he'd listened to with his old doctor friend, another reminder of happier times he couldn't get back.

The four teenage thugs jumped out and surrounded Phinn, only a few feet from the Sound's shore—and freedom—brandishing bats and chains. They hooted and jeered something about having driven around looking for him ever since that night, ready to dole out violent vengeance.

In the darkness of the alley they'd apparently not got a really good look at him. Now that he was exposed in the moonlight, they were both shocked and amused.

"Look at them fat lips!"

"And them little beady eyes!"

"And that bald monkey head!"

"He ain't nothin' but a bleached nigger, all right!"

Phinn was tired, passive as they beat him to the ground with their weapons, then tied him up with rope and threw him in the back of the truck.

They drove him to a remote corner of Lake Washington in Magnusson Park, while Phinn thought back on his days, his misfortunes, his triumphs, his lives—all of them—since that black lagoon so long ago.

When the truck ground to a halt, he knew it all mattered not, just one more bruise, one more knot on his existence. The thugs dragged him out and threw him on the ground beneath a large tree next to the water. They used the rope that entangled Phinn to string him up on one of the stronger branches, and an old produce crate to keep him stable, for the time being.

"Any last words, nigger?" the leader of the mob asked him as Gene Vincent's song died out in the background from the truck's radio.

After a pause, Phinn said, "It was not my choice to be brought here to walk among you. I meant you no harm. I only wished to assimilate and be left alone to live my own life, in peace. Now you choose to destroy me. Why?"

The four thugs stared back at him, seeming dumbstruck into silence. Phinn could almost see the confusion, maybe even comprehension, wash over their faces.

Then "Endless Sleep" by Jody Reynolds came on the radio, breaking the moment.

The leader grinned and kicked the crate out from under Phinn's once-webbed feet. He could no longer swim against the tide of his own fate.

WILL "THE THRILL" VIHARO is a pulp fiction author, cat daddy, dog walker, and lounge lizard at large. For many years he was the producer and programmer of the cult movie cabaret Thrillville, *featuring classic B films in 35mm with live burlesque acts all around the Bay Area and beyond, which he presented with his wife, Monica "Tiki Goddess" Cortes Viharo. Currently he is host and organizer of* Noir at the Bar Seattle. *His "gonzo grindhouse" novels include* A Mermaid Drowns in the Midnight Lounge, Freaks That Carry Your Luggage Up to the Room, Lavender Blonde, Down a Dark Alley, Chumpy Walnut, *and* Love Stories Are Too Violent For Me. *Swing by his cyber pad anytime for virtual cocktails at* www.thrillville.net.

NOBODY MEANT FOR THE PIGGLY WIGGLY TO burn down. Or any of the rest of what ended up turning to smoking rubble, not exactly. So let's clear that up right now.

You never really see these things getting out of hand until after they do. Up to then, it's all just normal stuff, going about your usual day. Like any other typical late Friday afternoon, me and Maddox in his old Dodge Coronet that looked like a rocket ship, with the huge fins and the four taillights poking out like shooting flames, making his rounds as his customers got fortified for their weekends.

Sugar Grove was a sleepy little college town, a fact you'd never

I Was a Teenage Shroom Fiend

BY BRIAN HODGE

He was the last greaser in a world of hippies . . .

know from the side we lived on. Cruising from south to north was like going to a whole other town. Once we got there, Maddox would wheel into the park near the campus, next to the big splashing fountain, or in the lot by the pond with all the weeping willows around it, or near the brick bathrooms, and pretty soon some sleepy-looking guy would amble over. Different guys in each location, but the same long hair to his chest and same stars on his pants or rainbow on his shirt, and the same vacant smile on his face. They looked like they never had a worry in the world, and I found an appeal to that. It had to be more than the drugs. I hoped.

I'd have the glove box open and as often as not Maddox had a better idea what the customer was after than the customer himself, so he'd tell me what to fish out.

"Gimme the baggie with the little green footballs," he'd say. Those were the chloral hydrate gel capsules.

Or, "That one, with the little tiny ones, whites and yellows and blues." Valium.

Or, "The one with six of the big yellow round ones." Percodan... the Cadillac of downers.

All that, plus codeine, Darvocet, Darvon... Maddox carried it all. He had a guy inside a pharmacy, a part-timer named Jimbo, a year behind me in high school, who did deliveries and things like that. You couldn't steal the good stuff outright. They'd notice that. But the system had a weakness ripe for exploiting. The pharmacy supplied two hospitals and several nursing homes, and they were always returning meds that had been prescribed but never used. Most of it could go back into circulation. But there were certain controlled classes of drugs that couldn't. When those came back, they were supposed to be destroyed. Which was Jimbo work. It seemed like a huge waste, but that was the law. So Jimbo would pop them all out of their blister packs into a gallon-size plastic ice cream tub they kept in the back, and when that got full, it would be time to empty it into the outside dumpster. Only Jimbo got really good at skimming the cream of the keepers.

Maddox would exchange the pills for cash, then we'd rumble along to meet the next customer while I sorted the money and kept the denominations arranged. We didn't get away quite as clean with the day's last one, a guy with a droopy mustache almost as long as his hair.

"Hey man, what about those mushrooms I asked for?" He curled his fingers over the driver's door. "Any luck with the shrooms?"

"I'm working on it. I got a line on a source a couple nights ago." Maddox gave the fingers a look as dirty as their nails. "Don't make me peel those off."

The guy backed away looking nine kinds of surprised, like he didn't even know what his fingers had been up to. As we drove away, he was all apologies, and looked that way in the mirror for as long as I could see him.

Maddox grumbled and shook his head. "Holy Jesus, but I hate hippies."

"Then why do you sell to them?"

"Cause their money spends better than they smell. And none of them ever tried to rip me off." He looked across at me, a good half-acre of front seat between us. "Bikers, they're the ones you have to watch out for. They're not the ones buying downers, either. They're speed freaks. You roll up to do business with a biker whose pupils are already down to black pinholes, there's trouble brewing already."

"Then what are you complaining about the hippies for? Next to that, they don't seem so bad."

Maddox had to grouse a little more, then relented. "They're not, I guess. A bath might go a long way toward raising my opinion with most of them."

"The girls are cute. Them too?"

Maddox uncorked his cigarette from the corner of his mouth and stuck it by the window so the slipstream would blow away the ashes. "They seem pretty free with the goodies, and that makes up a lot of ground for the b.o., but they're not really all there when you bone 'em. Their heads are off in Middle Earth or someplace. It's weird."

This sounded like a problem I wouldn't mind trying to overcome.

"Shitty music, too. I don't know how they could listen to it if it wasn't for the pills and the reefer. It doesn't ever seem to end, or go anywhere in the middle. Holy Jesus, but I hate that music of theirs. Speaking of, let's have something else."

Manning the eight-track player was another duty of mine. Maddox made tapes off his albums at home, and he never got tired of listening to anything, just eager to hear the next one, nothing but wall-to-wall twang and double-time stomp and crazy yelping vocals like the singer was ready to jump through the speakers. Give Maddox enough Charlie Feathers and Duane Eddy and Link Wray, and he'd run out of gas before he ever ran out of road he wanted to get down.

We weren't done for the day yet, though. Maddox hated frat boys most of all, but not so much he wouldn't sell to them, too. Closer to campus he cruised a stretch of main drag with a lot of cheap restaurants and cheaper bars, then whipped into an alley and met a guy who looked like he was waiting for us, even if I didn't recognize him and Maddox didn't either. Preppy looking, Sigma Chi, not a hair out of place and creases on his slacks sharp enough to cut the hair.

"Nice wheels," the guy said, except I couldn't tell if he really meant that or not. "It's still from the twentieth century, right?"

"Fifty-nine, motherfucker." Maddox looked him up and down. "I don't know you. Where's Scott?"

"I'm Heath. Scott has his necktie hanging from the doorknob to our room. Which means he's having more fun right now than all three of us put together."

Heath dropped down for a look inside over at me, I guess to make sure I wasn't having extra fun. He stared too long, like I knew he would, with a *hoo-weee* expression blooming across his face.

"Hey kid! What time are you supposed to be back at the circus? I want to catch your act!"

"Eight o'clock," I told him. "But stick around. It's *nnn*—" I hung stuck on the N, the way I sometimes still did, but sliding through it was less a giveaway than grinding at it like an engine that wouldn't start. "—*nnnot* just the eyes. If you're *llllucky*, I'll bite the head off a chicken, too."

Motherfucker was right.

Maddox drummed his fingers on the top on his door, a galloping sound. "You bring Scott's money with you or was this a wasted trip for me?"

Heath slipped it from his pocket and handed it over. Maddox let the baggie of little green footballs slip from his fingers to the alley, with an "Oops, sorry." When Heath bent over to pick it up, Maddox levered the door open and banged it into his head. As the frat boy tottered backward holding the top of his skull, Maddox slid out after him.

Six lanky feet of gristle and bone with a pompadour—that was Maddox. When his little brother Hazel and I were still kids, I used to think Maddox was the coolest guy on earth. And I guess he was still up there in my estimation, but now it was more that I admired him for sticking to his guns. He was the last greaser in a world of hippies. Outnumbered 10,000-to-1 by bellbottoms, he wore pegged jeans so tight that, even if someone got in a lucky punch and knocked him out, the jeans might have kept him standing. I never knew how he could even move in them, let alone stash a bicycle chain in his back pocket, but he could, and did. He whipped the chain out and around and up from below into Heath's balls. It got the expected reaction.

"I've got a bigger chain in the trunk. Just right to fit around your ankles so I can drag you up and down this alley a few times, and then we'll see who's ready for the circus. I'll make a lizard man out of you before sundown, you'll look so scaly." He grabbed onto an ear and dragged Heath over and slammed his head on top of the door. "Or you could apologize. It's your choice."

Heath burbled and sputtered, but squeaked it out all right.

Maddox peeked in across at me. "Does that cover it for you, Wyatt?"

"It'll do. Thanks."

Maddox yanked him away and pushed him aside. Skull, balls, and now his ear, Heath needed a third hand just to cover all the hurt.

"Have a good weekend," Maddox told him. "And tell Scott I said for him to run his own errands from now on. If he sends you again, I'll massacre you both faster than Sitting Bull on Custer."

We were a couple blocks away, and he was in a happy mood again, when he asked if I was okay for a detour before we got something to eat, and I asked where.

"What I was saying earlier," he told me. "I got a line on some magic mushrooms. Heavy on the magic, maybe."

I THOUGHT HE'D BEEN LYING, just to shut the hippie up or string him along, since I already knew good and well that a couple nights ago—which is when Maddox said he'd learned about the shrooms—he'd been spending a night in jail for drag-racing out on Route 44.

Maddox didn't see a contradiction. "Where do you think it was I got that line on them in the first place?"

"Oh. Okay. I guess that makes sense."

"The trick to a successful night in the hoosegow is to keep the idiots talking while you don't give up anything."

He made this sound like a pearl of wisdom I should hang onto for future reference. I supposed if I kept hanging around with Maddox, sooner or later I'd need it.

Didn't many people want me hanging around with them, but Maddox was always cool with it, now more than ever. His brother Hazel was the first friend I ever had, the two of us going back so long I don't even remember meeting him. Hazel and I were tight before he knew better, that he was supposed to make fun of the same things about me that everybody else did, but by the time they tried to set him straight, it didn't matter to him. Hazel took my crummiest years and made them better. Until he drew a bad number in the draft and got shipped over to Vietnam, so until he got back, I guess to Maddox I was the next best thing to having his kid brother around.

I didn't care what he did or what all mischief he got up to. Maddox stuck up for me, and there'd never been a line of people waiting to do that.

From way back I had the lazy eye and the stutter, and because of the eye I could be clumsy. In school most everybody treated me like it was catching. And they were the nice ones. With the others, my spot in the pecking order was as one of the main tackling dummies for pecking practice. The day isn't complete until you put the retard in his place. I mostly got over the stutter but the eye still did its own thing. By then, though, the damage was done and never going to get better. I could wear a big pair of Ray-Bans like Maddox's and keep my mouth shut, and the past was all anybody else was ever going to see or hear.

As we tooled back down to our side of the tracks, he told me the story of the other night, how after the cops had shut down him and Hunter Sykes, doing their Snake & Mongoose routine out on 44, he'd been cooling his heels in his cell for a couple hours when they brought in a sad, jabbering case of humanity starting to come down off what sounded like a pretty bonkers high, and deposited him in the next cell.

"Jail's just like study hall," Maddox told me, "only your neighbor has better stories."

The guy had gobbled a few mushrooms earlier, and by half past nine, the cops had been called to come scoop him off the floor of the Voodoo Mama Lounge. He'd taken up permanent residence down there, but not like your average passed-out drunk. No, he was busily engaged in being an active weirdo, pressed out as flat on the wood as he could get, heaving and humping and splorching along through the night's swamp of spilled drinks, trying to climb up people's legs and telling anybody who'd listen, "I'm a blob! I'm a blob!"

"Johnny Law assumed he was hopped up on goofballs and let it go at that, but I got the straight skinny out of him. It was homegrown he was on."

"Was he the one who grew it?"

Maddox shook his head. "Nah. He just helped himself."

He drove us to where the southernmost edge of town petered out toward the river bottoms. The air always felt wetter and heavier down here than anywhere else around, and smelled like mud, and two minutes in you couldn't help but break an extra sweat to flush the mucky feel back out of your skin. He pulled us up to a peeling bungalow set in a cluster of old trees that looked like they'd been gagging on the air for the past two hundred years.

"This is where he said he got the mushrooms." Maddox shut down the engine. "You know Sheena Halliday? She waitresses at the Voodoo."

"How would I? I'm not old enough to go in there yet, you know that."

Maddox sighed. "We gotta get you a fake I.D., that's all there is to it."

He leaned on the horn to announce himself, then we got out and weren't three steps away from the car when what had to be Sheena barged out through the bungalow's front door. She was the realest unreal thing I'd ever seen, in a leopard print skirt and high heels and a busy lime green top and hair as red as anger piling around onto one shoulder. If they all dressed like that at the Voodoo Mama Lounge, I couldn't get that fake I.D. fast enough.

"Was hoping to talk some business," Maddox said.

"Could you pick a less terrible time? My shift starts in thirty."

"How about Erik? Is he here?"

She hesitated just enough for the silence to catch my ear the wrong way. "Erik's not seeing company right now."

Maddox must have noticed it too. "He was seeing company a couple days ago, for no good reason at all, it sounded like. At least I got a reason."

"Who? Who was here?" She looked suspicious now.

"They call him Trenchfoot Tommy—you know who I mean?"

"Oh, god. *He* was here? Was this before they hauled his loser ass in?"

"Right. He said he came over in the afternoon to play something he called 'booper balls.'" Maddox wasn't the type to go uncomfortable and shuffle his feet, but now he did. "I, uh . . . I don't know what that meant and didn't want to ask."

Sheena nodded like she knew anyway, and didn't like any of it. "Pong. It's this stupid new game that connects to the TV. Like ping-pong, but on the screen. It makes a boop sound. It's fun for about two minutes unless you're brain dead."

Maddox and Sheena looked at each other for a second, then they both just nodded. *Yup. Tommy.*

"What else did he tell you?"

Maddox gave me a tap on the elbow and leaned in close enough to mutter, "Flash some greenbacks." So I held up a shy fistful of everything we'd collected from the hippies and the frat boys.

"It was more what he implied. That there might be an opportunity here for some mutual benefit. Supply and demand, and all." Maddox poked me to raise my hand a little higher. "I figure you have a sweet little crop of something or other growing out back. This is a good place for it. I could always swing back by when you're not here, but I don't want to be that way. I may be a dirtbag, but I'm no thief."

Eyeing the cash, Sheena gave her head a big dramatic toss and whirled around with an impatient wave for us to follow. "Then get yourselves inside, you idiots."

You could see the bluish glow of the TV at the windows, and in the living room it was the only light at all, if you didn't count the big purple lava lamp doing its slow motion churning along one wall on a table next to a bong. The log stretched out on the couch, facing the big console TV, must have been Erik.

"There he is, if you can get much of a rise out of him," she said.

Maddox stepped up to say hello, then jumped straight back with the loudest "Holy Jesus!" I ever heard leave him.

Sheena stood with her arms crossed. "There's your sweet little crop of something or other. You still want to talk business?"

I couldn't see around Maddox yet, and wasn't sure I wanted to, then he got brave again and crept a little closer.

"He just lays around like that all day. And night. Twenty-four-seven, just about. It's been weeks since he's come to bed."

Maddox looked up. "Let me be the first to say that's a crying shame."

Sheena snorted a cute little laugh. "You're not the first, and not yet, it isn't. If you want to know the truth . . . " She dropped her voice to a whisper. "I kinda like him better this way."

Maddox glanced over his shoulder at me, still hanging back near the door. "Get your bony butt up here, Wyatt. I bet you pay closer attention in science class than I ever did."

Sheena looked at me with camaraderie and my heart melted down into my shoes. "That's a low bar." She hitched her thumb at Maddox. "He never showed his face in science class at all."

Maddox put his hand on my shoulder and steered me the rest of the way toward the couch. "What do you think?"

What did I *think*? What was I supposed to think? I think I would rather have been back in the Dodge topping 100 m.p.h. with the speakers thumping Duane Eddy so hard they were about to tear themselves off the rear deck. But no, instead he had me looking down at a long, skinny guy stretched out watching *I Was a Teenage Werewolf* on

TV, with glazed eyes and mushrooms growing from his skin. They were a blue-gray color, speckled with purple spots... big fat ones popping from his neck and down his chest and belly, between the sides of his open shirt, and a bunch more little ones across his forehead like a fresh outbreak of zits. He had a few more on his cheeks, but not so many they got in the way of his eyes. I didn't want to know what things looked like under the rest of his clothes.

Maddox leaned in close to my ear. "That's not normal, right?"

"What are you asking me for? I'm not the one who works in a pharmacy!" I looked over at the movie on TV, at the werewolf in a varsity letter jacket. *Yeah, people bug me too, Tony.* "Maybe it's normal for him."

"It started last week," Sheena said. "I came out here one morning, ready to get coffee going, and he was like this."

"No doctors? No trip to the emergency room?"

"He said he was feeling fine. Look, he hasn't worked in almost a year. I hardly notice the difference. I don't think he does either." She jabbed at the TV screen. "I bet he's watched this three times the past month alone. They run the same spookshows over and over, and every time one comes on again, you'd think it was the first, he's so fixated."

Maddox slipped right up between the couch and the coffee table. He clicked open his switchblade, then scraped at one of the mushrooms on Erik's chest. After a moment of working it, it popped free and tumbled to the cushion next to some Cheetos. He speared it with the tip of the knife and held it up for inspection.

Erik's eyes finally left the TV and tracked us, then he broke into a hazy smile. If he wondered who I was, he didn't show it. "Hey, man. When did you guys get here?"

"A few minutes ago, is all." Maddox held the mushroom out and down, to make sure Erik saw it. "This may be a delicate question, but you do know about these, right?"

Erik processed things slowly, but it all got through eventually. "Sure. It's kind of weird, but... it's no big deal."

"These don't hurt?"

"I don't even remember they're there half the time."

Maddox popped off another one. "How about now?"

Erik only giggled. "That tickles!"

"So you're not worried about this?"

Erik just shrugged. "I figure it's just how I sweat now."

"Are these the only ones there are, or . . . "

"No, they keep coming. I broke some off and put a couple bags of them in the icebox the other day."

"Good man. Sorry to interrupt," Maddox said, then stepped back and turned to Sheena again. "Honestly, I don't see as there's a problem either. You got the best of both worlds here, you know. If you'd like for him to start earning again, I don't think he has to do a thing different than what he is now." Maddox held up the shroom on the knife point again. "There should be a solid market for these, if Trenchfoot Tommy's reaction was anything to judge by."

Sheena only just now got it. "You're telling me *that's* what wigged him out the other night?" She looked like she was about to gag.

"You'd be providing a valuable commodity—look at it that way. A lot of these dope fiends and hopheads, what they put inside them, nobody even knows where it comes from, or if it's purely what it's supposed to be. With this, at least we know."

Sheena stood tapping her toe against the floor while looking up at the ceiling. "Why can't people just get drunk anymore? Drunks leave tips." Then she looked us both in the eye. "Okay. If you can sell them, you're welcome to them. Just keep them from getting anywhere near the Voodoo again, or somebody's balls are getting cut off."

I laughed, until she showed us the scissors.

NEXT DAY, MADDOX MADE some calls that made some hippies happy, then we made the run back up to the north side and met in the park to make them even happier. The one who'd asked about mushrooms the day before had brought friends, and they'd all brought money, so I figured I was happy too and just didn't know it.

One of them, so hairy there wasn't much of his actual face to see, held his baggie to the sky and gave it a good eyeballing. "They're pretty. But these don't look anything like psilocybin shrooms."

Maddox held out his hand for cash or return. "That's part of the magic, Sasquatch. You want 'em or not?"

Of course he wanted them. They all wanted them.

Once the transactions were concluded, Maddox called over their ringleader with the droopy moustache. "Are you guys planning on sticking around here in the park while you take them . . . commune with nature, that kind of thing? That's what you do, isn't it?"

He grinned like he'd never heard a better idea. "That's our bag, man."

"Then live long and prosper. Or whatever else it is you do."

We watched as they trailed away from the fountain and off among the trees, then Maddox fired up the Dodge and found another spot to park, close enough to still keep an eye on them but far enough away we didn't have to hear the clash of acoustic guitars and bongos.

"Are you worried the mushrooms aren't any good?" I asked. "Is that it?"

He unrolled his pack of cigarettes from the sleeve of his T-shirt and lit up a fresh one. "These walking stinkbombs would get high off them no matter what. But I've got a feeling there's *something* to them. I just want to put out a test batch and see what it is."

I held up one of the remaining baggies to do some eyeballing of my own. "How do you think they work? Science class or not, I can't even guess."

"Now that I've had time to think about it . . . ? Well, back at Sheena and Erik's, you saw the bong. Guaranteed there's a lot more there you didn't see. I think he's hit it all so hard for so long that it's built up inside him and now it's coming back out of him however it can. So it's just as well he's not boning Sheena these days. Can you imagine her knocked up from him now? That's one baby who'd be doing good to pop out with nothing worse than two heads."

Which made me wonder anew. I'd never blamed my parents for the lazy eye and the stutter, but then, how much did I know about their habits before they had me? It wasn't like I'd never caught them in lies before. Maybe all that clean, virtuous living they yapped about at me was more of the same.

And I couldn't take my eyes off the shrooms. I hadn't even eaten one, yet they still seemed to pulsate and dance. Even an inexperienced dork like me knew that, when it came to weed dealers and pill pushers, you had to be a mighty stupid one to get high on your own supply. But the longer we sat and I looked at these, the easier it got for me to forget about their growing medium, because they looked like most any other normal dirt-grown mushrooms, only prettier, and to wonder what would it feel like, just a few, for just a while—?

Maddox snapped his fingers in front of my eyes. "You best not be thinking what it looks like you're thinking."

"You're not tempted? Not even a little bit?"

"You pick your poison, and that's not mine. If they're going to scrape me off the Voodoo Mama Lounge's floor, let it be because I'm puking on someone's shoes, not because I'm trying to eat them." Then he sighed and dialed it down. "I used to not mind a puff of reefer every now and then, but the hippies stole it away from the jazz cats. It doesn't have the same appeal anymore. The only thing I'll tolerate for myself is speed, and that's mainly because there's times you need to fit thirty-six hours into a twenty-four hour day. The rest of it is there's a heritage to it." He reached down to give the eight-track player a gentle pat. "All this righteous musicality I'm honored to introduce you to, most of what you're listening to is the pure, headlong, drive-it-over-a-cliff sound of Benzedrine in action."

"No joke? I didn't know things were like that back then."

"You've just got yourself a watered-down view of history. Fuck *American Graffiti*. Fuck *Grease*. And fuck *Happy Days* twice."

He flicked his butt out the window and fired up a fresh smoke.

"You think Elvis got his break at Sun Studios because the guys there were touched by the fact he wanted to record a gospel song for his mama? Like hell they were. Nobody took him seriously until he started bringing in bottles of mama's diet pills. Then he seemed like somebody worth keeping around."

Maddox shook his head with great sadness.

"Seen him lately? He should've just stuck with the speed."

So we sat and whiled away the afternoon, and every so often we'd take a stroll and watch the hippies frolic among the trees. So far, so good. A little later, as evening settled over us, that's when most of them began to run around looking a lot more agitated, and snarl and howl and fight each other, and as far as Maddox was concerned, this was a million times better.

I THOUGHT CRAZED HIPPIES were just something from the movies, like in *I Drink Your Blood* that double-featured with *I Eat Your Skin* at the drive-in theater a few years earlier. Which I only got to see because the Dodge Coronet had such a big trunk that it could've fit four of Hazel and me when Maddox snuck us in, with room left over for a giant bag of popcorn. But those were Satan-worshipping hippies who got rabies from infected meat pies. I would really have liked for that to be true, but it didn't match up with how I'd seen the real ones out in the wild. They seemed pretty docile all around.

So curiosity got the better of me. Two plus two equals... what, here, exactly?

Erik had been watching a lot of *I Was a Teenage Werewolf,* and next thing you know we had a pack of shroom-gobbling hippies baying at the moon. But what about Trenchfoot Tommy? Oozing around the Voodoo Lounge's floor trying to engulf people from the ankles up, calling out how he was a blob... suppose he wasn't just any blob. Suppose he thought he was *the* Blob.

I opened up the *TV Guide* for earlier in the week before Mom could pitch it out, and started flipping through the pages, and there it was:

THE BLOB (1958). *Steve McQueen, Aneta Corseaut. A shapeless creature from another world lands on Earth and gets bigger with every meal.*

Open and shut, your honor.

I brought my findings to Maddox, showing him right there in the *TV Guide,* and told him how it may not have been the reefer and who knows what else coming back out of Erik. Or at least not exclusively.

The real mojo was in the movies. I knew that much from growing up with them, my best place to go to get lost. They were my rock to hang onto, and the strength to do it. Where Maddox had his way-back music, I had movies. Sometimes they were all that got me from one day to the next, or through the weekend before the start of a new school week. When you're the resident human piñata, there's nothing a TV or theater screen can show you that's more horrifying than the idea of another Monday morning.

I'll take a werewolf or a rabid hippie or a flesh-eating zombie any day before I ever take a second-string football player looking to entertain his buddies for the next five minutes. Nobody has to convince me of the power of movies.

So it seemed like a sound theory to me: Erik lying back on that sofa for the best part of a year, soaking in the TV's blue glow 24/7, and the area where they lived was dank anyway, and the air probably lousy with spores . . . something was bound to mix and mutate.

"Interesting," was about all Maddox had to say about it. "You could be onto something."

I wasn't sure how I expected him to react. Me, I was thrilled he took it seriously.

"I wonder what else he's been watching lately." Maddox grinned like he'd been watching too many movies himself, nothing but devils and rogues. "You want to find out? Give everybody up there one last blowout for the weekend?"

"You don't think they've had enough for this one?"

"As I see it, it'd be doing them a favor. Did you *hear* them last night? They sounded more alive in one night than I've seen them in two years. They need more of that, don't you think? Life is more than rainbows and tree-hugging."

When we cruised back down to Erik and Sheena's, she wasn't any happier to see us this time than she'd been the first, not until I handed over their cut of the sales. She was out of her Voodoo garb now, in cutoff jean shorts and a halter top, and when she gave me a bouncy hug, there wasn't anything I wouldn't have done for her short of murder, and that was still on the table.

"And people are actually buying this?" She hadn't yet moved beyond disbelief. "They really are getting high off this?"

"You on-shift tonight?" Maddox asked.

"No, thank god."

"Then come with us and see for yourself."

She was right on the verge of saying no, I could tell, that she'd seen all of it she wanted to the other night, when Trenchfoot Tommy blobbed out on the floor. But then she looked around, caught between the purple light of the lava lamp and the blue TV glow of *The Creature From the Black Lagoon*, and something else came over her. Like she maybe started to get the idea that automatically saying no to too many weird things was how she'd landed here, in a neighborhood that smelled of mildew with a boyfriend so inert that mushrooms were growing on him.

If the weird is going to take over your life anyway, you might as well go out and find it first, so you have some control over the situation.

"You know, I think I will," she said.

Ten minutes of harvesting, and we were back on the road.

I LEARNED SOMETHING NEW that day: If you have a half-price sale, even people who wouldn't normally buy something like magic mushrooms get to thinking, well, why not? The hippies definitely didn't need convincing. Quite a few of the vegetarians even mentioned that the previous batch had given them a new appreciation for meat. Next, after we found the Sigma Chi house and sought out Heath from the other day, with Maddox claiming to be bringing a peace offering, we got to be pretty popular along Fraternity Row, too. They wouldn't want to know us tomorrow, but today we were gold.

After that it was just a matter of going to the park and waiting for the show to begin.

As the sun started to dip low, it was like a drive-in movie come to life around us, the biggest monster mash ever. We heard it before we saw anything, with the howls of more born-again werewolves rising in the distance. After that it was all moms grabbing their kids off the swings, and boyfriends and girlfriends running for cover. As the park began to fill up and be overrun, you could chart Erik's viewing habits and tell who'd ingested what by the way they moved. The werewolves were the most agitated and erratic, and the only ones who went up into the trees after the squirrels. The vampires skulked and tried to bite. The Frankenstein monsters blundered along with a low frustration tolerance, slamming into things and knocking them over. The mummies, they more or less just plodded. Then there were the ones who scurried around on all contorted fours, like giant ants, and worked together in teams to go after their quarry. They'd scuttle up on the roofs of cars and lift their heads for a better overview, and you could almost see antennae twitch before they scampered on their way again.

"This may be getting out of hand," Sheena said.

"In this dead-ass town?" Maddox said. "Something needs to."

After a time, he kept the Dodge in gear and kept us on the move, motoring from one vantage point to the next as the hubbub became a rolling wave through town. Any six men could overturn a car, I remembered one of the characters telling another in *Night of the Living Dead*, and where zombies were concerned that may have been true, but seeing our human ants scale the sides of buildings was a display of strength on an altogether different level.

When the Greeks showed up, though, that's when it all went to hell in a hurry, a sweaty tide of screaming frat boys and fire sweeping in from the opposite direction. It only made sense in hindsight. If you're going to have monsters on the loose, sooner or later you're going to have a mob.

"What are they carrying?" Sheena asked. "Where did they get all of those in such a hurry?"

In my whole life, I'd never seen Maddox mortified. Not until now.

"Tiki torches," he said. "Leave it to these smug assholes to get everything wrong."

They're pretty much universal laws: Monsters run from fire. And mobs, once they're stoked, aren't going to be satisfied until they burn something. Really, though ... did they have to start by torching the Piggly Wiggly? I guess they did. I tend to think that, under threat and under the influence, a herd of otherwise harmless hopheads and shroom-gobblers are going to take shelter where they instinctively feel safest . . . and the place with the most munchies was it.

Once the smoke started to billow, they scattered, and so did the loudmouthed guys with the torches, in pursuit. One fire became four, turned into eight, and within half an hour, the night was full of red lights and sirens, and you couldn't see the moon for all the smoke, and three blocks of the campus-adjacent downtown was either burning or had its front windows smashed in. And the one thing definitely looked to be true: Any six men *could* overturn a car.

But not ours. Any time anyone got too close, Maddox jumped out whirling the bicycle chain to drive them away. Which we should've done for real, but the three of us felt like we had an obligation to see it through, to bear witness to this chaos we'd set in motion, as it whirled toward its blazing zenith.

The downtown bell tower clock was out of the danger zone, and by the time it bonged midnight, we were scuffing and scraping along a sidewalk full of ash and grit, taking it all in, while the fire crews kept busy hosing things down a block ahead of us.

"You know I never meant for this dealing thing to be permanent," Maddox said. "I always told you, as soon as I get my grubstake together, it's shit through a goose time for me, I'll be so gone-daddy-gone."

This was true. He'd been talking about his grubstake for years. Either it had to be sizeable enough by now to get him anywhere he wanted, or it was all talk and no cash. Either way, this time he meant it for real.

"Tell me you've got room for three," Sheena said.

"You've seen that beast I drive. I've got room for four, if it comes to it."

A couple minutes later he said he had an idea, and slipped through the smashed glass storefront for Featherstone TV & Appliance. Another couple minutes and he was out again, lugging a little portable television, a floor demo plucked off a shelf.

"It runs off batteries," he said. "We can use that."

I didn't move. Maddox may have been a dirtbag, and now maybe an arsonist by proxy, but he had standards. The stutter was coming on, the way it still did when things mattered most, so I battled through until I got it out: "I thought you weren't a thief."

First mortified, now sheepish. Tonight was full of firsts.

"You're right. Hold this," he said, and stuck the TV in my hands while he dug in his pocket for a wad of cash, and ducked back inside.

WHEN THE SUN ROSE on the north side of town, they were still raking through the ashes when the three of us southsiders finished packing.

Sometimes all it takes is a whisper in your ear to tell you it's time to move on, that your future lies down a road you won't recognize until you're on it. Other times, it takes a fire under your ass. Maybe we'd all three been hearing the whisper for a while, and ignored it until the heat came.

We picked up Sheena last, because the logistics made sense that way. Then we stood around outside under the sky and the wet, heavy trees, the world so quiet we could hear the rushing of the brown river water a block away.

"If I never smell mud and wood rot again, or feel some drunk's hand trying to get up my skirt, it'll still be too soon," Sheena said, then got in the car while Maddox and I hung back to wrap things up out here.

We looked down into the trunk. Maddox had rigged the portable TV to an aerial on the car, and we had lots of batteries, so it seemed like the arrangement would do for now.

"You hear about this new thing they're coming up with in Japan?" he said. "It's called a VCR. Video Cassette Recorder. Anything you want to see, anytime, anywhere, it'll be on the tape. You just load it in and press play."

"Wow. He'll like that." The existence of such ingenuity made me smile. "Go on, get the motor started, I'll finish up."

If, back in our drive-in sneaking days, the Dodge's trunk could've held four of Hazel and me, it meant Erik had all the room he could ever need. I reached up and took hold of the trunk lid.

"Do you need anything else before we get going?" I asked him.

He didn't answer, didn't even look at me, just smiled a slow, hazy smile, like he'd heard me from somewhere down by the river. He was good. He had everything he needed.

Just before I shut the lid on him and the blue glow, I looked around to make sure nobody was watching, then popped a couple growths as big as drawer knobs off his forehead and gobbled them down quick as I could.

We were somewhere around the county line on the edge of tomorrow when the shrooms began to take hold. Link Wray was tearing it up on the speakers and Maddox was drumming on the steering wheel and Sheena's hair was streaming in the wind and I couldn't believe how my hips were wanting to move.

How 'bout that Erik? Somewhere into the mix he'd thrown an Elvis movie or two. And the road ahead may have been winding, but for a kid with a lazy eye, I was seeing straighter than ever.

Called "a writer of spectacularly unflinching gifts" by no less than Peter Straub, **BRIAN HODGE** *is one of those people who always has to be making something. So far, he's made thirteen novels, around 130 shorter works, five full-length collections, and one soundtrack album. His novella, "The Same Deep Waters as You," was recently optioned by a London-based production company for development as a TV series.*

He lives in Colorado, where he also likes to make music and photographs; loves everything about organic gardening except the thieving squirrels; and trains in Krav Maga and kickboxing, which are of no use at all against the squirrels.

Connect through his web site (www.brianhodge.net), Twitter (@BHodgeAuthor), or Facebook (www.facebook.com/brianhodgewriter).

EDITOR'S REQUEST

D EAR READER, FAN, OR SUPPORTER,
It's a dreadful commentary that the worth of indie publications is measured by online 5-star reviews, but such is the state of current commerce.

Should you have enjoyed this book, gratitude is most appreciated by posting a brief and honest online review at Amazon.com, Goodreads.com, and/or a highly-visible blog.

With sincerest thanks,

Eric J. Guignard, editor
Pop the Clutch: Thrilling Tales of Rockabilly,
Monsters, and Hot Rod Horror

ALSO FROM ERIC J. GUIGNARD AND DARK MOON BOOKS:

A World of Horror

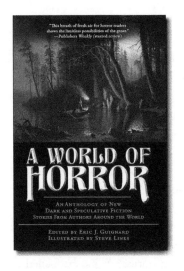

Every nation of the globe has unique tales to tell, whispers that settle in through the land, creatures or superstitions that enliven the night, but rarely do readers get to experience such a diversity of these voices in one place as in *A WORLD OF HORROR*, the latest anthology book created by award-winning editor Eric J. Guignard, and beautifully illustrated by artist Steve Lines.

Enclosed within its pages are twenty-two all-new dark and speculative fiction stories written by authors from around the world that explore the myths and monsters, fables and fears of their homelands.

Encounter the haunting things that stalk those radioactive forests outside Chernobyl in Ukraine; sample the curious dishes one may eat in Canada; beware the veldt monster that mirrors yourself in Uganda; or simply battle mountain trolls alongside Alfred Nobel in Sweden. These stories and more are found within *A World of Horror*: Enter and discover, truly, there's no place on the planet devoid of frights, thrills, and wondrous imagination.

"This breath of fresh air for horror readers shows the limitless possibilities of the genre."
—*Publishers Weekly* (starred review)

"This is the book we need right now!"
—*Becky Spratford; librarian, reviewer,* RA for All: Horror

"A fresh collection of horror authors exploring monsters and myths from their homelands."
—*Library Journal*

Order your copy at www.darkmoonbooks.com or www.amazon.com
ISBN-13: 978-0-9989383-1-8

ALSO FROM ERIC J. GUIGNARD AND DARK MOON BOOKS:

Darkness exists everywhere, and in no place greater than those where spirits and curses still reside. In *DARK TALES OF LOST CIVILIZATIONS*, you will unearth an anthology of twenty-five previously unpublished horror and speculative fiction stories, relating to aspects of civilizations that are crumbling, forgotten, rediscovered, or perhaps merely spoken about in great and fearful whispers.

What is it that lures explorers to distant lands where none have returned? Where is Genghis Khan buried? What happened to Atlantis? Who will displace mankind on Earth? What laments have the Witches of Oz? Answers to these mysteries and other tales are presented within this critically acclaimed anthology.

Including stories by: **Joe R. Lansdale, David Tallerman, Jonathan Vos Post, Jamie Lackey, Aaron J. French,** and twenty exceptional others.

"The stories range from mildly disturbing to downright terrifying... Most are written in a conservative, suggestive style, relying on the reader's own imagination to take the plunge from speculation to horror."
—*Monster Librarian Reviews*

"Several of these stories made it on to my best of the year shortlist, and the book itself is now on the best anthologies of the year shortlist."
—*British Fantasy Society*

"Almost any story in this anthology is worth the price of purchase. The entire collection is a delight."
—*Black Gate Magazine*

ALSO FROM ERIC J. GUIGNARD AND DARK MOON BOOKS:

Death. Who has not considered their own mortality and wondered at what awaits, once our frail human shell expires? What occurs after the heart stops beating, after the last breath is drawn, after life as we know it terminates?

Does our spirit remain on Earth while the body rots? Do the remnants of our soul transcend to a celestial Heaven or sink to Hell's torment? Can we choose our own afterlife? Can we die again in the hereafter? Are we given the opportunity to reincarnate and do it all over? Is life merely a cosmic joke or is it an experiment for something greater? Enclosed in this Bram Stoker-award winning anthology are thirty-four all-new dark and speculative fiction stories exploring the possibilities *AFTER DEATH . . .*

Illustrated by Audra Phillips and including stories by: **Steve Rasnic Tem**, **Bentley Little**, **John Langan**, **Lisa Morton**, and exceptional others.

"Though the majority of the pieces come from the darker side of the genre, a solid minority are playful, clever, or full of wonder. This strong anthology is sure to make readers contemplative even while it creates nightmares."
—*Publishers Weekly*

"In Eric J. Guignard's latest anthology he gathers some of the biggest and most talented authors on the planet to give us their take on this entertaining and perplexing subject matter . . . highly recommended."
—*Famous Monsters of Filmland*

"An excellent collection of imaginative tales of what waits beyond the veil."
—*Amazing Stories Magazine*

ALSO FROM ERIC J. GUIGNARD AND DARK MOON BOOKS:

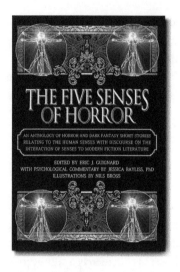

The Five Senses of Horror:

Hearing, sight, touch, smell, and taste: Our impressions of the world are formed by our five senses, and so too are our fears, our imaginations, and our captivation in reading fiction stories that embrace these senses.

Whether hearing the song of infernal caverns, tasting the erotic kiss of treachery, or smelling the lush fragrance of a fiend, enclosed within this anthology are fifteen horror and dark fantasy tales that will quicken the beat of fear, sweeten the flavor of wonder, sharpen the spike of thrills, and otherwise brighten the marvel of storytelling that is found resonant!

Editor Eric J. Guignard and psychologist Jessica Bayliss, PhD also include companion discourse throughout, offering academic and literary insight as well as psychological commentary examining the physiology of our senses, why each of our senses are engaged by dark fiction stories, and how it all inspires writers to continually churn out ideas in uncommon and invigorating ways.

Featuring stunning interior illustrations by Nils Bross, and including fiction short stories by such world-renowned authors as John Farris, Ramsey Campbell, Poppy Z. Brite, Darrell Schweitzer, Lisa Morton, and Richard Christian Matheson, amongst others.

Intended for readers, writers, and students alike, explore *THE FIVE SENSES OF HORROR*!

Order your copy at www.darkmoonbooks.com or www.amazon.com
ISBN-13: 978-0-9988275-0-6

ALSO FROM ERIC J. GUIGNARD AND DARK MOON BOOKS:

Exploring Dark Short Fiction #1: A Primer to Steve Rasnic Tem

For over four decades, Steve Rasnic Tem has been an acclaimed author of horror, weird, and sentimental fiction. Hailed by *Publishers Weekly* as "A perfect balance between the bizarre and the straight-forward" and *Library Journal* as "One of the most distinctive voices in imaginative literature," Steve Rasnic Tem has been read and cherished the world over for his affecting, genre-crossing tales.

Dark Moon Books and editor Eric J. Guignard bring you this introduction to his work, the first in a series of primers exploring modern masters of literary dark short fiction. Herein is a chance to discover—or learn more of—the rich voice of Steve Rasnic Tem, as beautifully illustrated by artist Michelle Prebich.

Included within these pages are:

- Six short stories, one written exclusively for this book
- Author interview
- Complete bibliography
- Academic commentary by Michael Arnzen, PhD (former humanities chair and professor of the year, Seton Hill University)
- . . . and more!

Enter this doorway to the vast and fantastic: Get to know Steve Rasnic Tem.

Order your copy at www.darkmoonbooks.com or www.amazon.com
ISBN-13: 978-0-9988275-2-0

ALSO FROM ERIC J. GUIGNARD AND DARK MOON BOOKS:

Exploring Dark Short Fiction #2: A Primer to Kaaron Warren

Australian author Kaaron Warren is widely recognized as one of the leading writers today of speculative and dark short fiction. She's published four novels, multiple novellas, and well over one hundred heart-rending tales of horror, science fiction, and beautiful fantasy, and is the first author ever to simultaneously win all three of Australia's top speculative fiction writing awards (Ditmar, Shadows, and Aurealis awards for *The Grief Hole*).

Dark Moon Books and editor Eric J. Guignard bring you this introduction to her work, the second in a series of primers exploring modern masters of literary dark short fiction. Herein is a chance to discover—or learn more of—the distinct voice of Kaaron Warren, as beautifully illustrated by artist Michelle Prebich.

Included within these pages are:

- Six short stories, one written exclusively for this book
- Author interview
- Complete bibliography
- Academic commentary by Michael Arnzen, PhD (former humanities chair and professor of the year, Seton Hill University)
- . . . and more!

Enter this doorway to the vast and fantastic: Get to know Kaaron Warren.

Order your copy at www.darkmoonbooks.com or www.amazon.com
ISBN-13: 978-0-9989383-0-1

ALSO FROM ERIC J. GUIGNARD AND DARK MOON BOOKS:

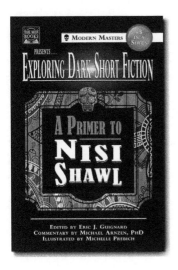

Exploring Dark Short Fiction #3: A Primer to Nisi Shawl

Praised by both literary journals and leading fiction magazines, Nisi Shawl is celebrated as an author whose works are lyrical and philosophical, speculative and far-ranging; "...broad in ambition and deep in accomplishment" (*The Seattle Times*). Besides nearly three decades of creating fantasy and science fiction, fairy tales, and indigenous stories, Nisi has also been lauded as editor, journalist, and proponent of feminism, African-American fiction, and other pedagogical issues of diversity.

Dark Moon Books and editor Eric J. Guignard bring you this introduction to her work, the third in a series of primers exploring modern masters of literary dark short fiction. Herein is a chance to discover—or learn more of—the vibrant voice of Nisi Shawl, as beautifully illustrated by artist Michelle Prebich.

Included within these pages are:

- Six short stories, one written exclusively for this book
- Author interview
- Complete bibliography
- Academic commentary by Michael Arnzen, PhD (former humanities chair and professor of the year, Seton Hill University)
- ...and more!

Enter this doorway to the vast and fantastic: Get to know Nisi Shawl.

Order your copy at www.darkmoonbooks.com or www.amazon.com
ISBN-13: 978-0-9989383-4-9

THE CRIME FILES OF KATY GREEN by GENE O'NEILL:

Discover why readers have been applauding this stark, fast-paced noir series by multiple-award-winning author, Gene O'Neill, and follow the dark murder mysteries of Sacramento homicide detectives Katy Green and Johnny Cato, dubbed by the press as Sacramento's "Green Hornet and Cato"!

Book #1: DOUBLE JACK (a novella)

400-pound serial killer Jack Malenko has discovered the perfect cover: He dresses as a CalTrans worker and preys on female motorists in distress in full sight of passing traffic. How fast can Katy Green and Johnny Cato track him down before he strikes again?

ISBN-13: 978-0-9988275-6-8

Book #2: SHADOW OF THE DARK ANGEL

Bullied misfit, Samuel Kubiak, is visited by a dark guardian angel who helps Samuel gain just vengeance. There hasn't been a case yet Katy and Johnny haven't solved, but now how can they track a psychopathic suspect that comes and goes in the shadows?

ISBN-13: 978-0-9988275-8-2

Book #3: DEATHFLASH

Billy Williams can see the soul as it departs the body, and is "commanded to do the Lord's work," which he does fanatically, slaying drug addicts in San Francisco...Katy and Johnny investigate the case as junkies die all around, for Billy has his own addiction: the rush of viewing the *Deathflash*.

ISBN-13: 978-0-9988275-9-9

Order your copy at www.darkmoonbooks.com or www.amazon.com

About Editor Eric J. Guignard

E RIC J. GUIGNARD IS A writer and editor of dark and speculative fiction, operating from the shadowy outskirts of Los Angeles, where he also runs the small press, Dark Moon Books. He's won the Bram Stoker Award (the highest literary award of horror fiction), been a finalist for the International Thriller Writers Award, and a multi-nominee of the Pushcart Prize.

He has over 100 stories and non-fiction works appearing in

Photograph by Jeannette Guignard

publications such as *Nightmare Magazine, Gamut, Black Static, Shock Totem,* and *Dark Discoveries Magazine.* As editor, Eric's published five other anthologies such as *Dark Tales of Lost Civilizations, After Death...,* and *A World of Horror,* a showcase of international horror short fiction. Additionally he's created an ongoing series of primers exploring modern masters of literary dark short fiction, titled: *Exploring Dark Short Fiction* (*Vol. 1: Steve Rasnic Tem; Vol. II: Kaaron Warren; Vol. III: Nisi Shawl; Vol. IV: Jeffrey Ford; Vol. V: Han Song; Vol. VI: Ramsey Campbell*).

Read his short story collection *That Which Grows Wild: 16 Tales of Dark Fiction* (Cemetery Dance Publications), novella *Baggage of Eternal Night* (JournalStone), and watch for forthcoming books, including the novel *Crossbuck 'Bo* to be published in 2019 by JournalStone.

Outside the glamorous and jet-setting world of indie fiction, Eric's a technical writer and college professor, and he stumbles home each day to a wife, children, cats, and a terrarium filled with mischievous beetles. Visit Eric at: www.ericjguignard.com, his blog: ericjguignard.blogspot.com, or Twitter: @ericjguignard.

About Illustrator Steve Chanks

R aised on a steady diet of Tom & Jerry, Star Wars, Freddy Krueger, and Marvel Comics since the late '70s, STEVE CHANKS has distilled the very best of his distorted pop culture view into a big-titted, puss-filled, pulp daydream.

Photograph by Justin Borucki

With a drawing style that's been described as Disney meets *Mad Magazine*, Steve has inked his way into such mags as *Maxim*, *Revolver*, and *Guitar World*, and has clothed the fans of bands like Mastodon, Lamb of God, Trivium, and Avenged Sevenfold.

Steve lives in scenic Queens, New York with his heartthrob wife Jessica and their daughter Claudia where they enjoy their dumb cats, upstate hikes, crap collecting, and BBQ.

You can see more of his work at www.SteveChanks.com.

Lightning Source UK Ltd.
Milton Keynes UK
UKHW010754150822
407319UK00002B/629